HANNAH GREEN AND HER UNFEASIBLY MUNDANE EXISTENCE

Hannah Green and Her Unfeasibly Mundane Existence

MICHAEL MARSHALL SMITH

HARPER
Voyager

Harper*Voyager* an imprint of
HarperCollins*Publishers* Ltd
1 London Bridge Street
London SE1 9GF

www.harpercollins.co.uk

First published by HarperCollins*Publishers* 2017

1

A catalogue record for this book is available from the British Library

ISBN: 978-0-00-823791-2 (HB)
ISBN: 978-0-00-823792-9 (TPB)

Set in Sabon LT Std by Palimpsest Book Production Ltd, Falkirk, Stirlingshire

Printed and bound by Clays Ltd, St Ives Plc

MIX
Paper from
responsible sources

FSC
www.fsc.org   **FSC™ C007454**

Acknowledgements

My thanks to those who spent time in the Behind with Hannah, and helped encourage her (or me) along the tangled path: Chris Schelling, David Smith, Stephen Jones and Jo Fletcher; to Cas Austin, Deborah Beale, Craig Zerf and Patrick Goss for comments and kindness; to my editor Jane Johnson for – as always – helping me kick it into shape, and to Natasha Bardon and Lily Cooper for their contributions; to my agent Jonny Geller; and finally to my wife Paula, for convincing me this story was worth showing to someone, and for everything else.

For Nate,
who heard some of this first,
and without whom it wouldn't exist.

One's destination is never a place but rather
a new way of looking at things.

—Henry Miller

Big Sur and the Oranges of Hieronymus Bosch

Then

Imagine, if you will, a watchmaker's workshop.

In fact, please imagine one whether you wish to or not. That's where something's about to happen, something that won't seem important right away but will turn out to be – and if you're not prepared to listen to what I'm saying then this whole thing simply isn't going to work.

So.

Imagine that thing I just said.

If it helps, the workshop is on the street level of an old and crumbling building, in a town some distance from here. With the exception of the workbench it is cluttered and dusty. The watchmaker is advanced in years and does not care about the state of the place, except for the area in which he works.

It is a late afternoon in autumn, and growing dark. Quite cold, too. It is quiet. The workshop is dimly lit by candles, and the watchmaker – you can picture him in the gloom, bent over his bench, if you wish – is wearing several layers of clothing to keep warm. He is repairing a piece he made several decades ago, the prized possession of a local nobleman. It will take him perhaps half an hour, he estimates, after which he'll lock up his workshop and walk through the narrow streets to his house, where since the death of his wife he lives alone but for an elderly and bad-tempered cat. On the way he will stop off to purchase a few provisions, primarily a bag of peppermints, of which he is extremely fond. The watchmaker. Not the cat.

The timepiece he is working on is intricate, and very advanced for its time, though the watchmaker knows that were he to embark upon crafting something like it now he'd do things quite differently. He has learned a great deal since he made it. He doesn't make anything new any more, however. He hasn't in a long while. The story of his life has already been told. He is merely waiting for its final line.

Nonetheless, his eyes remain sharp and his fingers nimble, and in fact it only takes ten minutes before the watch is working perfectly once more. He reassembles it, and polishes the outside with his sleeve. Finished. Done.

He stands with the piece in his hands. He is aware, through his profound understanding of its workings, of the intricate mechanisms involved in its measuring of time, the hidden movements. He feels these as a subtle, almost imperceptible vibration, like the murmur of a tiny animal cupped in his hand, stirring in its sleep.

And he is aware of something else.

Not one thing, in fact, but a multitude – a cloud filling his mind like notes from a church organ, soaring up towards heaven. He is aware of children, and a grandchild. They cannot be his, because he has none: his marriage, though long and comfortable, was without issue. Aware, too, of the people who had come before him, his parents and grandparents and ancestors, aware not merely of the idea of them but their reality, their complexity – as though he has only ever been the soloist in the music of his life, supported upon the harmonies of others.

He's aware also that though the candles in the workshop illuminate small areas, there are patches of darkness too, and parts that are neither one thing nor the other. That his entire life has been this way, not forever pulled between two poles but borne instead along far more complex currents, of which ticks and tocks are merely the extremes.

How did he come to be standing here on this cold afternoon? he wonders. What innumerable events led to this?

And why?

He shakes his head, frowning. This is not the kind of thought that usually occupies his mind. He is not normally prey, either, to a feeling of dread – though that is what is creeping up on him now. Something bad is about to happen.

Something wicked this way comes.

He hears footsteps in the street outside. He half turns, but cannot see who is approaching. The windows are grimy. He has not cleaned them in many years. Nobody needs to see inside. His venerable name on the sign is advertisement enough, and as he has gradually withdrawn from the world so he has come to value the privacy the windows' opaqueness confers.

But now suddenly he wishes he could see who's coming. And he wonders whether his life is over after all.

He waits, turning back to the bench, busying his hands.

And the door opens.

No, no, no. Sorry. Stop imagining things.

I've got this completely wrong. I've tried to tell the story from the beginning.

That's always a mistake. I've learned my lesson since, and have even come to wonder if this is what I was dimly starting to comprehend on that cold, long-ago afternoon. Life is not like a watch or clock, something that can be constructed and then wound for the first time, set in motion.

There is no beginning. We are always in the middle.

OK, look. I'm going to start again.

PART 1

A story is a spirit being, not a repertoire,
allegory or form of psychology.

Martin Shaw
Snowy Tower

Chapter 1

So. This is a story, as I've said. And stories are skittish, like cats. You need to approach calmly and respectfully or they'll run away and you'll never see them again. People have been spinning tales for as long as we've been on this planet, perhaps even longer. There are stories that are *so* ancient, in fact, that they come from a time before words – tales conjured in gestures and grunts, movement of the eyes; stories that live in the rustling of leaves and lapping of waves, and whose ghosts hide in the tales we tell each other now.

Be good, and be careful.

Beware of that cave; that forest; that man.

Some day the sun will go dark, and then we will hide.

But all stories – and I'm talking about proper ones here, not stories about sassy teens becoming ninja spies or needy middle-agers overturning their lives in a fit of First World pique and finding true love running a funky little bookshop in Barcelona – need us to survive. Humans are the clouds from which stories rain, but we are also shards of glass that channel their light, focusing them so sharply that they burn.

Humans and stories need each other. We tell them, but they tell us too – reaching with soft hands and wide arms to pull us into their embrace. They do this especially when we have become mired in lives of which we can make no sense. We all need a path, and stories can sometimes usher us back to it.

That's what happened to Hannah Green. She got caught up in a story.

And this is what it is.

Hannah lives in a place called Santa Cruz, on the coast of Northern California. It has a nice downtown with organic grocery stores and a Safeway and coffee shops and movie theatres and a library and all the things you need if you want other towns to take you seriously. It is home to a well-regarded branch of the University of California and also to a famous boardwalk, where you can go on fairground rides and scare yourself witless should you be so inclined. The boardwalk features a house of horrors and a carousel and shooting galleries and the fifth-oldest rollercoaster in America (the famed Giant Dipper, which Hannah had ridden only once, with her grand-father: both emerged shaken from the experience, and he later described the contraption as 'potentially evil') and places to buy corn dogs and garlic fries and Dippin' Dots. It is a matter of lasting chagrin to the childfolk of Santa Cruz that they're not allowed to go to the boardwalk every single day.

Though outsiders have been visiting for many years to walk on the beaches or surf or eat seafood, the town – as Hannah's mother sometimes observed – is rather like an island. Behind it stand the sturdy Santa Cruz Mountains, covered in redwoods and pines, cradling the town and providing a barrier between it and Silicon Valley and San Jose. Once these mountains were home to wolves and bears but the humans got rid of them to make the place tidier, and for the convenience of those who wish to hike. South lies the sweeping bay, where not much happens except for the cultivation of artichokes and garlic and other unappealing grown-up foodstuffs, until you get to Monterey, and then Carmel, and finally the craggy wilderness of Big Sur. On the northern side of town there's mainly emptiness along seventy miles of beautiful coast until you reach San Francisco, or 'the city', as everyone calls it in these parts. Santa Cruz could therefore seem somewhat cut off from the rest of California (and indeed the world), but luckily almost everyone who lives there is content with this arrangement. So Hannah's mother sometimes said, without much of a smile.

Hannah hadn't heard her mother say much recently, however. Before Hannah became embroiled in the story I'm about to tell, she was already a participant in several others, starring in *The Tale of Being an Eleven-Year-Old Girl*, *The Story of Having Annoyingly Straight Brown Hair*, *The Chronicles of My Friend Ellie Being Mean to Me for No Reason*, and *The Saga of It Being Completely Unfair that I'm Not Allowed to Have a Kitten*. One story had come to dominate her life recently, however, looming so large and changing so many things in such enormous ways that it drowned out all the rest.

It's an old and sad and confusing tale, called *Mom and Dad Don't Live Together Any More*.

Hannah knew the exact moment when this story began, the point at which some malign spirit had furrowed its brow and wondered 'What if?' and started messing around with her life.

It was a Saturday, and they were in Los Gatos. Hannah's mom liked Los Gatos. It's neat and tidy and has stores they didn't have in Santa Cruz. Hannah's dad was never as keen to make the half-hour journey over the mountains (the most doom-laden highway in the world, according to him, attractive but luridly prone to accident, and it's hard to be completely sanguine about the fact it actually *crosses* the San Andreas Fault) but between the Apple Store and a coffee shop and the nice square outside their favourite restaurant he seemed able to pass the morning pleasantly enough while Hannah and her mother shopped.

Lunch afterwards was always fun. The restaurant they visited was bright and airy and the waiters were friendly and wore smart uniforms and before you got your food they brought baskets of miniature breads and pastries which Hannah's parents would try to stop her eating. Meanwhile they'd talk and sip wine and Hannah's mom would show her dad some of the things she'd bought (though never, Hannah noticed, absolutely everything).

All of Hannah's memories of Los Gatos were good, therefore, until the time six months before, when she happened to glance up while nibbling a tiny muffin and saw her mother looking out of the window. Mom's face was blank and sad.

Surprised – lunches in Los Gatos were always cheerful, sometimes so cheerful recently that they might even have seemed a little shrill – Hannah looked at her father.

He was watching her mom. The expression on his face was not blank, though it was also sad.

'Dad?'

He blinked as if waking from a dream, and gave her a hard time for starting another pastry, though she could tell his heart wasn't in it. Meanwhile her mother kept staring out of the window as though watching something a long way away, as if wondering if she were to jump up from the table *right now* and run out of the door as fast as she could, she might be able to catch up with it before it disappeared from sight.

Food arrived, and everybody ate, and then they drove home. They didn't go to Los Gatos again after that. As far as Hannah was concerned, that lunch was when it all started to go wrong.

Because two months later Hannah's mom moved out.

*   *   *

A lot of things stayed the same. Hannah attended school, did homework, went to French class on Tuesday afternoons (which was extra, because Mom thought she ought to be able to understand it, even though the nearest place anybody spoke French was probably France). Dad had always done the grocery shopping and cooked the evening meal – as Hannah's mom travelled a lot for work, all over America and Europe, and had always seemed baffled and infuriated by the oven – so that was business as usual.

There's a difference between 'Mom being away until the weekend', however, and 'Mom is away . . . indefinitely.' The kitchen table goes all big. The dishwasher sounds too loud.

Her grandfather came to stay with them for a week – or, at least, his meandering path through the world brought him into Santa Cruz – which was nice. He did the kind of thing he usually did, like making odd little sculptures out of random objects he found on his walks, and dozing off in an armchair (or spending periods 'resting his eyes'). He cooked dinner one night though it wasn't entirely clear what it was, and tried to help Hannah with her science homework, but after ten minutes of frowning at the questions simply said that they were 'wrong'.

Hannah also saw her Aunt Zo, who came down a few times to keep her company. Zoë was twenty-eight. She lived in the city and was an artist-or-something. She had alarmingly spiky dyed-blond hair and several tattoos and wore black most of the time and was her dad's much younger sister, though it seemed to Hannah that Zo and her dad always looked at each other with cautious bemusement, as if they weren't sure they belonged to the same species, never mind family. Hannah didn't know what an 'artist-or-something' even was. She'd intuited it might not be an entirely complimentary term because it was how her mother described Zoë, and Hannah's mom and Zo had not always appeared to get on super-well. It had to be different to an 'artist', certainly, because extensive tests had demonstrated that Aunt Zo couldn't draw *at all*.

She was friendly, though, and fun, and had gone to a lot of trouble to explain that the fact Hannah's parents didn't live together right now didn't mean either of them loved her any less. Sometimes people lived together forever, and sometimes they did not. That was between them, and the reasons could be impossible for anybody else to understand. Sometimes it was because of something big or weird and unfixable. Sometimes it was merely something 'mundane'.

Hannah hadn't understood what this word meant. Aunt Zo waved her hands vaguely, and said, 'Well, you know. Mundane.'

Later Hannah looked it up on the internet. The internet said that the word came from the Latin *mundus*, meaning 'world', and thus referred to things 'of the earthly world, rather than a heavenly or spiritual one'. That made zero sense until she realized this was only a second thing it could mean, and that usually people used it to mean 'dull, lacking interest or excitement'.

Hannah nodded at this. She didn't see how Mom and Dad not living together could be without interest, but she was beginning to feel her life in general most certainly could.

The next time she saw Zo was when her aunt came to babysit overnight because Hannah's dad had to fly down to a meeting in Los Angeles. Hannah dropped the word into conversation, and was pleased to see her aunt smile to herself. Emboldened, Hannah tentatively asked whether maybe, next time, rather than Zo coming to Santa Cruz, Hannah could come up to the city instead. She did not say, but felt, they could be girls together there, and have new and unusual fun that would not be dull or lack excitement. Zo said yes, maybe, and how about they made some more popcorn and watched a movie.

Hannah was old and smart enough to understand that whatever 'mundane' might mean, 'maybe' generally meant 'no'.

Otherwise, life dragged on like a really long television show that was impossible to turn off. She went to school and ate and slept. Mom sent her an email every couple of days, and they spoke on Skype once a week. The emails were short, and usually about the weather in London, England, where she was working. The phone conversations were better, though it sometimes felt as though the actress playing her mother had changed.

Hannah realized it wasn't likely that, even when (or if) her mom did come back, she was going to come and live with Hannah and her dad. Straight away, anyway. Missing her mother was tough, but bearable. Hannah put thoughts of her in a box in her head and closed it up (not too tightly, just enough to stop it popping open all the time and making her cry) and told herself that she was welcome to look inside however often she liked. In her imagination the box was ornate and intricate and golden, like something out of a storybook.

Missing her dad was worse, because he was right there.

He hadn't gone away, but he had. Virtually everything about him with the exception of his appearance (though he often looked tired, and didn't smile with his eyes) had changed. He hugged her at bedtime. He hugged her at the school gate. When something needed to be said, one of them said it, and the other listened. But sometimes when Hannah came into a room without him realizing, she would look at him for a while and it was as though there was nobody there.

Otherwise, nothing much changed.

School.
Homework.
Food.
Bed.
School.
Homework.
Food.
Bed . . .

. . . like waves lapping on a deserted shore. Life was flat and grey and quiet, all the more so because every other adult with whom she came into contact – teachers at school, her friends' moms and dads, even the instructor at gym, who'd always been snarky with literally everyone – treated her differently now. They were polite and accommodating and they always smiled and seemed to look at her more directly than before. They were so very nice to her, in fact, that the world no longer had edge or bite. It lost all shape and colour and momentum, and any sense of light or shade. It was like living in a cloud.

Late one autumnal afternoon, as she sat watching through the window as a squirrel played in the tree outside, looking so in charge of its life, having so much fun, Hannah realized that her own life had become 'mundane'.

Horribly, unfeasibly mundane.

So I suppose that's where we'll begin.

Don't worry, things will start to happen. This hasn't been the actual story yet. It's background, a few moments spent sifting through the tales already in progress in order to pick a moment in time and say: 'So *now* let's see what happened next.'

And we will.

But before we get any further into Hannah's story, we need to go and meet someone else.

14

Chapter 2

Because, meanwhile, an old man was dozing on the terrace of the Palace Hotel, on Miami's South Beach.

The hotel stands amidst a half-mile of art deco jewels restored to their former glory in the 1980s, and – like many of the others – was determinedly now running back to seed, as though that was the state in which it felt most comfortable. The old man had a local newspaper on his lap but he had not read it. To one side, on the table supporting the umbrella protecting him from the sun, was a glass of ice tea that had long ago come up to ambient temperature. A large bug was swimming in it, a leisurely freestyle. The waiter working the terrace had approached the table several times to see if the gaunt old buzzard wanted his glass refreshed. Each time he'd discovered the man's eyes were closed. His position had not changed in quite a while.

Nonetheless the waiter decided to try one more time. In half an hour his shift would be over. In most ways that was awesome. The afternoon had been hellishly humid and the waiter was looking forward to returning to his ratty apartment, taking a shower, sitting out on his balcony and smoking pot for a couple of hours before hitting the town in the hope of finding some margarita-addled divorcée or, failing that, simply getting wasted. Business on the terrace had not been brisk, however. He was below quota on tips (and behind on his rent), and that was why he decided – now it was approaching five – it was worth one final attempt to upsell the old dude in the crumpled suit into a big glass of wine or, better still, an overpriced cocktail.

He went and stood over him.

The old man's head was tilted forwards in sleep, showcasing a pale forehead dotted with liver spots, a sizable beak of a nose, and combed-back hair that, though pure white, remained in decent supply. Large, mottled hands rested on knees that appeared bony even through the black linen of his suit. Who wore black in Florida, for God's sake?

The waiter coughed. There was no response.

He coughed again, more loudly.

Consciousness returned slowly.

It felt as though it was coming from a great distance, and that was because this was not a normal awakening. It wasn't merely a matter of rising from sleep. On this day, the old man woke from a far deeper slumber.

He opened his eyes and for a moment he had no idea where he was. It was hot. It was bright, though the quality of the light suggested it must be towards the end of the afternoon. He could see the glint of some ocean or other, past the stone terrace on which he sat.

And there was a young man, wearing a white apron, standing in front of him and smiling the kind of smile that always had financial outlay attached to it.

'Refreshed, sir?'

The old man stared confusedly at him for a moment, and then sat up straight. He peered around the terrace and saw young couples at other tables, and a few older people wearing hats and looking out at the ocean as if waiting for it to do something. Hotels on either side. Palm trees.

He turned back to the waiter. 'Where am I?'

The waiter sighed. The old fart had seemed fine when he ordered his ice tea earlier. Evidently a day in the sun had fried what was left of his wits.

'Wondered if I could interest you in a cold glass of Chardonnay, sir? We have an intriguing selection. Though perhaps a crisp Sauvignon Blanc would be more to your taste? Or a Martini, a Bellini, or a Sobotini? That's the signature creation of our in-house executive mixologist, Ralph Sobo, and features a trio of—'

'Did I ask you to recite the entire drinks menu?'

'No, sir.'

'So?'

The waiter smiled tightly. 'You are on the terrace of the Palace Hotel,' he said, offensively slowly. 'South Beach. Miami. The United States of America.' He leaned forwards and added, loudly enough for people nearby to turn and smile to themselves, 'Planet Earth.'

The man frowned. 'How long have I been here?'

'In this spot? The entire afternoon. The hotel? I have no clue. I'm sure reception can assist you with that information, along with your name, if that's also slipped your mind. Now – can I help you with a beverage, or not?'

The man shook his head. 'Just my bill.'

The waiter walked off, bouncing his tray against his knee, vowing that he would use everything within his power to make sure that the wrinkly old fool received his bill only after a very significant delay.

This waiter had only been working at the Palace for a couple of days, and didn't yet know many other members of staff. Otherwise he might have heard, in passing, whispers about this particular old man. Rumours that in the three months he'd been resident in a suite on the thirteenth floor, it had proved impossible to place guests in the accommodation on either side. The hotel's sophisticated computer system appeared to have developed an intermittent glitch that meant those rooms showed up as occupied, even when they were not. Any attempt to override or ignore this resulted in double- or even treble-booking, with the inevitable fallout of enraged guests, and so for the time being reception had stopped trying to allot the rooms. They had also temporarily halted attempts to get to the bottom of the means of payment the old man had presented. His credit card, though unimpeachable in status and hue, proved impossible to retain reliably in the system. As a result – and to the hotel manager's increasing disquiet – no charge had yet been levied against it. The technical department claimed this would be fixed very soon. The manager hoped this was true, though it was not the first or even third time he'd been given this assurance.

The waiter didn't know any of this, however. So he went over to the register and surreptitiously tore up the old man's bill, before hanging up his apron and leaving the terrace, whistling a tune to himself.

It'd only take the senile old bastard ten or fifteen minutes to get a new bill from the next waiter, but any inconvenience was better than none.

The man sitting under the umbrella didn't wait that long, however. He laid ten dollars on the table, securing it under his glass. He stood. For a few moments he didn't move any farther, apparently becalmed, his face blank.

Then suddenly he smiled.

It was not a simple smile, one of pleasure or joy. It was complicated, rueful. If you'd been watching, you might have thought he'd remembered something, a matter that was not urgent but which he felt foolish for having neglected.

He took a last look at the ocean and then turned and walked towards the doors to the hotel lobby, moving with a good deal more grace and speed than you might have expected.

An hour later, after a shower and in the middle of his second joint, the waiter from the Palace Hotel was relaxing on his balcony when it suddenly collapsed, dropping him forty feet into the chaos of his downstairs neighbour's scrap of yard, where he died, reasonably quickly, as a result of a sheared metal strut which punctured his ribcage and heart.

This was not a coincidence.

Chapter 3

It was seven in the evening, and Hannah was waiting.

Waiting.

Waiting.

She'd been waiting since breakfast, during which her father had been even more distant and insubstantial than usual; and waiting since he'd dropped her at school, saying goodbye with a hug and a kiss but an odd look in his eyes. He had forgotten to shave that morning, she noticed. He'd forgotten the day before, too. She hadn't waited during the math homework they'd endured after pick-up, as she knew she had to pay attention. Her dad had more than once described helping her with math as his punishment for all the evil things he didn't remember doing in a previous life, or *lives*, and while she doubted this was true she understood his patience was not limitless, especially now.

She then waited while he cooked dinner, her favourite, a creamy pasta dish with bacon and peas that he'd invented for her when she was small and the very smell of which made her feel safe and warm even when she knew that the world had changed. In fact, as she sat in the corner of the kitchen reading while he cooked, she wondered whether it was accidental that he happened to be cooking creamy bacon pasta this evening, or if it was in some way related to whatever it was that she knew – without having any reason she could put a finger on – that she was waiting for. The menu had been notably random in recent weeks, occasionally featuring complicated things she'd never seen before, but then frozen pizza three nights in a row.

And now tonight, suddenly, it was her favourite.

Waiting.

They ate at the kitchen table. Her father asked about her day, and listened, seeming more 'there' than for the last day or two. He didn't eat much, though.

Afterwards Hannah carried her plate to the dishwasher and went to the living room to wait some more. Finally her father came through holding a cup of coffee. He perched on the edge of the sofa. 'I need to say something,' he said.

For a dire moment, Hannah was convinced he was going to tell her that Mom was never coming back from London, or that Hannah had to leave too, or he'd decided they needed to move to another town or something. She stared at him, barely able to breathe, but saw that his eyes looked soft, and so she thought probably – hopefully – it wasn't something as bad as that.

'What?' she asked.

He pursed his lips and stared down at the carpet. He looked tired. Some of his bristles were grey. Had they been that way before Mom left? Hannah wasn't sure. He'd never forgotten to shave when Mom was around.

'I'm not handling this as well as I'd like,' he said. 'Your mom being . . . not here, I mean. I'm trying to do what needs to be done. And it's working, right? We're doing OK?'

Hannah nodded dutifully. Most of the time it sort of was OK, but even if it hadn't been, she understood he hadn't asked the question in order for her to answer it. Grown-ups did that a lot, saying something they believed to be a fact but putting a question mark at the end. It was meant to make you take the fact more seriously, or something. You learned that you weren't expected to say anything in reply, just as you learned that if you were a girl you didn't always want to mention your video-game scores to boys, especially if yours were higher.

'But . . .' He stopped. He didn't seem to know what he wanted to say next.

'You're sad,' she said.

He laughed, surprised. 'Well, yeah. You are too, I know. It's, uh, it's a strange time.'

'I'm sad,' she agreed. 'But not like you are.'

'What . . . do you mean?'

'You're badly sad.'

He stared at her, nodding, and she was intensely scared to see that his eyes were full. She had never, *ever* seen her dad cry. She didn't want to see it now. She knew life sucked but if it turned out it was bad enough to make her father *cry*, it was far worse than she realized. That would be beyond mundane.

'Did I say something wrong?'

'No. You said something smart.' He sniffed briskly, and stopped looking like he was going to cry. 'I need some time,' he said. 'Firstly . . . well, all this.' He raised his hands, referring to the house, and what was in it, and what was not in it any more. 'Plus . . . work. I'm getting behind. One or the other thing, I could handle. Both at once, not so much. It seems.'

Hannah understood that her father typed for a living, for people who lived down in Los Angeles, helping them make stories. She knew this was a hard job sometimes, partly because – so she had gathered, from overhearing conversations between him and Mom – almost all of the people her dad worked for were assholes and idiots, with the creative acumen of mosquitoes and the moral sensibilities of wolverines. He said things like this very quietly, though, as if concerned they might be able to hear him from over three hundred miles away.

'OK, look,' he said. 'Here's the thing. I wondered if you'd like to go stay with Granddad for a while.'

Hannah wanted to say 'yes' immediately, but dimly understood that she should not. 'Granddad?'

Her father was watching her carefully. 'Yes.'

'Why not Aunt Zo?'

'Zo-zo's busy.' He sighed. 'Got an exhibition coming up, or a performance, or some . . . thing. Plus you've seen her apartment. She has to stand up when she goes to sleep.'

This was an old family joke and Hannah smiled as always, or tried to. It felt different now. In the past there would never have been any question of her staying with Aunt Zo. Now it had evidently been considered, and rejected. That made Hannah feel rejected too. 'And I was thinking . . . of you going for more than a couple of days.'

'How long?'

'A week. Maybe two.'

Two whole *weeks*? 'When?'

'Tomorrow.'

'But . . . what about school?'

'I talked to Teacher Jen. She said it would be OK.'

Hannah looked hard at her father, and knew he was not telling the truth. Not the whole truth, anyway. He would have talked to her teacher, yes. You couldn't just yank a kid out of school without clearing it with mission control.

But it struck her now that, though he had not shaved, he'd been wearing smart chinos and a shirt when he dropped her at school that morning – the first time in ages he hadn't been wearing the raggedy jeans he used to only wear at the weekend. She didn't think you could bail your kid out of school for two weeks just by saying 'I'm having a hard time.' So probably he'd said it was something to do with working for the wolverines instead, which is why he'd been wearing business clothes. Things to do with work were always incredibly important for grown-ups. They were respected without question. Far more, it sometimes seemed, than things to do with children.

'Have you asked Granddad?'

'Yes. I spoke to him last night. Well, emailed. There's no phone signal there.'

'Where *is* he now? Where on earth?'

Her father smiled, and this time it looked genuine. It made Hannah realize what a long time it had been since she'd seen that kind of smile on his face.

'Washington State,' he said, as if this meant the far side of the moon. 'God knows why. But where he's staying sounds pretty cool. I think you'll like it. And he says he's really looking forward to seeing you.'

From the moment Dad first mentioned the idea, Hannah had wanted to go. She loved her dad's dad, and the prospect of getting out of Santa Cruz for a while, doing something – anything – other than plodding through her mundane existence, felt desperately attractive. She'd held back from leaping at it because she knew she shouldn't seem as if she wanted to get away from her father. That also meant she had to say what she said next. 'But I'll miss you.'

As soon as the words were out of her mouth, she realized how true they were. How badly true.

Her dad's lips clamped together, the way they sometimes did when he was mad. His eyes didn't look mad, though. Not at all.

'I'll miss you too,' he said. 'But we can Skype, and email,

and it's not so long. And when you get back, things will be better here. I promise.'

'OK,' Hannah said. 'Can I watch some Netflix now?'

'Sure,' he said, wrong-footed.

'Yay.'

She jumped up and ran to the den and switched on the big TV. As she was waiting for her show to load she glanced back into the living room and saw that her father was still sitting on the edge of the sofa, shoulders bowed and head lowered. She could not see his face or eyes.

His shoulders seemed to shake, for a moment, and then shake again. Presumably he was laughing at something.

Chapter 4

The driver pulled over to the side of Ali Baba Avenue and turned to look at the guy in the back of his cab.

'You sure this is where you want to be?'

The old man had been silent throughout the long journey into Dade County from South Beach, successfully resisting Domingo's attempts to involve him in conversation. Domingo was *good* at conversation, too. His game was tight. He didn't mind listening either, a much rarer gift, and so he could usually get customers to chat with him, and he did this out of a simple desire to tell people things and to hear stuff about where they'd come from and where they were going, not just because it meant a bigger tip, though that was always welcome.

This customer, though . . . he wasn't buying it. Anything Domingo said, he'd said nothing back, remaining relentlessly and noisily silent. He was currently looking out of the window at the twilight, his big, pale hands resting on the knees of his suit. 'Yes,' he said. 'This looks perfect.'

Domingo laughed briefly. 'Right. You want to get mugged or score some dope that's gonna put you straight in ER, that may be true. This could be Heaven on earth right here.'

The passenger held out a few bank notes to signal their

business was concluded. Domingo was not to be so easily dismissed, however.

'The hell you want to come to Opa Locka for, anyway? Some dumbass website say there's authentic down-home cooking? They lied, brother. The only specialty they got around here is rat boiled in meth. You want food, I can take you places, good places, back where the locals don't eat each other.'

The old man opened his door. Domingo tried one last time. 'Look. At least take my card, OK? How the hell else you going to get back? Don't you be flagging down no cab here, even if you see one, which you won't. For real. They'll take you round the corner and rob your ass. If you're lucky.'

The man got out and walked off down a street that looked as though it had recently withstood a minor hurricane and hadn't been remotely picturesque before that. Domingo thought about going after him, but this was, bottom line, not a neighbourhood where he wanted to linger any longer than necessary.

So he drove away.

The old man spent an hour strolling the streets as the light faded. He saw low storage buildings of indeterminate purpose, fortified with barbed wire. He passed squat one-storey dwellings interspersed with clumps of stunted palm trees, houses set apart from each other not for the luxury of space but as though the inhabitants didn't trust their neighbours enough to live in closer proximity. There were no sidewalks, so he walked down the middle of the streets, which were pitted and patched and ragged at the edges and sprouting grass in many places: the kind of broken roads you'd expect to see down the dusty end of country towns that had been dying for decades. It was stiflingly humid.

He encountered few people. Every now and then a child would run past, but never stop. A woman stared at him from the stoop of her small, battered house, as if wondering what kind of fool he might be. A couple of times he observed men loitering outside corner grocery stores, their eyes following him. He passed slowly, in case it would be one of these who'd show him where he needed to go. None moved, however. They seemed winded, listless, as though they couldn't summon up the energy to rob a frail-looking old man who was evidently a long way from base.

But eventually he hesitated.

He felt something.

He turned in a slow circle, sniffed the air, and then set off up the next cross street. The houses were even farther apart here, and few showed a light. It felt . . . right.

When he saw the abandoned warehouse down the end, looming in dark isolation, he knew for sure that it was.

They looked up as he entered.

It was a large, empty space, the heart of the disused building. A fire built of fallen palm leaves and broken furniture burned in the centre.

Five men stood around it. Three white, one black, one half-Latino, none of them kids, all in their late twenties or thirties, but dressed in hoodies and ragged jeans all the same. Each looked as though it would be their pleasure to hurt you quite badly. There were a lot of candles, a hundred or more, spread over the floor and flickering in cavities in the walls.

One of the men, the tallest of the white guys, laughed. 'Whoa,' he said. 'Holy crap, are *you* lost.'

The old man kept walking until he was within ten feet of the fire. He put his hands together as if in prayer, and looked at each of the men in turn.

'No,' he said in a calm and thoughtful voice. 'I believe this is precisely where I need to be.' He pulled out his wallet and threw it on the floor closest to the man who'd spoken. 'Let's get that part over with. I'd hate us to get distracted by mere theft.'

The tall guy frowned.

One of the others picked up the wallet. He leafed through it with a professional eye, and whistled. 'Six hundred,' he said to the tall guy, evidently the leader. 'And change. We going to kill him now?'

The tall guy said nothing. His real name was Robert. That's what his mother had called him, anyhow. She was dead and had been for a long time, along with his father and two sisters, and these days most people called him Nash instead. He'd been alive for nearly forty years – a long story by local criminal standards – and during that period had done many things. It'd be hard to come up with something he hadn't done, in fact. Suffice it to say there were women, and men, and children, who woke in the night with his face in their minds as they lay sweating with the terrible memories they had acquired at his hands. Nash had stolen and beaten, and he had killed, via the media of gun and knife and bare hands and the sale of drugs cut with everything from toilet cleaner and chalk to concrete dust idly swept up off the street.

Bottom line: Nash was a very bad man, and in the last six months he'd started to explore whole new realms and means and levels of being not-good.

He was, however, also not-dumb. The way the old guy was presenting said you didn't simply kill him. Not yet. 'What do you want?'

'Tell me about the candles.'

The other three guys glanced at each other. 'We're Satanists,' one said proudly, the guy who'd rifled through the wallet, and still clutched it in his hand.

'Shut up,' Nash said.

The old man seemed intrigued. 'Is that so?'

The guy holding the wallet didn't want to stop talking. 'You don't believe us?'

'You say you are, you are.'

'You'd better bel—'

Nash turned to the wallet guy, his eyes hard. The other man went silent. He froze, his mouth open in mid-word. It looked as though he was trying to close it but could not. Eventually, after a great deal of effort, he managed to. Sweat had broken out on his forehead and his hands were trembling.

The old man watched all this with interest.

The trembling man retreated into the shadows. The others followed suit, leaving only Nash standing opposite the old man.

'Going to ask you one last time,' Nash told him. 'What do you *want*?'

The old man shrugged in a friendly way. 'I'm curious. I have a fondness for ruins, the abandoned, the lost. I was walking, and saw this place. I decided I'd take a look. I was assuming it would be empty or that I'd find a few homeless or addicts sprawled over the floor. Instead . . .' He gestured around. 'Candles. They look well enough. But you don't seem the *Martha Stewart Living* type. So I'm curious.'

'Who are you?'

'Merely what I appear to be. But who are you, Robert? What are *you* these days?'

Nash stared at him. 'How you know that name?'

'It's just a game of mine. Whenever I don't know someone's name, I call them Robert, that's all. So tell me. Was what he said true? Are you gentlemen really Satanists?'

Nash elected to tell the truth, not because he considered the practice to be important or valuable, but because it was time to let the weird old dude know exactly what – and who – he was dealing with.

He lifted his right hand, raising it to chest height. His eyes on the other man's, he coughed, once.

A small glow puffed into life in his palm, at first very dim, but quickly growing into a little ball of bright orange fire, about the size of a golf ball.

The old man watched the flame. 'Huh,' he said, as if impressed.

'Right,' Nash said, closing his hand and lowering it back to his side. 'That answer your question?'

'I suppose it does.'

'Good. Got any more, or are you going to leave? Or I guess you could stay, and we could beat up on you for a while. For practice. That could work.'

'How'd you do it? The fire.'

'It's a gift.'

'From whom?'

'From him. The Dark One. For doing his work.'

'How? What kind of thing?'

'We pray to him,' Nash said. 'Every day. And we make sacrifice.'

The old man nodded as if someone was explaining an important change in the terms and conditions of his health insurance. 'What kind? Animals? People?'

'No.' Nash laughed scornfully. 'That's retro bullshit. You do the wrong thing with the right intent, you don't need that Dennis Wheatley crap.'

'So what do you do?'

'We break, we burn. We spoil.'

'You say "we"?'

The other men watched from the background, silent, as if knowing this conversation was out of their league.

'Me, mainly. These guys . . . they got a ways to go.'

'So show me something. The kind of thing you do.'

Nash hesitated. On the one hand the situation was kind of whack. He didn't have a clue who this guy was. Could be a cop for all he knew. But if so, he couldn't have anything on Nash or he'd have come with back-up and guns – even assuming Miami PD kept detectives on the payroll after they got so old they looked like they should have their feet up on a porch, waiting for the grandkids to come visit so they could go to Disneyworld and waste enough money to feed an Opa Locka family for a month.

The other thing was that Nash *did* want to show someone, someone other than the hangers-on lurking in the shadows. He'd shown those guys what to do, countless times, but none of them was making progress. They couldn't get it to click, and that failure was holding him back. Nash understood that it wasn't enough to walk this road by yourself. You got status from how many you dragged along with you. It was a gift you had to keep on giving. Day after day. Night after night.

He put his hand in his jeans and pulled out a small cardboard container, about the size of a pack of cigarettes. He held it up.

'What's that?'

Nash opened it. The interior had been padded with cotton wool. Lying in the centre was a tiny box. He removed this and held it up for the old man to see.

The man leaned forwards and squinted, seeing an intensely shiny black surface over most of the box, apart from the lid. There, someone had spent a great deal of time painting a detailed winter scene: pine trees and snow and a horse-drawn sleigh with two people on it, wrapped in old-fashioned coats and furry hats. It was so precise that it looked as if it must have been painted with a brush of a single hair, white and green with highlights of intense red and purple and dots of gold, all the more striking for the blackness of the box. It was extraordinarily shiny, too, as if coated with many coats of colourless varnish. In its detail and lustre it reminded the old man of something else, a far larger box he had once commissioned to be built.

'And?'

'Old guy who lives a couple blocks from here,' Nash said, putting the tiny box carefully down on the floor. 'I heard him talking in the store. His wife's dying of cancer. Her mother was from Russia. The one thing she brought with her from the old country was a box like this. A lacquer box, they call it. It got stolen when this guy's wife was a kid, but she's remembered it all these years. Like it stood for her mom, or some shit. So this guy, he knows his wife's dying, and he's got cash salted away she doesn't know about. He's been saving all these years for the right time, putting a buck away here, fifty cents there. He figures this is the right time. So I overhear him telling all this to the guy behind the counter – who doesn't give a crap, I mean he really could not care less – telling him that he's blown this money, seven hundred fifty dollars, on buying one of these on the internet. Spent weeks tracking down a box like the one he's heard his wife describe all these years. It's her birthday in a week. He's going to give it to her then. Or . . . he *was*. Until I paid a visit to their house, last Sunday morning when they were at church.'

'You stole it. Nice.'

Nash smiled. 'Right. But that's not it.'

He raised his right foot and paused, closing his eyes as if in supplication, and then brought the heel of his boot down on the lacquer box, smashing it to pieces.

He was quiet for maybe ten seconds, relishing the moment. Then he opened his eyes.

'*That's* what he likes.'

The old man was motionless, as if listening for something. After a few moments he shook his head. 'I got nothing,' he said. He seemed irritated, and something else. Disconcerted, perhaps.

Nash was confused too, having anticipated a very different reaction. 'What?'

The old man stood there, lips pursed, furrow-browed. Up until this point he'd seemed relaxed, as if their discussion had been quite interesting but no big deal. He didn't look that way now. He looked unhappy, and thoughtful. He looked serious.

'What's *up*, dude?'

The old man glanced at Nash as though his mind was already on other things. 'What's up? I'll tell you what is up. I like your style, but there's a problem.'

'What kind of problem?'

'A big one. I don't know who you've been sacrificing to, my friend, but he is not the Devil.'

'Oh yeah? How do you know he's not?'

'Because I am,' the old man said.

He turned to the man in the shadows who was still holding his wallet, held up a hand, and clicked his fingers.

The man exploded.

There was utter silence. None of the men standing there, sprayed though they were with blood and brains and internal organs, said a word or made a sound or moved a muscle. It was so very quiet that it seemed possible they might even have stopped breathing, until they all blinked, in unison.

'Don't try that at home,' the old man said, bending down

to pick up his wallet from where it had landed conveniently by his feet. 'Otherwise, keep up the bad work.'

He walked out into the night, purposefully, a man who'd determined that it was finally time to get down to business.

Chapter 5

The flight was OK except that a woman from the airline kept coming to check on Hannah, talking to her like she was five years old. At first, Hannah had been glad. She was a little nervous at the prospect of the journey, never having flown by herself (though also excited, as it would be the most compelling proof yet that she was, in fact, extremely grown up). Her dad was there to see her off, of course, but he still had not shaved and his voice was quiet and he was blinking an awful lot. He hugged her tightly when it was time for her to get on the plane and stood watching her walk down the corridor until she had to turn the corner and couldn't see him any more. A kind-looking old lady with long grey hair told her not to worry, she'd see him again soon. Hannah didn't think it was any of the lady's business, but said thank you anyway.

She didn't like to think of her dad driving back over the hill to their house and walking into the silence all by himself. So she did not, and read her book instead.

The flight passed, as they all do, eventually.

The first person she saw when she walked out of arrivals in Seattle was Granddad, standing with his hands in his corduroy trousers, chubby and pink-faced and irrevocably bald. His face lit up when he saw her, and she ran over and buried her face in his sizable stomach.

'It's OK,' he said, putting his arms around her, smelling as always of peppermint. 'Everything will be OK.'

Half an hour later they were in Granddad's car on their way out of Tacoma. It was, Hannah believed, the same car he'd had when he came to visit in Santa Cruz – though it was hard to be certain. He seemed to delight in changing them regularly, and in picking vehicles in colours that had no name, somewhere on the spectrum between brown and green and sludge, hues of which it was impossible to imagine someone ever thinking: Ooh, yes, let's make it look like *that*. Their shape was also hard to describe beyond that they looked like cars, the kind a small boy might draw. The sole constant – and this is what made it tough to tell if this was a new one or the same old one – was that the inside would be flamboyantly, outrageously untidy.

When Granddad opened the trunk to stow Hannah's bag he had to move a birdcage, two bags of old alarm clocks, a broken DVD player, quite a lot of shoes, a length of green hosepipe, two large metal springs made of copper, and a stuffed raccoon. Hannah wasn't sure whether she was allowed by law to ride in the front of the car with him, but there wasn't any choice as the back seat was full of too many things to list unless you had a piece of paper ten feet long, a pencil, and a sharpener.

From time to time Granddad would make odd sculptures, one of which – apparently fashioned from the insides of a small television, some watches, a toy mouse, and other things she didn't have names for – graced the bookshelf in Hannah's bedroom. She had no idea what it was supposed to be but she liked it anyway. He had given her parents several such works in the past, too, but Hannah's mother had evidently decided they would be seen to their best advantage in the garage.

When she sat in the passenger seat Hannah had to angle her legs because there was an ancient suitcase in the footwell. It was made of leather and had a dusty dial on the front. She asked, politely, if it was possible to move it.

'I'm afraid not,' Granddad said. 'It has to be there or the car won't go.'

As often, Hannah wasn't sure whether this was true or not, but managed to get her legs comfortable. 'So where are you living now, Granddad? Where on *earth*?'

'You'll see.'

'Will it take long?'

'Quite a while. I'm going to take the scenic route.'

'Should I chatter senselessly the entire way, or gaze quietly out the window instead?'

He looked at her and smiled, putting deep, kind lines in the skin around his eyes. 'That, my dear, is entirely up to you.'

As he pulled out of the parking lot, Hannah settled back into her seat and took a bite of the sandwich he'd brought for her, knowing she'd probably do a bit of both.

Hannah had learned early in life that the thing about her grand-father was he didn't live anywhere in particular. He did not fail to live anywhere in the way most people did, like the ones who sat on street corners in Santa Cruz, displaced or unplaced, submissive or cranky, overly tan and wary of passers-by, the people her mom and dad had taken pains to explain deserved as much politeness and goodwill as everyone else, possibly more. Those people didn't have homes because they couldn't afford them, or due to being unwell in body or mind.

Granddad was different. He didn't have a house because

that was the way he liked it. For a long time – before Hannah was born – he'd had a home. He lived with Grandma, whom she never met, in a house in Colorado. Even then he would have preferred a more itinerant life, but his wife felt differently and they had children to bring up – Dad and Aunt Zo – and so he'd consented to being shackled to one particular house, one particular road, one set of grocery stores and local news stations and weather patterns and group of people and ways of being, and a ludicrous little dog belonging to a neighbour who'd barked the whole damned time for years and years, a memory which evidently still rankled.

Once he'd got over the death of Grandma, however, he'd done what he'd always wanted. He sold the house and everything in it, and went on the road. That was twenty years ago. Now he was a quantum elder, and there was almost no means of predicting his whereabouts at any given moment – where on *earth*, as Mom and Dad always put it, rolling their eyes, the old man might be. He rattled around the United States (and occasionally other countries, like Russia and Mozambique, but mainly he stayed in America) in a succession of battered cars (or perhaps one car, of surprising longevity, no one was sure). Sometimes he'd hole up for several months, renting an apartment or cottage or shed. At other times he'd pause for only a few days, lodging in a hotel or motel or even, Hannah's mom speculated darkly, somewhere so far off the beaten track that there *were* no places to stay, which meant he was presumably sleeping in his car.

Hannah thought this was an exaggeration. Having seen Granddad's car/s, she was confident there would simply never be enough room for him to stretch out.

They drove for a few hours. At first it was busy city streets and highways, and Hannah kept quiet because her grandfather was concentrating. He drove at a consistent, sedate pace, which from time to time provoked irritation in other road users, manifested by honking and the waving of fists. Unlike her father, who responded to this style of criticism in kind, Granddad hummed serenely – before suddenly stepping on the gas and leaving the other cars for dust, out-smarting them with deft multi-lane manoeuvres. Just occasionally you might feel inclined to close your eyes during one of these dogfights, but you rarely believed there was a genuine chance of dying.

Soon they were out of the city and driving around the Olympic Peninsula. For a while he played music on the car stereo, the kind of quiet, complicated music he liked, which he said was called 'baroque', but when it ran out he didn't put on any more. At times he took them close to the woods and at others he drove along the cold, craggy coast, flicker-lit by sun glinting off the ocean between stands of silver and paper birch. Sometimes they talked, about school and stuff, and where Granddad had lived recently (he'd been lodging at their destination for several weeks now, a long stay by his standards: before that he'd tried a spell in the hills of somewhere she'd never heard of, called Syria, but hadn't liked it much, too dusty and hot).

For much of the time, as the afternoon wore on, they drove in equable silence. Something she liked about her grandfather was that if you wanted to talk then he'd listen, but if you didn't want to talk, he'd listen to that too. His mind wouldn't immediately fly away to work and emails or all the things that seemed to have Mom and Dad in their tractor beams. With them you had to talk all the time to keep their attention, to remind them you were *there*. Not with Granddad.

And sometimes, when a lot has happened in your life, much of it inexplicable, silence is what you need to say the most.

After a while she fell asleep.

*   *   *

40

It was almost dark when she woke, stirred by a sudden decrease in the car's speed. Hannah pulled herself upright, blinking, as her grandfather turned off the highway and on to a narrow two-lane road leading into the hills.

'Are we here?'

'We're always here,' he said. 'That's important to remember. But in the specific case of the place to which we're going, we very nearly are.'

'What?'

'Sorry. "Yes" is what I meant to say.'

The road wound up and over the hills. At the top you could see the ocean for a few minutes through the trees, and then the road headed down again on the other side.

At the end of it stood a hotel, an old-looking two-storey lodge made of wood, but Granddad turned towards a crop of cabins dotted along a pathway that meandered along the low bluff above the beach. He parked in front of the last of these.

'Welcome to Kalaloch.'

The cabin was made of wood and painted white and grey, though not recently. It was clean but had a musty smell, like old sea breezes retired into stillness. There were two bedrooms, a bathroom with a tub so tiny Hannah thought she might have difficulty stretching her legs out in it, and a living room with two chairs and a couch but no TV. At all. Not even a small one. She checked several times, baffled by this over-turning of the natural order.

The outside wall of the living room was taken up with a pair of sliding glass doors, with a view out over the path to the ocean. When he'd put her suitcase on the bed of her room, Granddad opened the doors and led her out on to the path, past a couple of battered plastic chairs evidently designed for enjoying the view from the minuscule deck, assuming you'd brought a thick sweater or two.

The beach was twenty feet below the edge of the bluff, a wide stretch of grey sand reaching out towards an even greyer sea. A few pieces of driftwood, large and very white, were strewn across it. There was no one down there, no footprints even. It looked like the end of the world. The ocean seemed as though it went on forever and then a bit more.

A gull sailed by, high overhead, and disappeared.

Even with Granddad only feet away, Hannah felt very alone. Her hand folded around the iPod in her jeans pocket. 'Is there Wi-Fi here?'

'Not in the cabin. There is in the lodge, though, when we go over there to eat dinner.'

Hannah nodded.

'You want to Skype your dad?'

She shrugged. He looked out at the ocean for a moment, then put his hand on her shoulder. 'I don't know about you,' he said, 'but it's been a long drive, and I'm rather hungry already.'

She smiled at him. He always heard.

Chapter 6

Meanwhile, about a thousand miles away, a man was sitting at a table in a diner called Frankie's Food Fiasco, situated at the edge of a small town in North Dakota. The man was called Ron – though a lot of people had another name for him.

The restaurant had got its name because it was owned by a guy called Frankie: sometimes that's the way it is. Frankie was a capable cook, and his diner was regarded as pretty much the only place you'd voluntarily eat in town. Less well known was that Frankie had never wanted to own a diner. He'd wanted to be a movie star. For a while it looked like it might happen, too, after he scored a lead supporting role in a TV series about a maverick chiropodist turned surfing detective, called *Undertoe*, which by odd coincidence was the first show Hannah's dad worked on. It was also the only one that had got a second season, and thus constituted his biggest and, kind of, only success. Frankie had played the star's dour buddy, prone to mutter the word 'Fiasco!' whenever things went wrong – which became a moderately popular running gag in society at large for about five minutes.

Once the show got cancelled and he'd realized the world of entertainment appeared not merely willing, but keen, to get along without him, Frankie had enough smarts to head back to his home town, where he used his savings to buy a failing restaurant, largely because he had no idea of what else to do. Through trial and error – and a degree of bloody-mindedness – he'd rewritten himself as a cook, and now if you wanted to eat out in Shendig, North Dakota, Frankie's Food Fiasco was where you'd go.

Frankie could have been content with this state of affairs, but he was not. He wished he was still an actor, and in the intervening years had developed a churning resentment of the people who frequented his diner. What did *they* know about the life he should have had? Nothing. Zip. Nada. They just wanted their burgers and wings and fries and beer. They sat and stuffed their greedy faces not caring that the food they were shovelling down had been prepared by a man who, were this a fair and just world, should be lounging on the deck of a beach house in Malibu, stupefied with money and success.

In revenge for this, every night Frankie would, at random, screw up a single dish. He'd put in way too much salt, or a big dollop of hot sauce, or mix untoward ingredients in such a way that the result tasted quite unlike anything you'd generally regard as food. Though it was never explicitly discussed, some of the restaurant's customers realized the danger, incorrectly assuming it was a recurrent accident. You couldn't say anything should you be unlucky enough to be served the booby-trapped dish because Frankie was prone to banning people if they got uppity, and you didn't want that to happen as the only other place to eat in Shendig (apart from Molly's Café, which was dependably disgusting) was the Burger King downtown. If you received Frankie's nightly food bomb you forced down as much as you could and politely told the waitress you were full, declining the opportunity to have the remainder boxed – knowing that statistically you were unlikely to get the booby prize again for a while.

Unless, that is, you were Ron.

Ron ate at Frankie's at least once a week. It was just down the hill from his apartment and he enjoyed the low ceilings, the wood panelling, the fact that the music was never too loud. He also liked the food, though it seemed like his entrée tasted *really* weird about one time in three. Ron hadn't heard the rumour about the food bombs. He just shrugged and put it down to fate.

Ron put a lot of things down to fate. He had to. Like the fact that the booth he was sitting in tonight – and he couldn't move, because the place was packed: people liked to come in when it was busy, as it lowered the probability of receiving a dish that tasted like it had been cobbled together from things that had died out on the highway and then spent a few days simmering in snot – happened to be right under a spot in the exposed piping hooked to the ceiling that had developed a leak, and was intermittently allowing droplets of very cold water to fall on to his head. He'd tried moving to the other side of the booth, but it happened there, too. Except the drops were boiling hot.

Tonight his ribs tasted great, but he was barely aware of them. He was concerned instead with two other matters, the first being that he'd totalled his car that afternoon. It had snowed heavily a couple of days before and while most people had managed to avoid the very obvious icy patch at the end of the road, Ron had not. As he'd recently lost his job at the picture framer's after dropping (and damaging, cataclysmically and beyond hope of repair) what had turned out to be a rather valuable painting, Ron wasn't in a position to get his car fixed. Without one, it was going to be hard to find a new job.

The second thing on his mind was his girlfriend, Rionda. Or rather, he realized gloomily, his ex-girlfriend. She worked at the Burger King and was the nicest person he had ever met. She'd seemed to like him too, but their association had been plagued by disappointing events, including him setting fire to her favourite dress when lighting a candle that was supposed to be romantic, and accidentally backing his car over her foot.

She'd put up with most of this reasonably well, but the last weekend had seen a new low point. Invited for the first time to meet Rionda's parents, Ron became entangled in a series of calamities during a visit to their bathroom that he still didn't understand, but which had ultimately led to a need for the services of not one, but two teams of emergency plumbers, working in shifts, an estimated refurbishment bill of six to ten thousand dollars, and an odour which experts were now saying would probably never go away. When Ron had trudged away from the house at the end of the afternoon, Rionda and her mother were standing on the porch in floods of tears, and her father had been brandishing a shotgun.

Ron guessed that was probably the end of it.

He sighed and reached for his soda, not realizing until too late that he'd dipped his sleeve in his barbecue beans, at which point this distracted him sufficiently that he knocked his drink over. Not all of it dripped through the hole in the table on to his trousers, but most did.

It was this kind of thing that caused many people, behind his back, to call him Bad Luck Ron.

As Ron was tucking into a slice of pecan pie and wondering why it tasted so strongly of fish, he looked up to see a man standing at the end of the table.

The man was old, with white hair pushed back from his forehead and large hands. He was wearing a crumpled black linen suit. He didn't say anything. He merely stood there, apparently watching the corner of the booth, the seat next to Ron.

He was looking at it so fixedly, in fact, that Ron turned to look too. The seat was empty, as he'd known it would be.

Well . . . it *appeared* empty. Ron couldn't see the strange, four-foot-high fungus-like creature sitting there, or the expression of utter surprise, tinged with guilt and nervousness, upon its gnarled beige face.

Ron turned back to the old man. 'Uh, can I help you?'

The man walked away.

Ron watched him head across the diner and out of the door without looking back. 'Huh,' he said.

He soldiered on with his pie a little longer, but eventually gave up. It was making him feel nauseous.

After he'd paid his bill, electing as always not to mention any problem with the food, Ron left the diner and stepped out into the freezing parking lot. He was disappointed to see snow was falling again. Driving home would have taken him five minutes. On foot, it would be half an hour up an icy hill. Oh well. Nothing he could do about it.

When he was halfway across the lot a figure stepped out from behind a car. This sufficiently startled Ron that he slipped on a patch of ice and fell down.

From his prone position he realized it was the old man he'd seen in the diner. Dots of snow swirled around the man's head. Ron thought it must be snow, anyway.

'Please stand up,' the man said.

Ron tried, but halfway through the attempt his foot hit the same patch of ice and he fell down again in approximately the same way.

The old man waited patiently.

On the third attempt Ron managed to get to his feet. 'Who are you?'

'That's not a question you need the answer to,' the man

said. 'Would you turn away from me, please? Carefully, so
you don't fall down again.'

'Why?'

'Just do it.'

Ron did as he was told. Something about the old man's
manner told Ron that doing what he said would be the wisest
course of action.

'Thank you. Now hold still.'

There was a pause; then Ron felt a pulling sensation, as if
something was tugging at his back. He glanced behind and saw
the old man remained several feet behind, so it couldn't be him.

'Face the front.'

Ron quickly turned back. The tugging sensation continued
for a few moments, getting stronger, as if something had its
claws in his clothes, or even *skin*, and was refusing or unable
to let go – and then suddenly stopped.

He heard the old man mutter something, followed by footsteps crunching away in the fallen snow.

'You may turn back towards me now.'

Ron did so, slowly, surprised to find the old man was still
there, now looking at him with a thoughtful expression, his
head cocked on one side.

'I can tell that you should not have received the attentions
of my associate,' he said. 'I shall chastise him for it.'

'What are you talking about?'

'I will give you one piece of advice, in recompense for your
troubles. Even when you think you've apologized as much as
you can, once more never harms. Your story can change.
Overnight.'

Ron watched the man walk away across the parking lot
to a large black car in the corner. Despite his age, he seemed
to have no difficulty navigating the patches of ice that had
proved unavoidably treacherous to Ron.

Oddly, the old man opened the back door of his car first. He stood with it open, waiting for a moment, as if for a tardy dog, and then closed it, got into the front and drove away.

Halfway home and already very cold, Ron had an idea. It didn't seem like an especially good idea, but he couldn't get it out of his head. He stopped, turned round, and trudged towards downtown instead.

He went to the Burger King, where Rionda ignored him steadfastly for an hour and a half. Eventually, however, she consented to listen as he said sorry for everything, up to and most definitely including the debacle the previous weekend at her parents' house.

Her parents' bathroom remained a sore point for Rionda, as the army had visited that afternoon and there was growing speculation that it – and the rest of the house, and possibly the ones on either side – might have to be destroyed in the interests of public safety, but Ron was so patently sincere that she couldn't help but soften.

He seemed different somehow, too, and when he walked her home at the end of her shift it was Rionda, rather than Ron, who slipped on ice going up the hill leading to her own little house. Ron caught her arm, and she did not fall.

She kissed him.

Five months later they were married.

They will play no further part in our story, but I'm happy to relate that they lived happily ever after.

Chapter 7

At around the time Ron arrived downtown, cold and snow-covered, and was plucking up the courage to go into Burger King, the old man in the black linen suit was sitting at the counter in a dark and dangerous basement bar only five streets away. To the casual observer it would have looked as if he was alone. He was not.

The imp called Vaneclaw was perched on the next seat. Bar stools are not designed for the likes of accident imps, and he kept slipping off. If you'd been able to see him, you might have thought the thing he most resembled was an extremely large mushroom, one of those exotic types, possibly a chanterelle. With a face, though, and spindly little arms and legs, covered in patches of hairy mould, like something you might find lurking at the back of the fridge after several months, and hurriedly throw away. Luckily – in common with all familiars of his class – Vaneclaw was invisible to the normal eye.

'You are a very stupid imp,' the old man said.

'Oh, I know.'

The imp did know this. Not only was he stupid on his own account, he came from an unusually stupid family, a line of imps celebrated for greater than usual dimness. His parents had once gone four years without contact, though they were plaguing two people in the same house, because they were too stupid to find their way from one floor to the next. This might have been more excusable had it not been a single-storey dwelling. Vaneclaw's grandmother was worse, so very dense that not only could she not even remember her own name (consistently referring to herself as 'that one, right here, where I am') but she also spent nearly thirty years plaguing *herself*. (In her defence, after she'd started, it was difficult to stop. Accident imps are sticky. Once they've bonded to someone they're almost impossible to get off.) The entire family was so intellectually torpid that they didn't even have the sense to apply to be stupidity imps instead, whose job is to cause otherwise smart people to behave stupidly, which seldom involves anything more complicated than access to alcohol and a member of the opposite sex.

'Explain yourself, Vaneclaw.'

'Well, boss. What it is, is this. Once you disappeared—'

'I did not disappear.'

'All right then, well, once you were, I dunno, *not around*, I was at a loose end. A lot of us were. And at first that was fine, because I'd been accidenting people for a thousand years by then, non-stop, and I didn't mind the thought of having some time off, right? But after a decade or so, it's like, I've had my holidays, what now? Accidenting's what I do. So I got back into it, and for ages everything was fine, honest. You should have seen me. It was top stuff. Calamity Central. But then one night I'm in a crowded pub and the woman I've been plaguing for the last twenty years has just died in a freak tofu-braising incident and so I'm ready for pastures new, and I spot this geezer. Total git he was. Perfect. So I thought, right mate, you're mine. Have some of *this*. And I threw myself at him, claws out. The bastard moved, though. So I flew right past and ended up stuck to the guy who was *behind* him, that Ron bloke you just pulled me off, who I freely admit did not deserve what I have put him through. But you know how it is – I was stuck.' Vaneclaw shrugged, causing himself to slip off the stool again, to land on the bar's dirty concrete floor with a quiet splat.

The old man waited while he scrambled back up. 'You're an idiot,' he said.

'Couldn't agree more. But whoa, boss, it's *magic* to see you. Let the bad times roll, eh? Where you *been*, anyway?'

The old man looked at the imp for a long moment. 'I fell asleep,' he said.

'You what?'

'The specifics of how I spend my time are not your concern,' the man muttered.

'Mine not to reason why, eh? Especially as reasoning has never been my strong suit. Never really understood what it even *is*, be honest with you.'

'Do that, yes, Vaneclaw.'

'What? Reason?' The imp looked uncomfortable, as if being asked to do something well above his pay grade.

'No. Be honest with me.'

'Oh, always! But . . . what about?'

The old man was looking at him very seriously. 'Have you been praying? Have you been making sacrifice?'

'Of *course* I have, guv.' The imp was bewildered to be asked the question. 'Morning, noon, and night, even when I was on holiday and not actively accidenting because of, you know, what I said earlier. First thing in the morning, last thing at night, and, well, somewhere around lunchtime, either before or right after, depending, I have prayed every single day to your infernal majesty, unhallowed be your eternal everlasting dreadfulness, et cetera.'

'What about sacrifices?'

'Yes! My every deed and thought is done in your awful name, for a start. Every single time I do something bad or disappointing, slip another mishap someone's way, I consecrate said deed to the glory of your appalling self.'

'Hmm.'

The old man seemed to be watching the only other patrons in the bar, a pair of very ugly men at a table in the corner. The men were talking in low tones, and even an imp as unsmart as Vaneclaw could tell they were not good people. After a moment the old man looked away, as if weary of the sight of them – weary, or extremely preoccupied.

'Boss?'

The man remained silent. The imp waited nervously. If you'd told him when he woke that morning (curled up on the roof of Bad Luck Ron's house) that he'd be seeing his lord and master that day, he'd have jumped for joy (and fallen straight off the roof). He still felt that way, but increasingly cautious, too. Something was on the old man's mind, and experience had shown that the kind of things that the big man had on his mind were seldom good. Vaneclaw felt it safer to remain very, very quiet.

Eventually the old man turned to him. 'I want you to do two things for me.'

'Anything, boss, you know that.'

'The first is I want you to look into my eyes.'

Vaneclaw suddenly felt very nervous indeed. He realized that what he'd previously been feeling hadn't been nervousness after all. It had been . . . something else. Maybe . . . solitude, or what was that other one that began with an 'S'? He couldn't remember. Speciousness? Didn't matter. The point was that what he was feeling *now* was nervousness. The imp knew very well that the old man could cause people to go absolutely shrieking insane merely by glancing at them. Not just humans, either, but imps and snits and demons and full-grown snack-ulars, whom even Vaneclaw found a bit creepy.

But, on the other hand, Vaneclaw thought if the old man looked into his eyes and drove him totally walloping bonkers, the imp would be unlikely to be able to do whatever the second thing was going to be, on account of being out of his mind. Saying you were going to ask two things of someone, and then preventing them from being able to even attempt the second, because of the first, was exactly the kind of mistake that Vaneclaw himself might make. But not the old man.

'All right,' the imp said, and slowly raised his eyes.

Precisely one minute later, the old man nodded. 'Very well,' he said. 'I see you speak the truth.'

The imp was so relieved that he felt as though he'd turned to jelly. It had been a very unpleasant sixty seconds. It was as if an acidic worm with spikes was crawling through every tiny, crooked nook and cranny of what passed for his mind; at times he'd felt also as though he was getting a glimpse in the other direction, seeing fire, and blood, and long-ago dust.

It was over now, though, and he'd evidently passed the test. 'So what was the third thing, boss?'

'Second thing, Vaneclaw.'

'Oh yeah, sorry.'

'Go now, throughout the district. Locate every one of our personnel in the area. Every single imp, demon and snackular, each familiar and shadow, soulcutter and schrank. Bring them here. Do it quickly. Do it now.'

'I am *so* on it, boss.'

'Not while you're still here.'

'Oh yeah.'

The imp slid quickly off the stool and scampered away into the night, leaving the man in the linen suit alone at the bar, looking intensely thoughtful.

And tired.

And old.

Ten minutes later the two ugly men from the table walked up to the counter, having decided that they would like to rob him.

'Look into my eyes,' the old man said.

One of the men left the bar five minutes later and killed a family in a house six streets away, before stealing a car and driving it into a wall, dying instantly.

The other staggered off into the dark, cold night and spent the short remainder of his days living in a box under a bridge, convinced that every time he breathed, his eyeballs filled up with spiders.

Meanwhile, the old man waited in the bar for the imp to return.

Chapter 8

Hannah picked at her food. It wasn't that she didn't like it. Everything she'd eaten in the hotel so far – dinner the previous night, breakfast this morning, and now lunch – had been good. Not as nice as when Dad had his game on but, on the other hand, not frozen pizza three nights in a row. She simply wasn't hungry.

She hadn't slept well either. She'd been woken several times in the night by the mournful sound of wind. It would sweep past the windows and over the roof of the cabin with a long, low howl, and then tail away as if it'd forgotten or come to terms with whatever tragedy had provoked it in the first place. It would be quiet for a while – a long, pregnant silence – and then suddenly do its thing again, much louder and with more keening this time, as if it'd realized that actually everything was far worse than it had originally feared, and the world needed to know.

It was cold, too. Granddad piled blankets and an extra counterpane over her when she went to bed, but in the dark hours it was freezing. Eventually, about six in the morning, she had wrapped herself in her dressing gown and a blanket and left her bedroom, padding out to the main room. She'd been surprised to find Granddad already there, fully dressed, staring out to sea, or at where the sea would be if it hadn't still been dark.

'You're up early,' she said.

'Hmm?'

Granddad took a moment to come back from whatever thoughts he'd been having, but then he said the hotel would be serving breakfast by now and why didn't they go get a big plate of eggs to warm themselves up.

He had been acting strange since, though. He seemed to lose focus every now and then, head held as if listening for something. After a moment of this he'd shake his head and be totally normal again.

They'd started the day by heading down the wooden steps to the beach, turning left and walking. They walked for an hour and then turned and walked back. The sea was grey and choppy. The sand was grey, too, punctuated by large, dark boulders. There was no one else around.

They talked of this and that. Looking back, Hannah couldn't remember exactly *what* they had talked about. Just . . . stuff. Mom and Dad always wanted to know how school had been, when she was going to do her homework, if there was the slightest possibility, ever, that she might tidy up her room. With Granddad it was more like waves on the beach. Coming in, and going out, none of them mattering but all of them real. It struck her as a shame that it was hard to remember this kind of talking after it was over.

'What are we going to do this afternoon?' she asked.

'Walk the other way. You have to. Or the beach gets un-balanced.'

'Really?'

'Oh yes. Like a seesaw. All the sand slides to one end. I wouldn't want that on my conscience. Or yours.'

Hannah raised a disbelieving eyebrow. Granddad just sat there looking innocent.

The only other person in the restaurant was a young waitress who spent her time looking as though she was in training for a competition to see who in the world could look the most bored, and had a real chance of placing in the medals.

'Don't you get lonely here?'

'I don't get lonely anywhere.'

'But how, if there are no people?'

'Loneliness isn't to do with other people.'

'But don't you want someone to talk to, sometimes?'

Granddad raised his hand in another vain attempt to attract the attention of the waitress. 'The problem, dear, is my age. When you're as old as me, if people see you in a corner with a book they think: Poor old fellow, he must be lonely – I'll go cheer him up. And so they come and talk at you, whether you want them to or not, and they always speak too loudly, and treat you as though you're incapable of understanding the smallest things, or as if you're simple in the head.'

'Really?'

The hand movement not having worked, Granddad coughed, extremely loudly. The waitress looked the other way.

'Almost always,' he went on. 'They believe that because older people move slowly, their minds must creep too. They forget that the way you get to be old is by living a long time, which means you've seen a lot of things. When you get to my age—'

'What *is* your age, Granddad?'

Hannah knew she shouldn't interrupt a grown-up but couldn't resist such a perfect opening. Granddad's age was a hotly debated topic. Nobody knew what it was, at least not for sure. They knew his birthday – 20 November – but not the year he'd been born. Hannah's dad and Aunt Zo had spent their childhoods believing that their father was born in 1936, which is what their mother had told them. But one Christmas when Hannah's mom mentioned this in passing – and when Granddad had enjoyed a few glasses of wine over lunch – he'd laughed very hard and said no, no, that wasn't when he'd been born *at all*. Concerted attempts to pin him down subsequently had been deftly avoided. Hannah's mom had more than once suggested this was because Granddad was losing his marbles, and couldn't actually remember. Hannah, on the other hand, believed he was just having fun.

'So very, very ooooooold,' he said with a wicked grin. 'Now – we need our bill. Please throw your spoon at the waitress. Aim for her head.'

The beach was wilder on the right. A river came down out of the hills, approaching at a jagged angle as though woozy after a long fight. The river widened markedly as it met the beach, became pebble-bottomed and choked with branches and trees, stripped of their bark, white and dead, washed down out of the mountains. Granddad sat to one side while Hannah explored the river mouth, but even for an only child used to being solitary, she needed someone her own age to make that kind of thing truly fun.

They walked further and found a stretch where the beach near the waterline was busy with sand dollars. These weren't just the shells, like the ones that – once in a blue moon – you might find fragments of on the beach in Santa Cruz. They were living creatures, as Hannah found with a start when she tried to pick one out of the sand (delighted to have found a whole one for once) and saw it burrowing away from her.

She found its being alive faintly disturbing, as though it was a pebble that had tried to scuttle off.

They walked on, and on. There was nothing along here

except wilderness, and thus no particular reason to stop. Neither of them had said anything for half an hour.

Eventually Hannah tired, and ground to a halt.

There was no one else on the beach. She was starting to feel like a piece of driftwood, washed up on this shore and left there forever. Like that, or . . .

Her father had once told her about something called the Watchers, a story set in the mountains of Big Sur. It was said that once in a very great while, at twilight, people caught a glimpse of figures – usually alone, but occasionally in pairs – standing in the deepest woods, or on a peak some distance away. Dark figures with no faces, not tall, cloaked in long black coats with hoods, or enveloped in shadows. They never did anything, or said anything, and when you looked back they were gone. Her father said people had been claiming to see the Watchers for a hundred years, and that the Native Americans had tales that sounded like they might be about the same thing, from even longer ago. Hannah had assumed her father might be making all this up – he did that kind of thing from time to time, testing ideas for whatever he was working on for the bastards and flea-brains down in Los Angeles – but then one afternoon her teacher had mentioned the Watchers too, and said that they were in a poem by some slightly famous poet who'd lived in Carmel, and John Steinbeck had put them in a short story, too, and John Steinbeck knew absolutely everything about sardines, so maybe he knew about that too.

Hannah felt like a Watcher.

Like something unknown, standing outside normal life, apart from it; right here, and yet far away. As if she lived in a secret country, hidden behind where everyone else lived, or as if some Big Bad Wolf – star of a fairy tale that had unnerved her as a young child, partly because it had been told to her by Aunt Zo, who really wasn't keen on wolves – had blown her whole house down, changing the world forever, stranding her in a place where her thoughts and fears were invisible to people who were always looking the other way.

'Can we go back?'

'No.'

'Huh?'

Granddad was smiling, but he looked serious, too. 'You can never go back, only forward. I read that in a book once.'

'Is it true?'

He shrugged. 'In a way. Time will slip sideways every now and then, but once something's happened it can't be un-happened. You have to make the best of how the world is afterwards. Lots of people make themselves crazy, or at least deeply unhappy, because they don't realize that.'

'Are Mom and Dad going to get back together?'

The question came out of the blue and in a rush. Granddad was silent for so long afterwards that she started to think he hadn't heard, or that she hadn't said it out loud after all.

'I don't know,' he said eventually. 'Perhaps.'

'Don't you hope so?'

'I hope they do what's right for them,' he said carefully. 'But I don't know what that is. I don't think they do either, at the moment.'

Hannah couldn't believe what she was hearing. 'What's right is for them to be together! We're a *family*. They have to be my mom and dad.'

'They are, Hannah. They always will be. Even if they stay apart.'

'That's not enough.'

'It may have to be, I'm afraid.'

'*No.*' She glared up at him. In that moment he didn't look like her granddad, someone whose face was so well known that it disappeared, allowing her to look inside. Now it seemed alien, a mask of lines and wrinkles holding a pair of sharp, knowing eyes – old man's eyes, the eyes of someone who'd witnessed so many things that it made him see the world differently.

Made him see it wrongly.

Unable to say any of this, she ran away.

He caught up with her, of course. Not by running – the idea of Granddad running would have been comical, had she been in the right mood. He caught up with her by walking, steadily, slowly, consistently. She ran out of steam. He did not. She lost her fury. He'd had none. That's how you win, in the end.

When they got back to the cabin she said she wanted to wander around the hotel grounds, by herself. Granddad agreed but warned her to be careful of the edge of the bluff, and he'd see her in the lodge in an hour.

She set off at a misleading angle – to make it look as though she was really going off to explore – but as soon as she was out of sight of the cabin she changed course towards the lodge. Once inside she got out her iPod Touch, found a private corner, and tried to Skype her dad.

There was no reply. In a way, she thought this was a good thing. He had Skype on his phone and both his computers, the big one in his study and his precious laptop. If he couldn't hear any of them it must mean he'd gone for a walk, done something other than the staring-at-a-screen routine he'd been in every day and night since Mom left, and which even Hannah knew could not be positive – especially as the staring sessions seldom seemed to be accompanied by the sound of typing. Good for him.

So she called her mom instead. Mom picked up on the eighth ring, as if she'd been a long way from the phone.

'It's late, honey,' was the first thing she said.

Hannah hadn't thought to check the time. It was after four o'clock. She did the math. That made it gone midnight where her mom was. 'Sorry,' she said, though she thought maybe her mom could have said something else first.

'Didn't Dad warn you what time it would be?'

Hannah hesitated. Mom evidently didn't know where she was. 'I didn't tell him I was going to try calling.'

'That's OK. How are you?'

'I'm OK. How are you?'

'I'm fine. Though it's very cold.'

'So why are you there?'

'What do you mean?'

'If it's so cold in London, why are you there? Why don't you come back home?'

'It's . . . it's not that simple.'

'So *explain* it to me.'

'I can't. It's work, and . . . I have to be here.'

'I hate you,' Hannah said.

'Oh, honey, I know this is hard for you. Hard and . . . very confusing. But you . . . you don't mean that.'

Her mom sounded upset. Hannah wanted to take the words back, but couldn't – not without having somewhere else to put them. The words were real things, and their story was real, and she realized that she'd needed to say them to someone. She wasn't sure if it should have been her mom, or dad, or even Granddad, for not being able to promise her everything would be OK. But *somebody* needed to hear, to hear right now and to *understand*, that everything was *not OK*. There was only one word for that. Hannah had never hated anyone or anything before in her life, but right now the word was there in the centre of her head. She couldn't see past it.

'I do,' she said. 'I hate you.'

'Honey, I really want to talk to you some more, but can you pass me over to Dad for a second?'

Hannah ended the call. She went to the part of the lounge where there were big windows, and sat looking out over the ocean. She watched as the light started to fade and the grey of the sea slowly rose to meet the grey of the sky, until eventually they joined.

Granddad arrived. They ate, they talked, though not much. They walked back to the cabin along the bluff. Her grandfather stayed in the chair in her room after Hannah had climbed into bed. For a long time they were silent together in the darkness.

'I know you want them to get back together,' he said. 'Of course you do. And that might be what happens. I certainly hope so. I love them both. But for the time being, trust that they both love *you*, and so do I. For tonight, that may have to be enough. And that's no small thing, either.'

She could see he wasn't lying. 'OK,' she said.

'What you feel now is serious, but try not to take it too seriously. Sleep, as deeply as you can. Dream long. Tomorrow things may feel different.'

''K.'

She closed her eyes and pretended to be asleep until her grandfather quietly got up and left.

Then she did fall asleep.

Granddad walked to the kitchen. He made a pot of coffee and took a mug of it into the living room. He sat in the big chair, facing out into darkness.

He settled to wait.

Chapter 9

Meanwhile, back in Miami, Nash and his remaining (non-exploded) associates – Eduardo, Jesse and Chex – were breaking into a second-hand store close to the warehouse where they'd encountered the freaky old man in the suit.

Most criminals avoid committing crimes on home turf, on the grounds that stealing from people with whom you might later come into contact tends to be a bad policy. People don't like being stolen from. It makes them angry and upset. In places like Opa Locka, where the stolen-from have a tendency to briskly take matters into their own hands, this can lead to violent confrontations, broken bones and general sadness.

Nash didn't care about this, despite the fact the store they were robbing belonged to a man called Mr Files, who even the dumbest locals knew was a dude on whose wrong side you most certainly didn't want to be. Mr Files knew everyone thought of him this way, however, and would therefore be able to guess that the only person likely to go ahead and rob him anyway would be Nash, whom Mr Files accepted was even scarier than he was. The situation was further complicated by the fact that half the goods in the store were in fact stolen, and Mr Files had acquired most of these from Nash himself. The items were, therefore, now being stolen a second time, and it was far from inconceivable that (after a suitable delay) Nash might resell them *back* to Mr Files; that some of these pieces of tech might spend the rest of their existence circulating back and forth between them like pieces of flotsam bobbing on a dead sea.

This is why you have to be quite smart to be a successful criminal. Keeping track of the interlocking illegalities and hierarchies can be hard, and if you get it wrong you don't just get a bad appraisal and the chance to buck up your ideas, but instead wind up floating in the bay, often in more than one piece. Men (and women) who were neither smart nor scary enough to work this system with confidence – men like Eduardo, Jesse and Chex – tended to find a leader and do what they were told.

Though robbing Mr Files's store made them nervous, they were glad to be doing something. In the couple of days since the encounter with the man in the black suit, morale among the group had not been high. The following night the three men had turned up to Nash's house to find their boss sitting on the tilting porch, beer in one hand, cigarette in the other, staring into the middle distance. He had not, as per his usual custom, got decisively to his feet, bounced down the steps, and led them into an evening of lucratively criminal behaviour.

He'd just sat there, alone, reaching after a while for another beer and another cigarette, saying nothing. After nearly an hour of watching this, the three men left.

A common trait amongst persons of a criminal nature is a lack of foresight. This is why so many of them end up in jail. It also means that rather than putting money aside for a rainy day, they live within narrow margins. Eduardo, Jesse and Chex were therefore soon in a position where they had no money.

And so they turned up at Nash's house again the next night,

because though they could have scraped together a little cash through muggings or small-scale robberies of their own, working for Nash produced a much higher return – plus there was the fact he was well known for exacting hideous revenge on anybody who messed with his people, and this made them feel a lot safer.

So though it was in none of their natures, they elected to be patient for once, and wait.

Tonight, Nash had come down off the porch. There hadn't been quite the usual spring in his step, but his guys supposed they could understand why. For six months he'd been trying to raise their game. Lift them from being mere thieves, drug dealers and criminals. Trying to make their actions pay off towards a larger goal – that of being truly evil. For a while on that evening in the abandoned warehouse it looked as though it had worked. But then the old guy in the suit had blown Pete to pieces, and left. Leaving Nash looking wrong-footed, rejected, and . . . a little dumb.

They knew this was intolerable, the very worst thing – especially in front of people who looked up to you. Leaders who've been made to feel dumb often feel the need to re-establish dominance through acts of flamboyant violence, and sometimes it's the people nearest them who wind up taking the brunt. Tonight, thankfully, Nash didn't seem like he was feeling dumb.

'So what's the plan, boss?' Jesse asked.

'Business as usual,' Nash said. And that was that.

Once they were inside Mr Files's store they fanned out. All had been in the building before, either to steal things or to buy. They knew what they were looking for. Not televisions, though twenty hung along the side wall. Nobody steals televisions any more, they've become too big and heavy. Game consoles were better. Smaller, lighter, easier to sell – even pro junkies need a game to nod out in front of. Laptops worked too.

And – especially and most of all – phones.

Eduardo went to the back and started putting the slimmest and newest-looking laptops into his bag. Jesse did the same with the consoles, picking through the available brands with a practised eye. Chex and Nash went to the other side, where the phones were. The interior of the store was dimly lit through the sturdy metal grille in front of the window, by the flickering neon sign outside and an occasional slow swish of passing car headlamps. Nobody was worried about people glimpsing shapes within the store and alerting the cops. The police knew better than to get involved in the complex criminal ecosystem, unless unusually high rates of fatality were involved.

Chex stood in front of the display with the Samsungs and LGs. He ignored the cheap, contractless handsets that people called 'burners', only ever of interest to drug dealers and those of no fixed abode, and started taking down smartphones and stowing them in his shoulder bag.

Nash walked further to the primo items, the iPhones. There were a lot, certainly more than when they'd last robbed the place. This could mean Mr Files had found an additional source of stolen goods, and that was something Nash needed to look into. A man in his position could not tolerate new thieves in his area, not least because if Mr Files stopped relying upon Nash then the balance of power could change. Nash knew he'd be able to resolve the situation, and the fact that spirited violence would be involved only made the prospect more appealing. Since the embarrassing evening in the ware-house he'd found himself increasingly drawn to the idea of hurting people, especially people who'd done him wrong. This, in fact, was what he'd been thinking about while sitting on the porch for hour after hour. Hurting. Causing harm. Breaking things and people so very badly that there would never be any chance of putting them together again. And then breaking them some more.

'What's that?' Chex had stopped plucking phones from the shelves and was standing with his head cocked.

'What's what?'

'I heard something.'

'No you didn't. Keep working.'

Chex didn't, however. Nash was self-aware enough to know these people worked for him mainly because they were afraid of him, and therefore when one of them didn't do what he said, there was generally a good reason for it.

So he became still too, iPhone in hand, and listened. At first nothing. But then, yes – a faint crackling sound. Not even quite a crackling. Quieter. More like a hiss. And then louder than that, more keening.

The other guys were talking quietly to each other as they gathered up stuff and didn't seem to have heard anything. No sign of anyone at the door in the back, through which they'd entered. Nash peered at the televisions hanging on the wall. There was something different about them. The screens were dark, but not the flat dark of an LCD or plasma when no power's going through. A faint swirling motion was visible within the muddy grey. On old-fashioned TVs a dead channel was bright and noisy and sparkling. Now it looked like electricity had been applied to all the televisions, but no signal.

Finally the guys at the back noticed. 'What's up?'

Nash held up his hand for silence. He'd already realized a possible explanation was all the TVs were on the same circuit, and had been turned on. Maybe from the back room.

Which meant someone was in here.

He was reaching for the gun lodged in the back of his jeans

when he noticed something else, however. The screen of the iPhone he was holding was doing the same thing. Instead of a black, shiny surface, it too was a swirling dark grey. And there was no way someone in back could have turned *that* on.

He glanced at Chex, saw he was staring down at the phone in his hand too. 'Hell's going on?'

Nash looked back at the phone. The variation in tones became more marked. He felt like he couldn't look away. The darker greys got darker, the lighter a little more light. It was as if there was something there, some pattern just outside reach – like one of those black-and-white pictures you stare at until they resolve into a Dalmatian or something. But moving.

Was it a face?

Was there someone *in* there, inside the phone?

Someone or something or maybe even a bunch of someones or somethings. If so, Nash believed they were there to talk to him – that this phenomenon was meant for him alone. He was wrong about this: something similar was happening in many places across the country, in front of similar men and women. The only difference was that Nash was able to perceive it clearly. It was not meant specifically for him, but it spoke to him far more strongly than anybody else. His soul was tuned to receive.

And so he was the only one who saw a digital compass slowly swimming up out of the swirling dots on the screen, its needle spinning so fast that it was a blur.

He was dimly aware of Chex staring down at the phone in his own hand, and the others gazing up at the televisions on the wall. But this wasn't for them.

Then he heard it, or felt it. The message. What sounded like a distant howl, something wild and feral heard from the other side of a mountain in the night, resolved into a number

70

of voices, speaking as one. Two words. A verb and a direction. He blinked, and felt the message settle deep inside.

The compass stopped spinning.

It pointed in one clear direction.

Then suddenly the screen was blank again, and the crackling sound was gone.

When they were back outside Jesse noticed that whatever had just happened, it had put purpose back in Nash's step. Their leader lit a cigarette and stood smoking in silence for a while. Then he nodded at the bags full of stolen goods each had hanging from their shoulders.

'Drop it all,' he said.

'Huh?'

'We don't need it where we're going.'

'Going? Where are we going?'

'West.' Nash dropped his cigarette to the ground and strode off towards the truck. 'We're going west.'

Chapter 10

The man in the black suit drove. You might think a person in his position would prefer an underling to perform that service, and often that would indeed be the case: him in the back seat, the passenger, looking out, casting blight with his gaze. The only being on hand tonight was Vaneclaw, however, and the last thing you want driving your car is an accident imp. With every hour that passed the old man was feeling more and more awake, too. He wanted to be active, engaged. He desired to be doing things.

And so he drove. Fast.

The big black car flashed along the highway, brushing the edges of small towns, where people would stir in their beds as if soured by a bad dream they would not remember; sometimes arcing long miles through wide, open country, where there was no one and nothing but the occasional nightbird or vole to look up and shiver as it passed.

Finally it got where it was going.

The man parked. He bade the imp stay in the car – on pain of things far worse than death. The imp pointed out, however, that just as allowing one of his kind to drive was a bad idea, leaving one unattended in a vehicle was not a great plan either. The last time he'd been left in a car it had somehow ended up at the bottom of a lake. Upside down.

The old man sighed, then said, 'Yes, come along then, but keep silent and out of the way,' on pain of things far worse than death.

'Right-o,' Vaneclaw said. 'I'll start being silent now, then, shall I?'

'Yes.'

'OK, bo—'

Seeing the old man's face, the imp closed his mouth, and followed him along a path towards the cabin at the end. One side of this was mainly made of glass. The interior was dark, but when the man walked right up to the sliding doors, he could see the Engineer sitting waiting inside.

The Engineer stood, came and quietly slid open the doors. He looked the old man in the suit up and down.

'Where the hell have you been?'

It was an old joke between them.

Fifteen minutes later the two men were sitting on the plastic chairs outside the cabin. The man in the black suit felt the cold but it did not bother him. The Engineer was huddled up in a sweater, two pairs of socks, an overcoat, and a blanket, and had a fresh cup of coffee cradled in his hands. He still felt chilled. Better to have this conversation here than inside, however.

'How did you find me?'

'I let my mind wander.'

'Of course. I felt it this afternoon, reaching out. Someone else did too. I merely wondered whether you'd also had someone watching me all this time.'

'No.' The old man raised an eyebrow. 'Were you trying to hide?'

'Of course not. I move around because it pleases me, and

for other reasons you know full well. Though I'll admit I was intrigued to see how long it would take you to track me down. Quite some while, it turned out.'

'No. I only started looking yesterday.'

The Engineer looked surprised. The old man shrugged. 'Before that . . . I don't remember. I woke up two days ago on the terrace of a hotel in South Beach, Miami.'

'Very hot, Florida.'

'You're telling me. Evidently I had been resident in the hotel for three months. I have no recollection of that period. Before that, according to receipts in my suitcase, I spent a number of years in Antwerp, of all places. Prior to that I do start to recall things. The wandering, mainly.'

'It's been fifty years. I'm not surprised you can't remember everything.'

'That's just it. I *do*, before the last few. I recall the moment where I decided that I no longer wished, for a while at least, to actively engage in the course I had pursued for a hundred millennia. I knew I had set countless black deeds and curdled paths in motion, given seed to chaos and sadnesses that would persist without my supervision – including wars that turned out rather better than I'd hoped. I remember decades spent travelling the globe, alone in thought, stalking the mountains and forests and backstreets, sometimes appearing as I am now, at other times as a woman in middle age, occasionally as a large black dog. Even, for a brief period, as a chicken.'

'How'd that go?'

'Not well.'

'But then?'

'It seems . . . I fell asleep. Not so that I stopped moving and doing, but so that I lost awareness of myself. I moved as if in a dream, a dream so deep that I was not conscious of either its contents or myself.'

'And now you have reawoken.'

'So it appears. Though . . .' The old man stopped talking. The Engineer let the silence rest for a moment. 'You're concerned about something,' he said then, quietly. 'What is it?'

'Last night I was in North Dakota.'

'Very cold, North Dakota.'

'Disappointingly so. But I tracked down the imp that is called Vaneclaw.'

'I remember him. Extremely dim.'

'But also very loyal. I interrogated him, then bade him gather all minions from the area, demons large and small. I looked into the dark void in the centre of each and every one. I found them still loyal too.'

'Of course,' the Engineer said, not surprised.

'Not of course, I'm afraid to say. I suspect it was this that finally drew me back from my slumbers.'

'I don't understand.'

'My doubts were first ignited in Florida, where I watched a bad man perform a sacrifice. It was a small act, a breakage, but good enough. It was evidently not the first that he had performed in my name.'

'So he claimed?'

'He did not lie. He had a trick that proved he had been rewarded for prior acts of a similar kind.'

'What strength of trick?'

'A minor thing with fire.'

The Engineer looked confused. 'I don't see the problem. Surely it's good that fresh acolytes have found the path to you, even while you were . . . dormant. And specious rewards ensue from their acts of fealty, conferred upon them by the black ether. It was ever thus. Sacrifice begets power.'

'That's just it, my friend. I did not feel anything at all from the sacrifice he performed right in front of my eyes.'

'*Nothing?*'

'Nothing. My meeting with the imps and demons of North Dakota confirmed my suspicions. They have prayed and made sacrifice, every day and hour. Countless lives have been blighted by their actions – yet none of that power has found its way home to me. I suspect this may even be at the root of how I lost awareness of myself. The dark charge faded to the point where I slipped into some kind of infernal standby mode.'

The Engineer looked serious now. 'That's . . . very strange.'

'When did you last check the machine?'

'Yesterday. It's working perfectly.'

The old man in the suit suddenly frowned, and turned his head towards the sliding doors.

Hannah had woken first a little before midnight, according to the clock on her bedside table. She was cold. She huddled deeper into her bed sheets and managed to drift back off to sleep.

She woke again an hour later. She was still cold, but something told her this was not what had interrupted her sleep. She lifted her head from the pillow and listened.

After a moment she heard a voice. It sounded like Granddad. Perhaps he was on the phone.

She fell asleep once more, but it was a shallow sleep, and her mind kept working, eventually popping up the observation that Granddad *couldn't* be on the phone, because there was no signal here, duh. This observation didn't know what to do with itself and so it wandered Hannah's dozing mind, bumping into other ideas and thoughts and fragments of dreams, until eventually it made enough noise to wake her up.

She listened blearily. There was silence, and then she heard a voice again. This time it sounded like an old man, yet not Granddad.

That was strange.

She raised herself up on one elbow, still half-asleep. She'd just about be able to believe that someone had happened to wander by the cabin and decided to stop and have a chat with Granddad, were it not for the fact that (*a*) he'd said he didn't know anyone here, and was glad of it, and (*b*) it was now after one o'clock in the morning.

Also, she thought she could hear the sound of running water, too. And a low, tuneless humming.

She got out of bed.

There was silence on the deck as the two old men watched Hannah approach the sliding doors.

'Who is this?'

'My granddaughter,' the Engineer said. 'She's the other person who felt the pressure of your thoughts today. It made the afternoon difficult for her.'

'She'll forget. But what's she doing here?'

'Staying with me.'

'Yes, I assumed something of the sort,' the old man said tetchily. 'I meant *why*?'

'Problems at home.'

Hannah reached the doors and slid one of them open. She flinched as the cold air crept quickly inside. 'What are you doing out here, Granddad? It's *freezing*. And who is this man?'

The man in the black suit stood slowly, towering over her, all the world's shadows ready at his command. 'I . . . am the Devil,' he said, his voice hollow with the echoes of countless millennia of howling darkness.

There was silence for a moment.

'I don't believe you,' Hannah said. She blinked at him, and yawned massively. 'Also, Granddad, there's an extremely large mushroom in our bath.'

Chapter 11

'But . . . but . . . but . . . *how?*' Hannah asked.

It wasn't the first time she'd asked. 'And also . . . *why?*'

It wasn't the first time she'd asked that either. She and Granddad were in the living room. The man in the crumpled suit had told the giant mushroom to get out of the bath and go wait outside. The mushroom, whose name seemed to be Vaneclaw, had done what it was told. A little later there had been a faint yelping sound, caused by it wandering too close to the edge of the bluff and falling over it. The man in the suit – or 'the Devil' as he kept insisting he should be called – said he'd be able to do less harm down there, and to ignore him for now.

After a while, however, the mushroom had started calling out, rather plaintively. The noise eventually got loud enough that Granddad became concerned it might get into the dreams of people in nearby cabins, and so the old man in the suit irritably went out to make the mushroom be quiet. He'd been gone for some time.

Meanwhile Granddad had listened to Hannah ask the same questions, again and again. How, and why, could he possibly know the Devil, the most evil and awful being in the universe, that a lot of people said didn't even *exist*?

Each time she asked, Granddad seemed to try to make a start at answering, but faltered. So she asked yet again.

'Let me tell you a story,' he said, finally.

Once, he said, there was a boy.

His name was Erik Gruen. Erik was thirteen years old and lived on a farm, a small farm, in the vast flatness of central Germany. It was not a very good farm. Every day Erik and his brothers and sisters helped their parents, tilling the land and planting seeds and looking after their straggly collection of livestock. Each year, the family barely scraped by. There was never much food, and Erik – the youngest of six children – went to work in the field every day wearing a selection of cast-offs not just from his elder brothers, but sisters, too. You might think that would have been embarrassing, but it was not, because everyone wore the same – torn rags and bits of sacking, held together with string. The point was not looking smart but being protected from the elements, because often it rained. It was cold a lot of the time, too, and windy.

It was a tough life, though they didn't know it. This hard, endless struggle was all they knew, all their parents had known, and all their parents' parents had known, back into the mists of murky time. The Gruens had been working this scabby patch of land for centuries. That was what they did, all they had ever done, and all they would ever do.

Except that one morning, when it was raining so hard there was nothing they could do outside and the entire family was crammed into the tiny farmhouse, sniping at each other, Erik decided to take a walk. He headed down the long, winding lane and got as far as the road (itself only a track slightly wider than the lane). He kept on walking until he'd gone further than ever before, and then he walked some more.

The sky was heavy and black, and the rain kept coming down. Eventually Erik noticed structures in the distance, buildings of a type he'd never seen before.

After another hour he reached the outskirts of the town. He was in awe. He'd never encountered anything bigger than his local village, which consisted of a few run-down wooden houses, a ramshackle store that never had anything in it except wizened turnips and the odour of rats living and dead, and a hostelry which he'd been warned never to go near because it was where people's fathers went to drink beer and shout and fall over. He was wholly unaccustomed to the sight of structures that were three and four storeys high.

He'd never seen so many people, either.

Going back and forth, rushing to and fro. People yelling at each other and hawking things, striding in and out of all the buildings. Hundreds and hundreds of them.

Thousands.

At first it was exciting but after a while Erik found himself dizzy and anxious. He wasn't used to being in the midst of so many souls. Out in the countryside you knew everyone. Your family, the people on the next farms, the folk in the village. This place thronged with so many people that it was quite clear you could never hope to know them all, not in a hundred years. How could you live amongst all these strangers?

When he happened upon an especially large building near the centre of the town he went in, hoping for respite from the crowds.

It was quiet inside. Erik realized it was a church, a hundred times bigger than any he'd seen. He sat on one of the chairs at the back. The church soothed him. There's something about the still atmosphere of a church – especially when no one else is around – that can make you feel yourself again.

And there were the windows.

Erik's life until then had been painted in shades of brown and grey. The mud of the fields where he spent every day working. The small, dull wooden buildings. The cloudy sky. Apart from the occasional spring flower, he rarely saw any colour at all. His universe was sludge-coloured.

The windows of this huge church exploded with every colour and shade and hue, even on an afternoon when the sun was barely leaking through clouds and rain. They showed pictures of Jesus, and the apostles, and other scenes from the scriptures, and they were in reds and blues and greens and purples and yellow so bright it looked like gold.

He sat open-mouthed, staring. They were the most beautiful and striking things he'd ever experienced. Or, at least, they were for half an hour, but then something else stole their thunder.

A door opened at the other end of the church and a man came in. He was tall but portly, and evidently didn't realize Erik was sitting at the back. He walked up to the organ and sat down.

Erik didn't know what an organ was. He'd never heard one. His parents and grandparents hadn't either. None of them had ever made it as far as this town, which was named Leipzig. Erik discovered later what the thing with all the pipes was called, but sooner than that, he discovered what it was for.

The man reached out with his hands and pressed his fingers on the keyboard. Some notes rang out, apparently randomly. The man stopped, and frowned, and looked up at the ceiling, as if waiting for inspiration.

After a few moments he reached out again with his right hand and played a few more notes, different notes, one after another. He stopped; then he tried once more. He seemed to like the sound better this time, and played the sequence again, and again, changing it a little each time, until he found an order that he evidently liked best.

Then he started playing with his left hand, too.

His right hand kept playing the first sequence. The left hand played something similar, but not exactly the same, and not at quite the same time. The two sets of notes spoke to each other, as if having a conversation.

They went round and round, changing, multiplying, until they became like two flocks of birds flying amongst each other, independent yet joined, and the sound got bigger and bigger and more and more complicated as more birds flew to join the whirl . . . and still, at the heart of it, you could hear the first simple sequence of notes.

Then the man started playing with his feet, too.

It turned out there was another keyboard down there, with big wooden pedals, and when he added another, lower line to the soaring music by stomping on them, Erik truly thought his ears were going to explode.

The stained-glass windows were no longer the most beautiful and astonishing thing he'd ever experienced. This music was. It was so extraordinary, in fact, that Erik let out a gasp.

The man at the organ heard – despite the music – and stopped playing, immediately.

Erik was bereft. It was as if someone had turned out the sun. The man turned to stare around the church. 'Who's there?'

Erik thought about trying to hide or run away, but his parents had raised him to be honest, and to take responsibility for his actions. He stood, rather scared. 'Me, sir.'

The man left the organ and strode down the central aisle until he was standing over Erik. He looked very stern. 'Who are you, boy? What are you doing here?'

Erik explained that he was from a farm, and had walked a very long way to the town and come into the church to be out of the crowds and the rain, and that he hadn't meant to trespass, and he was extremely sorry.

The man looked down at him. After a moment, his face softened. 'Well, then, what did you think?'

'Of what?'

'The music, of course.'

'It was . . .'

Erik tried to describe how it had made him feel. He didn't want to just say it was 'good' – it was so much bigger than that. He wasn't used to describing things like music, however. Most of his language skills were dedicated to conveying information about his family's farm, like whether the mud in the field was averagely wet and grim today, or notably deep and depressing.

'It was like mountains talking,' he said, feeling foolish. 'It was the things they say to each other when we're asleep, or looking the other way. Like every tree on the mountain saying how interesting it is to be alive, all chattering at once and yet always listening to each other.'

The man thought about this for a moment. 'Excellent,' he said. 'I like that. What's your name?'

Erik told him, and then the man told him *his* name, and explained he was choirmaster of this church. He was writing the music for a performance to be held on Sunday and so while he didn't mind Erik having heard what he'd done so far, he needed private time now to refine the music. He hoped Erik understood.

Erik did, though he was sad this meant he wasn't going to be allowed to hear any more. 'But how do you *do* that?' he asked. 'Make music?'

The man held up one hand, and pointed to his head with the other. 'Somewhere between here and here,' he said, 'is Heaven. You only have to open the door.'

Erik realized that though the man had at first looked forbidding, he was not, merely focused on his work of creation, and that what he meant was that somewhere between a person's brain and their fingers lay the power to create things that were bigger than the world itself. Bigger than the universe, perhaps.

'But how do you open the door?' he asked.

'You've already begun,' the man said. 'Once, a long time ago, I walked over two hundred miles to hear a man play. You've done the same today, without knowing it. You've found your door. All you have to do now is keep pushing against it for the rest of your life. Here. Take this to help you remember that.'

The man put his hand to his lapel and pulled out something that had been threaded through it, like an austere brooch. A pin, of a tarnished gold colour. The man threaded it through the rags of Erik's coat, winked, and strode back to the organ.

Erik left the church and walked back out through the streets. The people coursing through them did not frighten him any more because he realized their movements and the sound of their thousand voices were notes in a vast piece of music, a story made of sounds, sometimes dissonant – like the shouts of men trying to sell bits of meat, or old, rusty tools – and at others sweet and pure, like mothers fondly calling their children, or greeting their neighbours. What he'd heard in the church, along with the realization that these things did not just come out of the mind of God, but could be born in the fingers of men, changed him forever.

He walked home in the rain. It was a long, long walk, and he was very tired when he got home.

The next day it was only raining a little, and so everybody got back to work. Erik toiled alongside them as always, but from that day on he knew he would eventually leave the farm, and his family, and find a place where he could learn to do something like the man in the church.

Something that changed the world.

When he got to that part in the story, Granddad stopped.

Hannah frowned. It had been quite a nice story, though short on action and talking animals and events of interest to eleven-year-olds. She didn't get the point of it, however, or how it related to her key questions:

How did Granddad know the man in the black suit?
Especially if he really and literally was the Devil?

'Ask him the name of the man playing the organ.'

Hannah jumped, and saw the other man had re-entered room and was standing over by the window. The mushroom was still outside, looking cold.

She looked at Granddad. 'OK. Who was he?'

Her grandfather's voice was quiet. 'Johann Sebastian Bach.'

This was evidently supposed to mean something to her. It did not. 'I don't get it.'

'Kids today really do know *shit*,' muttered the man in the black suit. 'Even *I* listen to Bach, and he was *so* working for the wrong side.'

Hannah was scandalized. '"Shit" is a bad word.'

He glared at her. 'I'm the Devil. *I'm a very bad man.*'

'No. You're just a rude old person,' she said. 'But . . . what's that story even got to do with you, Granddad?'

Her grandfather smiled, ruefully, as if giving up a secret he'd been holding for a very long time.

'Hannah . . . Erik Gruen is me.'

Chapter 12

Granddad unlocked the passenger door of his car. The man in the suit lowered his head to peer inside. Hannah was confused to see he seemed to be looking at the big old suitcase-thing with dial attached to it, the object that had been in the way of her feet on the drive from the airport.

'Test it,' he said.

'I did yesterday,' Granddad said. 'As always. As I said, it was fine.'

'I need to see it with my own eyes. Not the daily check. A thorough examination. Now.'

'It'd need to be indoors.'

'So take it there.'

'I can't carry it by myself. That's why I keep it in the car.'

The Devil looked at Hannah.

'No,' Granddad said firmly. 'She's a child. If it's going inside, you're helping.'

The Devil looked speculatively at the large mushroom, who was standing some distance away in the darkness, so cold now that it had turned a rather ghastly blue colour.

'Seriously?' Granddad said. 'An accident imp?'

The Devil opened his mouth, but evidently saw Granddad's point. He sighed bad-temperedly and rolled up his sleeves.

* * *

Fifteen minutes later, after a lot of puffing and a certain amount of extremely bad language, they had the suitcase inside the cabin, standing upright on the floor. The Devil had taken up residence in the big armchair. Hannah and the imp had been told to sit on the sofa.

'I'm not sitting next to a mushroom,' Hannah said. 'It's icky.'

'I am not a mushroom,' Vaneclaw said, indistinctly, because his teeth were still chattering. 'I am an imp.'

'You're a mushroom.'

'I am not.'

'Well, you look like one.'

'That's merely how he appears,' Granddad said. He knelt on the floor near the old suitcase, wincing as his knees popped, and laid out a set of very precise-looking tools on the carpet. 'I'm surprised you can see him at all. I suppose you're still young, and flexible. It's the closest the human mind can get to a shape it recognizes. Other imps might look like gnarled trees, or rotting pumpkins, or empty coats.'

'Well, *he* looks like a mushroom. And I hate mushrooms.'

'Not keen on children, myself.' The mushroom sniffed. 'Unless I'm *especially* hungry.'

'Be quiet, the pair of you,' the Devil snapped. 'Let the Engineer concentrate.'

'Why does he call you that, Granddad?'

Granddad selected a screwdriver with a long, thin blade and started undoing the screws around the edges of the suitcase. There were a lot of them. They were very small.

He didn't answer her question directly but went back to his strange story. 'Erik Gruen eventually left the farm,' he said. 'He walked back to the city and supported himself doing whatever job he could find. Working in the markets, sweeping the streets, anything that would earn a coin or two. Then one afternoon – when he was walking back from listening to the man in the big church playing the organ again – he happened to pass a workshop, and saw clocks and watches inside. He was fascinated by them, their intricacy, and by what they were. Pieces of metal, working together, physical objects somehow capturing and describing something abstract and untouchable: time.'

Granddad finished undoing the outer screws and carefully lifted off the piece of leather-covered wood on the front of the case, and put it to one side. This revealed another wooden plate, with even more screws in it. He selected a different screwdriver, and got back to work.

'Erik went into the workshop,' he continued, 'and convinced the clockmaker to take him on as an apprentice.'

'If Erik is you, Granddad, why do you keep talking as if he's someone else?'

Granddad laughed. 'I suppose it feels that way, sometimes. Erik – OK, *I* – worked hard. I soon learned everything the clockmaker had to teach me. After five years I set up in business on my own, working on clocks and watches to my own new and improved designs.'

'Like a start-up,' Hannah said, having often heard her mother use the term approvingly, as though it was the most interesting thing anyone could possibly be involved in.

'Perhaps. It took a long time to establish myself, but after ten, twenty, thirty years, I had become by far the best watch-maker in the city. The best in the country, in fact. All the wealthiest citizens came to me to make their timepieces. The king himself wore one of my watches. I became, I suppose, a little famous for my work.'

Hannah grinned, feeling vindicated. She'd always known her grandfather was special, though Dad and Mom never seemed to behave as though he was, instead discussing him as if he was an erratic old buzzard who couldn't even be relied upon to stay in the same place for any length of time. Aunt Zo always talked as though she thought her dad was pretty cool, though. It was one of the things Hannah liked about her.

Meanwhile, Granddad continued to methodically remove screw after screw from the suitcase. 'I had a good life,' he said. 'I married, though we never had any children.'

'What? Yes you—'

'Listen, Hannah. I wore expensive clothes and I ate fine meals. Every week until he died I would go to hear whatever new piece of musical wonder the choirmaster conjured in his church. It made me feel glad to be alive every time, and the pin he'd given me remained my most treasured possession. But after a while . . . something happened.'

'What?'

'One of life's dreariest truths, my dear, is that something once wonderful can come to seem . . . ordinary. This doesn't matter if the thing was ordinary in the first place. But when something that once seemed extra-ordinary, perfect, even wondrous, stops being that way, it feels like a betrayal. It makes you bitter at the world. When that happens people may do strange things. They become desperate to change their lives in search of the intensity they once experienced – that feeling of being engaged and alive, of knowing they are a piece of infinity. They run after anything they think might make them shine again. They may even leave their perfectly good—'

He glanced at her, but shook his head. 'Never mind. The point is I was the best clockmaker and watchmaker I knew of. I had plenty of money, more than I could spend. But there were no challenges in my life. I came to work every day but

I was bored. Dreadfully bored. I wonder sometimes if this ever happened to Bach, though he was on a different level to me. To everyone.'

'You do yourself a disservice,' the Devil said, an unexpected note of kindness in his voice.

Granddad shrugged. He undid five more tiny screws. 'Now,' he said. 'I have to concentrate for this part. Move your feet back everyone, please.'

He pulled at the panel he'd unscrewed and it swivelled out at an unexpected angle. This caused another, thinner panel to appear, and this too swivelled, in a direction that again was contrary to what you would have expected.

This caused a further chain of new panels to rotate into view, and then the entire interior mechanism pivoted out, splitting into further parts that swivelled in yet different directions.

Granddad was completely focused on his task, hands moving over the workings as if it was a musical instrument. By the time he'd finished, something very odd had happened.

The machinery filling the interior of the suitcase had unpacked and unfolded itself into something significantly larger, about the size of a very large refrigerator – a full foot taller than Granddad – and four feet deep, and almost the same wide.

He slid aside a final panel, the door swung back, and the inner mechanisms were fully revealed.

Cogs, wheels, little spinning things, and springs. Thousands upon thousands of them. All working together, utterly silent, yet moving in such harmony that they seemed to hum, or sing.

'What *is* that?' Hannah asked.

'The Sacrifice Machine,' the Devil said.

Chapter 13

'One long, slow afternoon I was alone in my workshop,'
Granddad continued, using first one tiny tool, then another,
and then another; checking tightness, alignment, torque; reaching into the interior space to adjust this and that. 'My wife
had died several years before, and I had nowhere else to be.
The bell over the door tinkled, and I looked up to see an old
man with white hair and big hands. I was rather old myself
by then. I said hello, but he didn't answer. He walked around,
looking at things. Eventually he came over to my workbench.

'"Erik Gruen," he said.

'I said nothing. I knew that was my name, and it was on
a sign above the door. I continued with my tinkering, and
waited for something more interesting to happen.

'The man reached into his jacket and pulled out a piece of
paper. It was very thin paper, folded many times. "I want you
to build something for me," he said.

'I shook my head. I had stopped taking new commissions.
The only work I did was repairing items I'd previously made.
I had reached that stage in life where you start to circle in
upon yourself, as if waiting for everything to be over – like
a bird making loops in the air, dropping ever closer to the
ground, looking for a place to land forever.

'"You may change your mind," the man murmured. "Or . . . you may perhaps decide the challenge is beyond your abilities."

'This gained my attention, as he'd known it would. I was good at my job, famously good at it, and still proud of my skills even after I'd stopped caring about them.

'I looked up, ready to make an impolite reply. He was holding the folded piece of paper out to me. I took it, somewhat reluctantly, but intrigued. I unfolded it, and unfolded, and unfolded some more. By the time I'd finished, and laid it out flat on the floor, the paper had revealed its true size – it was over ten feet square. Upon it, someone had made a diagram. A fantastically intricate drawing of the insides of some kind of machine containing hundreds of thousands of parts. It was clearly not a clock. It was far too complicated for that. Too complicated for any purpose that I could possibly imagine.

'"What is this?"

'"It's what I want you to build."

'I took out my spectacles and spent a whole hour looking over the drawing, while the man sat in a chair on the side.

'Finally I shook my head. "It's impossible," I said. "This machine cannot be built."

'"Oh, but it can," the man said. "It already has been."

'My professional jealousy was stirred. "By whom?"

'"You will not have heard of him. And he could not have done it on his own. It took a very long time. I had to engage some of my . . . helpers to give him assistance."

'"So then why do you need another such device?"

'"His device is ailing now, as previous versions have before. He is unable to repair it. And what you see, this drawing, includes a number of significant improvements to the design. He is not up to the task of constructing it. I believe that you might be."

'I looked again at the diagram. I still didn't believe it could be possible for any one man – or even a team of the most skilled craftsmen in the country – to cut and shape the near-countless parts involved, never mind hope to get them to work together. And yet . . . and yet I found myself drawn to the task.

'For the first time in many years I felt challenged. Excited. I sensed the possibility that between my brain, my hands, and this drawing, I might be able to create something extraordinary, perhaps for a final time in my life.

'I realized that it would be a total commitment, however. To stand any chance of building this machine I would have to close down the rest of my business, turning down any other commissions, even repair work.

'"If I were to take on this job," I said, "how much would you pay me?"

'The man smiled a strange smile. "Nothing at all," he said.'

At that point Granddad stopped telling the story. He spent fifteen minutes inspecting different parts of the machine. Sometimes he leaned towards the interior – which was about the width of an old-fashioned phone box, but a little deeper – and then went and stood completely inside the machine.

Hannah watched, bewildered at how large the interior was. There would have been plenty of room for her to go inside too, though she did not, and did not want to.

After another few minutes, Granddad stepped back out and looked at the Devil. 'The machine is in perfect working order.'

The Devil nodded. 'I felt so too. It's a long time since I have been in its presence, but I recognize the aura of its proper functioning.' He sat back in his chair, perplexed. 'So what's wrong?'

Granddad was looking thoughtful. 'The problem must lie

elsewhere. In the . . . in that place to which this machine delivers its power, before it is channelled back to you.'

'And you can't check that from here?'

'No.'

Hannah stared into the machine, awed by its complexity. All those tiny wheels and cogs, made of steel and silver and . . . 'Some of them look like they're made of gold.'

'They are.'

Set into some of the cogs were minuscule dots of jewels, red and green. She looked closer, and realized that beyond the parts she'd seen were even more parts: many of the cogs were themselves made up of even smaller cogs, working together, and the wheels were made of even tinier wheels, rotating in unison. And then . . .

She stuck her head into the mechanism and saw that even these smaller parts were made of yet smaller parts. Scarcely able to believe this possible, she pulled her iPod out of the pocket of her nightgown and found the magnifying glass app on it. This showed that there was yet *another* layer after that, and after that, until even with her keen young eyesight she couldn't make out the next level. She knew it was there, however. She could feel it. But how could that be?

How could anyone, even her grandfather, whom Hannah was perfectly prepared to believe capable of special things, make parts too small to be seen with a magnifying glass, and then place those parts in perfect relation to each other, so that a hundred thousand points of contact ticked along in harmony, so closely and perfectly aligned that they didn't make a sound?

'How is this even possible?' she asked. 'They go on forever, don't they? Smaller and smaller?'

'Don't look too closely,' her grandfather said, moving his hands to obscure the workings from her eyes.

She had a glimpse then, in her mind, of what really happened inside this machine. That there came a point at which the parts were so incomprehensibly tiny that they were separate and yet joined at the same time – discrete, independent components fused into a solid mass, like a million people in a city, like the souls of everyone on the planet. She couldn't articulate this, but she did know that it didn't make sense.

That it wasn't, in fact, possible.

She noticed something sticking out of the wall of the interior. It was a pin, in a tarnished gold colour, with a dark red jewel at the end. A red that looked like old blood. It spoke to her. She slowly reached her hand out towards it.

'Don't touch that,' Granddad said sharply. 'You of all people. Leave it be.'

'What is it?'

'The last resort,' he said.

He stepped out of the machine and began to pack it back into its case, using a long and complex series of adjustments to cause the parts to fold back upon each other, somehow getting smaller with each pivot and swivel, until, ten minutes later, it fitted back into the old suitcase again. It was like being able to stuff a car into a shoebox. He put the first of the panels back in position and started screwing it in place.

Meanwhile the Devil – for some reason, after glimpsing the interior of this machine, Hannah felt more willing to think of him in that way – had gone to stand in the corner of the room. The big mushroom climbed down off the sofa and went to him. They started a quiet conversation that Hannah couldn't hear.

Granddad finished the first plate, and put the other one in place. Hannah watched. 'You made this?'

He nodded.

'But how?'

'It took a very long time.'

'But if you made this for him, and it was so hard, how come he didn't give you anything for it?'

Her grandfather looked uncomfortable. 'I didn't say that.'

'You did. In the story. He said he wasn't going to pay.'

'That's different to saying he didn't give me anything.'

'Well, then, what?'

Granddad sighed, but spoke quickly, as if he'd decided it was better to just get on with it. 'The meeting in my workshop took place in 1779.'

Hannah frowned. 'So?'

Her grandfather tightened the last screw. He put his tools back in the old leather bag they'd come out of.

'You really can't do the math?' This wasn't her grandfather speaking, but the other man. He'd finished his conversation with the mushroom and was now standing over them, as if impatient to get moving. 'That was nearly two hundred and fifty years ago.'

Hannah stared at him. '*What?*'

The man in the suit ignored her, and turned to Granddad. 'How soon can you be ready to leave?'

Chapter 14

Some hours before, in a hotel lounge five thousand miles away, Hannah's mother had spent a while sitting by herself. An hour previously she'd finished an early supper with a man with whom she was now close, a man who lived here in London, the man of whom she'd been thinking during that long-ago lunch in the restaurant in Los Gatos.

The guy, in short, for whom she'd bailed on everything that had previously been her life.

They'd gone to a place around the corner from her hotel, a discreet little Italian restaurant where, nearly a year before, their knees had first brushed during a meeting to set up the work Kristen was now here to conduct. It had been 'their place'. It still was. They didn't have to go there any more, of course. They could go anywhere, and did frequent other restaurants and bars, yet more often than not they gravitated back to the Bella Mare . . . though she'd now eaten everything on their menu at least once and if the truth be told it was all pretty average.

It hadn't used to taste that way.

Putting down her credit card at the end of every other meal – instead of paying in cash so it wouldn't pop up looking suspicious on the monthly statement – had stopped feeling interesting too. Even kissing him goodnight in the hotel's underground parking lot, one of the rituals of their short time sort-of-together, hadn't made her feel much at all.

Her date had gone home early – he had a breakfast meeting the next morning (life quickly turns practical even after cata-clysmic events of self-definition) – and Kristen decided to bring her iPad down to the hotel bar to clear the backlog of personal emails. That hadn't happened, however. There were several in her in-box, weeks old, that remained unanswered. Old friends, a few former colleagues back in the States. Her cousin, most of all.

Kristen was hiding from these emails and their enquiries and accusations, just as she was effectively still hiding each time she suggested they go to the Bella Mare instead of some-where new. And hiding here by the fireplace in this hotel bar, and even in the hotel itself.

Hiding from the feelings of guilt that laced her every waking hour. Having an affair is like running into the back of your spouse's car. It doesn't matter how slowly or erratically they were driving, you're the one getting a ticket – plus you may suddenly find it turns out you're responsible for every single ding or scrape in the relationship before that, going back *years*. Added to this were feelings of guilt relating to the not-great recent conversation with her daughter, which she was finding difficult to think about, and pushing away again for now.

But there was something more.

The first disquieting hints, perhaps, that while the man who'd spent most of dinner talking about work might have been a sharp enough needle to help unpick the seams of her previous story, he might not be the one to help her start making something worth replacing it with. That he might have been an effect rather than a cause. Kristen was scarred and battle-weary after months spent blowing through interior walls of 'if not now, then when?' She wasn't sure she had the resolve or strength to now tackle 'so – if not this, then *what*?'

At least, not tonight.

The waitress floated up and asked if she needed anything, disturbing this train of thought before it had time to get properly started, to Kristen's relief.

She ordered a hot chocolate – it was cold in London tonight, very cold – and tried once again to answer the email from her cousin Jill.

Instead she ended up thinking about a painting, one that hung on the wall of a house she hadn't seen in a while. The house that used to be her home, in Santa Cruz.

The painting, a passable watercolour of Big Sur by a Carmel artist, had only been three hundred dollars (framed) when Steve bought it a year and a half before. Not an insignificant amount, but hardly worth the strident muttering it had occasioned from Kristen. Steve very seldom bought things for himself. He'd effectively asked permission, too (or at least given her a heads-up of his intentions, leaving space for opposing counsel to speak their mind), and she hadn't said no.

So why the damning with faint praise and who-cares-where-it-hangs? Why the failure to engage?

Then, a few weeks after the picture came into their house, she'd been relaxing with a glass of wine in the yard while Steve put Hannah to bed. As she sat looking vaguely at the back of the house where they'd lived for seven years, the answer came to her as if dropped out of the sky.

For a long time Big Sur had been their dream place. They visited it every year, a long weekend or two at least. They'd taken Hannah on her first hike in its mountains, watched her play in its streams and on its windy beaches as infant, toddler and child. It had become part of their daughter's world and imagination as well as their own.

An aspiration they'd spoken of so often it had become bedrock was that when (not if) Steve finally wrote a hit series and money flooded in, they'd buy a cottage perched on the vertiginous wooded slopes overlooking the vastness of the Pacific. Renovate it while honouring its funky authenticity. Construct a crazy little tor of local stone, like Robinson Jeffers had, in which Steve would write further hit TV series. Build fires and relax around them on cushions in the soft-wind evenings, wrapped in artisan hand-woven blankets, sipping fine local wines and thinking wise and beautiful thoughts. Except . . .

Kristen didn't care about Big Sur any more.

It wasn't that she didn't want the cottage. The notion neither excited nor bored her. It didn't raise a blip on her radar, and that was what was strange. It was like walking up to a gate in a forest, one you've looked at longingly many times, believing that one day you'll open it and walk through and undertake a promised journey along the path on the other side; but then one afternoon discovering the view had been a painting all along, and nothing lay beyond. That there was no path, no adventure to be had along that road.

It was like discovering this, and not caring. Not feeling any loss. Just shrugging and turning away.

Kristen saw her husband trotting down the staircase inside the house, his head visible at intervals through the small, circular windows that ran down it. He went into the kitchen and poured a glass of wine that was local, but not fine (they were on another economy drive). He'd hang out there a while, she knew, catching up on email, then come out to join her.

She watched his face, so well known, as it bent over his laptop on the counter, his sequence of mannerisms. She'd known this man a long time, and been married to him for fifteen years, and yet she realized the prospect of him joining her caused no blip on her radar either; and this probably meant it was not only Big Sur that had lost the keys to her heart. She was the only person who had a set.

And so not only did she have to hold on to them very tightly, but there might come a day when she had to get in her car, and drive.

That day came. She drove away from home. A long way. But then she stalled.

When the woman spoke, she startled Kristen.

'Huh?'

'Your machine,' she said. 'It's going to fall.'

Kristen saw she was right. Her iPad was in danger of slipping off her lap. She moved it to safety, and smiled up at the woman, who despite appearing well into her seventies was rocking a head of long grey hair. This was a look you often saw back home, though never here in London. It made her feel homesick.

'Thanks,' she said. 'Miles away.'

'Yes,' the woman said in a less friendly way. 'You are.'

With that she walked out of the bar. A few moments later Kristen saw her leave the hotel and walk away down the dark street in the rain.

As she lay in bed later, alone and cold in the dark and finding sleep slow in coming, Kristen wondered what the old woman meant.

Miles away.

She rolled over, saw her phone on the nightstand, doing its

duty, waiting patiently to wake her at 6.15 a.m. as usual so she could run for an hour in the hotel gym. It would still only be late afternoon in California. She found herself wondering if she should call Steve. Check he was OK.

It was a strange thought, and she dismissed it.

He'd be fine.

PART 2

We like to think we live in daylight,
but half the world is always dark.

— Ursula Le Guin

Even good and evil dream of each other
from the depths of their loneliness.

— Jean Baudrillard
Cool Memories III

Chapter 15

They left just before the dawn.

Granddad had to take everything out of the trunk of his car to make room for the machine, and then almost everything out of the back seats to make room for Hannah and Vaneclaw. Hannah helped. The imp also assisted for a short period, but after breaking several things was told to go stand some distance away. The Devil spent the time standing on the path by the bluff, staring out to sea. Granddad explained he would be listening to the dark turnings of the stars. Hannah privately suspected he was just being lazy, or evil.

They piled all the stuff from the car in the main room of the cabin and Hannah tried not to think about the fact that the size of the pile made it extremely unlikely it could ever have fitted in the car in the first place. Granddad was the Engineer, evidently. He was good at wedging things into very small spaces. That was all.

When it was finally done, Granddad locked up the cabin and they set off. This time he did not take the scenic route but drove to the airport as quickly as possible. After a while he pushed a CD into the player, and as Hannah sat tiredly watching out of the window and listening to the music she realized that yes, it really did sound like the sky and trees

talking together, saying wise and kind things – and that sometimes not having to use words might make it easier to say
what you needed to say.

She was even more tired when they eventually landed at the
other end, but tired in that wide-eyed, brittle way that feels
like you're completely *not* tired and will never be tired again
but on the other hand if someone is rude to you you are
likely to bash them over the head with a brick until they are
completely flat.

She was surprised to be there at all. She'd realized as they
walked into Sea-Tac Airport that, if they really were going to
another country, she'd need her passport. She mentioned this
to Granddad but he said not to worry. Sure enough, when
they approached security it hadn't seemed to be a problem.
The Devil showed the man at the gate something that he
pulled out of his wallet. It didn't look to Hannah like any
passport she'd ever seen. It was too small, and a strange
colour. The man glanced at it, blinked slowly, then waved
them through as if checking passports was the most unim-
portant thing in the world. He seemed to recover his
dedication soon, however, because when she glanced back as
they waited to go through the X-ray machine, Hannah saw
the man giving somebody else's passport an oppressively thorough going-over.

Granddad had to go through the X-ray machine three times
because he kept setting it off on account of very small tools
or tiny bits of machinery he'd forgotten about, hidden in the
pockets of his jacket and trousers. The man in charge of the
machine started getting more and more suspicious, and began
to look like he might not even let Granddad pass, but the
Devil stared at him, and the man turned pale, as if something
in his insides was troubling him. Soon afterwards he waved

them all through. Hannah was glad to finally get to the other side but disturbed at the look she had seen the Devil give. It seemed likely that bad things would come of it.

She was right. The man who'd been in charge of the X-ray machine died of stomach cancer four months later.

They walked to the departure gate and waited until they were let through. They sat in a row on the plane together, the Devil stuffing the imp into one of the overheard lockers. The locker kept flopping open throughout the duration of the flight, to the increasing irritation of nearby passengers, but otherwise the journey was uneventful. Though very, very, very endless.

It wasn't the first time Hannah had been on a long-haul flight. She'd been to Hawaii twice before, and Paris, France, when she was younger. This flight seemed surreally long, however, as though time itself had stopped to take a break, re-evaluated its life, realized it was tired of always rushing forwards, and decided to remain still forever instead.

Granddad and the Devil spent the time in conversation, often in a language Hannah didn't understand. German, presumably. It got to the point at which she wished the mushroom in the locker were sitting next to her, so at least she'd have someone to talk to. But then the locker flopped open again, causing someone's handbag to fall out and land on the tray of a passenger trying to eat their meal, splashing it all over them, and she realized the imp was better off where he was.

Eventually the plane landed and they got off and trudged through an airport that was dark and cold and made of concrete. They went through a different type of security. Again, the Devil went first, and once more nobody seemed interested in Hannah or her lack of passport. Their party only had one small bag with them and so they walked straight across the concourse and out on to the street.

Hannah gasped out loud. She'd been cold in her life before, but this was . . . this was *something else*. The streets had ice on them and the wind felt like a knife.

'Good God,' Granddad said, shivering too. The Devil gave him a dirty look, but Granddad shrugged. 'It's just an expression.'

All the buildings looked as though they had been designed to make you feel small and sad. It was working, too. The few people battling their way along the road, wrapped up in thick coats and wearing big, furry hats, looked as if they would rather, given complete freedom of choice, be dead. It was so cold that it made you feel miserable and empty and afraid. Vaneclaw rapidly turned a distressing shade of purple, his teeth chattering so loudly that it made Hannah's jaws ache.

Granddad and the Devil went to the kerb to hail a cab, leaving Hannah and the mushroom shivering together.

'Why are we even *in* Siberia?' she asked.

'Search me,' it said.

They spent the night in a nearby hotel made of concrete. It was, by local standards, slightly not-ugly. It didn't look like it wanted you to feel bad, more as if whoever had designed the hotel simply didn't like buildings very much, and was encouraging you to feel the same.

By now Hannah was stumbling with tiredness but Granddad insisted they go downstairs to get dinner, on the grounds that this would help her get over the jetlag more quickly. The Devil and the imp did not come with them.

They sat alone in a cavernous room and ate something that was halfway between a soup and a stew. It had beetroot and other less identifiable things in it but was surprisingly tasty.

'Why does this town look so tired and broken?'

'It was an experiment,' her grandfather said. 'It didn't work out. But it was a brave idea.'

Hannah caught a note of wistfulness in his voice. 'You've been here before, haven't you?'

'Places like it. Long time ago. Some people tried to do an interesting thing. But . . .' He tailed off.

'What?'

'Wherever there are good people,' he said, 'there are also bad. The world is heavy. If it doesn't want to follow where you're leading, then in the end the dream will die. What replaces a dream is often thin and dry for a time. People do not show their best sides in such circumstances.'

'And is that his fault?'

He looked at her. 'Who?'

'Him. Upstairs. That man who says he's the Devil.'

'We are who we are, and so there are ways we cannot help but behave. Balance is all you can hope for, which comes from making the right choices. There's an old Native American tale you may have heard. Cherokee, I believe. About two wolves?'

Hannah shook her head.

'In the story, an old man tells his grandson that he has a fight going on inside him, and has done his whole life. Between two wolves. One is a bad wolf – a wolf consumed with anger, regret, resentment and sorrow. The other wolf is good, with a heart filled with kindness, compassion and hope. Even joy. The boy asks which wolf will win in the end. The old man looks at him very seriously and says: "The one you feed."'

Hannah thought for a moment. 'I don't get it.'

'No,' Granddad said, sadly. 'In my experience, most people don't.'

'Are you *really* two hundred and fifty years old?'

'Older, actually,' he said, suddenly cheerful again, as if glad of the change of subject. 'I was nearly seventy when I started building the machine. Though I flatter myself I don't look much over three hundred, on a good day.'

'What's it like? Being old?'

'Not dying is nice, but it might have been better if he'd come to my workshop when I was, say, thirty. But I wouldn't have had the skills to build the machine for him then, I suppose.'

'Why are we here?'

'He needs me to try to work out why it isn't working properly.'

'What's the machine even supposed to do?'

Granddad chose his words carefully. 'It might more accurately be termed a "device". Something that divides. When people behave in certain ways, their deeds have a dark sort of power, which is something he needs. The machine selects and harvests those deeds and transports their power to . . . another realm, for his use. But it seems to have stopped working.'

'But we had to leave the Sacrifice Machine in the car, in the parking lot back in Seattle.'

'It doesn't matter where it is. Bad deeds are everywhere.'

'But if it's to do with bad things, why did you agree to build it?'

Granddad sighed. 'At first, I'm ashamed to admit, because of the challenge. But then I realized its true importance. The machine absorbs the dreadful energy of evil deeds and transports it out of harm's way. Without it, the world would . . . well, it would be an even more difficult place than it already is.'

'So why isn't it working properly?'

'The device itself *is* working. As a piece of engineering. But for some reason it's not achieving what it's supposed to.'

'Why?'

'I don't know.'

Hannah didn't understand any of this, and was having increasing trouble staying awake. 'If he's the Devil then why can't he work it out for himself?'

'Nobody knows everything. Not even him. Not even God.'

'So . . . is God real then, too?'

'So I'm told. We've never met.'

'Couldn't the Devil just have magicked himself here? Instead of going on the plane?'

'Not while he has physical form. Fighting the laws of the *mundus* takes a vast amount of energy, which is precisely what he doesn't presently have. And you and I couldn't have travelled that way, even if he did. He is the only being who can be both here, and there, at the same time.'

'And he needs you here with him, to check why the machine isn't doing what it should?'

'Yes. And I wasn't going anywhere without you. Your father entrusted you to me.'

Hannah nodded quickly. Grandfather knew what she meant, as always. As soon as they'd reached the hotel, Hannah had tracked down some Wi-Fi. She'd tried Skyping her father, but again, he'd been too busy to pick up.

'We'll try again tomorrow,' Granddad said.

There was a loud smashing sound. They turned to see that a waiter carrying a large tray of plates and cups and saucers had somehow lost control of it, and dropped the entire thing.

Three seconds later, Vaneclaw entered the room. He walked carefully around approximately six thousand tiny pieces of shattered crockery to their table. He had returned to his normal unwholesome colour – the hotel, though not warm, was at least not utterly freezing – and looked very self-important.

'Boss says you have to go to sleep now,' he declared. 'We're leaving at sparrow fart tomorrow. By which I mean very early. So chop chop. Upstairs with you.'

Granddad smiled at Hannah, and reached for the menu in a leisurely fashion. 'Something for dessert, dear?'

Nonetheless they were on the road by five o'clock the following morning. It was still dark. The Devil drove. He drove much, much faster than Hannah's grandfather, and she spent most of the time with her eyes firmly closed.

Soon they were out into the countryside.

For an hour or two it was bleak and empty. Then the road took them into a forest that seemed to go on forever, hour after hour, tree after tree after tree. If these trees were able to talk, Hannah felt, their conversation wouldn't sound like Bach. It would be a cold, papery whispering, a muttering just below the threshold of hearing, and would mainly be about how cold they were, and the loves they'd lost, and whether it was worth the effort of killing themselves.

Then they were back out in open country again for a while, before plunging back into forest once more.

And still the Devil drove.

Finally, just after three in the afternoon, the Devil turned off what had passed for a highway – increasingly broken-up and ragged though it had become – and on to a smaller and even less well-kept road. It was icier, too, with wisps of snow blowing across it, and the Devil was forced to slow down. After an hour of this (by which point Hannah thought she was actually going to *lose her mind* with boredom) he stopped the car.

'We there, boss?'

The Devil didn't answer. He turned his head, like a dog trying to catch a scent. Then he started driving again.

Fifteen minutes later, by the side of a small hill, he finally pulled the car over to the side of the road and turned the engine off.

Hannah looked out of the window. She couldn't imagine anywhere more desolate. Half of what she could see was covered in lonely-looking fir trees. The rest was snow, with grass poking up through it. The grass was short and stubby and more blue than green, as if frozen. There were cracks in the ground. The sky was leaden grey, and getting darker by the moment.

'Where is this place?' she asked.

'Nowhere,' the Devil said. 'The very heart of it.'

Chapter 16

At first the Devil said she had to stay in the car. Hannah said that wasn't going to happen. She wasn't going to be left quite literally in the middle of nowhere, by herself, *in the dark*. Grandfather backed her up on this until the Devil pointed out that night would indeed fall soon, at which point the temperature – already well below freezing – would plummet further. Even though the humans were wearing several layers of clothing, it would be dangerously cold. Possibly fatally so.

Hannah could see her grandfather weighing the risks. In the end he said that unless they left the engine running it would be no better in the car than outside, and walking might help keep Hannah warm, and if she didn't come, he wouldn't either.

The Devil stared at him for a long time. Granddad raised an eyebrow, and waited.

They all left the car together, setting off into the wilderness.

After a while, Hannah noticed that the ground they were walking over was boggy. The water on the surface had frozen, but the ice was thin and brittle, unlike the rock-like hardness they'd been seeing all day. She asked her grandfather about it.

'The permafrost is melting,' he said.

'I know about permafrost,' she said. Her face was so cold
it was hard to move her mouth. 'We did it in the fourth grade.
It's where it's been so cold for so long that the earth freezes
for thousands of years. It's where they find woolly mammoths.
But why is it melting? It's so *cold.*'

'Not as cold as it used to be.' His breath puffed up in
clouds around his face. 'Global warming, they say.'

'Nonsense,' the Devil snapped. 'It comes and goes. Twenty
thousand years ago this was a meadow.'

Hannah sniffed. 'How do you know?'

'How do you think?'

He strode ahead. Granddad put his arm around Hannah's
shoulders, and they kept walking.

Half an hour later, Hannah could tell something had changed,
or was changing. It was almost fully dark by then but that
wasn't it, and her head had nearly frozen into a block of ice,
but she didn't think it was that either. There was something
different about the atmosphere. The terrain had altered, too.
What had started out as cracks in the earth had been getting
bigger. Some were now wide enough that you had to jump
over them.

The Devil stopped walking.

'Are we lost?' Vaneclaw asked, the words barely audible
above the chattering of his teeth. The imp had turned a colour
so extremely vile that it was impossible to name. Just looking
at it made your eyes want to swivel completely round in your
head, even if that meant you had to look at your own brains.

'No,' the Devil said, irritably. 'Imp – show yourself.'

Hannah was confused, as he obviously didn't mean
Vaneclaw, who was right beside her.

The Devil started walking in the direction of a particularly large crack in the ground. As they got closer, Hannah saw something standing all by itself at the edge.

'Eurgh,' she said.

You would have too. It was about three feet high, and squat. It was like the kind of thing you see sometimes by the side of the road, an animal that's been hit by a car and subsequently run over by another, and then left for several days in hot sun. It looked as though something like that had somehow survived, and managed to stand itself upright again, though in a mangled, lop-sided way. It was covered in short black bristles. On what was presumably its head were two eyes, one the size of a fist, the other of a tiny marble. Both were bloodshot. Its mouth looked like it had been cut into its head with a rusty axe.

'Soulfang!' Vaneclaw said in wonder. 'Well I never. Haven't seen you in *ages*, mate.'

'Well, I been here, haven't I?' The creature's voice was mournful and cracked and very deep.

'That explains it! How long?'

The squat imp turned its head to look up at the Devil. 'How long, boss?'

'Eight hundred years,' the Devil said. 'And?'

Soulfang shook his head. 'Ain't seen no one. At all.'

'What is that . . . thing?' Hannah asked, keeping well out of its way.

'They call them stop imps,' her grandfather said. 'Their job is to bar the way.'

'To what?'

'It depends. They're invisible to most people. Have you ever been walking somewhere, in a field, or forest, or the middle of town, and seen a path or road and started to walk down it, but then decided . . . no, I'll go another way? Without knowing why? That'll be because of something like

Soulfang, stationed to keep it private. Sometimes they'll be put in houses, too, in closets or drawers or the garage, to stop you finding something you've lost. They're particularly drawn to car keys and photographs of people who have died. And homework, of course. Then later you'll open the door or drawer and wonder how you missed it when you looked before.'

'Eight hundred years,' Vaneclaw said with some admiration. 'You must be *freezing*.'

'Not really,' the imp intoned. 'I feel no cold.'

'No, me neither,' Vaneclaw said hurriedly. 'Balmy, isn't it, eh? Lovely temperature. Bit warm, maybe. In fact, I wish I was wearing a coat, so I could take it off.'

'Come,' said the Devil.

He led them towards the edge of the crack, which was even bigger than it had first appeared. Big enough, in fact, that it was more like a canyon. The Devil started climbing down into it.

'I'm not going down there,' Hannah muttered.

'I couldn't care less what you do,' the Devil said as his head disappeared. 'But the Engineer will follow me.'

Hannah glanced at her grandfather and saw from his face that he had no choice, and so she lowered herself carefully over the edge and started clambering down the side.

The earth was rocky and slippery, and freezing cold on the fingers. What made it worse was that each step lower into the ground made you feel more afraid. Of what, you didn't know. It just felt like you should be going the other way instead, as quickly as possible, or maybe faster.

Granddad was doggedly scrambling down beside her, however, and Hannah decided that if he could do this, she would too. She saw the way he winced each time he had to move his shoulders, or knees, and how blotchy his face had become with

117

the cold. Whatever working for the Devil had done for him, he was still an old man. He looked after her.

She could look after him too.

It was totally dark at the bottom of the canyon, only a sliver of almost-dark still visible up above.

And it felt . . . dead. Hannah no longer felt what she'd felt on the way down. She felt nothing at all.

The Devil tapped Vaneclaw on the head, quite hard, and the imp started to glow, gently, like a huge nightlight, shedding sufficient illumination that you could see where you were. At the bottom of a huge, freezing, wet, nasty crack in the ground, a million miles from anywhere.

The Devil went to the canyon wall and brushed his big, pale hands over it. Dust and clods of frozen earth fell down, eventually revealing . . .

'Is that a gate?' Hannah peered at it. Yes, there was a gate stuck in the earth – a huge, ominous, iron gate. It didn't lead anywhere, of course, because it was bedded in the earth. It looked like a big metal gate had somehow fallen down a crack ten thousand years ago and got swallowed up.

'The only remaining physical access,' the Devil said. 'There were two others, but one is now far beneath a major city and the other wound up at the bottom of the sea after the geological upheaval that caused the Flood.'

Granddad looked as if he was preparing himself for something he didn't want to do. Vaneclaw seemed excited. The Devil looked as he always did, like a cross between the stern man in the library who would be the first to tell you not to whisper so loud, and the kind of person Mom or Dad warned you not to talk to even if he offered unusually interesting candy, and a kitten.

The Devil kept brushing with his hands, getting the earth

off this side of the gate, ultimately revealing a narrow slit in one of the upright bars, about an inch wide and four inches tall. He raised his left hand and put his fingers out straight, held together, like a karate-chopping hand. He moved it forwards and into the slit in the gate.

He turned it to the left. There was a clunking sound, low and somehow awful. It was like that feeling you get when you realize you've done something wrong, and deeply terrible, and won't ever be able to take it back.

The gate swung slowly open, and when it did, she saw there wasn't earth on the other side of it after all.

There was an opening, a tunnel.

Or a mouth.

Chapter 17

Hannah stuck close to her grandfather as they stepped through the gate and into the area beyond. It was less dark than the canyon – like the end of a cloudy afternoon, near twilight, the remnant glow of today fighting a losing battle against the oncoming of inky night. The ground was covered in short grass. A dusty path led across it into shadow. It was the kind of shadow you'd see in a forest, though there were no trees to cast it. There were a few low bushes dotted around. Nothing else. The shadows had come by themselves, bringing dust and silence.

After they'd gone ten yards along the path, Hannah glanced back. It was the same in that direction now too, stretching endlessly. The gate had disappeared.

Once you were here, you were here.

For a moment then she heard something – a clattering of plates, a low hubbub of conversation. Like a restaurant during a busy lunchtime. It faded, leaving the silence even more silent.

The Devil pressed onwards, head held high. He led the way along the path towards and across an old wooden bridge over a sluggish river, in which the water ran thick and black. Vaneclaw scurried after him, extinguishing his light. Though

Hannah tried to keep up with her grandfather she soon found herself falling behind. 'Wait,' she said.

He didn't seem to hear.

Then she was alone.

Some things were the same. The low, featureless sky dimly warmed by a tobacco-ochre glow. Quietness. Not quite a silence, now, but as if all sound had been turned down or was being heard from several rooms away, through thick walls. Other people's sounds, eavesdropped. Sounds that said you stood outside, a stranger, listening to stories that had nothing to do with you. Sounds that said you were alone, and always would be.

But she was walking along a residential street, lined with trees. It seemed familiar, but she had never seen it this way before. There were no cars. The leaves on the trees were grey. There were houses, or things that should be houses but were just oblongs with roofs. There were no windows or doors. They were the idea of shelter, nothing more. These houses were designed to keep you *out*. To make it clear that you were alone.

The street finished in a dead end. Beyond was a grassy area. The trees here were bigger. Pines, some eucalyptus, and a redwood or two. A few picnic tables, empty, old, forgotten. It looked like it had been a long time since anyone had tied a birthday-party balloon to any of them.

On the right there was an open patch, with a path leading across it. She walked this to the end, where the ground abruptly shaded away, and realized how high up she was. Then she saw the view, and realized . . .

This was Ocean View Park.

She blinked, looked back. Yes, she knew this place, of course she did. It was a park on the other side of Santa Cruz from where they lived now. They used to come here when she was younger and they lived on the east side, back when everything was good and all she knew was a rolling cycle of warmth and food and play and sleep – with occasional TV.

She took a few steps towards the edge, realizing something else was wrong. She should be able to see the boardwalk from this high vantage. The ocean too, of course, hence the name of the park, and the wide mouth of the San Lorenzo River, crossed by the old wooden hulk of the decommissioned railway bridge, but especially the boardwalk and the Giant Dipper, and . . .

None of it was there. It was just cloud.

She turned and hurried back up the path, calling for her grandfather, fighting to stay calm. She couldn't remember when he'd started not being with her any more. He wasn't here now, though. She could tell that. *Nobody* was here.

The place felt dead. Wholly, utterly dead.

Past the tall trees and the picnic tables was the first set of swings, the ones for little kids. Beyond that, down a shallow slope, the bigger swings. She could still remember the day when she'd graduated to these, when she'd judged she no longer needed to be held fast by the bucket shapes of the toddler swings but could perch on these stirringly adult contraptions instead, keeping herself in place by gripping the metal chains and allowing herself to be held by momentum.

Her father had been dubious at first, but she'd proved herself capable. 'Wow. Look at you,' he'd said. He seemed both happy and sad. 'Look at you all grown up.'

She remembered running across the grass afterwards to where her mother sat, and her mother folding her in her arms and telling her how big she was now. It was the moment when Hannah had progressed from toddler to a child, the first time she'd left part of her life behind.

The swings hung limply in the still air.

Hannah walked past to the park's banner attraction: the two long slides. They went down a full thirty feet, dropping from the park's upper section to a lower one with a climbing frame that she'd never had much to do with (it seemed to her to be a boy thing). The slides were made of metal, burnished by the passage of countless small backsides, often aided by small, scavenged squares of cardboard (which meant your bottom didn't get as hot, and you went twice as fast).

She stood at the top and looked down. She couldn't see the end of the slides. She didn't want to go down. She didn't want to be here at all. She turned, deciding to walk back out of the park the way she'd come, to do it now, and to do it fast.

She saw that one of the swings was in motion. Someone was sitting on it. Too large to be a kid. Someone with brown hair like her own, but wavier. And . . .

Hannah took tentative steps towards the swings. The figure didn't look up. She, or he, or it, kept swinging slowly back and forth . . . And Hannah suddenly realized that there was something deeply familiar about it.

'*Mom?*'

The figure jumped off the swing and ran.

It ran like a bundle of shadows, through the trees. It was making a noise like someone crying – though again, the sound seemed confused, broken up by other noises, like a swing door opening and the chink of wine glasses.

Hannah ran after it, ran as fast as she could, but the figure was moving at adult speed – the speed of someone who, like Hannah's mom, diligently did at least a 5K run three days a week, come rain, come shine. Hannah followed it along the path to the drop, towards the big cloud where you should be able to see the boardwalk, running until her breath was tearing in her chest, managing to keep the figure in sight.

It ran right to the end, where the bluff dropped away, not slowing, getting faster and faster.

And then it jumped – hurling itself into the cloud.

Hannah was scared to jump, but scared not to. The figure had been the only thing here. Now she was alone. She tripped but kept on running, trying to screw up her courage to follow, to jump into nothingness.

But then something grabbed her arm, and Hannah screamed.

It was Granddad.

'Don't go closer to the edge,' he said.

'Was that Mom?'

'No. Come on. Follow me.'

He tried to drag her away but Hannah didn't want to leave. She dug her heels in, eyes still on the cloud.

Behind them, she could hear the rusty sound of the swing still going back and forth. Swinging, swinging.

Why was it making that noise again? What was making it swing? Was the figure back there now? Was everything repeating?

'It's not there,' her grandfather said. 'What you're seeing and hearing isn't really there.'

'But how come, if you see it too?'

'I'm seeing it because you do. Until a few seconds ago I was somewhere else. I was beside an apple tree in a garden I knew long, long ago. Waiting for someone who never turned up. I'm only here now because your mind is young and very strong.'

'I don't believe you,' Hannah said. 'That . . . that was Mom. I have to go to her.'

Granddad gripped her arm even more tightly and swung

her round to face him. He looked strange and old. 'Turn away,' he said. 'Forget it. Leave her be.'

Hannah didn't want to. Once his gaze held her, however, she didn't seem able to free herself. She couldn't move. His hands gripped her arms tighter and tighter, like giant claws.

She heard the thing on the swing – her mother, she still believed it must be her – make a noise.

Then there was a clanking, chinking sound as the chains on the swing rattled, as the thing sitting on it climbed off, slowly this time, and started towards her.

'Hannah,' Granddad said very urgently. '*Look away.*'

She closed her eyes.

She opened them a moment later to find that she was standing again on the pathway in the place with the short grasses and the bushes. Ocean View Park had disappeared. The Devil was standing to one side.

The imp, Vaneclaw, was close to him. Its face looked pinched and tense. 'Boss? This doesn't feel right. At all.'

'It does not,' the Devil agreed. 'We should go.'

He set off up the path. Up, or perhaps down. Hannah and her grandfather followed. After a few minutes she was enormously relieved to see the iron gate in the distance. She sensed that she was not the only one to feel that way, as they all started to walk a little faster.

She was the last to pass through, and as she stepped over the threshold she turned, thinking she heard someone call her name.

'No,' her grandfather said. 'Don't look back. Never ever.'

When she was the other side the Devil closed the gate and slipped his hand into its lock. This time when he turned it, she felt the way you do when you're walking down a flight of steps and don't realize there's one fewer than you thought.

But hollow, too, and very sad.

After they'd clambered back out of the canyon, the Devil spent a few minutes in conference with Soulfang. At the end the imp nodded, looking somewhat dejected, and trudged back to stand guard once more at a crack in the earth in the back of beyond.

Then they started the long walk back to the car.

For hour after hour, the Devil drove through the dark emptiness. Granddad insisted Hannah ride in the front, to be closer to the heater. The heater wasn't very efficient and barely produced any warmth at all, but she loved him for the thought.

For a long time nobody spoke. Finally, as they came out of the second endless chunk of forest, and Hannah felt that they were far enough away that it might be safe to speak of what had taken place, she asked a question.

'What happened in there?'

'You got lost behind,' Granddad said.

'Left behind?'

'No. Lost. In the Behind.'

She turned in her seat to look at him. 'Did you find out what's wrong with the machine?'

He shook his head. 'No. All I learned is that it's worse than we thought.'

The Devil's eyes were on the road ahead, or what little of it could be seen in the light of headlamps fighting against the thick darkness. Hannah didn't think she'd ever seen someone look so serious in her entire life.

'What's going on?' she asked him.

He took a very long time to respond, and when he did she could see that the answer pained him a great deal. 'I don't know.'

*   *   *

They got back to the city just before dawn, the same time they'd left the day before, which made Hannah hope she might be able to pretend the whole episode had never happened, that she'd merely dreamed it, lost a day somehow through forgivable carelessness, and that life could go on as before.

As they were walking across the hotel lobby towards the elevator, Granddad's phone rang. He answered it, and listened, and then walked a distance away to listen some more, his eyes on Hannah all the time.

When he ended the call he stood motionless for a moment, looking lost. Then he walked back over to her.

'What?'

'We need to be calm,' he said.

Hannah immediately felt very un-calm. 'Why? Has something happened to Mom?'

'No. That was Zoë. Your father has disappeared.'

Chapter 18

In the beginning was the word. So what do you do when the words won't come? When you don't know what happens next?

You just keep typing.

Steve knew this all too well. You keep *doing things*. It's how life works, the engine of time itself. Breath follows breath. Day follows night. Homework has to be supervised and school lunches have to be made. Groceries need to be bought. Cars require to be filled with gas before you can do any of this, and those cars have to be paid for and your dad or mom or some steel-nerved stranger will have had to teach you to drive.

This follows that. That follows this.

It takes you a long time to grasp the fact that neither 'this' nor 'that' make a lot of difference, and in fact it's all the following that takes up your time. Whatever you do, whatever you say, will lead to another thing, and another – and before you know it you'll be riding some brave sentence out into the great unknown, driving it like a road into a future you create for yourself word by word.

Unless . . . the words stop coming.

She was beautiful. Beautiful and wild deep inside. Beautiful and bold and occasionally rash and yet always so practical, and fundamentally – Steve believed, and had always believed – several large strides out of his league. He had tried selling himself the idea that perhaps their leagues lay side by side, like different breeds. If it's true that every dog still has a touch of the wolf in it, then Steve's was heavily domesticated, glimpsed only in an occasional twitch in the feet as he dozed and dreamed by the hearth after a long day working the farm. Kristen's inner wolf had her pacing up and down along the fence every evening, sniffing at the cold winds coming down from the mountains, eager to run and explore. To be Out There.

Yet somehow they'd come together. Come together and started weaving a life, sharing the same page. In your twenties you unquestioningly believe you're writing in pencil, a striking first draft. You do things with such confidence. You know you're so strong, so individual, wholly unique: that you have power over heaven and earth, and that the future and its wonders are either already in your hands or will be after you do the next thing, or the thing that follows naturally after that.

And so you bravely pick up the existential pencil and sketch a few opening sentences, the speculative first paragraph. You encourage the woman or man you love to write alongside you, relishing the co-authoring of this huge improvisational adventure, this big and beautiful game. You write and write and write and it all seems so very easy, and before you know it you're already on Chapter Sixteen and that's great because just *look* how much you've done, and how very good it is . . . or will be, definitely, when you've had a chance to give it an edit.

Until the lunch in Los Gatos when you realize there will *be* no second draft, that your wife doesn't love you any more, and you've been writing with indelible ink all along.

Before all that happens you get married, rather early. You have a child. You work. You buy a house. You prioritize one set of friends over another. You move to a bigger house. You tend towards one brand of instant coffee. You buy a mountain bike and feel guilty about never using it. You fall into the habit of visiting Big Sur, and hang your dreams upon its crags.

You do all these things, telling each other how serious they are, so mutually proud of how grown-up you're becoming – look at me, Mom! Hey, Dad, see how well I've done! – though in reality it still feels like a game, endless dress-up. And gradually you realize a lot of these haven't been actual *choices*, but words following words in the sequence that makes sense at the time. Or maybe just . . . happens.

Because sometimes, you come to fear, doing what made sense, word by word, has trapped you into sentences that don't in fact go where you expected (or wanted) to be led. But that's OK, because you're still in charge, right? Life is the ultimate creative act, as all the photo memes and Twitter quotes and the racks of bestsellers in the bookstores endlessly remind you. *You're the artist at work.* And so you take stock, judiciously, glad to be older and wiser now, and you pick up the Eraser of Maturity and bend over your story, ready to make the few minor adjustments required to get it back on glorious track.

But it won't rub out.

All those words and sentences, those previous chapters . . . turns out they're there for good. You rub and rub at them, and maybe you'll get some of the most recent words to smear, but the meaning remains in place, irrevocable. There is no future in them, no present, only the endlessly structuring past. You live in this house in particular, and are father to that specific child, and have a certain job, and you have become all the things you have done and thought, and now can't undo or unthink.

You push the paper aside, discomfited. Ignore the situation

for a while, continue to add the everyday acts of brushing your teeth and working and listening to your wife talk about a big contract she's considering taking in London and how good it would be for her career, and thus for the two of you, never realizing that by now she is thinking mainly of herself and her intangible needs – to a degree that even she is unaware of.

But then a few months later, when you return to the task, having convinced yourself in the meantime that it *must* be possible, you find that someone else has been covertly trying to change the story while you weren't paying attention, rubbing out your joint past far harder than you ever had courage to.

The words are all still there, still visible. But she's rubbed so very hard at them that the paper itself has started to tear right across the middle.

And in your heart of hearts, you don't blame her.

You've grasped by now that the situation is in danger of becoming desperate, that your story is going off the rails. The problem is that by the time you accept this, the world has already jumped tracks.

But it must be recoverable, right? There must be *something* you can say or do, some form of words, some astonishing paragraph that will fix everything and bring life back under control. You try and try, but the words won't come. If stories are like cats, then words are the most scaredy of kittens. The harder you chase, the deeper they hide, until the morning when the woman you love hands you back the piece of paper you've huddled over together for many years, and tells you that – apart from a few choice sentences, like the child you both love – it's your story and yours alone now.

And the next chapter is your sole responsibility.

So WTF happens next?

You realize then, far too late, that you were mainly good at the describing parts, the adjectives – and it was she who came up with the plot, the verbs, the doing words. You realize that your wife may even have a point, that you have become ossified and disengaged and becalmed (though doesn't her impulsiveness miss the target far more often these days, now she's stopped using you to ground her feet and steady her aim?). You come to fear that while some are good at writing their stories, you have a tendency to let your story write you instead.

Words will vanish under these circumstances, and this messed-up, anger-torn, and tear-stained piece of paper becomes all that remains of a life that not so long ago you were so proud of that you'd have hung it on the wall. Now it looks like something found screwed up in a drawer of an old person's house.

But it's all you've got. So you scribble. You type. You hack at it. Nothing makes a mark. You start to fear it never will, that all you can do is cross some of these once-loved words out. Until one night it occurs to you that maybe there's a more vigorous editing style left to try, a way of bailing from a story in which you don't even seem to have a speaking part.

That perhaps you have to be your own *deus ex machina*.

That you could take your piece of paper somewhere private. By yourself.

And set fire to it.

Chapter 19

Nash and his crew stopped again in Deming, New Mexico. Previous breaks had been pit stops, barely long enough to gas up, use the john and grab snacks. Otherwise they simply drove, hour after hour, taking shifts. Hammering the highway up through the centre of Florida, across Louisiana, and then the endless slog across Texas, swinging around San Antonio and up towards New Mexico.

Eduardo and Chex started lobbying for another stop around El Paso. Jesse, who was taking a turn behind the wheel, kept quiet. He knew the decision wasn't his. He also knew that Nash hadn't slept since they left Miami. When not driving, his boss had taken the passenger seat and sat staring straight ahead. Jesse liked the idea of a break very much. The truck was thick with cigarette smoke and stale sweat, and the flatulent after-effects of cheap burritos bought from gas station chiller cabinets had not contributed anything pleasant to the ambience. His ass was aching from three straight hours behind the wheel and his eyes were tired and dry. But he knew that Nash could hear the guys bitching in the back too, and if he hadn't agreed to take a break, it wasn't happening.

'You still don't know?' he asked Nash. The reason they

were driving instead of taking a plane was the boss apparently didn't know exactly where they were headed.

'Only that it's west.'

'You think maybe Los Angeles?' Jesse had always wanted to go to LA – even before he learned it was where they made all the movies and TV. His grandmother, born on its outskirts, often nostalgically referred to the city by a longer version of the old Spanish name – the 'city of angels'. Jesse was old enough now to know there'd be no angels there but he still wouldn't mind taking a look, in her honour. She'd been like a mother to him after his real mom ran away, but died when Jesse was twelve, bystander in an amateur-night grocery-store robbery that went badly awry.

Neither Jesse nor his boss knew that Nash had fired the bullet that killed her – that Jesse's grandmother had been, in fact, the first person to die at Nash's hand, and the only death that, once in a great while and in the deep dead of night, he could bring himself to regret. She had been the gate that opened in front of him and led on to his life's dark path.

'I don't know,' Nash said. 'Just drive.'

Deming didn't look like anywhere in particular, just another town on another highway. But then – for no reason Jesse could determine – Nash gestured towards the side of the road.

Jesse spotted a gas station/grocery store combo and steered gratefully into the parking lot.

The store was the kind of place where it looked like you could pick up a serious skin condition just by touching things on the shelves, but nonetheless had a counter in back where you could buy burgers and hot dogs. The cook was standing out near the battered table, glaring irritably up at a small TV hung from the wall. It wasn't showing anything. He reached up and slapped it. Nothing changed.

He turned to look at them. His apron looked like it had been run over by a tractor on a rainy day. 'Seriously?' he said. He was middle-aged and paunchy. 'We got robbed just last week. Someone tried, anyhow.'

'Here for food,' Nash said. 'Nothing else.'

'Glad to hear it. Dave's kind of pussy when it comes to shooting people, huh, Dave?'

This was addressed to the man behind the register by the door, who was tall and fat and had a shaved head and a tattoo of a spiderweb over one cheek. He smiled, kind of. It was a smile that said his colleague's previous statement had not been in any way accurate, and that there was a loaded weapon under the counter which he would be delighted to use.

Nash looked at him, then back at the cook, taking his time, and both men understood straight away that Nash was not a guy they wanted to mess with.

'Cheeseburgers,' Nash said. 'Fries. Make it fast.'

While they waited for the food Nash went to the john. This was in a detached block out back and not as bad as he'd expected. Someone, a woman most likely, and paid very little for the pleasure, kept it in a state hovering around the merely unpleasant rather than truly disgusting.

Nash stood in a stall and did what he needed to do. When he stepped back out he caught sight of himself in the grimy mirror above the washbasins. He looked the way he always did – rangy, stubbled chin, dressed in faded black denim – but he barely recognized himself. As he washed his hands he stared at his face. Was that him? Was he the guy inside that body, that shape? Why was he even asking this stuff? What did it mean?

He turned off the tap and wiped his hands on the back of his jeans. That face in the mirror . . .

That *was* him, right?

The restroom was quiet and so the noise of the mirror cracking was loud. It sounded like a stone being dropped on glass. The crack went from top to bottom, right down through the part holding Nash's face. The line went between his eyes.

Nash blinked.

The mirror cracked again, in the other direction. The crack was shorter this time, cutting right across the first, nearer the top than the bottom.

Nash waited, very still.

Scaring Nash was nearly impossible – he didn't care enough about his life – but this was the closest to scared he'd felt in many years. Neither of the cracks reached all the way to the edge of the glass, which struck him as weird. The cracks were also surprisingly straight. Taken together, they made a shape. A short line crossing a longer one, at right angles, their intersection nearer the top than the bottom.

A very well-known symbol. One familiar from every church, and from the front of every bible.

He heard a gurgling sound.

It was coming from the stall he'd visited, and the ones to either side. It was a liquid sound, but thick and throaty. Like a toilet flushing but in reverse.

As he watched, the water level in the bowl started to rise. At first the water was clear, but quickly turned muddy brown, and got thicker.

It started to smell, too. It smelled bad.

Then it was spilling over the edge, pouring out, in wave after wave, far too much to have been in the bowl or the local plumbing. A horrific reversal, a switch of direction, as if all the world's shit was gushing back out into this restroom.

Nash backed away and got out of there before it could reach his feet.

The others were at the table, munching their burgers in silence. Nash's was waiting on the counter. He didn't bother to tell the guys running the store about the issue in their bathroom – it wasn't his problem.

As he stepped up to grab his food he realized the TV screen on the wall was no longer dark. There was a faint, swirling light within it. A sound was coming from it, too, but it wasn't a faint crackling like they'd heard in Mr Files's store. It was like waves, and also voices. The voices were low, whispering. They weren't speaking in English. One word gradually started to stand out – 'Santa' – though it was nowhere near Christmastime.

Nash looked at the cook. 'Spanish stations all you got?'

'Funny guy.'

'What?'

'Cable's been out all day. That black screen and silence is all we get.'

Nash stood, eating his burger, watching the screen, listening to a language he didn't understand.

He took the wheel when they got in the truck, and drove in silence. The guys in the back fell asleep quickly. Only Jesse stayed awake, kept that way by a low feeling of unease in his guts, listening to the sound of their tyres flashing along the highway across the desert. At one point he thought he glimpsed something out of the side window, a rangy, four-legged creature loping along beside them through the brush, keeping pace in the darkness. Jesse abruptly turned to the front and watched the road ahead instead.

Nash meanwhile could feel something gathering at the edges

of his mind. A name of a place. Somewhere he'd heard about long ago. Somewhere on the west coast. To do with surfing, maybe?

'You know Spanish, right?'

'Some. From my grandma.'

'Whatever. "Santa" means "holy"?'

Jesse shrugged. 'Yeah.'

Nash thought about the shape he'd seen in the cracks in the bathroom mirror. 'So what would "holy cross" be?'

'Santa Cruz, I guess.'

Nash nodded, slowly. 'Then that's where we're going.'

Chapter 20

When they pulled up outside her house in Santa Cruz, Hannah ran to the door but then realized she had no key. Her father had been due to meet her at the airport, of course, so she wouldn't need a key. But . . . he *hadn't* picked her up.

Nobody knew where he was, and Hannah didn't have a key. How was she supposed to get back into her house, into her *life*, if she didn't even get through the front door?

She hammered on the door with both fists. 'Dad!' she shouted. 'It's me. Let me in. Let me *in*!'

She was sobbing by the time the door opened. It wasn't her father. It was Aunt Zo.

Hannah sat at the kitchen table. Her head ached. Zo had made her a sandwich, but the result suggested sandwich making was another thing – like drawing – that lay outside her field of expertise. Short of getting the thing inside out and putting the bread in the middle and the ham and cheese on the outside, or hiding all of the ingredients in different rooms, it was hard to imagine how she could have got it more wrong.

Hannah wasn't hungry anyway. She'd listened for an hour while Zo and Granddad talked. The talk was like the traffic on Mission, the main road through town. Sometimes they would talk and talk and you thought they'd never stop. Then there would be a gap, and you thought it would never start again. The talking was making her head hurt, but the gaps were worse. When you were talking, you were doing.

Bad things lived in gaps and silences.

Like Hannah, Zo had tried calling her dad. She'd made the same assumption – that Steve had elected to turn off the ringer or take a break from staring at screens, and that was probably a good thing, right? Granddad nodded when she said this, and Aunt Zo looked relieved. Evidently being twenty-six didn't prevent you from needing your dad to tell you that you'd done OK.

Steve.

Hannah knew her dad's name, of course. She didn't like hearing it, though. When things were OK nobody said 'Steve'. Hannah called him Dad. Her mom hadn't called him anything – because when people live together and are happy, they don't need targets to aim words at – you talk in someone's general direction and everyone knows who's meant.

In the weeks before her mother left, Hannah started hearing the word 'Steve' more often. A *lot* more often, by the end. Sometimes like a needle. Sometimes like a hammer. Sometimes like a sigh. It wasn't only Mom doing it, either.

Kristen – that's not fair.

Kristen – please let's talk about it.

Kristen – let's not do this now: she can hear.

When Zo hadn't got a response to another call, she'd sent an email. When that didn't get a reply, tendrils of real concern had started to wrap around her mind. If there was one area of life in which Zoë's brother could be guaranteed not to drop the ball, it was email. He was vague on things like birthday cards, yes; and Zo – like Hannah – had more than once heard him ranting how emails were the zombies of the twenty-first century. Didn't matter how hard you fought back, he said, they kept on coming. You cleared the compound each night and thought you were done, but next morning you'd find twenty-six more of the damned things, shambling outside the fence, tugging at it, reaching for your attention, wanting to eat your brains.

He was dogged with them, though – not least because a lot of his work was conducted this way, and he was used to whapping emails back across the net like a tennis player in an endless rally (also, Hannah's mom was heard to mutter, usually good-naturedly, it was a way of not doing any actual work).

Bottom line was if you sent an email to Steve Green – be you friend, foe, colleague or even relative – you'd get a response by end of play. You could count on it.

But none had come.

And so, not even sure why she was reacting this way (except that she knew how unhappy her brother had been since his power-dressing, Powerpoint-wielding wife moved out, and, like Hannah, had not failed to notice when he didn't shave), she'd driven down. Of course he'd be there when she arrived, baffled and irritable at her appearing on his doorstep without warning (her brother was not the world's most sociable person), but she could say she'd got bored and come on a whim and offer to take Hannah out for the afternoon, give him a little space.

Hannah looked up when she heard this. Aunt Zo had evidently not known about her going to visit Granddad either. Dad hadn't mentioned the plan to her, or to Mom. What did that mean?

'I've called his cell every couple hours since,' Aunt Zo said. 'I've sent a bunch more emails. Kristen called on the house phone, FYI. I told her I was here helping out for a day or two, that he was at a meeting in town.'

'Did she have anything to suggest?'

'We didn't . . .' Aunt Zo glanced at Hannah, as if she'd just remembered that she was there. 'We didn't, like, chat. But I got the sense she's hearing alarm bells too.'

Hannah jumped up and ran out of the room. She didn't want to hear this any more. Her dad wasn't 'Steve'. He was that big, daddy-shaped thing who should be here.

'Steve' didn't say who he was.

'Steve' said he was gone.

The Devil was in the sitting room. He was staring with distaste at a picture on the wall, one that Dad had bought for himself. It was a nice painting of Big Sur.

'Stop looking at that,' Hannah said furiously. She didn't understand why she said it, except she knew Dad really liked the picture – though Mom hadn't seemed so keen – and she didn't want the Devil looking at it in case he spoiled it.

'It will be a pleasure,' the Devil said. 'Though it has given me an idea. Tell your grandfather I have gone.'

'But you haven't.'

'What a sharp little girl you are, Hannah – and I am famously drawn to the details, after all. I *haven't* gone, yet. But I will have by the time you tell him.'

'Where are you going?'

'To find out what's going on. I've already wasted too much time.'

There had been a heated discussion at the airport in Russia about whether the Devil would allow Granddad to stay in Santa Cruz, or if he had to drop Hannah off and go fetch the Sacrifice Machine from Seattle. Granddad had stood firm. He'd said the machine would be safe in the trunk of his car at Sea-Tac, or as safe as it would be anywhere. It could not be opened by another person. The machine would not allow

142

it. The Devil could do what he damned well pleased, Granddad had concluded, but he needed to find his son.

In the end the Devil had flown with them to San Francisco. He had remained silent throughout the flight, but an hour before they landed a man in the row behind them had had a heart attack. The man, a middle-aged Italian on the way to America to be reconciled with the brother he hadn't seen in twenty years, survived the rest of the journey. He would not survive the night.

When the Devil opened the front door to her house, about to leave, Hannah ran and tried to stop him. 'We've got to find my *dad*.'

'I'll keep an eye out for him.'

'You don't even know what he *looks* like.'

'I know how he will taste.'

Hannah stared up at him, revulsion crawling over her skin. '*What?*'

'I've met you. I know your grandfather. Your father lies somewhere along the middle of that bloodline. I'll work it out. But in the meantime I need to go to Hell.'

'You can't go all the way back there.'

'I don't need to. I only had to make the journey that way because I was taking your grandfather, and you.'

'Because we're not dead?'

'You don't need to be dead. Hell is not a place. It's not a noun, child. It's a verb. I need to find someone doing it.'

'But you can't just *leave*. My granddad made that machine for you. He went all the way to the coldest place on the planet to try to help. You've got to help him.'

'No,' the Devil said, and walked past her on to the pathway.

She followed. Vaneclaw had been lurking in the front yard earlier, but wasn't to be seen now. 'You *do*,' she shouted.

'One of the great things about being me,' the Devil said,

143

'is I don't have to do *anything at all*. Especially not over something so insignificant as a single human soul.'

'I *hate* you,' Hannah said, to his back.

It sounded so weak. The first time she'd said these words it was to her mother. It hadn't been what she meant then, and it wasn't now. They were dumb words, useless sounds. They were arrows that didn't land. She needed words that were bigger and heavier and sharper.

The Devil smiled, however. A thin, horrible smile. 'There's hope for you yet,' he said.

In the kitchen, Granddad and Zo were *still* talking.

'What are we going to *do*?' Hannah asked.

'Well,' Granddad said. 'Zoë and I are going to take her car, check a few places. Zoë stayed here at the house all the time, in case . . . your dad came back. So now we're going to leave a note, and drive around a little instead.'

Aunt Zo smiled brightly at her. 'We wondered, honey,' she said, 'who's your best friend?'

'Why?'

'Someone you might be able to . . . go play with. For a few hours. Or maybe even a sleepover. That'd be fun, right?'

'No,' Hannah said firmly. 'I'm coming with you.'

Zo's smile faded. She turned to Granddad for help. Granddad shrugged.

'So let's get going,' he said.

Chapter 21

Though it was only four in the afternoon, the Devil headed straight to a bar. This was not because he wanted a drink. Though he enjoyed the taste of alcohol from time to time, preferably spiked with the blood of recently living things (or the dust of the long-dead), he normally only indulged when playing a favourite game, in which he sat with a stranger in a dark place, pretending to care, enabling their resentments and subtly goading them if necessary, in pursuit of the – usually successful – goal of causing them to stagger out of the bar to do something catastrophic.

This was not the time for such diversions, however.

He had sought out a bar because bars sometimes have a thing. The druids, a group the Devil found particularly annoying – along with vegetarians who eat fish, and people who style themselves as 'opinion-formers' or 'growth-hackers' – used to believe in 'edges': corners of the planet where the division between this world and the next is less rigid. They'd been right about this, though not much else. There are places where the wall between the *mundus* and other realms is thinner, and these areas are often associated with legends concerning ghosts or aliens, or feelings of nausea and dread (though these can also be the effects of an invisible stop imp, or eating too large a burrito). Some edge zones find their way into local lore, and are avoided – subconsciously – by people in their vicinity. Others have been long forgotten, and find themselves accidentally enclosed within houses or other buildings, which may subsequently change hands frequently, and attract rumours of hauntings.

And sometimes these buildings are bars.

Not the regular type, a location that could as easily be a restaurant or shoe store, where the waitresses are perky and children are welcome and there are crayons and an espresso machine. The kind of bars that wind up on edges are more hardcore. You don't go there to watch sporting events, celebrate birthdays, or hold impromptu brain-storming sessions about how to get Facebook to notice your pointless social-media app and buy it for a gazillion dollars. These are the kind of bars where you go to talk lonely bullshit to people who aren't listening, to slip your hand under the table to hold that of a married friend, or to simply be by yourself, in low lighting and with a line of stiff drinks, with no one around to engage with or love you, because being engaged with or loved can be very, very tiring.

Edges attract people for whom the constraints of their lives and reality are chafing, whose stories have stopped making sense; and over time many edges have wound up housing bars where the beer is cheap and the barman tattooed and pierced like a pincushion and the carpet reeks of despair.

That was the kind of place the Devil was looking for.

The first two weren't right. Though evidently establishments for committed drinkers, featureless oblongs near the highway with nothing but broken neon signs to attract passers-by, neither was truly grim enough.

The third was the real deal.

The Dragnet sat squarely on an edge, and the act of walking off the street into the dank interior felt like a journey of far greater distance than a single step – or would have, if its patrons hadn't been too inebriated or preoccupied to notice or care. A counter ran along one wall, solitary figures dotted along it on stools. Other individuals, predominantly male, held defensive positions in booths along the opposite wall and at the far end. The lights were low, a few red-shaded bulbs. The music was the kind you put on to show people how pissed off you are at the world, played 20 per cent too loud.

While the Devil waited for the attention of the barman he turned to the man on the nearest stool. 'Good afternoon,' he said.

The man looked up at him blearily. He was twenty-nine and worked nights stocking shelves at the Best Buy on the other side of town. He was extremely, albeit quietly, drunk, though the scatter of bills on the counter in front of him was supposed to be in an envelope on their way to his ex-wife in Watsonville to pay for clothes for her/their infant child, the name of which he presently, in all honesty, couldn't bring to mind, his former wife having changed it at least twice since she threw him out. Kyle, probably. Or Kylon? Some shit like that. Kryton?

'In what *possible* way?' he asked.

The Devil inclined his head, as if conceding the point. He bought a large vodka and left the counter, trailing his finger along the man's shoulder as he walked off. The man was too drunk to notice. Later that afternoon, however, he finally realized how much his room-mate's aged cat was getting on his nerves, and killed it, losing consciousness on the sofa with the animal's neck still gripped in his hands. Around midnight the room-mate returned, worked out what had happened (not a tough piece of deduction, profoundly stoned though the room-mate was), and stabbed him in the heart with a dirty ten-inch chef's knife. He died quickly, a faster resolution to his pain than the Devil would have preferred, but it was not an exact science. You put stuff out there, and you got what you got. It's a journey.

But before that happened, back in the present moment, the Devil selected a booth near the door, and waited.

A little before six o'clock a man came in by himself, and the Devil sat up and took notice. The man was in his forties, heavy-set, wearing jeans and a lumberjack shirt. He drank a beer at the counter while talking to the barman. They did not look as though they were merely passing the time of day, nor as if they were friends, exactly.

The Devil watched their reflection in the mirror behind the bar, though he already knew this was the kind of man he was looking for. He could smell it. The odour was hard to describe, but you might say it was kind of like brimstone. It's the scent of men and women who are the wrong kind of verbs, and always have been. After ten minutes the man at the bar finished his beer in a single swallow and left. The barman – himself not someone you'd want to meet down a dark alley at night, or even in a brightly lit library on a Tuesday morning – looked somewhat relieved that he'd gone.

The Devil followed.

He could have accosted the man on the street but he preferred it to be somewhere more private, and so he let the guy climb into his battered truck, quickly made arrangements for his own transportation, and followed.

The truck left town heading north on Highway 9, a winding two-lane up into the mountains. Fifteen minutes north of

Santa Cruz it would be hard to believe there was anything in the world but miles of silent redwoods and pines clinging to craggy slopes, the San Lorenzo River snaking far below. The vehicle continued up through small old logging towns called Felton and Ben Lomond, and nearly as far as Boulder Creek, before taking a side road. Ten minutes after that it took another turn, this time on to a one-lane county road whose surface had started to come apart long ago.

The Devil allowed himself to fall some distance behind to avoid detection. He was driving a cute little pink Fiat he'd stolen off the street. He didn't know that the vehicle was the pride and joy of a young woman called Luanne, who'd recently been making strides towards getting control of her life after a very shaky start, and who would likely react to the car's loss by sliding back into depression and substance abuse.

But, had he known, he would have been pleased.

Ten minutes later the Devil parked behind the truck, which had been left in front of the rusted metal gate that barred the way. Beyond this point the lane was impassable by motor vehicle. It could be that the man simply lived a long way off-grid, peaceably eating kale salads and living at one with nature, but the Devil didn't think so.

He walked into the forest, taking his time, pacing himself against the persistent slope. He felt tired. Physical bodies require energy, and he had neglected to eat, but that wasn't it. Without the constant redirection of millions of beats of black energy from the deeds and sacrifices of the world's dark ones, he did not feel himself. There was a potential source of back-up, a temporary ally, in pursuit of whom he had dispatched the idiot imp. Even that would only help a little, however.

He needed the Sacrifice Machine working properly again, directing the world's blacknesses through Hell and back into his soul. To determine the problem he needed access to Hell once more – the hell of people. Once that business was concluded he would be able to turn his attention to the broader question of *what on earth was going on*.

In the meantime he walked, steadily and implacably, up the slope between the trees.

It was forty minutes before he started to smell it. Not the odour of other worlds this time, but one born of chemical processes and cheap ingredients. It had something of stale cat urine, a touch of rotten eggs, an undercurrent of sickly sweetness. It was not strong, but it was persistent.

The Devil adjusted his course, and kept walking.

After a further half-mile he caught a glimpse of a rotting cabin in the trees ahead. He headed towards it, passing several dead patches of vegetation where spent chemicals had been discarded. As he got closer, he saw two men standing talking at a safe distance from the cabin.

Soon after that, they saw him. Both quickly put out the cigarettes they'd been smoking and came to attention.

'You want to turn around, buddy,' the first said. He was skinny and had an unappealing beard. His cheeks were dotted with small scabs, as were his knuckles. 'Now.'

'Really?' the Devil said mildly. 'But it's so beautiful up here as the light fades.'

The other man was the one the Devil had followed from Santa Cruz. He did not have the first guy's jittery energy, nor did he appear concerned at the arrival of a stranger. 'Seen you before,' he said.

'In nightmares, perhaps.'

'No. I'm thinking more likely the Dragnet. About an hour ago. Sitting in a booth. That was you, right?'

'You're observant.'

'You a cop?'

'No.'

'Good.' The man smiled. 'Kenny – kill him.'

The skinny guy did a double take. 'Huh?'

'Two words, Kenny. Kill. Him. You understand both.'

'But . . . he's just some old dude.'

'Then he's got nothing to lose. Make it so. Now. We got a cook to finish.'

The thickset man walked towards the cabin. Kenny reached reluctantly behind his back for the handgun lodged in his jeans. 'Sorry, sir,' he said to the Devil as the other man went inside. 'But you heard what the boss said.'

'You don't want to do this?'

'I actually don't, to be honest with you. I only killed one other guy before. And he was really an asshole. Seems like we could all walk away from this one, though, right?'

'Kenny . . .' The other man's voice came from inside the cabin. 'Just do the thing, will you?'

Kenny made an apologetic face and raised the gun, pointing it at the old man's head. 'I gotta do this,' he said.

'You've done enough already,' the Devil said. 'Your ticket's booked. Comfort yourself that I'm merely saving you the next few years of turning into something unrecognizable.'

'Whatever, dude,' Kenny said, and pulled the trigger.

He didn't notice that some unconscious impulse had caused him to alter his hold on the gun, so the barrel pointed towards his own face rather than the old man's.

The laws of physics noticed, though. There was a loud clapping sound, and then a thud as Kenny's near-headless body fell to the ground.

'Good job,' the other man called from inside the cabin. 'Free treats for you later.'

The Devil waited.

After a couple of minutes, the man called out again. 'Kenny, you coming back in, or what?'

'Doesn't seem likely,' the Devil said.

The other man emerged quickly from the cabin. He looked at the Devil, at Kenny's body on the ground – still holding the gun – and then back at the Devil. 'Who the hell are you?'

'I love it when people ask that,' the Devil said. 'It's so *ironic*.'

Chapter 22

First, Hannah led them to coffee shops. Her dad liked coffee. A lot. Coffee was non-negotiable. She'd seen her dad tolerate stunningly dull shopping expeditions (during some of which she'd personally nearly lapsed into a coma), and even children's parties – which she was gradually getting weren't the fun explosion for him that they were for her – purely because he was holding a cardboard cup of well-made coffee. It was one of those weird grown-up things like wanting the kitchen to be tidy, needing a little damned peace and quiet once in a while, and watching the TV news. You didn't have to understand these strange urges in the elderly, merely accept they were real and tolerate them as best you could.

So when Aunt Zo had driven them downtown, the first places they looked were Starbucks, Lulu Carpenter's, Verve, the Cruz Brewz, Peet's and two other places Hannah could recall being in with him on one of their Saturday-morning walks. She was methodical, leading Granddad and Aunt Zo to the coffee shops in order of probability, not merely because they sold those weapons-grade caramel shortbreads which Hannah loved but which even she had to admit gave her a sugar rush that was not pretty to watch.

No sign of Dad in any of them. Next they tried the bookstores. Hannah liked books. Her mom sort of did too, especially if they had a photo of a serious-looking businesswoman on the front. But Dad? That was some whole other thing. It was as well that none of the bookstores downtown housed a coffee shop, or you'd need a tractor to haul him out.

They went to Bookshop Santa Cruz. They went to Logos, which featured a second-hand basement into which Hannah's father had been known to vanish for half-days at a stretch. They even went to a small place down a side street that took her a while to find by herself and which only had books for smart people at the university, where Dad went when he was researching. The guy there always glared at Hannah as though he was afraid she was going to knock stuff over. He did it again this time.

While they were searching all these places it felt OK. They had a mission, and because Hannah knew downtown better than Granddad or Aunt Zo, she was the leader. Being in charge suggested there must be something that she was in charge *of*, which proved they were doing something and it made sense.

But they'd gone to all the places and still there had been no sign of Dad. She'd even asked, after insisting on a second look in Starbucks, if the people working there had seen him. Hannah recognized the barista, and he recognized her and knew who her dad was, but said he hadn't been in.

That news came as the tolling of a bad, cracked bell. Dad shared his love of coffee around, but she knew if he'd come down to the town the first thing he'd do was grab a double-tall two-pump vanilla latté from a major multinational beverage corporation. It was like walking fuel to him. If he hadn't come into Starbucks it was unlikely he'd come at all.

Afterwards they stood outside, Aunt Zo looking pointlessly up and down the street. 'So where now?'

Hannah realized she didn't understand what her dad did, what he wanted, where he might go: that she'd somehow lived with him for nearly twelve years without gaining any idea of what he was about. If he wasn't working or buying coffee or books or cooking dinner, what would he *do*? She knew these couldn't be the sum of him, but Santa Cruz was a different town for her dad. She didn't know where his streets led, except for the few points where they intersected with hers – places like home.

'It's OK,' Granddad said, sensing she was beginning to panic. 'Let's think laterally. Where else does he like to go? Where else have you seen him looking happy?'

The question scared her. She knew her dad was content sometimes, or had been. He laughed. He said silly things. He looked at her occasionally in a bemused and affectionate way, as if he was unsure how they'd come to be grouped into a family unit, but felt OK with the arrangement.

She didn't know what made him happy, though . . . and she couldn't remember him doing any of those things – laughing, smiling or being silly – for quite a while. From some time before Mom left, in fact. Was that why she'd gone? Because he hadn't laughed any more? Would you leave someone because of something like that? Did you have to keep laughing and smiling and seeming happy or else people would leave you?

'Twin Lakes,' she said suddenly.

And so they tried Twin Lakes, which – as Hannah realized in the ten-minute car journey over there – had to be where he was, as not only was it his favourite beach but it also had a coffee shop. Ha! She felt dumb for not having thought of it before. He liked the walk up to Black Rock, where the pelicans lurked during their season. He liked the Crow's Nest restaurant (though that was a family place, somewhere they all used to go together, and she and Dad hadn't been there since everything changed, and seeing it now gave her a cutting twist of sadness in the stomach) and he liked the Kind Grind coffee shop (specialty of the house, notably awesome oatmeal toffee cookies). So, duh.

Except, no.

They walked the length of the beach, though the light was starting to fade. It was almost deserted. At the far end, near Pelican Rock, there was no one at all. The sand was strewn with driftwood, large and small.

But no Dad.

'This isn't working,' Aunt Zo said.

And so later Hannah was back at the kitchen table in her house. Sitting where she'd sat earlier. Her place. Hannah didn't know that humankind has a deep-set belief in the idea that we create and maintain reality through ritual, that repeated actions are what keep the spheres in alignment. She also didn't know that it doesn't work, and that there are far older, more complex, and much darker designs in motion, ones that override ours as effortlessly as a crack of thunder blotting out birdsong.

And so she sat at her place in the kitchen, becoming more and more terrified that the fact she was there didn't seem to be magically putting the world to rights.

Meanwhile Granddad and Aunt Zo were talking in the backyard. They looked serious. Aunt Zo was even smoking a cigarette, which is one short step from genocidal lunacy. Hannah had only seen her aunt perform this dread act twice before. Once at a party her parents held a year ago, late in the evening, when everyone had been very cheerful indeed and the usual laws of the universe seemed to have been suspended (including the one that said Hannah should have been in bed); and then once in the last few months when Zo had been at the house babysitting for the afternoon and hadn't realized that – instead of sitting indoors reading, as advertised – Hannah had come to see what her aunt was up to. Zo had looked guilty when discovered, sad, and compromised. Like a grown-up Hannah didn't know.

She bent down to stub out the cigarette she was smoking now, and put the butt in her pack. The action looked tidy and sneaky at the same time. Her voice was muffled, but audible. 'At what point do we call the police, Dad?'

Now, Hannah thought, heart rising. *In fact, we should have done it hours ago.* That's what you did when something like this happened, right? When you couldn't find your dad. You called the police. And you called them NOW.

But then she thought instead: *Never.*

Because doing that would be like using Dad's name. Both 'police' and 'Steve' were sounds that could change the world. They were short, dark spells that turned stories on their heads, trickster words that turned off all the lights.

For a moment, Hannah actually wished the Devil was with them. He'd know about this kind of thing. He'd be able to warn them to stop using these words, to be careful. They might listen to him. Hannah was feeling bad that when she'd been leader they hadn't found anything. She'd failed. Now they wouldn't let her do it again, and instead would start saying the wrong words until they cast a spell that couldn't be broken and she never saw her father again. Unless . . .

Think, Hannah.

Think.

*　　*　　*

Ten minutes later she ran out into the yard.

'He's OK!' she shouted.

Granddad and Aunt Zo turned quickly, and it hurt her to see the hope in their eyes: hurt most of all because it showed they were as worried as she was.

'I don't know where he is,' she added hurriedly. 'Sorry. But I've looked everywhere. In his study, the living room, the den, the kitchen, *everywhere*. The bag he uses for it has gone, and the charger isn't where it normally is either. So he's taken it. He must have done.'

'Taken what, Hannah?'

'His *laptop*,' she said.

'Um, so?' Aunt Zo said.

'*So*,' Hannah said. There wasn't time to explain that Dad and his MacBook were joined at the hip, and wherever one was the other would be too. More to the point, that if he'd left the house with it then he'd gone somewhere to work, not to . . . She didn't even know what the alternative was, but she knew Aunt Zo was thinking about one. Something that was very serious, but not about working. If he had his laptop, it couldn't be that, whatever it was. 'So – he's gone somewhere *to work*.'

'But we've already looked everywhere,' Granddad said.

'I don't mean here,' Hannah said. 'The car's gone. If he goes downtown he always walks, because he says he sits on his ass all day and needs any exercise he can get. Twin Lakes is far enough that he'd take the car, but we checked and he's not there. So he's further. Another town, or . . .'

Suddenly she knew, without a shadow of a doubt, where her father had gone.

'Come with me,' she said.

They stood in the living room, in front of the painting the Devil had been glaring at before he left.

'It cost a *lot* of money,' Hannah said, reverently.

Granddad glanced at Aunt Zo, who looked as if she didn't know what to say. Beneath the face adults learned to wear (the one that stopped you being able to tell what they were thinking), Hannah could see confusion, and concern. Zo looked how Hannah felt inside, and that could not be a good thing.

'I don't know,' Zo said. 'What do you think?'

Granddad considered. Then he nodded. 'If he's not back by tomorrow morning, then yes.'

Chapter 23

All this took place while the Devil was sitting in the Dragnet, spotted the man who came in for a beer, followed him into the mountains by car and then on foot into the forest, caused the skinny guy with meth mite scars to put an end to himself and then waited for the other man to come back out of the cabin. That's the thing about stories. Lots happen at once, as I've said. If you could lay all the world's tales end to end so they took place one after another instead, it would be a lot easier to make sense of them. But you can't. Someone tried it once but the story got so long it went all the way around the world and eventually joined up with where it first started, creating an endless loop from which the poor guy never escaped. He became a story himself, a cautionary tale, which is what I've just told you.

Anyway.

The man outside the cabin stood looking cautiously at the Devil. He was cursing himself for not bringing his gun out of the lab, and wondering whether he'd have time to get to the one still clutched in Kenny's fingers, while simultaneously being aware that having a weapon hadn't seemed to help Kenny much.

The Devil knew what he was thinking, and was mildly interested to see what he'd decide.

After a few seconds the tension went out of the man's body. 'OK,' he said. 'What do you want?'

'You,' the Devil said. 'Though not for higher office. You've found your level and it looks like a dollar sign.'

'What's that supposed to mean?'

'Money. That's what drives you.'

'Anything wrong with that?'

'It lacks ambition, that's all. How much do you make from an operation like this?'

'Depends.'

'Answer the question, Brian.'

The man looked wary. 'How do you know my name?'

'I know everyone's name. Everyone like you.'

Brian didn't see how that could be, and he was starting to feel uncomfortable. This fragile-looking old guy was getting under his skin, like his dad used to. He was making Brian feel small and defensive, and as if someone needed to pay for him feeling that way. 'I was in Oregon before. Well established, distribution in place. Cops came for me, but I got out ahead. I'm starting again. Only been up three months.'

'How much?'

'About twenty thousand last month.'

'And that's enough?'

Brian swallowed. The forest had started to feel odd. It was as if darkness was falling more quickly than usual, or from the sides, or even seeping out from the old man's head. 'Well, sure, I'd like it to be a lot more, but it takes time to—'

'Oh, hush,' the Devil said. 'I don't want your business plan. I'm checking that's sufficient for you to overlook that the people who buy your wares from that barman in the Dragnet or other minions will wind up stealing and whoring, killing bystanders in car crashes or robberies, accidentally setting fire to mobile homes with children inside; all the while scratching their faces to shreds trying to get at bugs that aren't there, turning skeletal because they forget to eat and their teeth are all fallen out of rotting, bleeding gums, to the point where dying alone in a muddy culvert one night is a blessed relief. Don't get me wrong. Personally, I'm all in favour. This is good stuff, Brian. Solid workmanship. But I'm checking *you're* OK with it.'

'I don't make them take the crap.'

The Devil laughed.

'What? I *don't*. I don't force it into their hands. They come seek me out. They pay *me*. It's their fault.'

The old man nodded. 'You're perfect.'

'For what?'

The Devil drew the sides of his mouth back in something like a grin, and Brian realized abruptly that he *really* had to be somewhere else. Somewhere far away.

He couldn't move his feet, however.

He urgently wanted his life to be totally different and happening somewhere else and he knew all he needed to do was start the process of change by taking one small step, and then another; but when he tried to do this his feet seemed nailed to the ground and it was impossible to get going, or too hard, or simply easier to be where he was and keep doing what he'd been doing – even though he knew deep inside that with every second that passed the shadows grew closer, heavier and colder. In this way, for the briefest moment, Brian received a glimpse into the lives of his customers, as if their stories had suddenly been translated into a language he could understand, but it was far too late and he'd never been much of a reader anyway.

He gave up trying to run. His voice was strained, as if his chest was tightening. 'What are you doing to me?'

'Riding you to Hell,' the Devil said.

'I don't . . .'

'Look into my eyes.'

Brian had no choice. There was silence for a moment. Then there was not. Half a mile away a mountain lion heard Brian's screams. It shivered, and ran away to hide.

Later, the Devil sat on the roof of the Rittenhouse Building, the tallest structure in downtown Santa Cruz. A symbol of optimism in the reconstruction of Pacific Avenue after the Loma Prieta earthquake in 1989, the Rittenhouse has remained stridently empty ever since. This disjunction between hope and reality drew the Devil to it. It was precisely the flavour of disappointment he most enjoyed: the frailty of human dreams writ large. Also, it was tall. Sometimes you need an overview, and there's no better place – both figuratively and literally – than sitting on the roof of a very high building.

The Devil was not in the best of moods. The encounter with Brian had not yielded the results he'd hoped – and at the end had turned disconcerting. He'd reached into the man's soul, picking over the dreary details of his life and childhood and casting an amused glance at the root causes for his anger, insecurity and selfishness, before going deeper. A trickle of power leaked back, though nothing to write home about. Love of money is not the root of all evil. Greed is its own reward and its own motivation. Bad things are done by people in pursuit of wealth, and seeking material dominion over others involves diminishing their reality, and these are steps in the direction of evil.

But greed for neither money nor power has the heft and tang of doing wrong for the sake of it, and before long – well before, in fact, Brian had gone completely insane – the Devil had started to regret not spending longer with the guy he'd encountered in the Miami warehouse. What he called himself, was that his name? He'd been closer to the right verb. Much, much closer.

Eventually Brian's eyes rolled in their sockets and his body started to shake, sounds forcing their way up from his throat and from between clenched teeth. Even this hadn't been sufficient to cheer the Devil up, and he'd been about to cut the connection and drop Brian's body to the forest floor to die and be eaten by rats and insects, when something unexpected happened.

Suddenly the man's eyes rolled back forwards, snapping into focus. His body went still. At first the Devil thought the man had merely died ahead of schedule, but then he realized something was staring out from Brian's eyes.

Not Brian. Somebody – or something – else. Something very cold and very strong.

'Your days are over,' Brian's mouth said.

It was not his voice, however. It was deep and guttural – precisely the kind of voice, in fact, that it had often amused the Devil to cause to issue from the mouths of the possessed. It had been a particularly big hit in Salem, back in the day.

'Who are you?' the Devil asked.

'We are legion. We are the coming tide.'

The Devil felt the presence inside Brian start to push back at him, shoving aside the tendrils he'd insinuated into every part of the man's soul. Brian's mouth began to move, but now more than one voice barked from his throat, so many voices, and so loud, that it was impossible to tell what they were saying.

The Devil disengaged quickly.

Brian's eyes flared a final time; then his body dropped to the forest floor. Lifeless, suddenly small, merely another object amongst millions in the world: an object wrapped in other objects (clothes bought from Gap and the O'Neill store) and containing other objects (blood slackening to a standstill, the remains of the beer in the Dragnet, a Big Mac eaten at lunchtime) and associated via proximity with others in pockets (truck keys, a wallet and loose change, a receipt for an old photo of his parents he was having framed for their upcoming anniversary); now merely a pile of things in the woods, lying near another pile that had once been called 'Kenny'.

The Devil had seen death countless times before. Approved it, caused it, revelled in it. This felt different.

He was still on the roof of the Rittenhouse, mulling this over, when something dropped chaotically out of the sky and landed with a thud behind him.

'Bloody pelicans,' muttered a voice. 'Useless for riding on. Bony, flappy bastards.'

The Devil waited while Vaneclaw got himself to his feet and came to stand in front of him.

'Well?'

'Hello, boss. Had a good day?'

'No. Give me good news, Vaneclaw, or none at all.'

The imp stood there and said nothing.

Chapter 24

After three minutes of Vaneclaw remaining silent, looking increasingly uncomfortable, the Devil rolled his eyes.

'Imagine, imp, that for the time being I have lifted my recent proscription on the spoken word unless it contains news or information that I will find gratifying.'

'Eh?'

'Speak freely, you cretin.'

The imp looked relieved. 'Ah, well, that was my point, see. 'Cos you did give me clear instructions which boiled down to "Don't speak unless there's good news", and . . . well, you know, to be frank, boss, you can get tetchy if people don't do what you tell them. *Notoriously* tetchy. Remember Pompeii? Whoa. That was a blinder.'

'You weren't there. You weren't even spawned.'

'But I heard about it. Burying a whole town under volcanic ash, eh, just because they wouldn't glorify your despicable name? Classy use of natural disaster. Old school. But, so, you see, that kind of incident does make one a tad wary.'

'I'm waiting.'

'Right. Well. I had a look round this place, but, like you said, Santa Cruz hasn't got the right vibe. Too chilled. Too "it is what it is", and "can I have a soy latte?" So I headed south, thought I'd give the Santa Lucia Mountains a look, but I got a bit lost, be honest with you, so I came back up here, was just going to tell you I'd had no luck, but then I thought to myself: That's not going to play, mate; you know what he's like. He will smite you, big time.'

'Indeed.'

'Then I remembered something, and so I went *up* the road instead, to San Francisco.'

'I told you to seek out *wilderness*, Vaneclaw. Places where they might shroud themselves in seclusion. I specifically mentioned the Santa Lucias, and Big Sur.'

'You did, you did, which is why I went there. Or tried to go there. But then . . . I forgot. Well, I didn't forget, so much, as . . . All right, here's the thing. I remembered that I had a tip.'

'A tip?'

'Yeah. Few years ago, back when you was . . . not yourself. Having a nap. Whatever it was you was doing. Or not doing. Anyway, few years back I went to an imp convention up in Oregon, and you know how it is, awful lot of bollocks gets talked at those things, but I kept hearing rumours in the bar about San Francisco, and how maybe one of the Big Boys was lurking there. I thought, that's interesting; but I didn't know where you was at the time, and anyway I had to get home to North Dakota sharpish, to get back on that bloke Ron's case.'

'And you didn't see fit to mention this before.'

'Yeah. I mean, no. I forgot. Dunno how.'

'Because you're an idiot.'

'That's it. I knew there was a reason. Anyway, so I'm up in San Fran, having a nose around. Checking the underside of tricycles, the roof space of train stations, round the back of Nordstrom. All the obvious places. But I find nothing. So I'm thinking it's a bust, just a bunch of imps had a few too many and made shit up, and I should head back down here . . . but then I see this bloke. Complete arse, he was – could tell from across the street. And so – and I know you and I differ on this point, boss, but I am always drawn to plague people what are wankers to begin with – I found myself following. I wasn't going to throw myself at him, because we're busy on other things, but you know how it is.'

'Get on with it.'

'Right. So. He goes into this bar. It's crowded, and I lose him almost immediately. But then I see this girl. I could tell straight away she'd been touched. So I went up and asked her. Well, not personally, but I hopped up on the bar and stuck me tongue into the ear of the guy standing next to her, used a Naughty Trick to make *him* ask the question. He asks her: "Are you fallen?" and she gives him a look and then slaps him across the face. Which I'm assuming probably means "No", but I'm not sure, right? Especially because, now I'm closer to her, the feeling's even stronger. Anyway, she's storming out of the bar at this point and I decide to follow.'

'I trust there's a point to this, Vaneclaw. Or should I pulverize you into shards of broken tears right now, and get it over with?'

The imp started talking even more quickly. 'I followed her all the way to Chinatown, which is stupid busy; they got some festival or something going on. Almost lost her, in fact – and, to be fair, idiocy may have played a part in that – but then I spotted her again, going into this manky old grocery store. Madame Chang's, it's called. In I go. Total chaos. Like they started selling things a hundred years ago and got busy and never had a chance to tidy up. Locals picking over things in buckets, shouting at each other, all that. And the girl goes up to the counter, buys something, then . . . leaves.'

The Devil stared at him. 'Please don't tell me that's the end of the story.'

'Ah, no. Because, see, I realize the woman that the girl's just talked to behind the counter – *she's* the one that's been touched. The girl I been following, she comes in there every day for groceries and that, and so she's had a second-degree brush – but it's this older woman who's been *close*. And then she does something that makes it certain-sure. She looks *right at me*.'

'She could see you?'

'That's what I'm saying, boss. She's ninety years old or something, but she clocks me straight off. She barks out: "Who are you, mushroom?"'

'I said, "I'm not a mushroom."'

'"You look like mushroom."'

'"And you look like you been left out in the rain for a hundred years. So what?"'

'"You a mushroom."'

'"Shut it. Also – I know your game."'

'She folds her arms, looks down at me all cocky. "What you talking about? What you want?"'

'"I'm on a mission."'

'"Did you say 'mushroom'?"'

'"No, *mission*. And it's from the very, *very* top, you know what I'm saying? Or the very bottom, anyway."'

'"No, mushy – what *are* you saying?"'

'By this point I'm getting seriously hacked off with the old bat, and so I did a thing; I know I'm not supposed to do it, above my grade, but my old man taught it me, and it comes in handy from time to time. So I made her legs stop working. She drops down behind the counter, splat. I hop over it, jump down on to her chest.

'"*Where is it?*" I shout, and by now she's got the message that I'm not mucking about. "*Take me to it.*"'

'She's not happy about it, but she nods. I hop off on to the floor, and wait. She looks up at me, doesn't move.

'I put my fierce voice on. "Are you going to show me, or what?"

'"My legs not working."

'"Oh yeah," I say, "sorry."

'So I undo the thing and she gets up. She goes to the counter, yells at everyone, says she's shutting up for the night, they all have to bugger off. They do. She locks up, then comes back behind the counter, flaps her hands at me, tells me to move. And under where I was standing, turns out there's a trapdoor. She opens it and, oof, the smell's *terrible*, but there's a staircase leading down into darkness. She tells me to go down it. I tell her, "Ha ha, no – *you* go first." I mean, I'm an idiot, granted, but not a *total* idiot.'

'Yes, you are,' said the Devil.

'Yeah, fair enough. Anyway, the basement's *ghastly*, and I speak as a long-term servant, vessel and connoisseur of all that is unholy and vile. Piled high with broken boxes and furniture. Rotting vegetables and fish everywhere. Slime. Any normal person comes down here, they're going to turn around and run away and go stand in the shower for a week. But she lights a candle and leads me across to the opposite corner. Kicks aside a bunch of old, reeking crap, and underneath – there's another trapdoor.

'"You *sure* you want go down there?" she asks, sly, and to be honest with you, I'm not. I can feel it now. Really, *really* strong. I know I'm dealing with one of the Fallen. But I am your faithful servant, and to be honest I'm far more scared of you, cruel but fair though you have generally been to me personally, so I tell her "Yes". And she opens the trapdoor.

'We go down into the sub-basement. It's huge. Must be twenty feet high, loads more candles in those things on the walls, ponces, whatever they're called, and the space is so long I can't even see the end of it. There's stinking black water dripping down the walls. The old Chinese bint, she keeps well back, muttering prayers or incantations and whatnot. I go down the middle of the room until I could see something at the end. It's in shadow. You could call it a throne if you wanted, but really it's just a bunch of old fruit crates stacked together.'

The Devil was paying close attention now. 'And what was sitting on the crates?'

'A squirrel.'

Vaneclaw saw the Devil staring ominously at him and hurriedly held up his hands. 'No, seriously, boss, a squirrel. One of those black ones. Little wispy bits on its ears.'

'And who was it?'

'Couldn't tell, at first. I asked it to show its true form, but it just sat there looking like a squirrel. So I asked its name. It didn't say anything. So then I told it that you had sent me, and I used that word you told me to use, or I tried to: it's a bastard to pronounce. The squirrel just looked puzzled, so I gave it another go. Fifth or sixth attempt I must have said it right. The squirrel sighed, and . . . woo, I tell you, it was a big one. You could feel it rumbling through the walls, out under the streets and into the bay and then the ocean, rolling out to bounce back off Japan or somewhere. Going to be some monster waves at Maverick's tomorrow. Then there's silence, and after that it said, in a voice like distant, tragic thunder . . .

'"I am called . . . Xjynthucx."'

Vaneclaw stopped talking, somewhat out of breath, but looking very pleased with himself.

'Good grief,' the Devil muttered. 'Of all the Fallen Angels, you had to find *him*.'

*   *   *

'Oh,' Vaneclaw said, looking crestfallen. 'Is that not ideal?'

'Xjynthucx and I were once close, but have not spoken in over seven thousand years.'

'Bit of a spat, was there?'

'The last I heard, he'd buried himself in a hidden cave in the Rocky Mountains. I visited the area five hundred years ago. He would not show himself.'

'So what's he in such a snit about?'

'It is angel business, not yours.'

'Fair enough, boss. But why's he a squirrel now, then?'

'I have no idea. Did you put my request to him?'

'Yep.'

'What did he say?'

'Nothing, really. Just sat there repeating "My name is Xjynthucx", over and over again, and something about destiny. What's all that about?'

'Weakness,' the Devil said distantly. 'I will not be the only one affected by the failure of the Sacrifice Machine. If need be, I may be able to strike a deal with Xjynthucx, whose sense of duty and loyalty was always greater than most others. Our disagreement was over a trivial matter. The cost may be releasing him from eternal bondage, however, so that can only be a last resort.' He reached his large, pale hands up and rubbed his eyes, suddenly tired. 'I hoped,' he said eventually, 'to avoid having to speak personally with the other Fallen. I am beginning to fear it is unavoidable.'

'Your afternoon didn't go well, then?'

'I encountered . . . something perplexing.'

'That's a type of plastic, right?'

'No, you fool. Something that didn't make sense. Not then, at any rate. But I have thought further upon it since.'

'What was it?'

'I had gone looking for Hell a different way. Perhaps . . .

perhaps I found it after all. It may have changed in my absence. Become more private and secular. People in themselves.'

'Well, that bloke said that might happen, didn't he? That French berk you never liked. "Hell is other people."'

'I suspect one form of Hell was having a long conversation with Jean-Paul Sartre. Did you ever *meet* him?'

'No, boss. I've steered clear of France, in the main.'

'Did you perform the other task I set you, at least?'

'What? Oh yeah. Meant to say. Found a baby snackular in San Fran soon after I got there, not too creepy. Gave the job to her. She's fetching it tonight. The Sacrifice Machine will be in the back garden of Hannah Green's house by dawn, latest.'

The Devil stood. Had anyone glanced up from the street four storeys below, they might for a moment have glimpsed a spectral figure up on the roof, though the Devil was usually good at making sure that kind of sighting did not occur.

He stepped down on to the parapet, and the two of them climbed down the outer face of the building, head first.

'So what now, boss?'

'I'm hungry,' the Devil said.

'Me too. Could *murder* some fried chicken.'

'Not for food.'

'Oh, yeah. Right.'

They walked through the town to a dive bar down by the boardwalk. Their presence caused the almost immediate break-up of two long-term relationships and, half an hour later, a brief but spirited knife fight in the parking lot. Hardly a full meal, but enough to keep the wolf from the door.

Then, somewhat refreshed, the Devil, by dint of a short conversation, lit a fuse under a gawky young man who, several years later, would be responsible for the strangulation murders of six young women, along with his own mother.

Sometimes you had to play the long game, like laying down a fine wine.

On the other hand, the Devil left the car he'd stolen from near the Dragnet in the street outside the Rittenhouse, from where it was eventually towed. The city worker driving the tow truck happened to know the car's owner, Luanne.

She paid the fine. She got her car back. She kept on top of things. She went on to live a full and decent life.

The Devil, had he known this, would have been disappointed. But you can't win them all.

Chapter 25

Who comes and talks to you, in the long watches of the night? Whose voice do you hear as you lie brittle-eyed, oppressed by sheets and twisting in your skin? You assume it must be your own, because the voice knows so much about you – but this voice never soothes or celebrates. It needles and stirs. It speaks to you through twitches in your soul and a tightening in the guts, and it tells you that things are not OK, and it may be too late to fix them, or yourself.

You have to listen, though. It will be this voice that finally finds the words to get you to talk to the doctor about that lump, or call your father, or give up drinking. It may be this voice that levers up the endless coats of paint with which you have coated yourself, and reveals something rotting inside; or else convinces you that the interior is clean and true after all, and it is the work of others that has made you feel otherwise.

It was this voice that made Kristen realize that she really, *really* had to go home.

A call to the company travel office would have scored her a seat quickly and easily. She couldn't do that. Appearing to jump the corporate ship wouldn't play. So instead she spent the hour between 5 and 6 a.m. laboriously engineering a ticket through the airline's own site, and then their helpline, by the end of which she had – silently – wished Very Bad Things upon more than one customer service representative. The time she spent on hold at least gave her the chance to round up her passport and phone charger and shove a few items into her carry-on, so when she was finally confirmed on the 11.20 out of Heathrow, she could leave the hotel immediately.

She'd spent a few nights of the last weeks in a house in Hampstead, home of the man with whom she ate at Bella Mare, but was glad that this morning she was in the hotel. Otherwise there would be a need for Discussion. Something to be said for a marriage, even one where the communication machine has stopped working, is the shorthand of friendship and shared years. If she'd got up one morning and told Steve she had to go somewhere, urgently, he would have said fine, asked what time she'd be back and if she could pick up some avocados. He would have trusted that she had a reason and that it would be good enough. Trust like this has to be earned. It can be lost, of course.

She didn't inform reception she wouldn't be returning that evening. They wouldn't care: the company had the room booked for another five weeks. Not for the first time in recent months it felt as if she was undercover in her own life.

She went outside into the street and stuck up her hand for a cab. It was cold, and raining a little, of course. This was England. It was cold, and it rained. It was cosy and dark and old. You could hide here. From your past. From your future.

From everything.

A spell in Airportland, following its rituals and signs. Standing in line. Submitting to people in garish uniforms. The same questions as always, the same answers, and then a thin piece of cardboard that tells you where to go and when. Magazines and bottled water to take on board. A glazed wander around the kind of stores they have in airports, buying nothing. She didn't need any more expensive scarves. Strangers milling to and fro like clouds. What seem like hours of dead time, and then a hurried hike down a mile of affectless corridor and you're ready to go stand in another line, between people who are either making a big deal of how they do this every day, or otherwise are silent, and quite scared.

The plane. Dry air. A cursory nod at whomever you've been put next to, a sparkleless smile, wordless ways of saying *I mean you no ill will but let's keep our elbows under control – plus if you're wondering if I want to talk (or listen), the answer is a big fat 'no'.*

Watch the video that pretends that, should this thing drop out of the sky, the big issue is whether you bring your handbag.

Take off.

Have a drink. Sink into the iPad, cut with sessions on the laptop. Get ahead of next week's work, always.

Eat.

Restroom.

Laptop.

Repeat. Repeat. Repeat.

Kristen had done years of hard time on planes, to England, Europe, the Far and Middle East, criss-crossing the United States. Never like this, though. Never having attempted to call her estranged husband twice more from the airport – trying once what had been her home, once his cell and getting voicemail, Steve's message in his from-before voice, his ghost voice, the one recorded back when things were different and they told each other often that they loved one another with all their hearts. She didn't for a moment believe what his kooky sister had told her on a previous call (he wasn't in a meeting cycle at the moment, and even if he had been, he sure as hell wouldn't have been taking one in Santa Cruz, where the nearest thing to a television industry was hippies putting up rants on the public access channel about aliens and recycling) but she didn't know what else to think.

That wasn't why she was going home.

Steve was a grown-up, more or less – and in adding that proviso she wasn't falling into the cheap, patronizing habit of treating all men as if they were kids. She was old enough to get that *everybody* was half-child, herself included. Steve was functionally an adult. He could look after himself.

It was Hannah.

And what she had said, of course.

Kristen had finally confronted that conversation properly in her mind, and kicked herself black and blue. For asking Hannah if she knew what time it was. For Christ's sake. Hannah was a *kid*. Even grown-ups have a hard time getting their heads around time zones. And then for going on about how cold it was there. To be fair, she'd thought her daughter might like that. Hannah was an avid snow bunny and, born and raised in California, saw precipitation of any kind as an interesting diversion and talking point, not business as usual, like the Brits did. Come rain or shine, Kristen always told her what it was like out of her hotel-room window, wherever she was. It helped Hannah picture the scene, brought them closer when her mother was away, or so she'd thought. Not this time.

I hate you.

Parents hear those words more often than anyone, and always from those they love the most. Families are the crucibles that temper the toughest of love's swords. It gets intense in there sometimes. You know you're going to get slapped with those words sooner or later, when the little person in your charge glares hot-eyed up at you and flexes their soul. You'll joke about it with your partner before it happens, how someday this bundle of dependency will carve off sufficient autonomy to stab you with the cutting words. You figure it'll be in their teens, but in fact it starts a lot earlier. Kids are leaving you from the day they're born. They have their pens in their hands and start making marks on their own sheets of paper, their first words and sentences, their personal Chapter One. It's shocking to have those words hurled at you, but you come to take them for the spasm of frustration or low blood sugar they usually are.

It hadn't sounded that way this time, though. It sounded as if Hannah really meant it. That was what the voice had been telling Kristen in the night, telling her over and over, and try as she might, she hadn't been able to get it to shut up.

I hate you.

Everything Kristen had done in the last months had been considered ahead of time. Though she now lived in a world of choppy swells and impulse – and, God, wasn't it wonderful sometimes, after years of steady, even seas, to do whatever the heck your soul told you? – every decision had been deliberated. She'd tried to do the right thing, even when a week spent analysing the issues from every angle spat out answers that made her wince. She was good at this shit, too – for other people, at least. She spent her life holding their hands and helping them make decisions, tough business calls that affected many lives.

She'd discovered, however, that you can't hold your own hand. It was like wandering round some big department store, your paw safe and warm in your parent's huge hand, and getting separated. If you're a child and this happens you whirl about, before tearfully doing what you've been told a thousand times: going to find an adult in uniform and telling them you're lost, and it will be scary for a while but they'll give you a cookie and be super-nice and eventually your mother or father will come running, their face strange with fear and anger and guilt.

When you're an adult, those options don't exist. You do what you can, on your own, and sometimes you freeze. You block.

You get lost.

And everything falls apart.

Kristen closed her laptop. She flagged down the stewardess and got another glass of wine. She sat with it clasped in both hands, staring ahead, and willed the plane to fly faster.

I hate you.

Please don't, Hannah.

Because I love you with all my heart, and if you did but know – and you must never know – I would do anything you asked. Especially as I personally have no idea what to do.

About anything, any more.

Chapter 26

Things did not start well in Santa Cruz.

Though the Devil and Granddad were in Hannah's yard at dawn to receive the Sacrifice Machine, it did not arrive. Investigation eventually determined that Vaneclaw had given the baby snackular insufficiently precise instructions, and so instead of transporting the machine to Santa Cruz, California, it had moved it somewhere less convenient, namely to a town called Santa Cruz in Paraiba, a region in northeast Brazil.

The Devil, in discussions with Vaneclaw, was frank in his disappointment at this turn of events.

Further disenchantment was expressed by Hannah, Aunt Zo and Granddad, as the night had not seen the reappearance of Hannah's dad, nor the returning of further emails or phone messages. They were keen to get on with heading down to Big Sur.

The Devil forbade them from leaving. He demanded that the Engineer be on hand to recheck the machine once it had eventually been delivered, via the actions of a more reliable tier of demon. (If you want to wreak havoc, especially on a subconscious level, a snackular is ideal. They are volatile, however, and do not take instruction easily, especially in juvenile form.) Locating a demon of sufficient acuity took a while, because – for reasons that lie outside the remit of this present story – most demons are unable to cross large bodies of water, and nearly all of the ones that can had recently been sent back to the doom-nurseries in a sector-wide recall that saw the member of the Wakeful in charge banished to the Outer Reaches of Appalling Voidiness for eternity and a day.

Eventually the Devil was able to repurpose a demon that had been enthusiastically creating sadness in the Middle East for decades. This demon was on the brink of triggering an especially juicy atrocity, however, and dragged its feet for a while until it finally dawned upon it that it wouldn't be a good idea to make the Devil more irritable than he already was.

As the entirety of this negotiation was conducted by the Devil sitting silently in a chair and reaching out with the slick, dread tentacles of his mind, it looked like nothing was happening for ages, and Hannah – who'd barely slept with worry – was on the brink of explosion by the time a thick fog blew up from the bay, providing cover for the demon to deposit the machine retrieved from Brazil in the backyard, before flicking back whence it had come at a speed so great that it caused a sonic boom that rattled windows all the way to Los Gatos and scared the living crap out of a cat who had been dozing on the porch next door.

Later that day, the event the demon had been growing came to pass, when a grieving man carried a bomb into a crowded market square and detonated it, to avenge the death of an older brother during an Israeli military action. He killed himself and forty-two others, but the demon went into something of a decline for months afterwards, feeling that, had he been there to guide the final hours, the toll could have been so much higher.

Granddad meanwhile briefly inspected the Sacrifice Machine and pronounced it to be still in working order. Then he and Hannah, together with Aunt Zo – who had watched the morning's events in a quiet way, and clearly now had a growing list of questions to ask, not the least of which being who the old dude in the black linen suit was, and why everyone was doing whatever he said the whole time – carried the machine through to Hannah's room and slid it under the bed.

In an afterthought, Granddad went to Hannah's bookcase. He took down the odd sculpture he'd given her when he last came to stay, and pulled a tiny screwdriver out of his waistcoat. He flipped the object over and made an adjustment.

Hannah watched. 'That's not just a sculpture, is it?'

Granddad looked sheepish. 'Well, I hope it has *some* aesthetic appeal, but . . . no.'

'What does it do?'

'It, ah, repels.'

'What?'

'Bad things.'

'Like?'

'Soulcutters and dreamspiders, mainly. And other banes.'

'Like . . . an invisible nightlight.'

He smiled. 'I suppose so.'

'What did you just do to it?'

'I turned it up. A lot.'

'What about the ones that Mom keeps in the garage?'

'Ah. I wondered where they'd gone.'

'Do they do the same? Keep the bad things away?'

He nodded, a little sadly, and put the sculpture back on the bookcase. 'But evidently not well enough.'

Hannah noticed Aunt Zo watching this exchange with one eyebrow raised – adding yet another question to the list in her head – and so, instead of saying more, she hugged her grandfather around his stomach as tightly as she could.

'Thank you for trying,' she whispered.

So it wasn't until nearly four in the afternoon that they were all finally in Aunt Zo's car. Her vehicle was almost exactly the opposite of Granddad's. It was a nameable colour – 'Oh my *God*, that's red' – and the interior was spookily tidy.

Granddad went in the passenger seat. Hannah and the Devil sat in the back. Vaneclaw, who'd been keeping a low profile since the debacle with the Sacrifice Machine's delivery, offered to spend the journey in the trunk. Granddad opened it discreetly for him so that Zo didn't see, and gently shut it again once he was inside.

It doesn't take long to get down to Big Sur from Santa Cruz, and it was a route that Hannah knew well. At least once a year since she'd been born, usually two or three times, she'd watched out of the window as Dad drove Highway 1 south out of town and then around the flat, sweeping expanse of Monterey Bay, listening to the comforting murmur of quotidian parental conversation. She knew all the landmarks, including the large ruined wooden house a hundred yards back from the highway near Watsonville. Her father was fascinated by it, and every time they passed said he'd try to find some information about the house for her, but never got around to it. Once it had been quite something, a huge Victorian building with wraparound decks and an Italianate tower. It was as fancy as the most impressive old houses in Santa Cruz, and it seemed odd that it had been built out here. Though it was very dirty now and clearly long-abandoned, and boards had slipped, and it had been raised up on bricks, it still caught the eye. It looked somehow larger than it should, perhaps because it stuck up all by itself in the middle of flat farming land. It was strange to drive past and not hear her father's voice reminding her to watch out for it, and the lack made her stomach ache.

The Devil seemed very interested, even leaning into her side of the car to get a better look through her window.

'What?' she asked.

'I sense that good work was done in that house, long ago. I can hear the echo of screams.'

He turned back to face the front with a distant, gloating look on his horrid old face. Hannah decided that when (not if) she saw her dad, she'd find a way of suggesting there wasn't anything to know about the house – a teacher or something had told her so – and he shouldn't bother to try to find out.

Forty minutes later they skirted Monterey and then Carmel. They didn't stop, another thing that made the drive out of kilter. Mom loved Carmel, and at this stage there would always be a short discussion about whether they had time to take a break for lunch. Hannah estimated that her mother won this discussion on approximately 107 per cent of the occasions when it took place, concerned though her father always was to 'make time'. Hannah had never got to the bottom of what 'making time' meant. Her mother evidently didn't know either, or judged it of little account. Probably it was something that only boys were interested in, like farts.

By now the sky was starting to soften and darken around the edges. Aunt Zo kept driving down through the Carmel Highlands, where the coastline became craggier. The cliffs got steeper, too, and the trees thicker, yielding glimpses of increasingly vertiginous drops to the ocean.

Usually this was an exciting part of the journey because you knew you were getting close. Mom and Dad stopped talking and looked out of the window. The atmosphere started to seep into the car, carried on the smell of pines and birch and sea. It felt different today. Hannah knew this was partly because she was in a different car with different people (and with a talking mushroom in the trunk, instead of an overnight bag). But that wasn't the real difference. As she stared glumly through the windshield at the hulking mountains ahead, forbidding fist-shaped masses that reared up in knotted clusters and then dropped into the ocean as if someone had summarily severed the land with a rusty axe, it felt not as if anything had changed, but as though her eyes had been opened a little wider, enabling her to perceive something that had been there all along.

Big Sur was different to what she'd thought.

It was beautiful, but the austerity of its poise took it to a place beyond the normal. Large chunks of the Californian coast – and Hannah had seen pretty much all of it, from the Oregon border right down to Tijuana – had the same basic things going on. Jagged rocks, ocean, trees.

The place they were driving into, however, was more than the sum of those parts, with added mountains. As they drove over Bixby Bridge, the graceful arch that soars over the first of the big canyons that fall right into the sea, she realized the bridge did the opposite of what she'd thought. It didn't link Big Sur with what lay north.

It was a dividing line. A gate.

It said things were different on the other side.

Hannah shivered. She'd been the one who'd said they should come here, but now she wished she hadn't. She didn't want to be here. She wanted to be at home. She . . .

She should call her mom.

The thought popped into her head with a panicky certainty. Why hadn't she done it before? Why hadn't she done it in all the time they'd spent kicking around the house that morning? Why hadn't a grown-up suggested it?

'We should call Mom,' she said urgently.

'And we will,' Granddad replied immediately, as if he'd been waiting for the suggestion.

'Why not now?'

'We don't want to worry her,' Aunt Zo said brightly, as if this response had also been prepared ahead of time and stored in the fridge, ready to be put in the microwave when needed.

Hannah didn't want to worry Mom either, but hadn't Aunt Zo said something about Mom calling the house, when they first got home? Surely that meant her mother was already worried? 'But—'

'Stop here,' the Devil commanded suddenly.

Aunt Zo laughed. 'Excuse me?'

He leaned forwards so his mouth was disconcertingly close to Zo's ear. 'I wish this car to no longer be in motion, effective immediately. Is that more clear?'

Aunt Zo yanked the car to the side of the road. She turned crossly to give the Devil a piece of her mind, but he'd already opened his door and was climbing out.

'Unlock the trunk,' he said. 'Now.'

'Look, Mr—'

'It would be best if you did as he asked,' Granddad said, mildly.

'But—'

'It really kinda would,' Hannah agreed. 'Seriously.'

Aunt Zo muttered, but pressed the switch that unlocked the trunk. Hannah and her grandfather watched her as she watched the Devil go to the back of the car, open it, wait a moment – almost as if letting something out – and then close it again. Without, of course, having any visible reason for doing so.

The Devil marched away across the road, paying no attention to a large truck that came rocketing around the bend.

The truck's horn blared, but the old man in the linen suit didn't even turn his head. Instead he continued to the other side and then, without breaking stride, set off up the steep, wooded hillside, walking in an exact straight line. Within moments he'd disappeared into shadow.

'OK,' Aunt Zo said with the air of someone whose list of questions would wait not a second longer. 'Who the screaming blue nutsacks *is* that guy?'

'It's . . . a long story,' Granddad said.

'Excellent,' she replied. 'It's a good forty minutes from here to the motels. A nice long story will fill the time.'

'Oh, I'm not sure—'

'Spill it,' Aunt Zo said. 'Or we're going nowhere.'

Granddad looked at Hannah, as if unsure. Hannah was struck by the fact that Aunt Zo was Granddad's daughter – that he was to Aunt Zo what her dad was to her. With this came the realization that some stories might be tough for people to tell to certain other people. That stories could be hard to frame in one person's mouth, and easier to tell in a different voice.

'Once there was a boy,' Hannah said. She glanced at Granddad, to check he was OK with what she was doing.

He nodded, looking small and old.

Her aunt started the car. 'I'm listening,' she said.

Chapter 27

Hiking the thickest parts of Big Sur, far from trails and in the growing dark, is not for the faint of heart. At the lower levels the mountainsides are choked with knots of trees. On steeper inclines there's nothing but scrubby grasses and chaparral, which might sound easier to negotiate, but these are dotted with rocks and boulders that lurk above you in ways suggesting they've spent the last several million years mulling over this new-fangled 'gravity' idea and have decided this could be the night finally to check it out. The slopes vary from 'really very slopey' to 'am I *seeing* that right?' and the way is constantly blocked by jagged canyons, forcing the Devil into diversions.

After an hour of this Vaneclaw was badly out of breath and making frequent observations that now might be a good time to take a breather. Or now.

Or now?

Or *now*?

Eventually the Devil turned and stared at him.

'Just to be clear,' the imp said, 'the last thing I want to do at this point in time is take a break. No way. The best thing, definitely, is to keep walking forever.' He broke off to do a few air-punches and some running on the spot. 'I'm loving it. In fact – shouldn't we go a bit faster?'

Then he had to cough for a while.

To his surprise, when he'd finished, the Devil had not recommenced walking. Instead he seemed to be listening.

'Can you feel it?'

The imp felt the air with his gills, and looked around. There was nothing to see except the tree/rocks/encroaching darkness combo they'd been working for the last several hours, but . . . 'I can,' he said. 'Not just one, either, is it?'

'No.'

'Did you know?'

'I had reason to believe they had clustered together, and that these mountains were a possible location. That's why I instructed you to head down here yesterday.'

'Sorry.'

'But this is . . . more than I was expecting. It's as well that you did not encounter this conclave alone. I would not have wanted them to harm you.'

'Thanks, boss.'

'When the time comes for you to be shredded into howls of blackened despair, it will be at my hand.'

'Oh. Right.'

'The question is . . . where they are.'

Happy to change the subject, the imp rubbed his little hands together. 'Definitely. *Where*. That's the biggie, eh? And *why*? Plus also *when*? Or *what*, and *how much are the hotdogs*?'

The Devil was staring at him in a bad way now.

'But *where*, mainly,' the imp said hurriedly. 'Bingo. That's the one. And . . . what's the answer?'

'I have no idea.'

Vaneclaw blinked. The Devil *knew things*. It was what he did: the Knowing of Things. That plus all the evil, of course. The Devil played the endless ebb and wash of evil like a man standing in the ocean, sculpting the currents around him like a conductor. One movement of his hands was enough to reverse the direction of the waves, and hell followed after. There was no escape, no defence. Almost every story in the world has a back door through which the Devil can enter if he so chooses.

Yet now it seemed as though he was standing outside them all, unsure how to gain entry.

'Are we close, at least?'

'I believe so,' the Devil said. 'But we need a blind spot. They are choosy about their locales. We need virgin ground.'

The imp nodded sagely. 'Aha.'

Despite his justifiably renowned dimness, this was an area in which he could genuinely contribute. The reason Vaneclaw was invisible to most people is that imps are skilled at avoiding the eye. They're not actually invisible – if an imp is behind you and you happen to turn at exactly the right moment you'll catch sight of it. If you have a camera and fast reflexes you may even get a photo, though film has a way of clouding, and iPhones and digital devices often seem to crash, or get dropped and broken, at the instant the shutter is released. Accidents happen. As you might expect.

The chances are that you wouldn't turn at the right moment, however. That's the skill. Keeping out of everyone's vision like this is a heck of a dance, and a useful additional trick when you need a rest is being to locate virgin ground.

Wherever they roam, humans leave residue. Not just litter and pollution, or rusted old cars, or cigarette butts, but stuff that leaks out of their minds. Hopes, needs, memories. Once a human has stood in a place or passed through it, it's never the same again. This is our way of leaving a scent, marking new territory, bringing the chaos of the unknown into our ken and under our control. It's not a bad smell – it's a bit like nutmeg, apparently, with a hint of old newspaper – but it never goes away. Vaneclaw, for all his legendary faults, had a nose for it. And thus also for the lack of it.

'Follow me, boss,' he said.

The imp did a decent job, getting to within half a mile, but then seemed to lose focus – unnerved, perhaps, by the increasing weight of the air, an intangible thrumming that seemed to issue from deep in the rock beneath their feet, and the inaudible echoes of centuries of frowns and sighs. By these, and the occasional half-glimpse of figures, barely discernible in the gloom, high up on a far slope, and also possibly – though not definitely – there amidst a tangle of trees.

It was nearly dark by the time the Devil finally motioned to let him lead the way, and Vaneclaw was happy to hand over the reins. It was getting cold, and the silence was hurting his ears. He'd never felt the world this heavy, this bleak and lonely. The situation was getting further and further beyond his discomfort zone, and he wished he was back in North Dakota, hassling that bloke Ron. That had been a sensible, imp-relevant job, with prospects. It made sense. Even exhaustingly unsmart imps know when they're straying into areas where they're badly out of their depth.

Eventually the Devil slowed. He raised his nose and sniffed once. 'Close,' he said.

He walked another fifty yards, and then stopped. He cocked his head as if listening – the scent's not really a smell, and so it's not the nose that detects it, though it's not a sound either – and changed direction. Then he stopped, mouth half-open as if tasting the air, his old yellow teeth glowing in the tired end of twilight. 'Yes.'

The imp stood with him, and nodded as best a mushroom can. He'd found it all right. This patch of forest, perhaps a hundred feet square, had never suffered the passing of a human foot. Not once, not ever. Somehow, out of all the people who'd trekked through the region, exploring for king or country or the US Forest Service, hiking and hunting and fishing, or trying to peck out a living among these unforgiving mountains a hundred or five hundred years ago, not a single human being had ever crossed this particular space.

It was clean and clear and empty. It was virgin ground.

'Now what?' Vaneclaw whispered.

'You may wish to cover your ears.'

'Ah. Bit of a problem.' The imp held up its stubby little arms to demonstrate they didn't reach up that far. 'See?'

'No matter. It's possible you will not be harmed.'

'Um,' the imp said, feeling – for the first time in his eleven hundred years on the planet – genuinely and extremely afraid. 'I'm not loving the word "possible" in this context, boss. Any chance you can change it to "absolutely and completely definite and certain-sure"?'

The Devil wasn't listening. He stood bolt upright, body straight and tall, like a spike of ancient rock. His eyes had turned black. The darkness coursing off him was luminous.

Then he opened his mouth, and said the word.

There are words that are different to other words, ones that are dark and secret and unknown. They used to exist in many languages, the closely guarded property of shamans and wise women, held close as a source of power, ways to open strange doors. Over time we have lost nearly all of them, especially since science convinced us that numbers hold the keys to reality instead. As a few languages started to establish dominance, the few tongues that nurtured and cherished a stock of secret words withered and died, taking their magic with them – but in the process also closing windows on to the dark unknown: windows for whose lack we should, by and large, feel extremely thankful.

The Devil still knows those words, however. He uttered one that had not been spoken in nearly two thousand years.

Every leaf in the forest shivered.

Every insect and bug and worm in the ground froze.

The clouds high above stayed their course for a moment, before hurrying on their way. The ambient temperature dropped twenty degrees.

Vaneclaw was relieved to discover that he neither melted nor exploded. But when the sound of the word faded, it left the world changed.

Five minutes later, the first of them appeared. A column of hooded shadow, less than the height of a man, at the far edge of the virgin ground. Its presence was reluctant, but the summoning word was of an age and power that brooked neither resistance or denial.

Soon afterwards another could be seen.

And then another.

And then more, coalescing out of the darkness and from between the trees like wolves made of shadows. Within ten minutes, eleven of the entities sometimes referred to as Watchers were gathered within the space.

They stood at angles to one another, keeping their distance. None of their faces – assuming they even had such things – were visible. The silence was so deep that it would have made any normal person vomit. Even Vaneclaw felt nauseous, and had to keep reminding himself to breathe.

The Devil strode towards the middle of the space, head lowered. When he reached some nexus only he could see, a point where the lines between them crossed, he looked up at them.

The Fallen.

The angels with whom he had once tried to usurp God, to claim Heaven for himself, and the entire universe as his rightful domain.

Tried, and failed.

Chapter 28

Hannah's story ended just as the first motel lights started to twinkle a hundred yards ahead. By then they were in the heart of Big Sur – or as close as you can get to it by road – and the trees hung heavy in lowering darkness.

'I . . . see,' Aunt Zo said, after quite a pause.

'It was just a story,' Hannah muttered. 'To pass the time.'

'Of course. And the fact the man in your story is called Eric, like Granddad? And that Granddad's surname, and mine, and yours, is an Anglicized version of Gruen? These are mere coincidences?'

'No,' Granddad said. He had remained silent throughout Hannah's retelling of his tale, except for gently correcting her pronunciation of Leipzig.

'So, Father of mine. The machine that you – pardon me, Hannah – that the not-real man in your totally made-up story built . . . that's the old battered suitcase we hid under Hannah's bed earlier, right? After it had been dropped into the backyard out of the fog, in a way that some people might describe as "extremely unusual"?'

Granddad nodded.

'And that ominous ancient dude in the black suit who's bossing everyone around like he owns the place, the one who's off

196

in the woods somewhere . . . he'd be the man who instructed you – I'm *so* sorry, I mean who instructed the entirely fictional Erik Gruen, who only lives in made-up storyland – to build the machine, what, *how* many hundred years ago?'

'Yes.'

'Nice. OK – I'll go round once more on this carousel of the crazy. So who *is* he?'

'He's . . .' Granddad hesitated.

'We're here,' Hannah said.

Aunt Zo hissed at being diverted from the conversation, but they were approaching the first of the motels on the strip. It was called the Pennyweather Motel, and – like most accommodations in the area – consisted of a series of low, old wooden buildings gathered around a small central lodge, nestled among trees. Apart from a couple of more recent and outlandishly expensive places on long driveways off the road (establishments where, Hannah's dad had said with a sigh, children weren't allowed, which meant they obviously sucked) all the motels here were like this. You didn't come to Big Sur to watch Netflix on a big flat-screen TV or laze in high-thread-count sheets or order room service – or, if you did, you were destined for disappointment as none of the motels had any of these things. They didn't even have phones in the rooms.

'So what do we do?' Aunt Zo asked as she caused the car to slow. 'Go into each of these dives in turn?'

Hannah didn't know what to say.

'I need a decision,' Aunt Zo added.

'Where do you normally stay?' Granddad asked.

'The Creekside,' Hannah said. 'It's farther along. Not the next one, or the next. The one after that. But . . .'

She didn't want to explain in front of Aunt Zo why she knew the Creekside Inn would be a bust. It was a place she'd stayed every year of her life, whose every nook and cranny she had explored. They had big, rough-hewn wooden chairs in the river behind the lodge where you could sit and dangle your feet in the bracingly frigid mountain stream that gave the place its name. She could see, in her mind's eye, her mother and father perched together in the love seat there, holding cocktails in plastic cups, laughing as Hannah took their picture on her iPod.

When was that? Only last year.

But it might as well be a century ago, an incident from someone else's life. Right now it seemed harder to believe in than anything that had happened to Erik Gruen. Her dad didn't take her to the Crow's Nest any more, and he wouldn't have gone to the Creekside. Some stories end.

'. . . he won't be there,' she finished.

'OK,' said Aunt Zo, steering into the lot of the Pennyweather. 'So we're back to checking each in turn.'

'Drive on,' Granddad said, however. 'Go to the other place first.'

'But Hannah just said—'

'I know,' he interrupted, quietly but firmly. 'And she may be right, in which case we'll be searching them slightly out of geographical sequence, at a cost of approximately ten minutes, which I will do my best to make up to both of you. With ice cream, if necessary. OK, Hannah?'

'Sure,' she said glumly.

Even Granddad didn't listen sometimes.

Aunt Zo swerved back out of the lot and on down the highway. There was half a mile of forest between the Pennyweather and the next place, the Log House Resort, a bunch of cabins and camping spaces with nothing but a tiny office to tie them together.

Another long stretch of woods, and then the Forgotten Inn, kind of like the Creekside, but not as old or nice-looking.

Another patch of woods.

Then Aunt Zo was pulling into the Creekside.

She parked in front of the lodge. They got out of the car, Granddad wincing. It was all so much the same that it was bizarre. The portico in front of the entrance. The main building, the heart of which – as you can tell from the black-and-white photos on the walls inside – has been unchanged in a hundred years. The tiny gas station on the right; the little general store on the left where you buy water and sandwiches to take to the cove down on Pfeiffer State Beach, the most windswept place in the world. All of it in darkness, glow-lit with lamps. The still quietness that comes from being amongst redwoods, apart from the faint buzzing sound Big Sur seems to have, which Hannah's mom said came from its energy. It was all so much the same that it felt uncanny.

Aunt Zo spotted the door on the short right wing that said 'Office', and also that it was closed. 'So, where . . .'

'Inside,' Hannah said.

She led them under the portico and in through the wide wooden door. A rustic lobby area; a big river-rock fireplace with a log fire burning. The strong, familiar smell of woodsmoke. There was a stand-up desk on the side where you made dinner reservations, and this doubled in the evenings as a way of getting in contact with the people who ran the place if there were no towels or the lights in the bedroom had stopped working, neither of which were unknown at the Creekside.

Hannah ran to it, eager to be the one to ask if her dad was here, even though she was confident that he would not be. She didn't notice Granddad and Aunt Zo stopping in their tracks, staring across the casual lounge/restaurant area beyond at a table in the far corner.

'How did you know?' Zo asked him.

'I never thought he was running away,' Granddad said, though there was some relief in his voice. 'I believe he's starting to face the future again instead.'

He spoke Hannah's name. When she turned, he pointed into the far corner. Hannah's shriek caused a waitress to drop an entire tray of calamari and buffalo wing appetizers.

Hannah ran straight through the debris and threw herself at a tired-looking man sitting at a table with a laptop.

After a moment of bewilderment, he wrapped his arms tightly around her too.

Chapter 29

'What do you want?'

It was one of the farthest Watchers who spoke, or caused the shadows of words to be cast and their meaning to be known.

'To talk,' the Devil said.

'There is nothing to discuss.'

The Devil frowned. 'You'd rather hide?'

'We are not hidden. Merely unknown, through choice.'

'Always with the semantics,' the Devil said. 'You guys slay me. So – how've you been?'

None of them spoke. The Devil let the silence stretch, looking at each in turn. Eleven angels, all of whom, long, long ago, he had known almost as well as he'd known himself. He'd continued to work with them after the Fall, after he and they had been cast down to this ball of rock. They were his co-constructors of Hell, the Stygian Council of Pandemonium. In the glory days when, OK, so they might no longer be in Heaven, but there was new work to be done – dark, sour work – and great things had been achieved. The destruction of entire civilizations. Pestilence and terror that had killed nine in every ten. Wars so dire that history had shied away from even recording them; events whose horror had been sealed into black holes of silence from which neither light nor words could escape. A few of the angels had drifted away or turned their backs, but these others . . .

The Devil spoke to one of them, to whom he had been close. 'I don't merit a greeting even from *you*, Ytr?'

The Watcher in question remained silent.

Another, the one who had spoken first, caused his assumed form to suddenly be closer to the Devil. 'You summoned,' it said. 'We came. Our contract with the word has been honoured. Now we will leave.'

'The Sacrifice Machine isn't working,' the Devil said, cutting to the chase. 'It isn't channelling the dark currents to Hell and back to us in the way it should.'

'That is of no account.'

'It doesn't bother you to grow weaker and weaker every day? To steadily lose your power?'

Another Watcher spoke, the one that had been called Zhakq, using one of the Devil's old names. 'Tell me, Diabolos, what good did it ever do us? We did as you commanded, and we fell. We continued to do your bidding in the aftertime. We were not raised back up on high. The world here continued as it always had. We facilitated its inhabitants in death and spoilage, and still the waves rose and fell on the shores, and the sun shone, and life persists. Power that affects nothing is mere vanity.'

'You were always a weak link, Zhakq,' the Devil said in a low, hard tone. 'You only joined us because of a slight God committed by accident. I remember the day I talked you into our campaign, how pathetically glad you were to have something to cleave to. And yet now you lead a shamble into nothingness. Congratulations, angel. You've grown into your weakness.'

He turned and spoke again to the Watcher that had been

styled Ytr, and who had once been almost equal in darkness to the Devil himself. 'What about you, old friend? You didn't need convincing. You *fought* to be at my right hand.'

'Long ago, in a different place,' the Watcher said. Its voice was deep and dreadful still, a rumble that had once turned hearts to stone. 'Things change.'

'They certainly do,' the Devil said. 'And it will start happening faster if action is not taken. Is that what you want?'

'Your time is done,' Zhakq said. 'And we no longer wish to be your allies. Humans have become too distinguishable from one another. Their dooms and terrors are shifting, individual. Your precious Hell is no longer relevant. Nobody believes. Nobody cares.'

'Wow,' the Devil said. 'You see that imp?' He pointed at Vaneclaw, who'd been standing well back, trying – though he knew it was pointless in this company – to be even more invisible than usual.

'Hi,' Vaneclaw said, very quietly.

'Until this evening, I believed that imp was the most dull-witted entity I'd ever interacted with. I see now I was mistaken. Compared to you, he's an intellectual titan.' He directed his full ire at Ytr. 'Do even *you* not understand? You, who at least stayed with Xjynthucx and me long enough to see how things work here?'

The Watcher was silent.

'Once upon a long ago,' the Devil said, 'the creatures here had a life that made sense. They lived in caves, as animals should. They survived in collections of families. Everybody knew each other. They understood a duty of care, or at least knew that if they did wrong it would be noticed and brought to account. Then things changed. They gathered in larger numbers, in villages and towns and cities. Nobody knew everybody any more. The shadows and back alleys grew dark, and sometimes ran with blood. People stopped knowing how to behave, and most of all they stopped remembering *why*. They needed reasons to toe the line, and that was what they were given. Two reasons. Heaven, and Hell. Equal in resonance and moment. No one will ever be able to tell whether it has been the promise of Heaven or the threat of Hell that has kept this world from teetering into chaos ten thousand times. *That* is why Hell matters, and that's why the power of black deeds must always be directed there. Without evil there is no good, and without Hell's focusing lens there can be no true evil – just a great deal of extremely poor behaviour.'

The Devil's words rang out in the forest, but found no home. After a disrespectful pause, one of the Watchers who had not yet spoken suddenly came towards him.

'We are eleven gathered,' it said. 'Only one remains to fold in. Once we draw him to us, we will be complete. Our circle of twelve will close. You are lost and alone.'

'You should leave,' Zhakq added, and in its chill, inhuman voice lay a hint of deep satisfaction – and threat. 'Leave, and perhaps hide. We have power yet to harm. We are the tide now.'

The Devil threw a last look at Ytr. When we are betrayed, it is the actions of those who once stood closest that cut the deepest. Ytr, however, made no sign – Ytr, whose fierce roar on the morning of the Fall had been enough to split planets half a galaxy away, but who now looked like nothing more than a shadow-monk in the wilderness, something to trigger spooky campfire stories that nobody believed in any more.

'There are lost angels here, true enough,' the Devil snarled. 'But I am not one of them.'

The rage he felt was sufficient that, fifteen miles away, a father of three who was camping in the woods with two other families reached immediately for the axe he'd used to help build the fire upon which he and his best friends were about to grill steaks and deployed it to commit acts so appalling that they passed into local legend. Two heads were never found.

The Devil stalked away, Vaneclaw hurrying after him.

The Devil was so very furious, in fact, that only when they were two miles from the virgin ground, striding down the forested slope towards the highway, did he suddenly stop dead in his tracks.

'Of course,' he said. 'Oh, you foolish old god.'

Vaneclaw was so short of breath that he was incapable of speech. Instead he waved his short arms in a way that he hoped would communicate that, what with him being famously non-smart, further clarification was necessary, should the big man be so inclined, but if he wasn't, that was also totally fine.

This wasn't an easy gesture to pull off and towards the end of it Vaneclaw toppled slowly over on to his back.

'The tide,' the Devil said quietly. 'The voice I heard from the throat of the man in the woods . . . it used the same phrase. That was Zhakq, Vaneclaw. Him, or one of the others. Perhaps all of them together, disguised.'

'I don't get it, boss.'

'Everything we just heard was lies. They have already turned against me. It is *they* who have somehow prevented the Sacrifice Machine from performing its function.'

'So what are they going to do, boss?'

'They're going to attack. They are trying to finally claim this world for their own.'

Chapter 30

Kristen hesitated in the back of the cab, looking out at the house. It looked the same. Of course. She didn't expect Steve to have done anything to it in the meantime, not least because while he'd had the ideas often enough, it was pretty much always she who'd said 'OK, so let's get this thing done.'

It looked the same. It probably was the same. But now she was looking at it from the outside.

'Say hi to your husband for me.'

'Huh?'

'Your husband,' the driver said. He had been, thankfully, one of the silent types, not saying a single word since picking her up from San Jose. 'I drove him to the airport last year. Had a meeting in LA. He seemed like a nice guy.'

'He is,' Kristen said. She didn't know what else she could have said. Then she realized part of what the driver was probably saying was that Kristen been sitting looking out of the window for nearly a couple of minutes now and it'd be cool if she would move so he could get on with his actual job.

She climbed out. Waited until the driver had disappeared back down the street, then walked up the path.

She rang the doorbell.

No response.

She rang again, and stood patiently outside for a few minutes, but it was just too damned cold. She had a key. They were still married. Her daughter lived here. If you wanted to get right down to it, she paid the lion's share of the mortgage.

She let herself in.

The house looked the same inside, too. Though tidier. Kristen would be the first to admit she had a habit of leaving things around. Her rationale when pressed was that she tended to need the same things in the same places, so what was the point of moving them back where they'd come from – and also she was busy and for Christ's sake was it really so big a deal?

Seeing the living room and kitchen so very tidy, however, made her realize that to an unbiased observer it might appear as though the mess had been removed from these lives.

And that the mess had been her.

She took off her coat. Got the kettle on. Found the instant coffee – Steve had resisted buying a fancy espresso machine on the grounds that going out to buy a latte or Americano was the closest thing he had to a 'lifestyle' when in the word mines, and just about his only reason for leaving the house. The coffee was a different brand – why? – but in the same place as always, of course. Steve's muscle memory had been trained over the years to put it there. Hers had too. Memory also made you expect to find the same person in the same place. It got to the point where you could find your way around your life in the dark, or with your eyes closed. The problem was, once you'd noticed this, you might be prone to ask whether that was a good thing.

After all these weeks, she still wasn't sure.

She leaned on the counter, waiting for the water to boil. Her head dropped. She was very tired indeed.

*   *   *

Meanwhile a truck was turning into High Street. This wasn't the main road through the centre of town, as the name might imply. Instead it led from the highway up to the higher part of the west side, where Hannah's house stood.

Nash was driving. Jesse was riding shotgun, holding Nash's phone where he could see the screen. Eduardo and Chex were awake now too. Nobody had slept in a while – certainly not since arriving in California. Nash had been wondering how the next message would arrive, how he'd know what to look for. Then just after they'd crossed the state line his phone had blinked into life. It wasn't incoming SMS or email this time, though, incessant pings from customers back in Miami trying to get hold of drugs and wondering where the hell their normally reliable dealer had gotten to. It was the map app starting itself up, though nobody had been touching the phone at the time.

A dot appeared in the centre of the screen. The dot pulsed. It did not look the way it usually did, a cheery little blue flag. It was a dark, lustrous gold, like a treasure box.

It looked like the kind of thing you'd want. To sell, or keep for yourself. To own.

They set a course towards it.

Kristen drank her coffee sitting at the counter. She felt brittle and wide-eyed. A third of her soul was still back in London. A third was here in Santa Cruz. She had no idea where the other part was. She thought maybe she should try to find out. It might be the part that understood her life.

The couch in the living room was calling out to her. It was as if she could actually hear its voice. The couch was comfortable, she knew. Very, very comfortable. She could go and sit, wait for them there. That'd be nice.

Except she'd fall asleep. Of that there was no doubt. And

she didn't want to be discovered sprawled sideways, head back and mouth open and most likely snoring. Certainly not if her presence was unexpected. Not cool. Not dignified.

She wandered into the living room, phone in hand, trying to work out what to say. Her feet took her towards the couch, like cats silently herding their owner towards a feeding bowl.

In a minute, she promised them, and herself. First, I need to at least let him know I'm here.

She dialled Steve's number. It went to voicemail. She started talking.

Then she realized something was going on outside.

Nash got out and strode up the path without even killing the engine. Jesse reached across, turned off the ignition, and then he and the other two guys followed their boss.

They didn't know why they were here, heading towards some random nice-looking house in a town none of them had heard of. But someone was home, obviously. A ton of lights were on.

Then they saw a woman in the living room, on the phone.

Jesse felt his heart sink, and hoped this wasn't going to be some kind of messed-up home-invasion deal. He'd done bad stuff in his life, hell yes – but never one of those, and he didn't want to start now. Even bad guys have a line in the sand, a point past which they'd prefer not to go. Jesse knew all too well, however, that Nash's skill was dragging guys over lines.

The woman saw them coming. She disappeared.

Nash got to the door and hammered on it with his fist.

The woman didn't open up, obviously. Jesse sure as hell wouldn't have done either. And weren't you supposed to ease your way in, knock politely, say 'Hey, is that your dog in the road' or something, before pushing past?

Nash hammered on the door again, ever louder, totally blowing that option. Which was OK by Jesse, and – he could tell – the other guys, who looked as unnerved as he was.

And then, before Nash banged on the door a third time, it flew open and all the lights in the house went out.

Kristen saw the man heading up the path and knew that whatever this was about, it wasn't good. He didn't look like someone Steve would know. He didn't look like someone that anybody law-abiding would ever want to know. The others with him seemed less sure of their purpose. That didn't matter. That guy was the man. That was obvious. Whatever he did, they'd get dragged along for the ride.

She backed hurriedly away from the window though she knew she'd already been seen. Instinct told her to head towards the kitchen and the back door. She could get out into the yard from there and over the fence. Although the guy who lived next door was kind of weird, he was generally home. It'd be a start.

Except the back door wouldn't open.

The sound of hammering fists on the front door.

She yanked at the back door, finally spotting that the key wasn't in the lock. They *always* left it there. She and Steve did, anyhow. The only person who moved it was his ditzy sister, who thought it'd be safer up on the . . .

Yes – there it was. Balanced on top of the doorjamb. Why had Zo been here?

More hammering. Starting to panic, Kristen stuffed the key in the lock. But it wouldn't turn. The door hadn't been locked. It just wouldn't open.

The knob in her hand suddenly went ice cold and she heard the front door crashing open and realized she'd run out of time.

210

She turned and ran upstairs. There was nowhere else to go – and at least up there she could lock herself into one of the bedrooms and call the cops.

But when you feel the need to run, you want to run far, and so instead of heading for the room she used to share with Steve, she kept going to the end, to Hannah's.

Only when she was in it, dead-end committed, and could hear the sound of heavy footsteps heading towards the stairs, did she remember that Hannah's door key had long ago been lost.

Kristen was scared now. Really very scared.

She looked wildly around. Closets – but she knew they were jammed full of clothes and old toys and stuff that neither she nor her daughter had the heart to throw out. No room for her.

There was nowhere to hide.

Except . . .

She dropped to the floor and scrambled under the bed, knowing it was a lost cause, knowing that they'd find her – but when something's coming to get you, the body shoves the mind aside and keeps running for as long as it can.

Nash was thorough. Though he'd heard the woman running upstairs he sent two of the guys to check the downstairs rooms, to make sure there was no one else home. Meanwhile he took Jesse upstairs with him.

'Why's it getting so cold in here?'

'Don't know,' Nash said. 'Don't care.'

They checked the rooms one by one. 'Where'd she go?'

'What'd I just say, Jesse?'

Finally there was only one room left to search. Jesse followed Nash into it, confused now. The woman wasn't in there either, which made zero sense.

'But why are we even here? If it's not for the woman?'

Seemed like the room belonged to a kid, a girl. Nash wandered around, and eventually stopped in front of a bizarre-looking sculpture on the bookcase. It looked like it had been made from the insides of about six different types of machines.

Nash raised his hand, slowly. Held his palm out towards the sculpture. One of the little balls of fire he could do coalesced there. Without warning it suddenly zipped into the machine and exploded, showering Jesse with parts.

Nash turned, and smiled one of those smiles that said someone was about to get hurt. Jesse hoped it wasn't him.

Nash pointed to the bed. Raised one finger to his lips. Turned his other hand over, opened it out, and raised it.

Lift it.

Jesse realized it was the only place she could have gone. They'd found her. So whatever was about to happen here was really going to happen, and after that . . . life wasn't going to be the same. He thought about trying to talk Nash down but knew it was a lost cause. He'd never seen the boss like this before. It was like something had control of him. Something really bad.

So he bent over and got his hands under the side of the bed and lifted one side. But there was no one under there. Just a very old-looking suitcase, made of battered leather.

Jesse blinked. 'Huh?'

Nash grinned. '*That* is what we're looking for.'

Chapter 31

Aunt Zo let Hannah stay fiercely gripped around her father for five whole minutes, using every last jot of patience. Then, when her niece had finally loosened her grip and slid into the chair next to him, she strode up to the table.

'You're an idiot,' she said, and cuffed her brother around the back of the head.

Half an hour later, Hannah's father had said sorry to Aunt Zo enough times to stop her glaring at him in such a scary way. He'd apologized to Granddad, too, who merely shrugged.

'I'm glad you're OK,' he said.

'That's *it*?' Aunt Zo barked. 'No *questions* to ask?'

Granddad thought about it. He looked around the restaurant. 'Is the food here any good?'

And so – after some gentle encouragement – he got Aunt Zo to move with him to another table, where they ordered something to eat. Hannah didn't feel hungry. She stayed in the chair right next to her father. He seemed different, though she couldn't put her finger on how. He looked tired, not in the way he had started to before he sent her away to Granddad, but the way he was when he'd been working

213

especially long and hard on something, and came down from his study at the end of the day, distracted but content.

'I'm sorry,' he said again. 'When I suggested you go stay with Granddad, I didn't know I was going to come here. But I sat around the house for a day, alone . . . It was worse even than I'd thought it would be. I wanted to call Granddad and say I'd made a mistake, he should send you back, but I didn't think that would be fair to you.'

'I would have come back right away,' Hannah said.

'I know – that's the point. That's *not your job*. So I decided to come down here. To . . . well, to work. Only when I got here did I find their Wi-Fi is borked. And there's no data signal, as you know. I asked in the office if I could at least send an email to Granddad from their machine but it was borked too. It was late by then, and I'd just driven down, so I figured I'd stay the night and go home the next day. Except . . .'

Her dad looked away, across the lobby. 'Except I sat at this table,' he said. 'And . . . I remembered it all.'

'Remembered what?'

'All the times we'd been here. It was why I checked in here. At first I was going to try one of the other motels, but then I thought, No, that's dumb. There are too many things to avoid. Too many places we've all been together, too many things we've done. I can't turn my back on them forever just because it's painful the first time. If I take out everything that used to be me, or you-and-me and our family, all that's left is loading the dishwasher and chasing deadlines and that's no way to live. I remembered sitting at one of these tables when you were nine months. And eighteen months. And four years old, and eight. What you had to eat. What I had, what . . . your mom had. And then getting you to sleep afterwards in the room. Sometimes you'd drop right off. Sometimes it'd be like wrestling an anaconda. I never knew which it was going to be, which drives you nuts, but that's also what it's about. It's what reminds you it's real, actually happening, like spotting a grey hair on the head of the woman you love.

'Then, sitting out on the deck outside the room afterwards, sipping a beer with your mom and talking about . . . stuff. Nothing important. Whatever. Random happy words. That's what I miss the most. Now whenever I talk to people, it's always *about* something. On those evenings I just talked. And listened. It's . . . Christ.' Her father suddenly seemed to realize what he'd been saying. 'I'm sorry. These are not age-appropriate observations.'

'It's OK.' Hannah did not want him to stop saying things, whatever they were. She had never actually heard him say so many words in one lump before, and nor had anyone ever spoken to her as if they realized she was a lot more grown-up inside than she looked. 'But . . . why didn't you come home the next day?'

'Because after I'd thought about those things, I opened the laptop and tried to do some work. It's how I escape, when things aren't good. It was slow at first, but then it wasn't. When they closed down here for the night I went to my room and kept on working, and when I woke the next morning I made coffee and kept on going. I know . . . I know Mom and Dad's work probably seems dumb to you sometimes. Just a way of us not being there.'

'Kinda,' Hannah admitted.

'I get that. And I know sometimes I get too into it, or too stressed about it, when it's not the most important thing in the world. But . . . look, you know, we've had the conversation. Partly I work for the money. Everything costs, right?'

Hannah nodded. They had definitely had this conversation. More than once. She had learned during an early example that ATMs did not give out money to just anyone, but that you had to put money in them first. At the time she'd been baffled as to how you pushed the bills *into* the machine, but had developed a (slightly) more sophisticated understanding of finance since.

'But that's not it,' her dad said. 'There are a lot of things that matter in life, that are important to having a *good* life. Your family. Having fun. Being warm and fed.'

'And having pets. Like a kitten.'

'Um, right. And those are the most important things. But you've got to *be*, too. You've got to *do* things. You've got to live your life out loud. Do you see what I mean?'

'I think so,' Hannah said. She watched as a waitress put food in front of Aunt Zo and Granddad. Her stomach growled.

'I knew you were with Granddad, and he'd look after you. And I assumed they'd get the internet fixed, but they didn't. Still haven't. I was going to head home tomorrow, first thing.'

'It's OK, Dad.'

'It's not,' he said.

'No, really it is,' Hannah said. 'You've shaved.'

Her father put his hand to his chin, puzzled. 'Well, yeah. So?'

'Never mind. Can I have something to eat? I'm *starving*.'

And so Hannah and her dad moved to the other table, and she had a cheeseburger, and then it was time to head home. Hannah said she wanted to go in Dad's car, to be with him. And she did want this, very much, though she also thought it might give Granddad and Aunt Zo a chance to talk about the story of Erik Gruen.

As they were getting the check the Devil walked into the lounge. He looked far more irritable than Hannah had ever seen him before, which was saying a lot. Irritable and old and perhaps even worried. He stood by their table and glared around at the other people in the restaurant with evident dislike.

Finally he looked down at Hannah's dad. 'So, you've been found,' he said. 'How marvellous.'

'Who are you?'

'I am who I am. And you are an idiot.'

Hannah's dad blinked. 'Excuse me?'

'You heard the guy,' Aunt Zo said cheerfully. 'Though I can repeat it, if you'd like.'

'I am weary of this place,' the Devil muttered. 'I shall be in the car. Do not keep me waiting.'

Dad got his stuff from his room. Granddad, Aunt Zo and the Devil set off in Zo's car (Vaneclaw once more secreting himself in the trunk, for convenience, and also because he'd discovered it was actually pretty comfortable and smelled interestingly of gasoline) and Hannah rode in the back seat of her father's. After a few days in unfamiliar vehicles, it was nice to be back in one she knew.

Her dad didn't say much as they drove north, heading back towards Bixby Bridge and the gateway to the rest of California, the bits that didn't buzz. Hannah didn't mind. She knew he liked to concentrate when driving, so she sat quietly. She was pretty sleepy (and enormously full of burger) and thought it likely she might be able to pull off that trick where you travel home in an instant, by falling asleep.

Halfway across the bridge there was a long series of faint bonging noises, however.

'Phone's picked up data signal again,' her father said without enthusiasm. 'That will be emails, flooding once more through the breach in the fence. *Welcome back, Steve. We've been waiting. Got a bunch of crap we'd like to bug you about. That stuff I said earlier about work? Emails don't count.'*

Then there was a series of other sounds, pings this time. 'Voicemail.' Her dad sighed. 'Would you mind seeing who they're from? Ten will be from Zo, calling me rude words, but your mom may have called too. She's also likely to be . . .'

'Really unbelievably mad at you?'

'. . . eager to communicate.'

'We need to make her come *home*, Dad. We should tell her to come home.'

'It's not quite that . . . Look, would you mind just seeing who called?'

Hannah fished her dad's iPhone out of his jacket and read down the notifications.

'Yep,' she said. 'Five voicemails from Mom.'

'Christ.'

'One two days ago, then another one, two yesterday, and – oh: one only half an hour ago. Can we listen?'

'I guess,' her dad said, with the air of a man who knew he might as well take his lumps sooner rather than later. 'Put it on speaker. Hang on – half an hour ago?'

'Uh-huh,' Hannah said as she navigated to the relevant screen on the phone. It was her strident belief that she was more than ready to own a phone (the schism with her friend Ellie at school had started through Ellie's excessive tendency to show off hers), and took any opportunity to demonstrate her skills.

'That's weird. It's the middle of the night there. Or, what is it . . . almost nine here: plus three, so it's five in the morning. OK, but she's still up very early, even for her.'

'Probably really worried about you,' Hannah said.

'Thanks.'

Hannah pressed the on-screen button. '*Hey,*' Kristen's voice said out of the speaker. '*It's me. Obviously. Uh, been trying to get hold of you, dude. Which presumably you know. But.*'

There was a pause. Hannah waited, struck by how different her mother sounded. People evidently had different voices depending whom they're talking to, which begged the question of which was their real voice. Though Mom sounded tired, too.

'*Anyway. I . . . shit, Steve. Look. I would like us to talk, soon. The first message I left was because Hannah called me. She sounded . . . I don't know.*'

'You called Mom?' Hannah's father said.

'Um,' Hannah said.

'*She sounded very not-happy,*' her mom continued. '*Which is why I wanted to talk to you, but you weren't there, and have continued to not be there, and . . . It's been a while, and lately there's been this voice of . . . something or other, in my head, ranting on, and I couldn't sleep, and so I've done some-thing a little out of left field. Basically, I'm here. In Santa Cruz.*'

Hannah's heart leaped. 'Mom's *home?*'

'Shh,' her dad said quietly.

'*In fact, I'm in the actual house. Though neither of you are. I guess you're out. Well, duh. Clearly you are. So I just wanted to warn you that I'd be here when you get back because . . . I felt I should. Warn you. Or something. In case that's weird. Me being in the house. Because I let myself in.*'

Hannah looked at her father. He was watching the road ahead and his face looked very still. Hannah wondered if he was thinking the same as her, which was that Mom didn't usually sound this uncertain.

'*So, uh, that's what it is,*' her mom's message went on. '*I hope it's OK. It's, what is it? – OK, it's half past eight, so*'

I assume you won't be too long now. I'll be here. In the kitchen, probably, though right now the idea of the couch is . . .'

Her mom went silent for a moment. When she spoke again her voice sounded very different.

'*What the hell—*'

Then the line went dead.

Chapter 32

Hannah's dad drove fast. Not crazy fast, but still fast, looping round Carmel on Highway 1 and then shooting north.

'You OK?' he asked when they were on the home straight.

'What happened?'

'I'm sure everything's fine.'

'But why didn't she answer when I tried?'

'I don't know,' he said.

'Maybe she just dropped her phone? And . . . it broke. Which is why she isn't answering now?'

'Could be. Or she fell asleep on the couch in mid-sentence and is lying there snoring her head off.'

'Mom doesn't snore.'

'Oh, she really does.'

He was calm and sounded as if everything was almost certainly OK. But he didn't sound like he believed it.

Hannah sat clutching his phone in her hands, staring at the screen, willing the car home.

It was quarter to eleven when they pulled into the drive, providing the first sign that her dad was as anxious as she was. Usually he took this turn carefully because the slope over the kerb was a little steep and so otherwise it—

Crunch.

—banged the underneath of the car. He didn't swear this time, though. They walked quickly together to the front door. It was unlocked, but that made sense. Mom would have unlocked on the way in. Dad opened the door, letting it swing away from him into the hallway, holding his hand to the side to stop Hannah running straight in.

'Wait,' he said.

The house was silent. Oddly, noticeably, ostentatiously silent, in the way houses are when you catch them unawares, as if they've recently stopped doing something secretive and weird, and the furniture has only just got back into its usual positions.

The hallway lights were on. So were those in the living room. That was also to be expected. Dad had them on a timer system that he worked from his computer to ward off intruders, a bit like Granddad's sculptures, Hannah realized. It only worked about a third of the time and had driven her mom a tiny bit nuts.

Dad took a cautious step into the house. 'Kristen?'

'Dad—'

'Shh. Stay here, OK?'

He walked carefully down the hallway until he could see into the living room. She saw him moving his head around to look on all sides. Then he went farther along the hall, towards the door to the kitchen. 'Kristen?'

His voice sounded tight. Hannah decided she had had enough of standing out on the mat and ran in to him. He looked angry for a moment but then rolled his eyes. 'OK,' he said. 'But stay close. I'm sure it's all fine, but let's . . . do this properly.'

The kitchen. All the lights were on there too, blazing in the way Mom liked, and which had driven *Dad* a tiny bit nuts. Everything looked normal. The counters were clean. The spatulas were all in the right place. A piece of luggage that Hannah recognized stood on the floor near the table. Mom's carry-on. There was a coffee cup on the counter too. Hannah touched her hand to it. It was not quite cold.

The house was still not saying anything.

They went to the den, which was dark. Dad turned on the lights. It was empty. They checked the bathroom, and the room where they had dinner once in a great while, if there were guests. Both were empty.

Then they were back in the hall, her dad looking up the stairs. 'What are the chances of you staying down here?'

'Not good,' Hannah said. 'Really quite poor, in fact.'

He sighed. 'OK. But two things first.'

He leaned on the banister and peered up the stairs. The upper hallway light was on. 'She evidently flew in today,' he said. 'Which case, it's somewhat credible that she went upstairs and crashed out in the spare room. After she . . . dropped her phone. She could be asleep up there now, and when your mom's asleep, she's *asleep*. So I'm going to call louder, OK?'

'OK.'

'*Kristen?*'

Nothing.

Her father's face was pinched, as each attempt to prove this was a normal, explicable situation came up short. 'OK then. Second thing: try phoning her again. Just in case.'

Hannah held up her dad's phone, which she had ready and waiting. She pushed the button that would place a call to 'Kriz', Dad's shorthand for Mom.

They waited. There was no ringing sound from above.

'Stay three stairs behind me,' her dad said. 'And if anything happens, run.'

'What kind of thing?'

'Anything . . . unusual. Run next door, OK? Tell Mr Golson to call the police. Promise?'

'But Mr Golson's weird.'

'I know he is. But just do it, OK? Promise me.'

Hannah knew that a lot of very unusual things had happened to her in the last couple of days, and she hadn't run once. But she nodded.

They went carefully up the stairs, her dad craning his neck to get a better view. He held her back when he reached the top, then motioned for her to follow.

The upstairs hallway looked as it always did.

Dad pushed the door to his study first, reaching round to turn on the light as it swung open. Empty.

Next was her parents' bedroom. That was empty too. Dad held a finger to his lips before opening the door to the guest room, in case Mom was asleep in there. But she was not.

Her dad seemed less tense with each room that was proved empty. Hannah was too, though also confused. Where was her mom?

Only two rooms left. First he opened the small one where Mom had worked sometimes when she was home. *Had* been at home. It was empty in an extremely empty way, Mom having taken most of her stuff when she left. A couple of books wilted on the shelf, looking lost and left-behind.

Which only left Hannah's bedroom.

'Did you shut that?'

He meant her door, which wasn't normally ever closed. Granddad had shut it that afternoon, however, after they'd stowed the Sacrifice Machine under her bed.

'Yes,' Hannah said. 'I did it this morning. I just thought it looked . . . tidier.'

'Huh,' he said. He sounded pretty relaxed now. 'Maybe she decided to go check into a hotel or something.'

'But why would she do that? She lives here.'

'Your mom likes hotels.'

He turned the handle of Hannah's door, barely paying attention, checking this last room merely for the sake of completeness. But when he pushed, nothing happened.

'Oh. Did you lock it?'

'It doesn't have a lock. A key, I mean.'

'Right. Of course.'

There had been a phase in Hannah's life when she'd taken to locking her door while she did Important Things. The timing of these Important Things had a very high correlation with periods when she was supposed to be doing something else, like getting dressed or brushing her teeth or doing homework. After a few pretty major arguments on the subject the key to her room had mysteriously gone missing, never to be found.

Her dad shoved at the door again, then bent to peer at a point near the handle. 'Weird,' he said. 'It's definitely not locked. Something's blocking it on the other side.'

'Mom?' Hannah called. 'Are you in there?'

'Steve?'

They both jumped out of their skins, but it wasn't Hannah's mom. The voice had come from downstairs.

Aunt Zo. They heard her hurrying into the hallway below. 'You realize you left the front door wide open?'

Hannah and her dad ran downstairs. 'Yes, Zo, I do,' her dad said. He explained about the phone message and the strange way it ended and how they'd searched the house.

Granddad stood in the doorway. His face was serious in a way that Hannah didn't like. 'You can't open Hannah's room?'

'No,' Hannah said, suddenly hopeful. Of *course* – he must have done something to the door. Locked it in a special way to protect the machine – or maybe he'd accidentally turned the sculpture's power up so high that *nobody* could get in.

'Let's take a look.'

He led them back up the stairs. He twisted Hannah's door handle experimentally, and even in that small, everyday motion Hannah could tell a difference from when her dad had done it. When Granddad grasped and turned, listening while he did so, you could tell he understood the mechanics in a higher way. He was, she supposed, the Engineer – and in that moment she fully accepted, for the first time, the story of Erik Gruen.

'It's not locked,' he said. 'Something's blocking it.'

'Uh-huh,' her dad said drily. 'We'd figured that out.'

'Have you called out to her?'

'Yes, obviously.'

Her dad suddenly shouted Hannah's mother's name again, very loudly. Everyone jumped, then listened. There was no answering sound from the other side.

Granddad reached up and pressed his fingers on the top of the door, near the frame. He did the same on the left side, the right, and then pushed along the bottom with the toe of one foot.

'Curious,' he said. He took a step back, still looking around the doorframe. 'Nice cup of coffee wouldn't go amiss.'

'Excuse me?'

'That's a long drive for old bones, and it'll take me a few minutes to work out how best to tackle this. Always think much better with a coffee, I find.'

'I'll help make it,' Aunt Zo said in a way that made Hannah wonder whether some of her aunt's questions might indeed have been answered during the period she'd just spent with Granddad in the car. Either answered or at least dealt with in a way that made her willing to go along with what he said – for now.

Hannah's dad looked baffled. 'Whatever you say. You're not going to have to damage the door, are you?'

'Oh no,' Granddad said. 'Probably not.'

He waited until they'd gone downstairs and then half turned to Hannah, mind still on the problem at hand. 'Would you do something for me?'

'OK.'

'Please go fetch Vaneclaw.'

Hannah slipped downstairs, past the kitchen and out of the front door. The Devil was sitting in the back of Aunt Zo's car, staring straight ahead.

'What are you doing?'

'Trying to call in a favour,' he said eventually. 'On the back of old friendship. Time will tell. And the paths of destiny, as that's how he's always liked to style the way he operates in the world of the *mundus*.'

Hannah had no idea what that was supposed to mean and so she left him to it and went round the back to open the trunk. Vaneclaw was stretched out there, eyes shut.

Hannah coughed. The imp did not move. She coughed again, more loudly.

'I'm not asleep,' Vaneclaw said blearily, eyes still closed. 'Like a ninja, I am. Ready for action at a nanosecond's notice. Or sooner.'

'You were asleep.'

'Yeah, I was a bit, to be fair. So – what's occurring?'

He stretched his little limbs, hopped out of the trunk and followed Hannah up the path. Hannah was about to tell him to be careful, but realized Aunt Zo and her dad wouldn't be able to see him anyway.

Her dad spotted her passing the kitchen, however. 'Where have you been?'

'Um, checking if Granddad's friend wanted a coffee.'

'That was kind.' Hannah realized just how much she loved

him, and that she didn't want to have to lie to him many times in her life. 'Does he?'

'He's good,' she said, and then realized this was, strictly speaking, if not a lie then certainly a very inaccurate statement. 'I mean, he doesn't.'

She ran up the stairs, the imp scampering after. When they got to her room Granddad was still examining the door. He looked more serious. 'Getting this frame off would take me quite a while,' he said. 'Imp – how dextrous are you?'

'Dextrous?' the imp said. '*Dextrous?* Ha. You have no idea, mate. I'm thinking of getting a second name, just so I can put Dextrous in between them. I'd go as far as to say that if you was to ask any given imp or demon about my finest qualities, possibly even the big man himself, *dextrous* would be the first word that sprang to their minds. Some would probably go as far as to say I am super-dextrous. Or *ultra*-dextrous. The Dextrous One, they call me.'

'Seriously?'

'No. To be absolutely honest, I'm not a hundred per cent sure what it means. Bit like "treacherous", is it?'

'I need to get this door off.'

'Oh,' said the imp. 'Why didn't you say? Stand back.'

The imp stuck out his short arms, waggled his fingers, and breathed in deeply, eyes bulging.

There was the sound of footsteps running up the stairs.

'Don't,' said a voice. It was the Devil. His face was stern.

'What's going on?' Hannah's dad had come to see what was happening. Aunt Zo hurried up behind him, making the hallway rather crowded.

The Devil stood in front of Hannah's door. He took in the frame at a glance. 'Stand back, if you would.'

Everybody took a step back. The Devil raised his hands, palms upwards, as if about to accept a tray. He blinked.

Hannah felt a shiver at the base of her skull, as though something small and insectlike with sharp little feet had run into her ear and tunnelled into the back of her brain.

Nothing happened for a moment.

Then all three pieces of doorframe fell off.

Granddad grasped the handle with one hand and supported the door with the other. 'Ready?' he said.

The Devil nodded, and Granddad took a careful step back, pulling the door with him and tilting it towards the wall to reveal what lay beyond.

Hannah's dad's voice was a whisper. 'What on *earth* is that?'

Hannah knew, and knew also that it was not something of the earth. She'd seen it before at the bottom of a crevasse in the permafrost of Siberia, a thousand miles from anywhere.

It was the gate to Hell.

PART 3

There are heroes of evil, as well as good.

— La Rochefoucauld
Maxims

Chapter 33

An odour came off the gate. Acrid but insidious, the kind of smell that would pick your pocket rather than rob you at gunpoint. The heavy iron gate barred the doorway, securely fixed into the walls either side. The light was better here than it had been at the bottom of the crevasse in Siberia, and you could see how battered the gate was – as if someone or many someones had crashed into it over countless millennia, hurling themselves against it in a vain attempt to escape. You also understood how inconceivably old it was. A faint mist hung about the end of the hall, and the gate's surface was matted with tiny beads of condensation, as if it stood on a lonely moor.

The gaps between its bars revealed the room beyond. Hannah dropped to her hands and knees and saw that the machine had disappeared from under her bed. There was a phone lying on the carpet nearby.

'That's Mom's,' she said dismally. 'Isn't it?'

The phone's screen was shattered. It was surrounded by small bits and pieces of machinery.

The Devil flattened his hand and inserted it into the slot in the gate. He turned it, and the gate opened.

'Wait here,' he said.

He stepped into the room, slowly, carefully, his eyes passing over every corner, his nostrils twitching. When he'd inspected the space thoroughly – even looking thoughtfully up at the ceiling for a while – he gestured Granddad in with his head.

Granddad walked gingerly into the room. Vaneclaw followed, also looking extremely cautious.

'Hmm,' Granddad said.

Hannah saw him looking at her bookcase. The 'sculpture' he'd adjusted before they went to Big Sur wasn't there any more. That was where the cogs and wheels scattered over the floor must have come from, when someone or something had utterly destroyed it.

'How powerful was that device?' the Devil asked.

'A complete barrier to anything below an elder sleepdemon,' Granddad said. 'And after the adjustment I made earlier, it would have slowed down anything up to third bar soulcutter. For it to have been destroyed this comprehensively . . . that's not encouraging. It suggests one of the Fallen was here, or else a person acting with their sanction, to whom they have loaned great force.'

Hannah's dad pushed past Aunt Zo and picked the phone up from the floor. Hannah saw that her mother was no longer using the special case her dad had had made for it. He'd had it done online and it featured a picture of the three of them together on the deck of the Crow's Nest restaurant. She didn't like that her mom wasn't using it any more. Why would she stop? In case somebody saw it, someone who was only interested in Mom, not her and Dad?

Her father took the phone and started pressing things.

'Is it hers?'

'Think so,' he said. 'Well, it's the right model. I'd need to check the home screen to be certain, but it won't turn on.'

'It's dead,' Granddad said. 'The power unleashed in this

room will have fused the interior. The cracking of the screen
. . . that might suggest a struggle. Unless the change in temperature and pressure in this room was very large indeed, and
sudden, but if so . . . there would be other signs.'

'Like what?'

'Quite a large crater.'

'A struggle with – or between, or against – whom, exactly?'

Granddad shrugged awkwardly.

'O-K,' Hannah's dad said firmly. Hannah knew this tone.
It was the tone of voice that said it was time for her to stop
the avoidance tactics and focus on math homework, for fear
of YouTube bans of biblical severity. 'I'm done with the don't-
knows and receiving information in baby chunks, people. Just
tell me. What the hell is *going on?*'

Hannah and her grandfather looked helplessly at each other.

'So here's the deal, Steve-o,' Aunt Zo said breezily. 'Assuming
I've got this right, our father has been working for the elderly
gent in black for several hundred years. Said dude is, in fact,
the actual Devil.'

Hannah's dad frowned at her. 'Have they changed your
medication again?'

'Also, Granddad met Johann Sebastian Bach. And makes
machines that turn evil into electricity or something. Oh, and
there's an imp on the team who apparently looks like a big
fungus, but I can't see him and so presumably you can't either.'

'Fungus?' said Vaneclaw indignantly. 'That's just insulting.'

Hannah's father jumped, and looked around. 'Who said
that?'

'You can hear him, then,' Granddad murmured. 'Interesting.'

'And so what's the smell?'

Zo shrugged. 'I'm guessing that would be brimstone, bro.'

Hannah watched her father as he glared first at Zo, then
Granddad, then at the Devil. She was sufficiently familiar with

her dad and his imagination to know he wasn't going to do what people did in movies and shout that he couldn't *believe* it, he wasn't standing for this dashed nonsense, where are the hidden cameras, blah blah blah. Her dad was smart. He could see for himself that an eldritch iron gate had materialized in the doorway to his daughter's bedroom, and knew that she was unlikely to possess either the tools or patience to have installed it herself. He'd also heard a disembodied voice. His brain was wide enough to accept that something weird was going on, not merely reject it.

He was going to want to understand, though. Grown-ups always did, even when that only pushed the truth further away.

'Is this true?' he asked the Devil.

'Yes,' the Devil said.

'But so what happened to my . . . to Kristen?'

The Devil glanced at Granddad. 'Take him downstairs, Engineer. Explain enough to forestall further questions. We don't have time for them.'

'I'll tag along on that,' Aunt Zo said. 'Not absolutely sure I got all of it the first time around.'

Hannah started to follow them. 'No,' the Devil told her. 'Wait here.'

He waited until the others were out of earshot, then came and loomed over her. 'We passed through this gate once before, as I'm sure you recall.'

'I'm not going to forget in a hurry.'

'Tell me what you saw on the other side.'

'Don't you know?'

'That place is not mine to control. Everyone experiences something different. The gate transports each person to their own version of the Behind, constructed from their history and soul.'

'The Behind?'

'Another name for Hell, more accurate when the living are pulled into it. Reality has weakened in this house but it's still too strong for the gate to suck the structure in. But that could change if the Fallen gain control of the Sacrifice Machine. Tell me what you saw.'

'I was in a park.'

'A real park? One that exists in the world?'

Hannah nodded. 'Ocean View. It's on the east side of town, the other side of the river.'

'Did anything ever happen to you there, in real life? Something . . . very bad? Of which you have never spoken?'

'No. Never. It's a fun place. It was where I grew up a little.'

'In what manner?'

'I swung by myself for the first time.'

'You saw your mother there, in the Behind, yes?'

'Oh,' Hannah said quietly. 'Yes. Well, I think so. I couldn't see her face. She was shadows. It *seemed* like Mom. But it was as if I didn't really know who she was.'

She described what she'd seen up to the point where the bundle of tattered shadows had run past her to the end of the park, leaping into the cloud.

'And you felt as if she was trying to lure you?'

Hannah had only ever heard this word in connection with warnings regarding strangers offering too-good-to-be-true deals involving drives in their car. She didn't like hearing it in connection with her mother. She nodded nonetheless, and felt her eyes fill with tears. 'Is Mom . . . is she trying to hurt us?'

There was no reply. Hannah wiped her hand hurriedly across her eyes and looked up.

Her mom was standing in front of her.

She was wearing a dress she'd bought in Los Gatos that last time, in a green so dark it was nearly black. Hannah remembered

237

her showing it to Hannah and her dad in their favourite lunch place. Her mom's hair looked like she'd just come from the salon. She was wearing earrings. She was smiling.

But her eyes were dark. They were black in the centre, but the other part was black too, the bit that was usually blue.

'*Mom?*'

Mom didn't say anything. She cocked her head, smile fixed in place. She looked, Hannah realized, like a huge crow – a crow that had spotted a worm wriggling defencelessly on the ground.

A hungry crow. Or something worse. A dark, feral beast.

Hannah started backing away, her heart thumping . . . but then her mom wasn't there any more.

Just the Devil. 'An image from your mind,' he said. 'I dipped into it to try and get a sense of your vision of the park. What you just saw was only a reflection.'

'Of what?'

'The fear she's brought into your life.'

'But . . .'

'Your mother isn't evil,' he said. 'You can trust me on that assessment. It's what I do.'

'But . . .'

'Concentrate. I can only assume she has fallen into the Behind, dragging the machine with her.' He looked thoughtful for a moment. 'Unless it was the other way around – the machine tearing an edge to escape the clutches of the Fallen, or whichever agent of theirs came here tonight. It amounts to the same problem. She and the machine may be together.'

'What *are* the Fallen?'

'Bitter souls, once brutally strong – once triumphant but now lost. There is nothing more dangerous. If you were in that park, in real life, and you were to leap into the cloud you described, where would you go? If you flew in a straight line?'

Flustered, and scared, Hannah tried to think. 'The board-walk,' she realized. 'Yes. You can see it from there.'

'Hmm,' the Devil said, eyes distant. 'You rode on a machine there once with your grandfather, correct?'

'Yes – why? How do you know that?'

'He mentioned it a few days ago. Along with some suspicions he had concerning it. I wonder . . .'

He turned and walked quickly down the stairs in search of the Engineer. Hannah stayed where she was for a moment, and whispered a quiet message into the emptiness of her room.

Just in case anybody could hear.

Ten minutes later everyone was ready to go. Her father was standing by himself on the front lawn. Hannah went to him and slipped her hand into his.

'Are you OK?'

He looked down at her. 'I'm struggling to broaden my mind at a fast enough rate,' he admitted. 'And I'm worried about your mother. But otherwise, yes.'

'What did Granddad tell you?'

'What Zo said. But in more detail. He also told me about your adventures. You're up on me, pumpkin. I've never been to Russia. And he told me a little about this thing that's gone missing.'

'The Sacrifice Machine.'

'Right. But that's not how he explained it. He said it was more like a one-way pipe, to keep the power of bad things in the world flowing in the right direction, away from here to . . . some other place. That it's what keeps this world safe.'

'And . . . you believe him?'

He father shrugged. 'I guess so.'

'Do you *really*, Dad? I think . . . I think it's going to be important that you believe.'

'Really,' he said. 'He's my father, and if your father tells you something – however crazy – and appears to be serious, you should believe it. In this family, anyway.'

'So . . . when I was small and you told me lots of times there was a flock of wildebeests flying past my bedroom window, to get me to come upstairs because it was bedtime, but they'd always gone just before I got up there?'

'OK,' he admitted. 'Not that.'

The Devil came out of the house. 'Can I assume that you've been brought up to speed?'

'I believe so,' Hannah's father said. 'You're the Devil. And you've lost something my father made for you.'

'Both of those statements are true.'

'Not so much a *deus ex machina*, then, as a *deus sine machina*.'

'What?'

'A god . . . without a machine. It's Latin.'

The Devil stared at him. 'I know what it means. But do they *pay* you for that kind of thing?'

'Only intermittently.'

'I'm not surprised.'

'On the other hand,' Steve said, 'I haven't just mislaid the device that keeps the walls of reality in place against the howling void, so I guess we've both had better days?'

The Devil glared at him. 'It's time to go.'

Chapter 34

At first it all felt so familiar that Kristen didn't realize anything was wrong.

She was sprawled face down in a bed, in knickers and her sleeping T-shirt. The sheets smelled clean. There were lots of pillows. The bed was so luxuriously wide that when she stretched, none of her extremities poked off the edge. Cradled in that moment of just-awake, she felt rested and comfortable.

Then she frowned, and rolled over on to her back.

She was in a hotel room.

In itself that wasn't surprising. She spent a lot of time in hotel rooms. So much so that their standard layout – bed, nightstands, fancy lamps with non-obvious switches, desk that's never quite deep enough to actually work on, flat-screen TV, coffee maker, closets, bathroom with marble floor and heated towel rail and array of fancy unguents – felt like home.

But she shouldn't *be* in a hotel room. She should be at home – or the place that used to be home, at least. She'd *left* the London hotel, hadn't she? Got up in the small hours, booked a ticket, flown back to SJC and then cabbed to . . . yes. She had.

She remembered getting to the house in Santa Cruz and making coffee and noticing Steve had bought a different brand, wondering whether he'd always secretly preferred it or if he'd grabbed the jar in the market because it was right there or on offer, and in that beat of the unknown realizing how wide some of the gaps in her life had become. She remembered trying to get hold of him on the phone yet again.

But then . . . something else had happened.

Somebody had come. Men. She remembered running upstairs to try to get away from them. And then . . .

Blank.

She sat up.

So where the hell was this?

The walls were in one of those nameless pale hues that interior decorators think are soothing, and so she would have been hard pressed to say whether it was different or not – but the picture on the wall definitely didn't look the same. The proportions of the room were different, too.

The blinds on the wall were down.

Kristen got quickly out of bed and went to the window. The mechanism was awkward, and it took several seconds of fiddling to get one of the blinds to release. It zipped up with disconcerting speed.

She didn't recognize the view. It was night. There were big trees. A grassy area. A picnic bench. Swings. She couldn't place it immediately, though it felt familiar – enough to make her feel guilty and lost.

She turned back to the room, looking for more clues. Hurried to the desk. Her laptop was there. It was charging. She followed the cable with her eyes and saw it was plugged into the socket with an adaptor. The socket was one of the big ones they had in the UK, with the three stolid-looking rectangular holes.

So *was* this London after all? Just a different hotel?

But why would she be in a different hotel?

She went to the wall near the bathroom and flicked the light switch down. The light came on. That proved it. Lots of people didn't even realize in Europe you flipped a switch *down* to turn something on, rather than up, the way it was at home. Didn't matter how many times you got it wrong, it never quite internalized. A little beat of foreign.

That meant this *had* to be London . . . unless it was some other place in Europe where they had the same plugs. Germany maybe? She couldn't remember. It didn't matter. She shouldn't be here, wherever 'here' was. She should be in Santa Cruz, where light switches worked the way God intended.

She peered into the bathroom. It looked neither familiar nor unfamiliar. It could have been in America, Singapore or on Mars. Her wash-bag was not by the sink.

She looked in the closet. No clothes. No suitcase, not even her carry-on. An ironing board. A mini-fridge. Two robes. She grabbed one of these and wrapped it round herself.

The television blinked on.

She jumped. But they did that, sometimes. Tech-savvy hotels often had a wake-up system via the TV, with blaring sound and a big-ass time indicator that you could read from right across the room. Kristen had no recollection of setting this one, however. She never did. She used her phone like any normal person.

Images slid across the TV screen, generic stills supposed to convey how deeply cool it is to be here wherever you are, while not actually making it clear where that is. Street cafés, museums, boutiques, theatres, close-ups of expensive food, happy couples laughing in bars – until you spotted a recognizable landmark you could be anywhere: Paris, Chicago, Sydney.

But . . . in fact, she *did* recognize these images.

Twin Lakes Beach. Pacific Avenue downtown. The *board-walk*?

The screen was showing images of Santa Cruz. In London? Why the hell would they be doing that?

She reached for the phone. Stabbed the button to be put through to reception and waited, still watching the images on the screen. The harbour. The lighthouse. Big Sur.

The phone rang and rang.

Kristen put it down and strode to the door. Took off the chain and flipped the lock. Opened it, hoping the corridor beyond would help her remember where the hell she was.

It was dark out there. Not completely. A light flickered down the end. But too dark, nonetheless. Hotel corridors are always lit even in the dead of night, so weary travellers can find their way. Their light is eternal. Not this one.

She stepped cautiously out of the room.

The carpet felt thick and clammy under her bare feet. It was very quiet. The air was stifling, as always in hotel corridors, with their dead connective space. The hallways of nowhere. An environment no one ever lingers in. A place where you see strangers or no one at all.

She gently drew the door closed, letting it rest on the latch, remembering she hadn't brought her key. She turned towards the flickering light at the far-right end of the corridor.

It said 'EXIT'.

But that wasn't right, was it? She was sure the elevator was in the other direction. Though that was in the London hotel, of course, her usual one – and she wasn't even sure yet if that's where she was.

She headed for the light, passing closed doors. None had numbers on them. The carpet was covered in strange, intricate designs in gold and silver: cogs and wheels, like the insides of a weird machine. It didn't look familiar. None of it did.

Soon she was jogging, past door after door after door. She realized that part of her was expecting the corridor to suddenly stretch out, double or treble in length, but it did not. That only made it worse. That meant this wasn't a dream.

When she got to the end the 'EXIT' sign still flickered silently, but it was a lie. There was no door here. There was no way out. So why would you put up a sign? Why would you make it look like this was an escape, if all it did was trap you?

But it wasn't anybody else's fault, was it? She'd chosen to come this way. It was her fault.

All of this was her own stupid fault.

She could hear something now. It was quiet at first, then louder. She turned slowly towards the nearest room door. Like the others it was featureless, flat, dark wood. She reached out and touched it. It was smooth, cold. The sensation of the grain beneath her fingertips was absolutely real.

That confirmed this wasn't a dream, and so what she was hearing was probably real, too.

The sound of claws, scrabbling against the other side of the door. A dog? It'd have to be a big one.

A very big one. Or a . . .

Kristen backed away from the door – then turned and hurried down the corridor towards the darkness at the other end. Metal doors suddenly opened at the end, a sideways mouth leaking a sickly yellow glow. The elevator.

The way out. Thank God.

She ran in and reached out for the panel. There was only one button. It had a cross on it, upside down. She slapped at it and the doors immediately slammed shut.

The elevator dropped like a stone, flipping her stomach over. Then it stopped – so violently that she was almost thrown over. The doors opened.

She poked her head out cautiously. 'What the . . .'

She stepped out into a cold, grey space. The flat echo of her voice told her it was low-ceilinged, large, though she could only see a small portion of it. It smelled of concrete.

Then she recognized where she was, and finally knew this was her London hotel after all. That this parking lot was, anyway. Because over there was the spot where, standing by his car after a long meeting that had turned into drinks and then that first dinner in the Bella Mare, she'd first kissed someone.

The man for whom she'd upturned her life.

There was no car there now. No cars anywhere. The garage was empty. Cold and dead and silent. Except for . . .

Two figures were standing right at the point where the light faded into shadow. One tall, the other shorter. A woman and a child, their backs to her, holding hands.

Kristen took a faltering step towards them. '*Hannah?*'

Her daughter turned her head. Her face was sad but resigned.

'What did you *think* was going to happen, Mom?'

They stepped forward into the darkness and disappeared.

Chapter 35

Everywhere has an underside, and Santa Cruz has dark notes in its past. The city tends to keep quiet on the subject, naturally, focusing upon more cheerful things like surfing and the wharf and the fact that the town would make a super-convenient place for rich folks from Silicon Valley to come and live, and so they should do that, now, and bring all their money. Such locales attract darkness like a sticky thing attracts dust, however, like a former hotel on Beach Hill, a Victorian mansion where at least one murder has taken place and which also provided a home to one of two serial killers operating in the area in the early 1970s. The hotel has now been converted to an assisted-living facility, and while nothing notably appalling has happened there for many years a peep inside the dreams of its residents would confirm that the shadows there remain liquid and strong. It's the kind of place where the Devil himself would stay.

Nash found himself led elsewhere, however.

The town first came into being because a bunch of Spanish soldiers happened upon the San Lorenzo River and thought it looked nice. Mission Santa Cruz was established on a bluff a mile back from the ocean. The mission then immediately got on with doing what missions did, namely encouraging the local Indians to work for the church and become Christians, primarily through destroying everything they had previously valued. Many died in the process, and the rest suffered terribly. All missions have dark stains within them but Santa Cruz's was worse than most – so very bad that the Indians eventually rose up and slew the padre in charge: for which, naturally, they were then slain in turn.

Most of their bodies were unceremoniously buried in a patch of land on the other side of the area where they were forced to work the land, right at the edge of the bluff. This area is now a park, though not a popular one, as though people can sense what happened there.

And that was the place to which Nash found himself drawn.

They left the truck in front of the reconstruction of the mission building, and Nash carried the battered old suitcase. It was very heavy, but Nash was strong – and stronger tonight than ever before. Jesse and the others had long ago stopped trying to understand what was going on, and were simply doing whatever their boss told them.

Nash walked out into the middle of the park, which was cold and dark. He put down the suitcase, backed away a few steps, and lit a cigarette. The others did the same.

After a few minutes they noticed that as it drifted out across the park, their smoke was swirling around shapes, revealing where things stood.

Invisible things. Creeping towards them.

'Who's there?'

There was no audible response to Nash's question, but the temperature was dropping. It was getting noticeably colder. Eduardo shivered.

'Boss,' Jesse said. 'I'm not—'

'Quiet.'

Then suddenly something was in front of them, about ten feet away, on the other side of the suitcase.

Nash frowned. To him, the figure looked like Jesse's grandmother. The random woman he'd killed during his first robbery, when he'd been young and very scared but trying to look tough and do what was expected by the older guys who'd broken him into the life. He didn't know how the others saw it, but he heard sharp intakes of breath, as if they were also seeing something that cut them to the quick – reflections of events in their own lives that had changed or ashamed them.

Then it morphed into a figure in a dark cloak.

Nash dimly understood this wasn't its true form either, but an averaging out of all the ways it had been seen over thousands of years. Humans need something to look at, a direction to speak in. That's all it was. It wasn't alone. Nash could dimly glimpse more of them now, standing in a wide circle around them. There was an odd smell, like a pack of wild animals.

The one closest spoke. Its voice was deep and unpleasant. 'Who are you?'

'Nash.'

'That's your name, which is immaterial to us. I asked who you *are*.'

'You know who. You called. I came right the way across the country because you chose me.'

'No. Our thoughts went out across the land in every direction. I wonder why you heard us more clearly than most?'

Nash shrugged. So far as he was concerned the answer was obvious. He was badass. 'I—'

'No,' it said. 'Prior misdeeds will not have been enough.'

Suddenly it was closer to him. The other guys flinched. Nash managed to keep still, and stared back at where there should have been a face.

'I smell angel on you.'

'I don't think so,' Nash said.

'It is so. You have been in the presence recently.'

'Trust me, there are no angels where I'm from. The . . .' Nash hesitated. 'Though something weird did happen. A few days ago. An old guy. Wearing a black suit. He said . . .'

'. . . that he was the Devil.'

'How do you know that?'

The being appeared to turn its head towards the others. Jesse – who, like the other guys, was so scared that he was having trouble breathing – understood that this action was an illusion, that he was merely seeing what he expected to see, interpreting something utterly inhuman in human ways.

The other beings nodded.

The one close to Nash, the angel named Zhakq – who had always known what the Devil had taunted him with in Big Sur, that he regarded him as least amongst the Fallen, a terrible cut to his pride that had curdled and twisted inside him for millennia – turned its face or attention back to him.

'You work for us now.'

Nash didn't generally work for people. People worked for Nash. On this occasion, however, he didn't bother to disagree. 'OK. But this thing.' He gestured towards the suitcase. 'What is it?'

'A machine. We have done what we can from a distance – preventing the device from channelling power from here into Hell, so that instead it pools here on Earth. That has weakened the Devil, and doubtless even you will have felt how in the last few years this planet has become a darker place. That much we have already achieved. Now we desire to take the final step, reversing the direction of its flow entirely.'

'And filling the world with shit.'

'Precisely. I'm glad the symbolism of that event during your journey was not lost upon you. Humans always benefit from being given simple images to comprehend.'

'OK, well, it's here. Knock yourself out.'

'It is not that simple.'

Suddenly the being was right next to the suitcase. Its arm moved, so that its hand – if there had been one – should have touched the top of it. That didn't happen, however. It passed straight through as though the suitcase wasn't there.

'The dark one is cunning,' the Fallen Angel said. 'He engaged a human hand in the design and construction of the device, tainting it with the rigours of the flesh. Because of that, its workings are obscured to us. We in turn require a human hand in order to pervert it. That hand shall be yours.'

'What do you want me to do?'

'Break it.'

Nash smiled, slowly. This he could do.

Except he couldn't.

Half an hour later, he and the other men were standing around the suitcase. All were sweating from exertion. Most had aches in their hands and feet. But whatever they'd tried – from attempting to open the case, to punching and kicking and banging it with rocks, up to throwing it off the roof of the mission building – had achieved nothing.

They couldn't get the thing open, much less destroy it.

The Fallen Angels had stood silent and motionless during this process. Eventually Zhakq spoke.

'The protection is strong,' it said. 'The human who built this did his work even better than we feared. Until it's open, it cannot be reversed, that is clear.'

'So now what?'

'We require that Engineer. Either him, or someone of the same blood, a person whose flesh tastes the same.'

'You want us to go back to that house and wait?'

'No. They are not there now. We sense the location of the Devil, and they will be where he is.'

'Where's that?'

The being slowly raised one arm.

Nash looked in the direction it was pointing. From this high elevation you could see right out across the town that had grown up on the river plain below, the lights of human habitation. And at the far extent, where the land met the sea, the looming bulk of a funfair at the beach.

'We will go into the Behind,' the being said. 'In case they try to escape there from us. Meanwhile you will find the Engineer and cause him to open the machine.'

'And what if he won't?'

'Break him. But destroy those he loves first.'

Chapter 36

They all went in Steve's car. It was after midnight and the streets were empty apart from those people who are always walking or driving somewhere, who knew where, who knew why. Hannah had wondered sometimes – when she'd glimpsed them sleepily while being driven home from a grown-ups' party – if they were forever in motion, wandering the streets on feet or wheels, tracing some dark and uncertain web only they could see; wondered too what they did in the daytime, or if they only ever came out in darkness – if they were in fact in some way *part* of the night. She realized that the person (or being, or thing) sitting silently in the passenger seat of her father's car might know, but she didn't ask. Never ask questions if you might not want to know the answers, lest you are pulled into those stories and the truths they reveal. Sometimes ignorance is better. It would probably not be so popular otherwise.

Her father drove quickly through downtown and to the front. If Santa Cruz is an island, the boardwalk is an island within an island. It stretches almost the entire width of a beach between two headlands, half a mile long, with a gap at the northern end yielding access to the wharf, which stretches out into the bay. In front of this had once been a motley spread of cheap motels and vacation bungalows, but most of these are gone, razed into a vast parking lot to hold the summer crowds. Behind the lot is a big hill, with houses, which cuts all this off from downtown.

The boardwalk stood dark.

The parking lot was closed, so Hannah's father found a spot up a road nearby. 'I still don't get why we're here,' he said as they all got out.

Nobody answered. The Devil and Granddad set off quickly, Vaneclaw trotting after. They were the people who understood things (with the likely exception of the imp). Dad and Aunt Zo followed – the people who did not.

Hannah found herself somewhere in between.

The boardwalk is anchored at one end by a large building that was a casino and swimming baths and now holds slot machines and laser tag and conference rooms. Spaced along the landward side are structures holding the rides and attractions. There are fences between these, and entry gates. These were locked, of course, but Granddad was able to rapidly overcome this. There were signs all over the fences saying that the place was guarded by security.

'Won't someone hear?'

'No,' the Devil said. He did not elaborate.

They slipped inside and headed out into the promenade. On a summer's afternoon this would be packed with families from San Jose and Watsonville and Gilroy, stuffing themselves with corn dogs and garlic fries, about as cheerful and boisterous a scene as you could imagine. Hannah thought that as it was now, after midnight in October and deserted, it was like creeping into the body of someone who was so deeply asleep you'd need a doctor to tell you they hadn't actually died.

They walked the entire length, right to the end where there was a section of rides for smaller kids.

'What's that?' Zo hissed suddenly.

A man was lying on the ground near the mini-golf, flat on his back, arms outstretched. He was wearing a dark blue uniform. 'Security,' the Devil said.

'Is he . . .'

'Sleeping.' He turned to Granddad. 'Are you confident this mechanism will take us to the Behind?'

'I believe it was actually built for the role, by someone whose name and purpose is now lost. Whether it's still capable of performing it . . . that's a totally different question.'

'Lead on, Engineer. Quickly.'

Granddad took them back along the promenade, and before long Hannah realized where he was taking them.

The rollercoaster.

The Giant Dipper on the Santa Cruz Beach Boardwalk was built in 1924, making it the fifth oldest in the United States. Its tangled half-mile of track is constructed predominantly of wood, and tolerates – barely – speeds of up to fifty-five miles an hour along the fastest stretches.

Hannah knew all this (and she'd once known how many rivets it had too, but had forgotten, though she thought it was about twenty-one billion) because while you stood in line there was a video telling you. She remembered Granddad muttering that being informed it was the fifth *youngest* in the country might be more appealing at this stage. They'd climbed on when their turn came, nonetheless, side by side in one of its six blue carriages, each of which held four passengers. The two ladies in front had been nearly as old as Granddad, and said they'd been riding the Dipper every year since they were kids of Hannah's age. This was mildly reassuring, but then

255

as they'd been ratcheted up to the top of the first drop, Hannah experienced an abrupt change of heart, blurting that she'd changed her mind and would like to get off, immediately, like, urgently, totally *right now*.

Granddad had grasped the bar across their laps, and – looking serene and resigned – said that wasn't possible. All they could do was hold tight and go through with it.

She remembered almost nothing about the ride apart from violent creaking and flashing speed and getting her knees banged on turns which threw you around like a car crash. That, and screaming until her throat was hoarse.

When they had emerged at the other end, exhilarated but shaken, Granddad turned to her, somewhat pale, and asked if she'd enjoyed the experience.

'No,' Hannah said. It had scared her witless.

'Nor me,' Granddad said. He'd been looking up at the track towering above them with an odd expression on his face. 'Let's never do that again.'

And yet here they were, walking towards it.

Granddad led them to an area at the side where a door was discreetly inset into the wooden panelling, near the window where you could buy photos of yourself being terrified on the ride you'd just endured. This door had a 'NO ENTRY' sign on it.

After a minute's work with one of the endless series of tools he seemed to have secreted about his person, Granddad had it unlocked. The interior thus revealed was dark and shadowy. Granddad peered around to get his bearings, then set off in the direction of the machinery.

'I know I'm sounding like a broken record,' Hannah's dad asked, 'but *what are we doing here?*'

'Steve?' Granddad called from deep in the shadows of the machine. 'Come here a moment, would you?'

Hannah followed her father towards the sound of Granddad's voice. When they found him, he was experimentally moving levers and dials on some kind of control panel. The panel was old and battered and looked like the kind of thing you might find on an ancient tractor, rusting in a field, rather than something that governed the movement of the edifice that ducked and rolled high over their heads. On one side was a long lever.

'Could you see if you can move that?'

Hannah's dad grabbed the end. He tugged. It resisted for a moment but then rotated downward.

'Excellent,' Granddad said as he started to undo screws on the front of the panel. 'In which case, that's going to be your job. I couldn't even get it to budge.'

'Dad,' Steve said, 'what are you about to do?'

'Ever wondered what rollercoasters are for?'

'People ride them, get scared, go eat tacos.'

Granddad lifted off the panel. A tangle of wires and cogs lay beyond. He reached into his jacket for glasses, put them on, and peered into the chaos. 'That's what they *became*, yes. And of course, the ones they're building now, that's all they're for. Most people don't know the original purpose.'

'Which was . . .?'

'Why do you think people enjoy riding them?'

'No idea. Personally, I don't.'

'They enjoy it because they *feel* something. It's scary, yes, and thrilling too. But it can also make them experience . . . something else. A rollercoaster constructed in the correct way, with precisely the right twists and turns and rises and falls, running at a very particular speed . . . it can get behind.'

'Behind what?'

'That's very hard to explain. Aha.' Granddad reached into the jumble of wires towards a small dial, placed so deep inside that it looked as if it had been hidden.

The Devil appeared at his shoulder. 'Does that confirm its original purpose?'

'Yes. It doesn't prove it's still up to the job.'

'That's a risk we're going to have to take.'

'Wait,' Hannah's dad said. 'Whoa, hold on. We're not getting *on* this thing?'

'You're not, no,' Granddad said. 'That lever you pulled is the fail-safe. It will halt the entire machine quickly. And . . . hopefully safely.'

'I don't like the word "hopefully",' Steve said. 'It's especially not-good in this context.'

'It's the best I've got. We're going to stand here – me operating the controls, you with your hand on the lever. If I tell you to pull it . . . pull it. Right away.'

'No *way*,' Hannah's dad said very firmly, turning to the Devil. 'Hannah is *not* getting on this thing. Are you out of your *mind*?'

The Devil raised an eyebrow. 'I have no idea what the question means. Hannah must ride the machine. We need the strength of her bond to her mother.'

'But you don't *care* about Kristen,' Aunt Zo said, walking out of the shadows. Her arms were folded. 'Only about your machine. You think the two of them are together. This is nothing to do with Kristen. Not for you.'

'True. But for now, our interests coincide.'

'This is *not* happening,' Hannah's dad said. 'Think—'

'Steve,' Granddad said. 'He's right, I'm afraid. What we found at the house points in only one direction. This is the only feasible means of quickly getting to where it appears the machine and Kristen may have gone. There's no choice, and meanwhile she is in very great danger. The world, too.'

'So we call the police.'

'They can do nothing except waste precious time. This is our only option, I promise.'

Hannah's father swore and bit his lip.

She could tell that he really, *really* didn't want this to go ahead – but that he was remembering what he'd said to her: *if your father tells you something, then you should try to believe it.* She could tell also that he was starting to realize that his own father had more tricks up his sleeve than he'd ever imagined. 'It'll be OK,' she told him.

'I don't *know* that,' he said. 'How can I? Dad – what are you actually going to do?'

'Not much,' Granddad said. 'Just make it go a little faster.'

'*Faster?*'

'At fifty miles an hour, this is a rollercoaster. At higher speeds it becomes something else.'

'Yes – a rickety old antique that could tear itself apart.'

'It shouldn't,' Granddad said, with less than 100 per cent confidence. 'It looks quite well maintained.'

'To run at its *normal speed.*'

'There's no time for discussion,' the Devil told Steve. 'I can make it so that you are unable to intervene, but your father urged me to give you the chance to make a choice. I have honoured the Engineer's request, but I'm losing patience and we're running out of time.'

'I'll come too,' Aunt Zo said.

'But you hate rollercoasters,' Hannah said.

'I surely do. But I'll go with you.'

Hannah's father stared at her. 'But how does that help, Zo? It just means if this thing blows apart I've lost even more.'

'Dad says it's not going to,' Zo said. 'I believe him. And when . . . whatever happens, happens, I'll be with her.'

'We have to find Mom, Dad,' Hannah said, near tears. 'We *have* to. *Now*. And this is the only thing there is to try.'

Her father tried to find one further argument. 'OK, so, tell me this – what are we supposed to say if the cops hear the racket and turn up and ask what the heck we're up to?'

The man in the black suit winked. 'Tell them the Devil made you do it.'

Chapter 37

Aunt Zo found an interior doorway that led to the stairs to the embarking point for the rollercoaster, high above. She, Hannah, the Devil and Vaneclaw hurried to the top together.

There was silence as they stood on the platform, then a distant clanking from below. After a minute the carriages juddered into view from a side chamber.

The Devil indicated for Hannah to get in the front of the first, next to him. Aunt Zo got in behind, with Vaneclaw. The protective bar dropped into their laps.

Suddenly they were going forwards. For the first fifteen seconds they moved at moderate speed through a dark area, banking left and then emerging into the outside air. Hannah remembered from last time how the carriages chugged slowly up the first slope, before plummeting almost immediately.

Her stomach turned over in anticipation. There was a clackety-clackety sound as they were winched higher and higher and higher, and then there they were, right at the very top, the front of their carriage nosing out into the cold night air, the mouth of the San Lorenzo River visible quite some distance below, glinting in the moonlight.

'Dear God,' Aunt Zo said, very quietly.

'Wicked,' cackled Vaneclaw. 'Bring it *on*.'

And then it happened. The carriage teetered over the edge and was suddenly in rapid downward movement, feeling like a mistake. Just when you'd started to adapt to this it made a wrenching turn to the left, then right, then left again – after which it basically went nuts: up and down and left and right, hectic, ear-dunning downward clattering punctuated by brief periods of unpleasant suspense as the carriage sailed higher, in preparation for another vertiginous drop.

Hannah gripped the bar with all her might, trying to decide whether having her eyes open or shut was less terrifying. Eyes open meant you could see how high you were above the boardwalk, which wasn't good; but closing them meant you got no warning of the next abrupt turn, which felt like you'd left your stomach behind and might never see it again. It was *all* very loud and very fast and very scary. It went on for two dreadful minutes, though felt *so* much longer.

And then suddenly they slowed. The carriage pulled back into the interior, still decelerating. The ride was finished. The carriage stopped at the platform with a jerk. Aunt Zo made a quiet, unhappy noise.

Vaneclaw was bouncing up and down. 'Again! Again!'

The protective bar flipped up. Hannah looked at the Devil. His eyes were narrowed and thoughtful. 'Did you see anything?'

She shook her head. 'Though . . . there was one turn, right up high, where . . .'

'What?'

'I'm not sure. I had my eyes shut, and you know how it's dark and sparkly in your head when you do that? For a moment it seemed . . . it was much lighter, I think. Like a flash of white.'

'Probably brain cells getting crushed against the insides of your skull,' Aunt Zo muttered. 'May I get out now? There's a reasonably high chance I'm going to barf.'

'I saw that too,' the Devil told Hannah. 'Vaneclaw?'

'Boss?'

'*Explosively,*' Aunt Zo insisted.

The Devil ignored her. 'Go to the Engineer, imp. Tell him to turn it up.'

'Turn it *up*?' Zo shouted. 'Are you *insane*?'

'Awesome!' The imp hopped out, hooting with glee, and went haring away into the darkness.

They sat in silence but for quiet moaning sounds from Aunt Zo, who evidently really didn't feel well. Then they heard the sound of tiny feet pattering back up the wooden stairs.

'Her dad's not happy,' he said as he jumped back into the carriage. 'The Engineer neither. He said he'd put it up two more notches, but that's your lot. He won't vouch for it after that.'

'Then we shall have to hope it's enough,' the Devil said.

Three minutes later the clanking started, and the bar came back down. The prospect of doing the ride again made Hannah feel very scared indeed, but she knew she had no choice, and that if this was the only way to save her mom then she'd do it as many times as it took. As the carriage started to clunk its way up the first rise, Hannah saw Aunt Zo gripping on to the bar as if her life depended on it. Her face was pale.

'I never liked you,' Zo told her with a wan smile. 'And I'm never coming to Santa Cruz *ever again.*'

And then it felt like some giant reached down, picked the carriage up and *threw* it.

The increase in speed was very noticeable. When you're on a rollercoaster you often fear it's going too quickly, that centrifugal force and crafty design surely can't be enough to keep you on a narrow track when you're going *so* fast, that the clanking and thumps that come at you like a swarm of random bees mean the whole thing's going to fly apart. You tell yourself that's the point of the enterprise, that's why these things are supposed to be fun, and the idea may be reassuring.

But when you *know* the contraption's been hotwired to go at far greater than usual speed, there is no reassurance to be found.

We're going to die, you think.

Right here, right now.

Squish, splat.

The carriage flew up and down and around and back so fast this time that the big drops didn't seem that much scarier than the shorter ones. It was *all* dreadful, and after thirty seconds Hannah started to notice the framework making creaking sounds that definitely hadn't happened the last time.

'Oh crap,' Aunt Zo moaned. 'Oh . . . crap on a *stick*.'

Faster and faster it went, picking up yet more speed until its velocity started to feel wrong and utterly out of kilter with the possible. Hannah went from scared to very scared to flat-out terrified, unable even to see, head and body thrashed from side to side, eyeballs juddering in their sockets. She began to fear that Aunt Zo had been right, and the only question was whether her brain would burst before her neck snapped.

The carriage soared and ducked, sometimes lost in the tangle of tracks, at others points flying above it on a line high above the boardwalk. As it hurtled up to the top of the highest of these, Hannah discerned a new sound, hard to disentangle first from the mechanical cacophony all around her, but then clear as a bell.

It was a siren.

It was coming from ahead, but then the carriage smacked into another hairpin bend. Hannah wrenched herself round in the seat and saw that way down below, on the street that came from downtown, a police car was driving very fast towards the boardwalk, lights flashing, siren blaring.

Her dad had been right. Someone had called the cops. So now what? Were they all going to get arrested?

Right at that moment the carriage hurtled through the high and viciously banking turn where Hannah thought she'd seen a flash of light on the first ride – and in that instant, jerked for a moment out of experiencing the ride, her mind was slapped sideways. A combination of speed and sudden change in direction – and other dark forces that even Granddad didn't properly understand – ripped a temporary edge in the world, a gap that led to the Behind.

The flash of white light was very bright this time.

And then . . .

Chapter 38

. . . it was very cold.

Chillingly, oh-my-God cold. So very and extremely cold that the first thing Hannah thought was they'd somehow flown off the track and been flung all the way back to Siberia.

It was also pitch-dark.

She could hear, or feel, a faint humming. When she sniffed against the cold – which was so acute it started settling into her bones immediately – the sound was flat, as if she was enclosed. She felt around with her hands and determined that she was sitting on some kind of surface, in the exact same position as she had been in the carriage of the rollercoaster.

She stood, carefully, grateful not to have the coldness in such direct contact with her butt. Then she realized something was right behind her. She let out a shriek and jumped away.

'Hannah? Is that you?' It was Aunt Zo's voice. She sounded notably freaked out.

'Yes! Is that you?'

'I hope so. I mean, yes. Where . . . where are we?'

'I don't know. Siberia, maybe?'

'*What?*'

Hannah reached for her aunt's hand. When she had it, she

felt a little better. Zo's hand was just as cold as her own, though. Being this cold couldn't be good for them.

She turned back in the direction she'd been facing and felt in front with her other hand. It flapped about in space. She shuffled a small step forwards. Finally her fingers touched something. It was cold and smooth. It felt like metal.

'We're inside something,' she said.

She could hear Zo's fingers swishing as they moved around on the walls too. Then they stopped. 'Can you hear something?'

'Just you,' Hannah said. 'Why?'

'Shh.'

After a moment Hannah realized Aunt Zo was right. She could hear faint voices, and an occasional clang. 'What *is* that?'

'I don't know,' Zo said, sounding disconcerted.

'We have to get out of here.' Hannah's teeth had started to chatter. 'We have to go find Mom. Right now.'

'I'm going to try pushing. See if I can get this thing to open. It feels like there's some give.'

'OK.'

Aunt Zo pushed. Hannah could hear the sound of her straining against it. There was a loud *clunk*, and then a strip of light going from the floor to about six inches above her head.

The noise they'd heard was suddenly louder. It sounded like people talking and shouting – not as if they were angry, just busy. More clanks. And a hiss, as though something very hot had been put in cold water. More clattering, and voices.

Hannah suddenly knew where she'd heard this collection of sounds before. Right after they'd first entered Hell through the gate in Siberia. But what did that mean?

Zo gently pushed the metal door. 'It's heavy,' she said. She pushed harder – and it suddenly swung open.

Revealing a hectic kitchen.

Aunt Zo teetered forwards. Hannah followed. She looked back and saw a tall, shiny metal door hanging open. The space they'd emerged from was filled with neatly stacked piles and boxes of fruit and lettuce and steaks. It looked like the fridge at home when Dad had just got back from going nuts in CostCo.

'What the good goddamned *hell* are you doing here?'

A fat man in a buttoned-up white jacket was standing furiously in front of Aunt Zo, hands aggressively on his hips.

'Um,' Zo said. She couldn't for the moment come up with an explanation for where they were – in the middle of a large, frantically busy kitchen. Lots of people, most of them Latino and almost all men, rushed back and forth with pans and plates, or stood at stoves banging things, enveloped in steam and heat and rich cooking smells.

'Looking for the bathroom,' Hannah said quickly.

The man poked his sweaty face down towards her. Thinning hair was plastered to his scalp and he looked both furious and pleased at being furious, as if in his ideal world he'd be paid to be furious for a living. 'The *bathroom*?'

'We took a wrong turning,' Zo said.

The man bellowed at one of the cooks toiling nearby. 'Hey, Pez – this look like the *bathroom* to you, huh?'

'No, chef.'

'Sorry,' Hannah said.

'Go,' the man shouted, pointing imperiously. '*Go!*'

Hannah and Aunt Zo hurried away through clouds of rich-smelling steam and past smirking cooks and washers. At the end of the room they found a pair of swinging doors. They went through and into the relative calm of a corridor.

Then they were in a restaurant. 'OK,' said Zo, bewildered, 'this is . . . *what*?'

268

The dining room was spacious and had big windows, yielding views on to ornamental trees in dappled sunlight. It was crowded, tables and booths filled with people eating and drinking and chatting, all in couples or groups apart from one old lady with long grey hair sitting happily by herself, everyone attended to by willowy waitpersons in sage-coloured uniforms and neatly starched white aprons. The ambience was just so. The plates on which the food stood poised were needlessly large and modishly rectangular.

It looked very nice. Upmarket and expensive. It looked . . .

'I know where this is,' Hannah said. They ground to a halt near the centre of the room. 'It's Bistrotechnical. In Los Gatos.'

'Los . . . are you serious?'

Hannah totally recognized it now. This was where they used to come for lunch. The place with the pastries. The restaurant where she'd seen her mom staring into the far distance, as if—

''Scuse me, ladies . . .'

A waiter shoved past, carrying a tray loaded with entrées. Aunt Zo watched him go, baffled. Hannah grabbed her hand and led her towards the lobby, where a smartly dressed lady was standing behind the desk. Hannah had known exactly where it would be, which proved it. This was definitely Bistrotechnical, a name she'd found hard to remember until her dad explained that it was a play on words, something to do with French restaurants and discos and Los Gatos's proximity to Silicon Valley, and in his opinion the person who'd come up with it should be forced to go and stand in the corner until they were sorry for what they'd done, even if that took a thousand years.

'So . . . how did we get to Los Gatos? That's like . . . thirty *miles* from Santa Cruz, right? And how can it be daytime?'

'I don't know how,' Hannah admitted. The woman behind

the desk was smiling at them with big bright eyes. 'But the rollercoaster put us here. So maybe this is where Mom is.'

Aunt Zo spotted the big doors at the end of the lobby. 'Let's go outside and look there.'

'Good idea.'

They hurried down to the doors and banged through them into the wide, friendly stone-paved square. Except it wasn't there.

They emerged instead into trees. Not small, pretty trees like the ones visible through the windows in the restaurant, but massive, serious trees. They were slap in the middle of a deep redwood forest.

They looked back at the restaurant. In Los Gatos it was part of a block of buildings which had either been restored from old ones or artfully built to look that way. Now it stood by itself, the edges of the building jagged, as if it had been torn from its position and placed here in the forest. There were redwoods right up against the walls, so tall that they reached up until they became lost in the canopy far above. The forest stretched away forever in all directions. There were no roads or paths.

'This is not . . . working for me,' Aunt Zo said.

They went back into the building. 'Can I help you?' the girl behind the desk asked immediately.

'Um, we're good,' Hannah said. 'But I'm looking for my mom. Have you seen her?'

'No,' the girl said. She was somehow managing to keep smiling while she talked. Her grin was so wide it looked weird. 'I have seen no moms. You have a *great* day.'

'I don't need a great day,' Aunt Zo muttered, 'just one I can understand.'

The dining room was even busier than before, and noisier.

Everyone was talking and laughing at the same time, so much so that it seemed hard to believe anyone was actually listening. The waiters and waitresses were darting between tables so quickly they were nearly running. Hannah noticed that a few of the people at the tables looked anxious and pale.

They hurried past a line of booths filled with people laughing raucously. Hannah saw an old man picking up great gobbets of Shrimp Louis salad – the entrée her dad always had when they came here – with his hands, instead of a fork, and pushing it into his mouth. Pink dressing was dripping down his wrists and into the sleeves of his jacket. A couple of tables along, a thin woman, the age that moms are, tipped a huge glass up to her mouth. She kept tipping and tipping until red wine started to spill out either side of the glass, pouring down her cheeks and on to her blouse. She didn't stop. She kept tipping.

'I don't like this.'

'Me neither,' said Aunt Zo.

They hurried through the swing doors back into the kitchen and started into the billowing vapour, looking for a path towards the refrigerator. There was a smell of burning now – like sometimes happened at home when Dad or Mom got distracted and forgot something under the broiler and it started smoking and the alarm went off, at which point whichever of them *hadn't* been cooking would always make the same joke: 'Dinner's ready.'

Back then. Back when there were jokes.

It was hot, too, *really* hot, and as they made their way through the chaos Hannah caught glimpses of cooks, looming out of the steam like tall ships in a mist. The cooks were all very big, with huge muscles in their bare and tattooed arms, and they looked down at her in a way that made her feel . . . hunted. Inspected too hard and too long and for reasons she didn't understand. She didn't like it. She wanted to be . . .

'Ha!'

Aunt Zo skidded to a halt. Hannah crashed into her.

'And theeeeeeere you are,' the chef crowed. He was blocking the way. He was also holding a large cleaver.

'Move, please,' Aunt Zo said. 'We need to get past.'

'Still looking for the bathroom, are you?' He pouted. 'Do you need to go pee-pee?'

He started towards them, slapping the flat edge of the cleaver against his hand. Some of the steam and smoke and smells seemed to be coming *from* him, as if escaping from his sleeves and the collar of his chef's whites.

'I think we should go back out,' Hannah said urgently.

'Screw that,' Zo said. 'Look, asshole – *move.*'

The chef slashed out at her, ripping the knife through the air in a sudden, vicious arc. It missed Zo by less than a foot.

'If at first you don't succeed,' he said, 'try, try again.'

'Get *out of our way.*'

'Can't. The menu's set. You're on it. Today's special is going to be . . . very special *indeed.*'

Hannah grabbed Zo's arm and pulled. 'Let's *go.*'

The chef kept advancing, pulling back his arm for another slash. 'Prime cuts,' he said in a wet, gloating voice.

'*Please,*' Hannah shouted. 'Let's get out of here.'

This time she *heard* the cleaver cutting through the air. It missed Zo's face by a bare two inches. 'Yeah, OK,' Aunt Zo said, hurriedly. 'Let's do that.'

They turned and ran back the way they'd come. 'Raw,' the chef murmured as he strode after them. 'Lady sushi. Very raw.'

Hannah grabbed Zo's hand, yanking her faster towards the swinging doors. Her aunt seemed dazed. They slip-slided to the doors across the wet floor and crashed out into the corridor.

The restaurant was worse now, though.

Most of the people were still talking, but some looked strange. Their hands were moving in short, jerky movements. As they ran through the room Hannah saw that some people's skin looked sallow, yellow or grey. One woman, so emaciated that you could see bones sticking out of her shoulders, had pulled her lip in too far and her teeth were slicing down into it again and again. What was coming out of her gouged lips looked like wine.

They were nearly at the lobby when suddenly all of the strange-looking people stood up.

'Oh God,' Aunt Zo said.

None of the other diners seemed to notice that someone had risen from their table. They kept chatting and eating. The people on the move were slow at first, like zombies in a video game, but once they'd fought free of the tables and chairs they began to move faster.

'We have nothing available, I'm afraid,' a perky voice said. It was the woman behind the desk. Her grin now looked as though someone had put it there with a knife. It was far too wide. 'I'm sorry. We are fully booked forever.'

'That's OK,' Zo said. 'We are *so* leaving.'

The grey people were lurching towards the lobby, knocking over tables, plates and glasses crashing to the floor.

'But I can't let you go,' the woman said, moving to block the doors. 'You have no reservation.'

'We don't *want* one. We want to *go*.'

'You can't leave without a reservation.'

'Just watch us,' Aunt Zo snarled. She grabbed the woman by the arm and pulled at her, hard. The woman's arm came off. Zo shrieked, and threw it to the floor.

The woman looked down at her arm. 'That's not very kind, is it,' she said disappointedly. 'However will I write in the reservation book now?'

The grey people were now only twenty feet from the lobby area. They weren't fast. But they weren't going to stop.

'Help me,' Zo shouted to Hannah.

Hannah put her hands around the woman's middle and pulled. The woman tottered forwards, away from the door, still looking peevishly down at her arm on the floor.

'You are very silly people. I've told you. We have nothing under the name "Kristen". You will have to starve.'

'"Kristen"?' Hannah said. 'You said you hadn't seen her. That's my *mom's name*.'

'No it isn't,' another voice said. A man's voice.

The chef was shouldering his way through the shambling people. He still had the cleaver in his hand, which was big and white and pale, mottled with liver spots that seemed out of place on a man his age.

'You have no mom,' the chef said. 'You never did.'

'I did so!'

'No. That woman was only pretending.'

'That's *not true*.'

'Ignore him,' Zo shouted. 'Pull. Hard. NOW.'

The chef raised his cleaver. His face did not look angry any more. He looked as if he was trying to help, and was using his other arm to hold back the grey people. Behind them, in the restaurant, everyone else was still happily eating as if nothing out of the ordinary was going on.

'It's better this way,' the chef said. 'The future is hungry and unkind. It'll gobble you up, little girl. It will eat your heart.'

'PULL.'

Just as the chef's arm started to swing down, Aunt Zo yanked at the desk woman with all her might. Hannah pulled too, and the woman fell into them.

Zo dodged right and Hannah to the left, and the woman went crashing past them on to the floor, next to her arm.

'Oh, hello,' she said warmly to it. 'I've missed you.'

Hannah and Zo slammed out through the doors. The chef watched them go, his hair slowly turning white.

'Over to you, imp,' he said.

As soon as they were outside everything was silent. It was darker in the forest than earlier, but there was still a soft, golden glow between the trees, enough to see their way.

If they'd had any idea where to go, that is.

Hannah was panting, her eyes still on the restaurant doors, watching carefully. You could see shadows of the grey people right up against the inside, filling the frosted-glass panes. 'Can they get out? Can they still get us?'

'Don't know,' Zo said, backing away as more and more figures gathered on the other side of the door, scratching at it with bloody fingers. 'But I think we should run anyway.'

'Which way?'

'I don't care. Let's just run.'

Chapter 39

Meanwhile, other things were happening. They always are, and that's why it's so damned hard to keep track of the world. You put someone down and think, I'll come back to them later, but when you do, they've run off to be part of some other story. One of the perilous things about being an adult is there comes a point where the doors of your mind open far wider than required by your own concerns. There's no ceremony when this occurs, and no warning. It simply happens one day and suddenly you find there are seventy things going on at once and you're flinching amidst a maelstrom of love and lost opportunities and hard choices and the tenacious grasping hands of the past, not to mention tidying the garage. Adults are not distracted for the sake of it, so cut them a little slack. They're all searching for the brake to stop the world spinning, so they can take a moment and catch their breath.

Standing with his hand on an actual brake, and surrounded by clanking and banging sounds as the Giant Dipper hurled the carriages around its rickety track, Hannah's father was nonetheless able to hear the siren approaching.

'Fan*tastic*,' he said.

'Aha,' Granddad said. 'Look!' He pointed up through a gap in the machinery.

Hannah's father looked up in time to see the carriages hurtling past at the beginning of their second lap. 'What the . . .'

Both carriages were empty.

'Where . . . *where did they go?*'

'Behind.' Granddad grinned, looking relieved. 'Heck of a machine, this. I'd love to have met the man who built it.'

'What *is* this "behind", Dad? And don't just say it's hard to explain. I'm not ten years old any more.'

'Well, it *is* hard. It's . . . Well, it's the Hell you can get to without dying. It's where we are who we don't want to be. But in fact it's rather more complicated than that.'

'*More* complicated?'

Granddad kept his eyes on the control panel, making minor adjustments. The sound of the police siren was getting louder.

'Seeing things isn't only about the eyes,' he said. 'We see with our minds, too. If we *care*, that's a kind of seeing too – you see with your heart. To glimpse the Behind, or fall into it, or be dragged, a place – or a thing, or a person – has to be wholly outside the human mind and spirit, for a moment truly alone. Wild animals see it, often. The homeless, sometimes. The Behind used to be much bigger, and easier to find. Now you need to tear edge points to access it, via devices like this one. It's where you go to be afraid, and lonely. But also where fate's currents come from, the nudges that shape our lives.'

Hannah's dad nodded thoughtfully. 'Nope,' he said. 'Didn't understand a single word.'

'I'm not good with words,' Granddad admitted. 'I've always preferred machines.'

The siren outside now sounded very close.

'That stuff you said at the house – that can't be true.'

Granddad made a face that said it was.

'You're over *two hundred years old*?'

'Time's a tangled road, Steve. In the Behind it runs in loops, like the track above our heads. We've no way of knowing how long it's been for them in there. Could be years, it might be only a few seconds. We just have to give them as much time as we possibly can.'

'Did Mom know? About you?'

Granddad shook his head sadly. 'The rules of the deal were firm. That was one of them.'

'But . . . but you used to look younger. I remember. There are *photographs*.'

'Tricks, I'm afraid. Courtesy of my employer.'

'And he's really the . . .'

'Yes. He really is.'

They heard the police vehicle pulling up the slip road that led to the entry gates.

'How long have we got?'

'Depends,' Granddad said. 'I locked the door. If they have to go off to find keys, maybe ten, fifteen minutes.'

'If not? If they just break it down?'

'Oh, about five. At the most.'

'You can't . . . freeze them, or stop time, or . . .'

'I'm an engineer, son, not a magician.'

They held their ground.

A few minutes earlier, a battered truck had parked in a side street opposite. Nash killed the engine and watched as, a hundred yards away, the cop car pulled up in front of the boardwalk. Two officers got out and ran in.

'Hell are they doing here?' Jesse asked nervously.

'I'm thinking it's probably to do with the fact that rollercoaster is running by itself in the middle of the night.'

'How is that even happening?'

Nash slowly turned to look at him. Jesse was deeply unnerved to see his boss's eyes looked as though they'd become black, with a hint of gold around the edges. Couldn't be. They just looked that way because they were sitting here in the dark. Probably. Hopefully.

'OK,' Jesse said hurriedly. 'Whatever. So are we going to go try find this guy who can open the case?'

Nash turned back to the front. Was silent for a while. The cops at home, you knew what you were dealing with. There was a system. There were relationships, usually involving money handed over discreetly in brown envelopes in bars.

But they were a long way from home. And their mission tonight, he knew – though he'd be lying if he pretended that he wholly understood it yet – was too important to be derailed by a dumb confrontation with local cops.

'Not yet,' he said. 'We're going to wait and see what happens next.'

Chapter 40

Hannah and Aunt Zo ran far too quickly into the forest, panicked, and within five minutes both were gasping and out of breath. It didn't help that it was uneven underfoot, tangled with fallen branches and leaves and rocks. Aunt Zo was the first to grind to a halt. She put her hands on her knees and coughed for a while, sucking in deep breaths when she had a chance.

'It's times like this,' she rasped, 'that all the Marlboro Lites don't seem such a great idea after all.'

Hannah was happy to stop. She didn't think it made sense to keep running if you didn't know where you were going. What if they were headed in the wrong direction – assuming, of course, there was a *right* way to go? But there had to be, didn't there? One choice had to be better than the others. There *had* to be a way from here to Mom. You couldn't be in the centre of nowhere, a place from which there was no road, no way home.

Could you?

They were a distance from the restaurant now, at least. You couldn't see it behind. Nothing had come after them. The forest was silent in the way that only innumerable redwoods can pull off. Except for . . .

'What was that?'

'Don't know,' Aunt Zo said tersely. Her chest still rose and fell rapidly, but she forced it to happen quietly. They stood close and turned in a slow circle.

All they could see were ranks of trees in every direction. Redwoods enjoy clustering in groups, circles of five or more, like gossiping (and very tall) old ladies. The forest looked like a vast and infinite assembly of such women, amongst whom all conversation had suddenly ceased. It felt as if some of the trees could, at any moment, turn and show their ancient faces.

Was that what they'd heard? The sound of one of the trees starting to turn?

They heard the noise again – a whistling sound from above, getting louder. Then it changed to a rustling sound, still high above their heads, but getting lower and closer. It sounded like something moving high up in one of the trees nearby. They looked up, but couldn't see anything.

'What lives in redwoods?'

'How would I know?' Aunt Zo said. 'I'm city folk. Once you get past "Trees have leaves", I'd have to google it.'

The rustling got louder, and louder, until it was more of a crackling noise. And then . . .

'Look out!'

Aunt Zo grabbed Hannah and yanked her out of the way as something came crashing down through the lower branches of the nearest redwood and smacked into the forest floor with a loud burping sound. It bounced several times in a hectic way before ending up in a bush.

Zo backed away, pushing Hannah behind her. 'What the . . . heck was that?'

The bush moved. 'That was awwwwwwwwwwwwwwesome,' a voice crowed. 'I am *so* doing that again.'

Hannah frowned. 'Is that . . .'

281

Vaneclaw came striding out of the bush, grinning gleefully. 'Oh, wotcha. Fancy seeing you here.'

'Oh,' Aunt Zo said in a voice of quiet wonder. 'It's a giant mushroom. That talks.'

'Don't *you* start,' the imp said.

'You can see him now?'

'I can see . . . something,' Zo said, staring at Vaneclaw as though her sanity was on the verge of deciding this was the last straw. 'Though I wish I couldn't. It looks . . . *very* weird.'

'Funny thing is,' said the imp, 'to me, you look like a shaved ape. With silly hair. Anyway – what a ride that was, eh?'

Aunt Zo smiled. 'OK. I get it. That's why I can suddenly see the . . . that *thing*. Duh. We should have realized earlier.'

'Realized what?' Hannah said.

'This is a dream.'

'Is it?'

'Of course,' Zo said, very relieved. 'A restaurant you've been to before, crazy receptionist who says your mom's name, then we're in a forest just like Big Sur, where we were *only a few hours ago* . . . Thank God. This is just a stupid dream.'

'No it's not,' Vaneclaw said.

'It is.'

'Nope.'

'It *is*,' Zo insisted.

'Hang on,' the imp said. 'Give us a sec.'

He went scampering off into the trees, and then slowed, his head – or the top part of his body – lowered, as if he was looking for something on the ground.

Hannah was confused. Was this just a dream? That kind of made sense, but if so, didn't it mean it had to be *her* dream? Aunt Zo had never been to Bistrotechnical, so she could have no memory to get mangled and flipped into a nightmare, which is more what this felt like. So it must be Hannah's. How could you tell if you were dreaming? She did the only thing she'd heard of, and pinched herself on the arm.

'Ouch,' she said. Nothing changed.

'It's a dream,' Aunt Zo insisted confidently.

'Daddy says you're not allowed to do that in stories, though. The bastards won't allow it.'

'Who are the "bastards"?'

'The people he writes stories for. You're not allowed to have dreams and they're not keen on flashbacks or voice-overs, either. Which he says is dumb because you've got a voice going in your head all the time and flashbacks are just like memories. But it's not allowed. It drives him *nuts*.'

'You can't have made-up things in made-up stories. But in real life, you can.'

'What?'

'I know that doesn't make much sense.'

The imp came running back holding something in his little hand. 'Here we go,' he said triumphantly. 'And blow me down if it isn't an old mucker of mine.'

He was holding what looked like a pebble. About an inch and a half round, dark grey, and smooth.

'It's . . . a pebble,' Hannah said.

'Aha, no,' the imp said. 'Oi, Sniveldash?'

Two little eyes suddenly opened on the rock. They swivelled round, taking everybody in. Aunt Zo blinked at it. A small mouth opened next, revealing sharp, scythe-like teeth. It yawned.

''Sup, Vane?' Its voice was resonant and deep.

'What . . . is that?'

'This, my friends, is a soulcutter,' Vaneclaw said. 'One of your more prolific types of demonon.'

'Did you say "demonon"?'

'I did. Sub-class of demons. Don't get me started on all that, or we'll be here all night. And, to be frank, whatever I tell you will be almost completely and utterly wrong. But the key thing, your take-away bullet point, is that your soulcutters *only exist in the real world*. In the real world they're all over the place. One or two in every garden. A few on every beach, which is why you always want to make sure you sit on a towel.'

'Granddad mentioned soulcutters,' Hannah said. 'That sculpture in my bedroom was supposed to keep them away.'

'*Exactly*,' Vaneclaw said. 'Your soulcutter, as a breed, prefers to do its work while you're asleep. Don't you, mate?'

'Yeah,' said the pebble very deeply. 'We do.'

'Come in through the windows, or up the water pipes. Or sometimes people pick them up and take them home, thinking they look nice. Which they're not. They're why some people feel grim first thing in the morning. Little paper cuts on the soul. But, and here's my big point, soulcutters are only allowed in the real world, or the Behind, 'cos of a thing that they once . . . never mind. It was a long time ago, let bygones be bygones. But as a result, they're not really allowed in stories – so you're being a bit naughty popping up in this one, my son – and *definitely* not in dreams. Right, Snivel?'

'Sadly, that is the situation that obtains.'

'So, QED and thank you very much,' the imp declared to Aunt Zo. 'We're in the Behind. This is not a dream.'

'You'll excuse me,' Aunt Zo said imperiously, 'if I'm wary of accepting existential advice from the fleshy, spore-bearing, fruiting body of a fungus.'

But Vaneclaw wasn't listening. He turned around, peering into the trees. Hannah realized that in the time they'd been talking, it had got darker.

'What are you looking for?'

'I'm not sure,' the imp said, standing on tiptoe to look over her shoulder. 'Something's not right, though.'

The idea that things could become even more not-right caused Hannah to feel extremely nervous. 'In what way?'

'Don't know. Think we should move on.'

'To *where*?' Aunt Zo was sounding nervous now too. 'A different batch of exactly the same trees?'

'Which direction was you headed?'

'That way,' Hannah said, pointing. 'I think.'

Vaneclaw peered into the gathering dark. 'Nah.' He turned about thirty degrees. 'I'd say we'd be better off going that way. Snivel?'

'Depends where you want to go, mate, to be honest.'

While the entities had a short, heated debate, Hannah alternated between looking between the trees and glancing at her aunt. Zo had started to look twitchy.

'Are you OK, Zo?'

'Don't know,' Aunt Zo said. 'There's something . . . I don't know. I thought I saw something running in the trees.'

Hannah saw something then too, far away in the woods. It was gone too fast for her to make out what it was. All she knew was that it made her feel ill at ease.

And panicky. 'Something's coming,' she said.

Chapter 41

Vaneclaw came to stand with Hannah. They leaned forwards together, trying to see if there was anything in the shadows.

Aunt Zo and Sniveldash looked at each other. 'I like your hair,' the pebble said.

'Thanks.'

'Shh,' Vaneclaw hissed.

'I'm scared,' Hannah said. 'Where's the Devil, anyway? Shouldn't *he* be helping us?'

'Not sure what occurred with him, and to be honest with you,' the imp said, eyeing the trees cautiously, 'you're better off without him at this stage. I yield to no one in my respect for the big man, but bear in mind he is in fact the Father of All Lies. As such, his counsel can be misleading.'

'But this is his place!'

'Well, yes and no, as it happens. He can lay paths in here but he can't actually make you *do* things.'

Aunt Zo caught her breath. Deep in the darkness between the trees, she'd seen a figure. 'Someone's here,' she whispered.

'Was it the chef?'

'No. It looked like it was dressed all in black.'

'Ooh, that's not good,' Vaneclaw muttered. 'Wasn't wearing a pointy hat, was it?'

'I think so. Oh God – there's another one.'

Hannah could see them now, and there were more than two. At first you weren't sure if they were different to the other shadows. They felt like the emptiness in the last drawer you check when you've been searching for something you loved but which is now lost. They were like the silence that falls when you give someone a chance to reassure you that everything's going to be OK, and they still love you, but instead they hesitate. Like that all the time, permanently, and forever.

There were six of them. No, seven. They were moving now, like a pack of animals. 'Watchers,' Vaneclaw said dismally.

Eight. Nine.

Hannah blinked. 'The Watchers are *real*?'

Ten. Eleven.

'Yes. My advice is we run away, very fast. Snivel – can we count on you?'

'Always.'

'Cheers, mate,' the imp said, and tossed the pebble on to the forest floor between them and the tattered shadows hovering between the trees. He turned to Hannah and Zo. 'Run. Now. Imagine nearly a dozen Fallen Angels are right behind you.'

'Will that help?'

'Might do. Also, it happens to be true.'

And so again they were running, crashing through the trees and darkness that seemed to be tugging at them as they passed.

Hannah glanced back and saw the pebble spinning on the ground, causing something to happen around it. The air went glassy. It looked sharp. It seemed like it would cut anything that came near it, but as though the wounds would be nowhere that you could see.

'What's it doing?' she gasped to Vaneclaw, who was sprinting alongside her.

'What he does best. He's well harsh at it, too, but those things are miles out of his league. They're out of *everyone's* league. If they come after us . . . it's bigly un-good.'

Hannah started running even faster.

Aunt Zo was ahead, trying to keep an even pace and to avoid twisting her ankle on the rocky ground, and at the same time fighting an impulse that horrified her – namely to run as fast as she possibly could and worry later about what happened to everyone else. She knew she couldn't do that, but she wouldn't have been human if the idea hadn't occurred to her. She too risked a glance back, and was bewildered to see the pebble – now spinning so quickly it had become a blur – being joined by something that jumped down out of the trees.

It looked like a squirrel. One of those black ones, with the tufty ears. It landed next to the pebble and stood on hind legs, holding its paws up in front.

Then it opened its little mouth and made a sound like a storm cloud rolling over in its sleep, a deep boom that seemed to shake your bones from the inside.

'Blimey,' Vaneclaw said, very unnerved. 'It's all kicking off. Faster, people.'

And faster and faster they went through the trees but it was hard to keep going as the ground started to thump and shudder and cracks of jagged black lightning shot between the trees from the conflict behind them, turning everything they touched to ash and blood.

'There's something up ahead,' Aunt Zo panted.

Hannah could barely see her now, it was so dark. 'What?'

'A light of some kind.'

'Vaneclaw, what is it?'

'Dunno,' the imp gasped. 'But we'd be better off spending the night up Beelzebub's arse than stuck out here with that going on behind us. Head for the light, whatever it is. Quick as you like.'

And they ran, and for a while it seemed as if the light ahead wouldn't get any closer, which gave Zo a chance to hope the imp really was as stupid as everyone said and this was a dream – or nightmare – after all.

But finally they started to gain on it, and Hannah shouted, 'That's my house!'

Zo saw she was right. Inexplicably, non-dream though this allegedly was, her niece's house was ahead in the forest, lights blazing. That *had* to be a good thing, surely.

A very, *very* loud noise came from the forest behind, a sound that could mean nothing but destruction. It was the kind of rupturing crack a bad planet might make in the moments before splitting apart to let all the dead babies out.

Hannah found speed she'd never realized her legs were capable of, even managing to draw level with Aunt Zo, whose lungs were giving out on her again, and then they were only yards away from the house – her house. She sprinted for the door, hand outstretched, but stopped so abruptly that she skidded in the leaves.

'Why aren't you going in?' Zo asked. 'Open the door!'

The imp was trying to see what was going on behind them in the forest. 'Yes. Seriously, love, it's getting well out of hand back there. Open the door.'

'But will it be safe?' Hannah asked. 'Will it be my *actual house*? The restaurant we were in wasn't real.'

'Yeah, it was. You was just seeing it from behind.'

Hannah looked at the windows of her house, glowing yellow and warm. 'But what's the Behind going to be like in *there*?'

'Dunno, love. But if the Fallen get one tince more fractious, it's game over. There's a lot of posturing and push-and-shove with that lot, but sooner or later one of them will genuinely lose his rag and the universe will have a new black hole. You do *not* want to be in the middle of that action, trust me.'

Still Hannah hesitated. Another dull boom came from behind. A beat later, a hundred trees burst into flame.

'If your mom's going to be anywhere,' Aunt Zo said gently, 'it'll be in here, don't you think?'

Hannah didn't know what to think. But home is home is home.

She opened the door.

Chapter 42

They all ran through it, and Aunt Zo slammed it shut again behind them. Hannah felt a wash of unbelievable relief at the idea of being back somewhere that she recognized, that was hers.

It lasted less than a second.

They weren't in her house after all.

Instead they found themselves standing nervously in the middle of the junction of two dimly lamp-lit streets. The sky was low and cloudy, the same murky, suffocating ochre dark-ness Hannah had seen when they entered the Behind through the gate in Siberia.

'Oh, bollocks,' Vaneclaw said. 'You're having a laugh, aren't you? Where the monkey nuts is *this*?'

'Downtown,' Aunt Zo said.

The door they'd come through had disappeared. The street now continued behind them towards another crossroads. The road and sidewalks in between were deserted. No cars, no people. Leaden silence. It was a place with all the life taken out.

'Downtown?' Hannah said. 'Santa *Cruz*?'

'Look.' Zo pointed across the junction. 'We've had dinner there, right? A few times.'

A family-friendly restaurant called Tinga, where they did pasta and pizza and some nights a glitter ball would drop from the ceiling and the staff would start suddenly dancing to disco music and spinning dough and then just as suddenly stop and go back to what they'd been doing before. Hannah had always loved it. Her mother grudgingly admitted it was 'fun'. Her dad said it was how the restaurants would be in Hell. Maybe he'd been right.

'So where *is* this place?' Aunt Zo asked the imp. 'Is it what it appears to be?'

'Oh yeah,' said the imp. He was still checking round warily, but seemed relieved to at least no longer be in the forest. 'Everything always is. That's the shocking thing.'

'So we are in Santa Cruz? The real one?'

'We are. But behind.'

'What *is* this "behind" thing?'

'It is what it is, love.'

'Try harder, mushroom, or when we get out of here I'm going to sauté you in butter and thyme.'

'You know, for a non-demon,' Vaneclaw said, 'you're genuinely quite scary.'

'You don't know the half of it. *Talk.*'

The imp looked pained. 'Look, I was not put on this planet to be the go-to entity for explaining things. But what happened to you guys in the restaurant in the forest?'

Hannah told the imp – from coming out of the fridge, to their interaction with the woman on the door, to what had happened to some of the diners and the chef.

The imp made a face. 'You was lucky, to be honest. Lot of places, you'd have seen far worse.'

'*Worse?*'

'Basically,' he said, 'your grey-looking ones are lost. People who weren't really *there*, 'cos they got something going on

292

in their heads, crowding everything else out. Anxious people. Depressed. Worried, or missing someone so much that the real world seems like shadows. People with secrets, too. Like that woman with the red wine you mentioned – she'd be a drinker, but fighting it, white-knuckle style. Spends lunch worrying how often she can take a sip without someone thinking, whoa, she's knocking it back. Can't hear what people are saying. Can't even taste her food, though she'll force it down for appearances. In her head it's just: Can I have another drink yet? Or now? Or *now*? She's on her own in the crowd, always, stuck in a hidden life going on behind everyone else's.'

'I don't understand,' Hannah said.

'Good,' Aunt Zo said firmly. 'What about the chef?'

The imp shrugged. 'Dunno. Could be he's spent a lot of time wondering what it would be like to . . .' He coughed, looking at Hannah. 'Do . . . bad things.'

'And everyone else seemed normal because . . .?'

'At that moment, their life makes sense to them.'

'And this is what the world's actually *like*?'

''Fraid so,' the imp said. 'Back in the day, before there was so bloody many of you, humans were a lot better at seeing the Behind. Now it's only your shamans and what-not, your forty-days-in-the-wilderness types. The Behind's a lot closer when you're alone, too – which is why people are so mad keen on company, even if it's only Arsebook or Tweetagram or whatever. It's what keeps the back door from opening in your head. Noise. Distraction. Idle hands and lonely souls do the Devil's work.'

Hannah ran across to Tinga and looked in through the window. The inside was empty. No chairs or tables. Dark. Dead. Forlorn. 'But how come,' Zo insisted as she and the imp followed her, 'if the restaurant was real, we stepped right out of it into redwoods? And from there to here?'

The imp appeared to be attempting to sound wise. 'If you love someone, then you're together even if you're a thousand miles apart. But when you're kept apart, a day can feel like a month. Time and space don't mean nothing. It's more about what connects to what, and to who. Or is it "whom"? Dunno. The Behind is the little bit of Hell in all of us, bottom line.'

'And that means . . .?'

Vaneclaw looked sheepish. 'I have absolutely no idea. Heard the Devil say it once, though, so it must be true. Or else a total lie, of course. You know what he's like.'

'But if this *isn't* my house, where do we look for Mom?' Hannah said desperately. 'Stop all this *talking*.'

Before the imp had a chance to answer they heard a voice from a dark alley on the side of the road. The voice was soft, but carried. It called out a single word, or a name.

And then Zo was running. 'That's her!'

Hannah was so caught out that for a moment she froze on the street corner, watching Zo disappear into an alley on the other side of the road.

Vaneclaw evidently understood nothing about this turn of events either. 'What's all that about?'

Hannah ran across and into the alley, the imp following. There was no sign of her aunt, but she could hear footsteps in front, running. 'Aunt Zo!' she called. 'Stop!'

Hannah ran as fast as she could towards the right angle at the end of the alley, but the imp caught up with her and slipped around the corner first. They were back on the main street now, just along from the Rittenhouse Building, close to her dad's favourite Starbucks. 'Now what?'

Hannah looked around, glimpsed a shadow disappearing around a corner on the other side. 'There!'

They ran across the street and into another alley. This led towards a two-storey parking lot. 'Know this place?'

'Yes,' Hannah said. 'It's where we park if we drive downtown.' She heard the sound of footsteps. 'She's in there!'

They sprinted into the lot. There were no cars inside, just two empty lanes under a low concrete roof. Columns stopped you from being able to see the entire space in one go.

'I'll look the other side,' the imp said.

He ran away. Hannah walked up her lane, looking hard – but Aunt Zo wasn't there. Vaneclaw came pelting back. 'Nah,' he said, looking worried. 'We must have gone wrong.'

But then they heard footsteps again, still running. A voice calling out – Aunt Zo's. She wasn't calling for Hannah, though, and because of the echoing space it wasn't clear what direction the sound was coming from.

The imp looked up at the ceiling. 'Is there another floor?'

'Yes.' Hannah sped back out of the side and towards the ramp to the higher level. She started running up it, but then felt the imp grab hold of her again – this time grasping her hand.

'Go easy,' he said. 'Got a bad feeling about this.'

Hannah shrugged him off and kept running. When she got to the top of the ramp she found herself in a wide, roofless open space. The sky was now shot with striations of violent, dark-orange cloud, as if a storm was coming. Pale lamps stood at each corner of the space, shedding enough light to show there were no cars parked here, and no sign of Aunt Zo.

There was *something* up there, though. A large shadow in the gloom at the end. About as tall as a child, but wider.

'What's that?'

'Oh,' Vaneclaw said, arriving a moment behind her. 'That . . . would be a wolf.'

'A *wolf*? A make-believe wolf?'

'Maybe not. Lot of animals took to hiding in the Behind, once you lot invented guns. They slip in and out when nobody's looking.'

At that moment the wolf raised its head and looked straight at Hannah. Its eyes burned golden yellow.

'Though, to be honest,' the imp added, sounding very unnerved, 'real wolves don't normally do that.'

'Is it . . . safe?'

'And they call *me* stupid,' Vaneclaw muttered, grabbing Hannah's hand and tugging her back towards the slope. 'No, love, it's not safe. Let's go. Now.'

'But what if it got Aunt Zo? She's really scared of wolves.'

'It didn't. We'd've heard all the chewing.'

Hannah continued to fight him until she heard the sound of running once more, this time from below – and Zo's voice calling out again. This time Hannah heard what she was shouting.

Aunt Zo was yelling her mom's name.

So she allowed the imp to pull her back down the slope, keeping her eyes fixed on the wolf until they'd gone far enough to turn and run. They hurtled back into the lower level, where Hannah was consternated to see that things had changed at the opposite corner. Instead of being an exit back on to Walnut Street, now there was another ramp – leading downwards.

'*Nuts*,' Vaneclaw said glumly. 'I hate it when that happens. That ramp's a bloody metaphor, innit.'

'A what?'

'Posh name for structuring imps. Twisty little bastards. They infest stories like head lice, chucking symbols around. She'll be down there, for sure.'

They ran halfway down the ramp. The scant light from above ran out, and they were staring into a very dark place. They slowed, going carefully, trying to judge the length of the slope.

When it flattened out, it was almost totally dark. Hannah hurried out into the silky black space, her hands held out in front, and then remembered something. She quickly reached out and patted Vaneclaw very hard on the head.

'Oi – what's that for?'

'He did it. In Siberia. It made you light up.'

'Right, yeah, he can do that. You can't.'

Hannah looked steadily into the darkness. She'd long ago learned that if you do this, your eyes eventually begin to adjust and may pick up detail you can't see at first.

Nothing doing, though. There simply wasn't anything to be seen. Then suddenly Aunt Zo called out.

'Hannah – hurry! She's here!'

Chapter 43

Kristen was lost.

Utterly lost. She had been running around the basement parking lot for what seemed like hours, or days, or years. She'd been on the move as soon as she'd seen her daughter and the other woman disappear into the gloom, and she moved fast. She'd been a runner her whole life and her body was ready to go, and keep going. But they weren't there.

Either the lot went on forever or she kept getting mixed up and turned around. She'd soon had to slow down, too, to avoid repeatedly smacking into concrete pillars, invisible in the darkness. There didn't seem to be a pattern to them – sticking to one line didn't help. Wherever she went, whichever direction she tried to go, something was in her way. She couldn't even seem to find the walls, or any way of judging the extent of this freezing space – she was lost somewhere in the middle.

She called Hannah's name but heard nothing back. She'd gone. Hannah had walked away and she wasn't coming back. She'd disappeared into the future with someone else.

Kristen tried again, desperately, her voice breaking.

And this time . . . heard something.

*   *   *

Hannah raced down into the darkness of the lower level, leaving Vaneclaw behind, heading for where she thought Aunt Zo's shout had come from.

'Zo? Where are you?'

'Shh!'

Hannah changed her direction and ran faster. Now her eyes were starting to adjust she could make out her aunt, thirty feet away, enveloped in the heavy gloom. Zo was standing very still, head cocked on one side, listening hard.

'What are you *doing*?' Hannah asked, taking her aunt's hand for a moment. 'We shouldn't *be* in this place. We need to look for Mom.'

'I *am*. She's here somewhere.'

'She can't be.'

'She is.'

Hannah shouted for her mom. The sound rebounded off the walls and fell to the ground. 'She's *not*. Or she'd come to us.'

Zo held up her other hand for silence. Hannah was about to get really, really mad – this was dumb and a waste of time and they needed to run back up to the streets and find somewhere else to look for Mom, *anywhere* else – but then she heard something.

The sound of feet sprinting past behind them. Bare feet.

Hannah and Zo whirled around together.

But there was no one there.

Kristen ran to where she thought the sound had come from. She banged into a pillar once more, hard, and almost fell, but kept going, doubled up against the pain. She called Hannah's name, again and again. There was no reply.

But she knew what she'd heard.

She'd heard her daughter, shouting her name.

She stopped moving and stood, turning slowly in the darkness. Listening. 'Call for me,' she said, trying to sound calm. 'Call for me again. Please.'

She kept saying it, over and over, not realizing how wet her cheeks were becoming.

Hannah and Zo looked at each other.

'You heard that, right?'

'I heard *something*,' Zoe said. 'And I heard her calling your name before, when we were on the street. That's why I ran over. But she's not here.'

'Or . . . she's not *quite* here,' Hannah said.

'What do you mean?'

'The Devil said it's different here for everyone. Maybe she's close, but can't find her way to where *we* are.'

'So what do we do?'

'Try again.'

They both shouted, several times. Nothing happened. Hannah was beginning to panic badly now. She knew Mom was near. She could feel her, nearly smell her. She was almost here but she was so far away, and Hannah knew time was running out.

'Mom,' she shouted. 'Come *here*.'

But then suddenly she had another thought. If everything *was* individual in the Behind, if it *was* all about you, then they needed to find a place where their paths overlapped – somewhere that was both of theirs, something that was about *them*.

'Mom,' she said, more quietly this time, picturing her mother in her mind as clearly as she could. 'Forget that. Don't come here. Go home, Mom. *Go home*.'

There was a crashing sound. Kristen turned to see a glow from the elevator doors, now standing open, having appeared – or been revealed – thirty yards away.

She ran over to them and into the elevator, stabbed the button. It was slow this time – very, very slow, and made a clattery, rickety noise, like an old piece of machinery near the end of its life – but eventually the doors opened again.

The same corridor.

She ran along it, convinced that she wouldn't be able to find her door, that all she'd done was swap one futile search for another. But no, there it was, the nearest thing she had to a base now: the door to her hotel room, a tiny bit ajar, propped against the latch, as she'd left it.

The room looked exactly as it had. The television was still on, showing the same scenes of Santa Cruz.

The phone on the desk rang. Kristen lunged for it, but there was nobody on the other end. She slammed the phone into the cradle to reset and then put it back to her ear, jabbing at the button for reception.

'Hannah!' she shouted into it. All she heard was her voice slapping against the walls of the hotel room.

Which . . . was now half the size.

Kristen slowly put down the phone, looking around. The room had got smaller. The bed was still a couple feet from her shins, but the side walls had closed in. The windows were almost within reach of the bed now.

The ceiling was lower too. It lurched down with a sound like ancient machinery, metal wheels on cracking tracks.

The TV screen went blank.

The ceiling dropped another inch.

Kristen ran back to the door while she could still get there – the area outside the bathroom was narrower now too, barely wider than the door itself. She tugged and pulled and kicked but it wouldn't move now. It wouldn't open. She couldn't get back out into the corridor. She was stuck here.

She threw herself on to the bed, reaching for her iPhone

on the nightstand. The foot of the bed was now right up against the desk, buckling the legs of the chair. Her phone's screen was cracked. How had that happened?

It had no signal.

She screamed at it. There was still no signal.

The walls were only a couple of feet from either side of the bed, inching closer to touch the nightstands. These had been hewn from fashionably chunky wood and looked sturdy enough to resist a lot of pressure, but . . .

Kristen looked up. The ceiling was now only two feet above her head, and getting closer. There was nothing to stop it coming all the way down to the bed. Nothing but her. Would her body, her muscles, be strong enough to hold it back?

Her *bones*?

The area by the bathroom had narrowed to less than a foot wide. She wouldn't be able to get down it even if she'd thought it worth trying the door again. The foot of the bed was now completely under the desk, the mangled remains of the chair crushed against the wall.

The bed was holding. The bed was strong enough.

She had to hope so, anyway.

Clutching her phone to her chest, Kristen rolled to the side of the bed and slipped over the edge on to the floor, just as the ceiling dropped another foot.

She pulled herself under the bed frame, scrambling into the middle of the space. She lay there watching as the walls finally reached the nightstands, and shoved them against the bed frame.

There was a series of tinkling sounds as the bedside lamps broke, but the tables held. She could hear the bed frame creaking as pressure mounted at the head and foot . . . and then a change as the ceiling came down on to the top of it.

There were thick square legs in each corner.

Would they hold?

A chirping noise. Kristen cried out, not recognizing it, thinking it was the sound of part of the bed frame cracking. Then she realized her phone was vibrating.

She shifted so she could angle the hand holding it up to her ear. 'Help me!' she shouted. '*Help me!*'

For a moment she couldn't hear anything. Then, as if from a very great distance, a quiet, calm voice:

'Go home, Mom,' it said. 'Go *home.*'

Chapter 44

It took only minutes for the cops to park and come running into the boardwalk. They were stymied by finding the service door to the Giant Dipper locked. The younger officer, Ray, was all for kicking it down. Ray was big on kicking things down. He was good at it, too.

The older cop, a twenty-year veteran called Rick, said no. Time had shown him that kicking things down, unless there was no alternative, had a way of coming back to bite you on the ass.

'So, what then?' Ray demanded.

'Find a security guy. He might have keys.'

'But—'

'Look,' Rick said, pointing up at the rollercoaster track. After a moment the carriages rocketed through their view, spilling noise behind. 'There's nobody on there.'

'So?'

'So *relax*, Ray. No one's in danger. Let's try to fix this the peaceful, easy way, and not spend the rest of the night filling in ten-page forms. Go, find someone. Shoo.'

Ray trotted away down the promenade. He swept his head back and forth, keeping an eye out for anything out of place. He ran in a tight, boxy style, like the guy he'd seen in an action movie the night before, though sadly Ray wasn't carrying a pump-action shotgun. He was alert nonetheless, ready for anything.

Rick watched him go. 'Good grief,' he muttered. He turned back to the service door to the Giant Dipper, and banged his fist on it. 'Open up,' he shouted. 'Police.'

The men inside looked at each other.

'Now what?' Hannah's dad asked his father.

'They don't have a key, and they're holding off on battering it down. We hold tight.'

Hannah's dad had spent a lifetime avoiding situations in which a functionary with official power would have cause to *address* him, much less issue a command. On the few occasions on which it had nonetheless happened – the security line at airports, or a super-officious dental receptionist – he had taken care to do exactly what he was told, immediately. He wasn't scared of these people, not as such. He simply understood that they held the potential to bring great disappointment into your life.

To 'hold tight', therefore, when someone in a uniform was banging on the door . . . that took resolve.

'Yessir,' he said.

Ray made it to the end of the boardwalk without seeing any sign of the security guys, which didn't surprise him. Most likely they gave it a quick walk-around every couple of hours and spent the rest of the night holed up in a basement bar a mile away.

Then he saw the body on the ground near the entrance to the kiddie section. He stopped, pulled out his gun.

'Stand up,' he barked, training his weapon on the chest of the supine figure. 'Stand up *now*.'

There was no response. Ray approached, carefully, doing it by the book, moving in a wide arc around the body.

Before long he caught sight of a badge on the figure's chest, and a similar one on its shoulder. First Response. The firm that ran security on the 'walk'. The guy on the ground was breathing, he could see that. So . . . was he *drunk*? Gotten himself so blasted that he'd fallen flat on his back on the job?

'Seriously,' Ray said. 'Get up, asshole. This is the real cops.'

Ray went right up, his gun still pointing steadily down. The guy's eyes were open. As Ray watched, he blinked. Then a few seconds later, he blinked again. Ray nudged him with his foot.

Nothing changed. Ray took a couple of steps back, reaching for his radio. Rick needed to see this.

He froze with the radio halfway to his mouth, however, staring into the darkness on the other side of the supine security guard. Another shape lay in the shadows. This wasn't another guard, however, at least not a human one.

It was an Alsatian. The dog was flat on its side. Ray could see its chest gently rising and falling too.

Maybe a local bar would let a dog in, but Ray doubted they'd let it drink enough beer to pass out, even down here in Beach Flats.

He held up his radio, composing the most profession-al-sounding way to convey this information. This was going to go *big*. It would probably even make the *Santa Cruz Sentinel*. He wanted to get his lines right. His mouth felt dry, though.

Suddenly very dry.

He turned. The security guy was still flat on his back. The dog remained out of it too.

He kept turning in a circle, gun held out. He thought it would be kind of nice at this point to have an additional hand, so he could use his flashlight too. He didn't want to let go of the radio, so he didn't know what he could do about that.

'Who's there?'

It was hard to be sure because of deep shadows, but it looked as though a tall figure was standing at the end of the concourse, watching him.

When he blinked, though, it was no longer there.

Ray decided that, from a purely tactical and strategic point of view, it might be better to get the hell back to Rick and tell him in person about what he'd found.

He started backing away, fast.

Chapter 45

In the parking lot, Hannah and Zo were startled by a sudden smashing sound behind them, very loud. They whirled round to see Vaneclaw running towards them down the slope.

'We need to go,' he said. 'Sharpish.'

A broken piece of wood was lying on the ground. It had originally been painted white but was now cracked and faded by years of sunlight.

Zo looked up at the low concrete ceiling of the parking lot, only a few feet above their heads. 'Where did that even *come* from?' She followed the imp and Hannah as they jogged the length of the basement towards the ramp. 'And where are we going?'

'Don't know,' the imp said tersely, peering up the slope. 'But we need a way out of the Behind, with a quickness. The edge isn't holding. If we don't get out before it folds then we're stuck Behind forever.' He coughed. 'Well, you are, anyway.'

'I'm not leaving,' Hannah said as they emerged back on to the street. The clouds now looked angry, flash-flickering as some terrible kind of lightning sparked deep within, arcing back and forth. 'We *have to find my mom.*'

'We don't even know for sure she's here.'

'She disappeared from Hannah's room,' Aunt Zo said. 'From behind a locked gate. Where else *could* she be?'

'Look, fine, yeah. She's in the Behind somewhere. But the big man gave me one job, and one job only. Have a look for her and the machine, then get you two back safely. All right, that's two jobs. Whatever. And bear in mind he's evil, and only cares a tiny bit, because you're the Engineer's family. Anybody else, I'd be long gone, trust me. See those flashes up above? That'll be the Fallen, on their way. Snivel was only going to be able to hold them back for so long.'

'But you don't even know *how* to get us out.'

'True. I am hoping to address that strategic shortfall. But it's not going to happen from here, that's for sure.'

'Home,' Hannah said. 'We need *to go home*.'

'But we've *tried* that,' Aunt Zo said. 'Remember? We got in here through what looked like the front door to your house.'

'This whole *town* is my home,' Hannah said. 'But home is *really* home. That's why I told her to go there.'

'Told who?' Vaneclaw said.

'My mom. She was here – or nearly here. We need to go home. That's where the gate is.'

'The . . . Oh,' Vaneclaw said. 'Interesting. I see what you're thinking.'

'I don't,' Zo said.

'It's the entrance to Hell,' Hannah said. 'If we go through it . . . maybe that'll get us back *out* again. And it's the place where our paths here cross – me and Mom.'

'I don't have any better ideas,' the imp admitted. 'But then I am famously dense. How far's your gaff from here?'

'About twenty minutes, if we run.'

Hannah led them across the next street but then lost her sense of direction. Hannah's dad had a habit of never walking home the same way twice, with the intention of giving her a sense of how it all fitted together. What he'd actually achieved was to fail to provide a dependable route. As she stood confused on the corner, turning in a circle, it struck Hannah this happened all the time – grown-ups trying to teach you things in the wrong way, *their* way, that only made sense if you already knew what you were trying to learn.

'So . . .?'

'Um,' Hannah said. She pointed across at what had long ago been a small hotel. It still had the rusted sign outside, though now held a burrito shop. 'I think it's that way.'

'But . . . that's north, isn't it?' Aunt Zo asked.

'I don't *know* about north,' Hannah shouted, frustrated and afraid. 'North' was another incredibly annoying adult thing. 'I just think it's that *way*.'

They ran across and up the street, and then it started looking more familiar. The buildings changed, became more functional as downtown shaded into the nameless bit between the shops and where the houses started. The road began to slope as they approached the big hill, and Vaneclaw was soon puffing.

Aunt Zo grabbed Hannah's arm. 'Watch out!'

A piece of wood fell out of the sky and shattered on the ground between them and the imp. It was the same kind that had landed in the lot – old, white-painted, knotted with ancient rivets. Hannah stared at it. 'Is that . . .?'

'Yes,' Aunt Zo said, sounding scared. 'It's from the Giant Dipper. That can't be good.'

'This would be my point,' Vaneclaw said. 'Come on – run.'

Mission Hill is *steep*. Hannah remembered times not so long ago when she would wail and moan to be carried; now here she was, sprinting up it, overtaking Aunt Zo. Vaneclaw was having trouble keeping up. Hannah grabbed his hand

and tried to help. Her own legs were aching but she knew it was only another hundred yards until the slope levelled out at Holy Cross Park.

'What was that weird noise?' Zo panted.

Finally they reached the flat part, and Hannah led them into the park – the one sometimes called the Homeless Hotel by the kind of parents that made her mom glare and mutter rude words under her breath. There was nobody there now. There was a noise, though: she could hear it now too. A rustling sound, like wind rushing through a canyon in the night, or the muffled sob of a child locked in a closet.

Hannah steered them across the park towards the darkest corner. The imp regarded it dubiously. 'Are you sure about this?'

'Definitely,' she said. 'It's our secret shortcut. There's a bridge over the highway.'

Round the corner was a dead end that stopped at a chain-link fence. Thirty feet below it ran Highway 1. Hannah took them to the footbridge. It wasn't actually 'secret', but not many people seemed to know about it, so she'd always thought of it as belonging to her and her dad.

'Oh,' Vaneclaw said as they reached the top of the stairs. 'That'll be what's making the noise.'

It was suddenly much louder, and from the bridge you could see that there were eleven shadowy figures down on the highway.

Looking up at them without faces.

And screaming.

Chapter 46

Inside the Giant Dipper, two generations held tight. Hannah's father remained in position with his arm held up, ready to pull down on the lever. Granddad kept an eye on the controls as the machine went round and round, sending the carriages over the soaring loops and falls of the tracks above their head.

And he listened, increasingly carefully, trying to hear beyond the sound of the cop hammering on the door.

Officer Rick was growing tired of banging on the door. It wouldn't be long before he came round to Ray's way of thinking and went with the plan of kicking the damned thing down.

He took a step back, hands on hips, preparing for a final shouted warning – and saw his partner backing rapidly towards him along the concourse, gun held out.

'Heck are you doing, Ray?'

'I found one of the guards – and a dog. They're out cold. Not dead. But, like, eyes open.'

'Huh,' Rick said.

'And then . . . I saw something else. A guy, I think.'

'Huh,' Rick said again, placing his hand on his holster. 'Where?'

'Down the other end. In fact . . . I dunno. He seemed more like shadows than an actual . . . guy.'

Rick got ready to say something sarcastic, but then realized his partner was genuinely scared. Ray might be young and dumb and gung-ho, but a scaredy-cat? Not so much.

He unclipped his holster. 'Well, we don't like random guys standing in the shadows freaking people out,' he said, to Ray's relief. 'Let's go take a look.'

But before they could even take a step, every single light on the boardwalk lit up.

Both officers were blinded. To go from middle-of-the-night dark to tens of thousands of bulbs all on at once – tiny lights on all the rides, all over the food concessions and the souvenir stores, in every shade from white to yellow and red and green and purple, all maxed out as if the power had been turned up as high as it would go – was a change you could have seen from space. All you could do was slam your eyes shut.

When they managed to open them again, they still had to squint, it was so bright. Rick had instinctively pulled out his gun in the meantime.

'Jesus,' Ray whispered.

Then most of the lights went out, only those on the structures ten yards either side staying lit, a pocket of illumination. The glow they shed was enough to reveal that something had joined them on the concourse. Both officers stared at it.

'Heck is that?'

'It's . . . a squirrel.'

The squirrel was black and had tufty ears. It stood staring at them with beady eyes, panting after its abrupt transferral from another place. The cops trained their guns on it.

'Now what, Rick?'

'I don't know.'

'Are we going to arrest it?'

'Ray, it's a squirrel.'

'Not just that,' a voice said from behind.

The cops whirled round. A tall, old-looking man in a black suit was now standing a few yards feet away, also having rapidly transferred from another place. He had a big nose and pale, mottled hands. He did not appear in the least disconcerted to have two policemen shakily pointing guns at him.

'You need to leave,' he said. 'Now.'

The cops, because they were cops, held their ground.

'What do we *do*, Rick?' the younger one whispered.

Rick thought about it, keeping his gun trained on the old man's chest. In theory the answer was straightforward. You read the guy his rights and take him into custody and try not to make the rap sheet sound too bizarre. Trespass, that'd do for now.

Rick had been a policeman for a long time, however. He'd handled a hundred domestic disputes, fielded a thousand weekend warriors with beer-pitcher hard-ons, seen the ten thousand things that people will do when they think the Man isn't watching. Somewhere in between these events and encounters he'd learned to taste a common flavour, and he knew in his heart that right now he was standing in front of its motherlode.

That this man was where all the bad things came from.

He didn't know what that meant, and didn't care. Rick was smart enough to know that your real and only job in life is to get to the next episode without your character being cut.

'This something to do with the Dipper running?'

The old man nodded.

'Anybody going to get hurt?'

'Not if I can help it. But time is of the essence.'

Rick lowered his gun and put it back in his holster. 'My partner and I will return to our vehicle,' he said. 'We're going to hang there maybe twenty minutes. After that, anyone on the boardwalk who shouldn't be here is going straight to jail.'

'Good enough.'

Ray was staring at him. 'Rick – are you *serious*?'

'Come on,' Rick said. 'And put that thing away. I've got a feeling it wouldn't do much good.'

When the younger officer had holstered his weapon, they turned. The squirrel was still there, its hard black eyes seeming to sum up and judge them.

'I am the Squirrel of Destiny,' it said.

Rick and Ray walked stiffly up the concourse towards the gate they'd entered by, expecting at any moment to feel a sudden, fatal impact in the back.

The old man in the suit turned to the squirrel. 'Go back to the Behind, Xjynthucx,' the Devil said. 'I will return there myself in a moment. This is taking too long. Do what you can, but fall back if you can't find the machine soon. I have no especial desire to destroy this town. Yet.'

The squirrel scratched itself vigorously behind the ear for a moment, then folded itself into a ball, tighter and tighter, and smaller and smaller, and disappeared.

Inside the Dipper, Hannah's father swapped hands on the lever. Granddad tended the controls. They had no knowledge of what had just happened outside, but the cessation of the banging on the door was welcome.

It did however reveal that the machinery surrounding them was sounding different.

'What's going on?'

'I don't know,' Granddad said. He peered up into the chaos of tracks above their head.

There was a grinding sound. A moment later, a short section of wooden support came tumbling down out of the darkness to smash to pieces on the floor between them.

'What the . . .'

'It's coming apart,' Granddad whispered.

The Devil waited until he was sure the two policemen were going to keep their side of the bargain. A man called Nietzsche once observed that there is no such thing as moral phenomena, only a moral *interpretation* of them. The Devil had a certain amount of time for Nietzsche, despite the moustache. He'd understood. We look at a squirrel and say it is jumping; but we might as well think about a jump in its essence, and claim that the *jump* is *squirrelling*. We do bad things, in other words, but the bad things also do *us*. This is almost never a successful defence in a court of law, but it's true.

Good things are part of us, too – and so you can't always resist the temptation to do them, either. Whoever you are.

So the Devil stepped back into the Behind, appearing from nowhere in the middle of its version of downtown. He paused a moment, then smiled, causing the immediate death of a nearby mouse.

He stretched out his arms, roared up at the sky – and changed.

Chapter 47

'*Are they those* . . .' Aunt Zo whispered.

'Yeah,' Vaneclaw said. 'Which is very poor news.'

'What do they want?'

'Oh, to kill us. Definitely.'

'What happens if you die in the Behind?'

'A fate far worse than death. So let's go, eh?'

They sprinted along the bridge and down the spiral into another dead-end street. Ten feet ahead, another section of track support plummeted out of the sky and crashed into the fence, exploding into a blizzard of splinters.

There was silence from the highway for a moment. And then the howling sound of the Fallen gliding up the embankment and towards the breach in the fence.

Hannah, Zo and Vaneclaw turned as one and ran up the hill. Hannah knew that they had to get up this stretch and then take a right up a road so vertically inclined it was called 'High Street'. But off this lay another locals' shortcut, a sharp set of old steps that would get them to within a few hundred yards of home.

Aunt Zo and the imp were panting badly, and Hannah wasn't much better. Part of this was sheer panic. The sounds of the Fallen were getting louder and louder. The breached fence was still obstructing them for now, but a rending sound as one of the metal poles sheared made it clear this wouldn't last long.

Vaneclaw was starting to fall behind again, partly because of his little legs, but also because he kept glancing back. There was an expression on his gnarled, beige face that neither Hannah nor anyone else had ever seen there before.

An expression that was thoughtful. Considering.

'Stop looking round,' Hannah shouted. 'Just *hurry*.'

She led the way to the steps. These ran between two houses, a shortcut to avoid the switchback of the road.

'You've got to be *kidding*,' Zo moaned when she saw the stairs. But then they heard the crash of the fence finally coming down. They kept running.

There were fifty-one steps. Hannah knew this, having counted them on the times she and Dad walked back from their Saturday excursions. Fifty-one short, concrete steps. That's all.

Fifty-one can feel like a lot, though.

Before she was even a quarter of the way up she slipped, barking her knee. The pain put tears in her eyes and for a moment she considered not moving ever again, but Aunt Zo grabbed her by the scruff of her neck and pulled her back to her feet. On to her hands and knees, anyway – which was how she tackled the rest of the climb. Zo was effectively doing the same thing, pulling herself upward with the rusted metal handrail, panting like a steam train nearing the end of its life.

The imp was at the back, still wasting precious moments by looking behind him. Hannah fixed her eyes on the top. There was enough moonlight to see her goal: the place in the very top step where whoever built them had made an impression of two horseshoes into the concrete. She kept going, ignoring the blood dripping from her knee, trying to match Aunt Zo step for stair.

Twenty steps.

She risked a glance back. Vaneclaw was right behind. She saw the first shadows appear from the street below. She heard the roar as the leader of the pack of Watchers caught sight of the stairs. She turned back round and started climbing even faster.

Thirty steps. Breath like knife-jabs in the lungs. The sound of claws on concrete as the Fallen Angels came towards the path. Thirty-six. Thirty-eight. Forty. Forty-six . . .

And then the horseshoes. Hannah was prepared for what came next but her aunt was not. Another stretch of steep road, and only after that did it level out. 'We're screwed,' Zoe wailed.

'Just keep *going*,' Hannah panted.

Zo sat down on the road. 'I can't. I just can't.' She had nothing left. 'I'm sorry, Hannah. I . . . oh dear God.'

Hannah turned to see what Zo was staring at, and saw it wasn't just the Fallen after them now.

The wolf from the top of the parking lot had reappeared. It snarled at the Fallen and they shrank back for a moment, enough for the wolf to get ahead of them . . . and then start after the people who'd just reached the top of the stairs.

This was enough to get Zo back on her feet – perhaps the only thing in this world or any other that would have done it. She grabbed Hannah's hand and they tried to run together, but Hannah's legs felt boneless, jelly-like, muscles worn out and empty. Vaneclaw meanwhile crested the top of the steps.

He made it another few yards, but then stopped. 'Go on,' he gasped. 'I'll keep it back.'

'*How?*'

'Um, dunno. I'll think of something.'

'We can't just leave you here,' Hannah said.

'The big man vouchsafed unto me a mission, and my non-life won't be worth not-living if I don't get it done. *Go.*'

She darted forwards and kissed the imp on his crumpled cheek. 'Thank you,' she whispered.

Then she ran back to Aunt Zo. 'You heard him. Let's go home.'

They started up the final part of the hill. After a few seconds they heard the imp shouting 'Banzai!' as he leaped on to the wolf.

The wolf snapped at him with enormous, spittle-flecked jaws, but the imp rode it like a bronco, grabbing fistfuls of fur and swinging himself around on to the vast animal's back, the position from where an accident imp always does his best work.

The wolf tried to ignore the infuriating little entity but the imp's claws were in it now and he was whispering distractions and confusions into the creature's huge ears, and as the wolf thundered up on to the road it tripped, crashing forwards on to its face with a thump that shook the entire hillside.

But wolves don't get discouraged easily. It was quickly back on its feet, clawing and pulling its way forward.

Vaneclaw didn't give up either, however.

He did his best.

Meanwhile Hannah and Zo gasped their way up to the point where the road went over the bridge that covers the top of the canyon, flanked by tall, fragrant eucalyptuses, and levels out.

They ran up the centre of the street. None of the lights in the houses were on. Things started raining down out of the dark and cloudy sky.

Rivets.

Chunks of white-painted wood.

Worst of all, a short piece of structure which had once been painted red, which Hannah knew must be a part of the Giant Dipper's actual *track*.

But there was nothing they could do except keep going, dodging the objects as they fell, until at last they turned the corner and Hannah's house was just there: the only building in the neighbourhood that blazed with light.

When they got to the front door, Hannah turned the handle and it opened. The corridor beyond looked like it should. They hurried in and shut the door firmly behind.

It was Hannah's house this time. There was no question.

But it was very, very cold.

Back at the steps, Vaneclaw was fighting a last-ditch battle against the wolf: clinging on to its shoulders with one tiny fist, using the other to bang heroically (although wholly ineffectively) on the creature's head.

'You can stop that now,' said the wolf as it stopped running. 'They've got to the house.'

'Oh,' Vaneclaw said. 'It's you.'

Chapter 48

'That's some serious air con,' Aunt Zo said, shivering. 'It wasn't on earlier, was it?'

'We don't *have* air conditioning,' Hannah said, feeling betrayed. They were in her house now. Her *home*. It wasn't right for things to be wrong. But everything *was* wrong.

It wasn't home any more.

They flinched at the crash of something landing on the roof and sliding down the tiles. A moment later, a piece of track support fell past the window.

'Upstairs,' Hannah shouted, her breath condensing in a thick cloud around her face.

There was a thin layer of ice on the floor of the hallway, and they slipped several times before making it to the staircase. The carpet crunched under foot. Every step made them colder. The upstairs hall was like an ice cavern. The carpet was a solid sheet of it, and long icicles hung from light fittings. It was so appallingly cold that it felt as if sharp nails were being hammered along your bones. Breathing was like rubbing sandpaper on your lungs.

Hannah's bedroom door hung open. The gate was still in place but you couldn't see through it now. The gaps between the bars were frozen solid. The keyhole was a block of ice.

'What is it with this *cold*?'

'The gate's doing it,' Hannah said, teeth chattering. She went up to it and moved her head from side to side, trying to see through the ice into the room beyond. 'How do I get *in*?'

'The Devil used his hand,' Aunt Zo said. She was shivering so badly it was hard to make out what she was saying.

'The slot's frozen over.'

Aunt kicked the gate with her heel. Nothing happened except she hurt her foot. She tried coming closer and smacking the keyhole with her elbow. The ice didn't budge.

There was a soft *thunk* from down at the other end of the corridor. Another piece of the Dipper landing on the roof, they assumed.

'We've got to *hurry*.'

'Hang on,' Aunt Zo said. She pulled out her cigarette lighter and knelt in front of the gate. She held it up close to the slot. The glow from the flame warmed the hallway for a moment, but then seemed to become trapped, reflected into the ice and held there.

After a few moments the ice started to go glassy, and a tiny droplet of water formed on the surface.

'Ha,' Zo crowed. 'Being a social pariah has upsides.'

Then she said 'Ow' and dropped the lighter as it got too hot to hold. She let it cool on the frozen carpet for a few seconds, and tried again.

Hannah stood with her ear as close to the gate as she could without getting frozen to it. She still heard nothing from beyond. '*Hurry*,' she said.

'It's physics,' Zo said, wincing as her fingers got burned again. 'Yet another thing over which I have annoyingly not been given total control.'

They heard another noise from the other end of the corridor.

It wasn't a *thunk*, however, and they realized it wasn't something falling on to the roof after all.

It was coming from Hannah's dad's bedroom.

It was a growl.

Aunt Zo slowly stood up. Hannah moved back from the gate. They looked down towards the bedroom.

It was dark in there, but a patch in the back was darker still, as if all the shadows had gathered into a solid shape.

The shape raised its head, revealing a pair of glowing golden eyes.

'Oh . . . *crap*,' Zo said.

It was one of the Fallen.

It looked like a bundle of black stinking rags. It smelled like something pulled out of a lost lake after many weeks. It felt like the hearts of the people brought to look at a briefly uncovered face in a morgue, to confirm that yes, this had been someone they loved.

Aunt Zo pushed Hannah back towards her bedroom.

'Can we run past it?' Hannah whispered, heart beating in her chest.

'Too late.' Aunt Zo handed her the lighter. 'Keep trying.'

Hannah crouched next to the door and inexpertly flicked the wheel. It took three tries to get it to light.

Meanwhile Zo stood guard. The Watcher took a considered step towards them, shifting its weight.

Hannah hissed as the lighter got too hot to hold. She blew on her fingers and sparked it up again. The ice was running freely around the lock, and she rubbed and scrabbled with her fingers, getting a couple of small chunks to slough off.

The Fallen Angel was now only a few feet from the doorway. It was getting larger.

Hannah chipped another piece of ice from the lock. But

what if she managed to clear the whole thing, put her hand in – and nothing happened? This was the Devil's business and the Devil's lock. And why wasn't he *here*? Why wasn't he helping them? Why should it come down to her and Aunt Zo?

'It's not *fair*,' she said, but for the first time realized those words – which she'd used a thousand times in her short life – had never meant anything. The Devil didn't deal in fairness, and neither did the world at large.

'How's it going?' Zo asked, her voice ostentatiously cheerful, as the Watcher started to glide slowly out into the hall. 'Running out of time here.'

'I'm *trying*.'

'That's OK, honey. Keep going.'

Hannah switched hands. The lock was over halfway exposed now, the ice melting quickly.

The Fallen Angel laughed, very quietly. It was an awful noise. It sounded as though its throat was rotting. The shape of its shoulders changed as it gathered itself for attack.

Hannah dropped the lighter and started frantically scratching at the lock with the nails of both hands. 'It's coming off,' she shouted.

Aunt Zo had already realized what was going to happen next, and didn't reply. Instead she took a step down the hallway towards the Watcher, putting herself between it and Hannah.

'What are you *doing*?'

'Keep going,' Zo said calmly. 'It'll all be fine.'

'Zo, we could still run . . .'

'No. You need to get in your room.' Zo risked a glance back at the gate, and saw Hannah had prised the last piece of ice off the lock. 'Go get your mom.'

Hannah slipped her hand sideways into the slot. 'But that thing's going to get you!'

'It's certainly looking that way.'

Hannah's hand felt as if it was inside a deep, frigid glove, as if she was shaking hands with the thing that lives under everyone's beds. She braced, ready to use all her strength and be denied, but in the end it started to turn easily.

'But you don't even *like* Mom.'

Aunt Zo laughed. 'Of course I do, silly. We're just different, that's all. Now . . . go, Hannah. Go bring her home.'

There was a loud, resonating *clunk* from the lock. The gate swung open inwards, and Hannah fell into her bedroom just as the Fallen Angel flew at Aunt Zo.

Chapter 49

Her bedroom didn't look like her bedroom. It was much smaller than it should be and there was a queen-sized bed taking up almost all of it, like the kind you always found in hotels. Hannah fell through the gate and on to the counterpane, cracking the thin sheet of ice across it.

Her window had moved. It was now where the door was supposed to be. The door and the gate had disappeared. The view out of the window in its new position was familiar, but she didn't have time to care. There shouldn't even be a view at all – one there should show the *inside of the house.*

Her bookcase was gone. Everything else too. There was just the bed. No one here. There wasn't any room for anybody else.

'Mom?'

They'd got it wrong. They'd come to the wrong place and now Zo was out there being destroyed and it was all because Hannah said they should come back to her home, and she'd been a terrible leader and she'd been wrong and she understood why now.

She didn't *have* a home any more. The building remained but everything that had made it her refuge and egg and comfort blanket had been stolen away. There was no laughter, only echoes; no conversation, only two-thirds of an attempt to fill silence; now music except the kind you could play with one hand. It was lack and nope and not-any-more.

Her house itself *was* the Behind. Its sad, silent heart.

She closed her eyes, pulled in a great gasp of cold air. She heard a quiet ticking sound.

She froze.

There was something under the bed.

Outside, Aunt Zo stared bewildered at the thing in the hallway. Something had happened to it, halfway through a leap destined to bring it into close proximity to Zo's throat – indeed, to see them occupying the exact same space, with presumably painful and fatal results.

With a quiet popping sound, the Watcher had changed into something else in mid-air. Something much smaller, but just as black, with the same tufts on its ears.

It landed on the ground and stood in front of Zo, poised, looking up at her with beady black eyes.

'Wh . . . *what?*' Zo said.

'I am the Squirrel of Destiny,' it declared. 'And I like your hair.'

Hannah carefully moved towards the edge of the bed. Nothing bad happened.

She moved a little farther. Slowly lowered her face past the frozen counterpane, and down past the mattress, and then – after a deep breath – farther still, so she could see into the space beneath the bed.

Somebody was under there.

Lying flat against the floor, squeezed into the incredibly narrow space. Eyes closed, skin blue with cold, hair obscured with ice. The ticking sound Hannah had heard was of teeth barely chattering, in a face where the muscles had seized almost to the point of forever stillness.

'Mom!' Hannah shouted.

The chattering stopped. There was silence, then an audible cracking sound as eyelids fought their way open.

Blue eyes blinked at her. The mouth opened, closed, then opened again. 'Hannah?'

Mom's voice sounded like it was coming from five thousand miles away. Hannah understood the cold had nearly finished her, and she needed to get her mom out from under the bed, *right now*.

She jumped down into the space between the bed and the wall and reached for Mom's hand. Her mother's arm was frozen up against her body, and could barely move.

Hannah took her hand and interlaced their fingers, and pulled and pulled. Slowly her mother began to unfold.

Hannah kept tugging and her mom started to move her legs and arms, to inch her way closer, ice falling out of her hair and melting from her face.

Hannah scooted to the end of the bed to give her more room. Her mom finally got her head out, and managed to get an arm and leg out too. Hannah helped as best she could as Kristen started to be more out than under, and winced her way on to her side, and then her knees.

Hannah couldn't wait any longer. She threw her arms around her. Her mom hugged her back with limbs that were stiff with the cold buried deep inside them.

'I never hated you,' Hannah whispered.

'Yeah, you did,' her mom said, her voice dry and cracked. 'That's OK. Better hate than nothing at all.'

There was a loud crash on the roof. Kristen cried out, still holding her daughter tightly, staring at the ceiling. Soon after there was a sound like a hailstorm. Rivets, Hannah guessed. 'Mom, we have to go.'

'I can't.'

'It's not safe here. We have to go.'

'I can't leave,' her mom said, near tears. 'Ever. There's no escape. There's *no way out*. I have to hide.'

'There's always a way out,' Hannah said.

'You don't understand,' her mom said. 'I made my bed and I have to lie in it. It's my fault. *I have to stay here.*'

'No you don't,' Hannah said, standing on the bed and pulling her mother to her feet.

When her mom had managed to clamber up on to the bed with her, still protesting, Hannah opened the window, ushering in a smell of eucalyptus and pine, together with a faint hint of the sea. 'Do you know where that is?'

Her mom shook her head miserably. Trees, a picnic bench. It still meant nothing to her.

'You will,' Hannah said.

It wasn't easy to get Mom through the window. Her frozen limbs weren't moving fluently, and she was a lot bigger than Hannah. She went in head first and for a minute it looked like she was stuck, but she managed to get purchase and pull herself further, though then there was the question of the four-foot drop on the other side. In the end she inched forwards until the shift in her centre of gravity did the work. There was a soft thump as she landed on the grass.

Hannah had to stretch her leg up over the frame, but after that it was easy until she too had to confront the drop – which suddenly looked kind of high.

Her mother was on her feet by then, however, and reached up with her arms. Hannah let herself fall into them. Kristen had to put her down quickly afterwards – Hannah was far too heavy to carry now, and had been for several years – but for a beautiful moment Hannah experienced that old sensation of being held up high on Planet Mom.

Hannah led the way towards the path. 'This . . . this is Ocean View Park,' her mother said, confused.

'Of course.'

'But how?'

'Doesn't matter. Come on – push me,' Hannah said, running off through the trees towards the swings.

Kristen followed, staring all around. The stand of redwoods on a hill, old picnic tables battered by generations of birthday parties with cake and carrot batons and taco chips, relatives standing round with folded arms and smiling eyes. Wooden houses nearby, a couple of which they'd looked at when it came time to move, before realizing there'd come a point soon when Hannah would be too old for the park and so buying proximity to it made less sense than heading to the West Side, where the schools were better. Calculations, decisions, always weighing the future instead of the present, worrying about the second and third acts when the first is still going on all around you. Welcome to adulthood. Please leave your dreams at the door.

Kristen glanced along the path that led towards the ocean, expecting to be able to glimpse it and the boardwalk, but there was only cloud.

'Come on, Mom!'

Kristen made her way through the trees to the swings, surprised to see that her daughter had ignored the grown-up ones and instead wedged herself – barely – into one of the toddler buckets. 'You're too big,' she said.

'I know. But please.'

And Kristen did, bending way down to nudge the seat forwards. Hannah had to hold her legs up high to stop them dragging along the ground, and looked kind of like a grass-hopper, and felt like one, or so she said, and soon they were laughing, the sound strange in the quietness.

Kristen pushed harder and harder, and eventually they got a rhythm going and Hannah soared up and down, until her mom's arms got tired and had to stop.

Hannah kept her legs up, letting the swing run out of momentum by itself, reaching the end on its own. After it was still she reached up the chains and pulled herself out.

When they were standing together again Mom looked down at her, trying not to let sadness rule her eyes. 'We can't get back here,' she said.

'I know.'

'I've messed that story up, Hannah. It's broken. I can't fix it any more.'

'You don't want to, though, do you? I mean . . . even if you could?'

'You can't ever go back.' Her mom was crying now. 'It doesn't work. I'm sorry. It was so good here.'

'I know. And it's sad. It's nice to come visit, though, even if we can't stay.'

Her mother nodded jerkily, and Hannah finally yielded to a suspicion which had been tickling the back of her mind since they'd got here, and which she'd pushed away while she was on the swings, wanting a last go on them.

She looked across at the tops of the long slides and saw things were now emerging from them. Black shadows, with pointed hats.

All the dreams that never happened. The winds that blow your house down. She could only see four for now, but she knew there would be more on the way. There was a buzzing, whispering sensation in her head. The sound of Big Sur. The aura of the Fallen. The underlying currents. The things we do.

'We need to leave,' she told her mom.

'There's no hurry. We can—'

'Actually, there is.'

The shadows were arriving more quickly. They weren't stopping at the top of the slides, either, but advancing across the grass with firm intent, as if shepherding them.

Mom noticed where Hannah was looking, turned and saw for herself. 'What . . . the hell are they?'

'They're "it's time to go".'

They hurried down the path. 'But . . . go where?' Kristen said, scared. 'I don't want to go back through the window.'

'We can't anyway. It's gone. You can't get back in that house any more, Mom.'

All eleven shadows had appeared now. The buzzing was much louder: the angels saying their names, over and over, repeating their own darkest spells. Eager to act through people, because without us the gods are only empty words and old ideas.

'But . . .'

'Just follow.'

Hannah grabbed her mother's hand and began to run. Kristen stumbled at first, her legs still stiff with cold, but started to pick up speed. They sped together down the gravel path, past the tall trees, through air as soft as the breath on your forehead when someone bends over to kiss you good-night.

Hannah ran faster and faster, and her mom kept pace alongside. The path led onward, she could see, but she knew that it led to a precipitous drop, and that where the view of the ocean and the boardwalk should be, there was only space.

'Where are we *going*?' Kristen panted.

'Trust me,' Hannah said.

'I do. But . . .'

'We're leaving.'

And they ran to the edge, and Hannah gripped her mother's hand to stop her ever letting go, and at the end of the path they leaped together into the cloud.

Chapter 50

The moment they left the park, the Behind folded in upon itself. Once Hannah had glimpsed the workings of the grown-up story of which she was a part, and shed upon it a child's clear light – which does not comprehend every shadow but is nonetheless exceedingly bright – the Behind ejected everyone who'd been pulled into it like a cat coughing up a hairball, and the edge resealed itself with a sound like a thunderclap.

Granddad and Hannah's father were enormously relieved – right on the verge of pulling the lever, afraid the Giant Dipper was going to finally shake itself apart – to see people suddenly sitting in the rollercoaster's front carriage again. Hannah, Kristen, Aunt Zo. A squirrel, who quickly bounded away. And the Devil, in the second carriage, with Vaneclaw still riding on his shoulders.

Hannah's dad yanked on the fail-safe with all his strength, the edifice of machinery above him clanked and sputtered, and the carriages rapidly slowed. The rollercoaster completed a last decelerating lap around the track's swoops and falls before pulling into the disembarkation area, where it finally came to rest, accompanied by a monsoon rainfall of rivets.

Everyone climbed out of the carriage, hugging one another, laughing with relief, and hurried out of the building.

Where they found four men barring their path.

The suitcase holding the Sacrifice Machine was on the ground in front of them. Nash was holding a gun.

'We can do this the easy way or the hard way,' he said, raising the gun and pointing it at Granddad's head. 'Personally I hope you choose the tough one.'

Hannah also saw that eleven dark figures were perched in a circle around them, up on the roofs of concessions and rides. Watching. Waiting. She felt the heft of their sadness and hatred, a weight so immense it made you feel nauseous. She understood that their combined power was such that the Devil could not simply kill the man with the gun, that he might in fact not be able to do anything at all.

And she knew the world was about to end.

'I know you,' the Devil said. 'The warehouse. Miami.'

'That's right,' Nash said. 'You seemed to think I wasn't good enough for you. Or bad enough, maybe.'

'I was wrong, evidently. And now you have something that is mine. It was never in the Behind after all.'

'Right about that, too. Except now it belongs to me.'

The Devil laughed sourly. 'Really? You think it's possible to *possess* something like this? What would that even mean, to *own* it? What would it say?'

'That I have it and you don't,' Nash said.

'It would be more accurate to say that it has *you*, but never mind. What do you intend to do with it?'

'Make it work in the other direction.'

'You don't want to do that,' the Devil said. 'Do you have any conception of what would occur if all the evil wrought since the dawn of time came flooding back into this world?

Someone tried it once on a much earlier iteration of the machine. That device was barely a fraction as efficient as the Engineer's, but the results were still dire enough to become enshrined in the legend of Pandora's Box.'

'Never heard of it.'

'It does not end well.'

'Good,' Nash said. 'I like that kind of story.'

The Devil glanced up at the shapes on the rooftops. 'And what have they promised you? My former associates?'

'Nothing.'

Jesse glanced at Nash, surprised and dismayed. He'd assumed a deal had been struck – that when the boss had received the messages of these beings in his head, some payment structure had also been agreed. He'd got that it probably wouldn't be as simple as something like cash or a really cool car, that money and things had only ever been a poor substitute for real rewards like power. But *something*, surely?

'True evil is never done for recompense,' Nash said. 'Only for its own sake. It stands alone.'

'I underestimated you,' the Devil said.

'Yeah. And now it's too late.' Nash nodded towards the suitcase. 'That thing is going to be opened now, and reversed. Sounds like there's only one person who can make that happen. The old dude here.'

'That is true,' Granddad said calmly. 'And therein lies a problem, I'm afraid.'

'And what's that?'

'I'm not going to do it.'

Nash nodded. 'I figured you'd say that. Sell your soul to the Devil and it stays sold, right?'

'No,' Granddad said. 'You don't understand. There is no cost too high to prevent you from going through with this.'

'Not even your life?'

'Certainly not something that insignificant.'

'Plus if I shoot you, I'm screwed, right? I had already thought of that. I'm not dumb.'

Nash moved his arm until the gun was pointing at Hannah's father's head. 'So how about I shoot your son?'

Hannah saw the expression on her grandfather's face change. How it went from resolute to beaten in an instant.

'Don't do it, Dad,' her father said, however.

'Seriously?' Nash said irritably, lowering the gun for a moment. 'Has this entire family got a death wish?'

He flipped off the gun's safety with his thumb. The click was very audible. It sounded like the last tick of a clock before it stopped, never to work again.

'Dad, no,' Hannah's father said. 'If I understand even a tenth of what's at stake here, or a ten-thousandth, you can't.'

'But, Steve . . .'

'No.' Hannah's father's voice was firm.

'The machine is my responsibility. I built it.'

'And I'm your son. So it's mine too now. It's part of our family. Our history. Do not do it.'

'Jesus,' Nash said. 'People apparently just aren't taking me seriously here.' He raised his arm so the gun was pointing straight at Hannah's father's head again. 'And here's how we change that. Bye, dude.'

Terrified, rooted to the spot, Hannah saw the man's finger tightening on the trigger.

'Stop,' the Devil said.

The world went still, and quiet. Nash's finger remained exactly as it was, an infinitesimal twitch away from firing the gun. Each of the Fallen Angels seemed to lean forwards.

The Devil turned to the Engineer. 'Open the machine.'

'You know I can't do that,' Granddad said.

'You can. You will. This man will not stop at your son.

338

You serve me, and have served me well. Your responsibility passes on to the second generation, and unto the third. The child has your blood too.' The Devil glanced at Hannah for a moment, his gaze boring into her. Then back at Granddad. 'Open it.'

For a long moment, Granddad didn't move. Then his shoulders seemed to slump.

'Very well,' he said.

Chapter 51

Granddad stood in front of the suitcase, looking down at it as though it were his own tombstone. He reached into the pockets of his waistcoat and pulled out a couple of tools. Lowered himself to his knees on the cold ground and ran his hands over the worn leather of the case – as if it were an old, much-loved dog, rather than the most dangerous thing in the universe.

Then he applied one of the tools to an area near the handle, and began. Everybody watched in silence. Hannah knew that neither her father nor mother had any idea of what they were about to witness, or much idea of what it meant. She could feel the glee of the angels: the dreadful joy of shadows who had waited a long time for revenge against both the world in which they had found themselves imprisoned, and the being who had dragged them down here with him when his rebellion failed.

She got a glimpse of what it would be like if all the dreadful, terrible things humankind had done were to come back into the world, back into everyone's lives, instead of being corralled into Hell's domain as they were supposed to be. Just a glimpse, because the mind cannot handle more than that.

More than a glimpse is stark madness.

Meanwhile, Granddad lifted off the front of the case, revealing the first of the inner panels. He undid further screws. There was nothing any of them could do, except . . .

Hannah looked at the Devil. If anybody could stop this, surely it would be him? Even though he'd told Granddad to do this, even despite the terrible strength of the Fallen Angels up above? The Devil was simply watching the process, however. It was impossible to tell what he was thinking.

She looked then at the bad man with the gun, while her grandfather undid screw after screw and then swivelled a panel aside, giving the first glimpse of the wondrous, golden mechanism within. He folded part of it out, starting the process of expanding the device to its full, impossible size. The other men were staring at the process, bewildered, awestruck. But the bad man remained focused, his arm still held out, unwaveringly pointing the gun at her dad. He would not be distracted.

He was here to do what he was going to do.

She glanced back at the Devil and realized he was looking at her too now. 'You must be able to do something!' she shouted.

'There is nothing I can influence here,' he said, keeping his eyes upon her. 'Sometimes there is no . . . last resort.'

And still her grandfather worked.

Until eventually, ten minutes later, he nudged the levers and touched the dials that caused the final unfolding.

Everybody watched as the machine unfurled to its true size. Then Granddad pressed the button that caused the front to swing open properly, revealing the mind-melting complexity of wheels and gears and cogs of the interior space.

'That's impossible,' Jesse whispered.

'Be quiet,' Nash said. 'Now what? How do I reverse it?'

'It's simple,' the Devil said. 'Too simple, perhaps, in retrospect. A single switch is all it takes.'

'So flip it.'

'I cannot. This machine was built with human hand because it is for humankind's sake. I cannot make the change myself. But I can show you how. If you truly insist.'

'Show me.' Nash handed the gun to Jesse. 'The old guy tries anything, you know what to do.'

Jesse nodded glumly, and pointed the gun at Hannah's father.

The Devil stood in front of the machine. 'Follow me.'

'Tell me what I'm looking for.'

'All I can do is lead you inside. One switch will be yours. You have to make your own choice as to which it is. That's how it always works. That's free will.' He crooked his finger at Nash. 'Come.'

He backed into the machine. Tall though the Devil was, there was still a clear six inches above his head. Nash took a step closer, keen not to be left behind.

The Devil took another backward step and disappeared full-body into the interior of the device. Disappeared, that is, apart from the reflection of his eyes, which Hannah glimpsed in the sparkling gold of the interior.

His dead, black eyes – once more seeming to look straight at her.

Nash stepped halfway into the machine. Hannah saw that Granddad's face was pale, as if he was finally accepting what was about to happen, that a thing he had made with his own hands was about to bring about the downfall of the stars. She also saw a tear slowly rolling down her mother's face.

'So where are the switches?' Nash asked as he prepared to take the step that would have him fully inside.

'All around,' the Devil's voice said. 'Don't you see?'

342

'Whoa,' Nash said as he saw.

'One of them will be yours. If you're really going to do this, you will know which it is.'

Nash stepped inside. And as he did, he revealed something: he stopped blocking Hannah's view of something she'd seen before, the first time she'd witnessed the interior of this infernal machine.

A pin, with a jewel on its head – a jewel that was the red of old blood.

And she remembered the Devil saying: *The child has your blood too.*

She blinked. Took a small step closer to the machine. Nobody noticed.

And then remembered him saying something else: *last resort*.

She knew that her grandfather had used these words, too – back in Kalaloch. When he'd said there was something that should not be touched, least of all by her.

Nash's voice echoed from inside the machine. 'I see it,' he said. He sounded excited, triumphant, as if all the small, narrow dreams he'd dedicated his life to had fallen away, and he'd realized there were dooms that were so much bigger . . . terrible, world-ending, but magnificent.

But he also sounded like a child, the person he'd once been long ago, before all the bad things had happened in his life. 'I see it.'

Hannah saw the reflection of his arm as he reached out for something, his switch, deep in the interior of the machine.

And before he could touch it she darted forwards, got her fingers around the pin with the dark red jewel, and pulled.

It slid smoothly out of the mechanism.

And the Sacrifice Machine fell apart.

* * *

It happened all at once, as if some force field had been holding it together instead of mechanics, and the device's ten million parts suddenly no longer had any connection or relationship to each another. One moment it was an eight-foot-tall cabinet, deep enough for two grown men to stand inside. The next it was a shower of cogs and wheels and screws and levers and switches, like a rain of tiny piece of precious metal. They dropped to the ground in a circle twenty feet wide.

And the machine was gone.

Nash was nowhere to be seen. Nor the old guy in the suit. Jesse blinked. 'Where the hell did they go?'

'Precisely there,' Granddad said. 'And what happens now is up to you. You can either follow them or not.'

Jesse tightened his finger on the trigger. He knew what Nash had said. That if anything happened, he should shoot.

But Nash wasn't here any more. Nash had gone to where part of his soul had always lived, the place where his path led. Nash had found Hell. That didn't mean Jesse had to join him.

He dropped the gun and ran. Eduardo and Chex followed.

They fled the promenade just as the cops arrived from the other direction, having finally decided they'd given the weird old spook in the suit enough leeway and it was time to start banging heads and taking names.

They were confused to find no sign of him, but instead a bunch of completely different people – they didn't seem to be able to see the dark shapes still roosting above – but Granddad gave them a long and detailed non-explanation of the events they'd witnessed earlier, involving an entirely fictional clandestine task force of rollercoaster troubleshooters.

Officer Ray looked dubiously down at the bazillion or so glinting pieces of finely worked metal strewn over the ground. 'So what are these things?'

'Spare parts.'

'And who are these other people?'

'Interns.'

Ray peered suspiciously at Hannah. 'She's, like, ten.'

'Eleven,' Hannah said indignantly.

Officer Rick assessed the situation, decided it would take at least a cubic yard of paperwork to encompass and that life was too damned short. He encouraged Officer Ray to return to the car with him and to forget any of it ever happened. Ray eventually agreed to go along with this and so on the way back into town Rick pulled over near an abandoned garage on a quiet back street and let Ray kick its door down. After a while, Rick got out and joined in. Then they went to Ferrell's and had donuts.

Next morning while on patrol Officer Rick came across three men huddled together in a doorway. All were wide-eyed, intensely scared by something they refused to describe, and evidently hadn't slept all night. Officer Rick dealt with them gently, shared coffee out of his flask, and encouraged them to be on their way. Jesse, Eduardo and Chex never stole another thing in their lives. They wound up as waiters in a beach restaurant in Los Angeles, and – so far as I'm aware – are there to this day.

By an odd coincidence (or perhaps not), Nash is also engaged in kitchen work. He is washing pots and pans for the restaurant in the Behind, his hands blistered from constant plunges into water that is hotter than the sun as he tries to keep up with an infinite amount of dishwashing while a chef with a cleaver stands behind him whispering about the meals he would like to prepare from his liver. But don't feel too bad for Nash. He will be allowed to progress to other things.

In about a hundred million years.

*　　*　　*

In the meantime, after the cops left, Hannah and her parents and grandfather remained on the promenade. They, and the things still standing up on the roofs of the boardwalk structures.

All was still for a moment, and then a wind started to pick up. It gathered fast, like a gale – coming not from the sky but the angels. This was their fury, Hannah knew, the terrible vacuum of their lack. Their anger at being thwarted, their need to damage and hurt. She looked up at the nearest.

'Go away,' she said. 'You're not wanted here. You're not wanted *anywhere*. You're nothing.'

The wind rattled and screamed down the promenade, like a whirlwind, blowing all the parts of the machine away.

And then they were gone.

Leaving only the humans, and Vaneclaw. Hannah turned to her grandfather. 'I'm sorry about your machine,' she said.

'I'm not.' He smiled, putting his arm around her shoulders. 'And I'm more proud of you than you'll ever know.'

She handed him the pin she'd plucked out of the inside. 'At least there's one bit left. Is this what the man gave you? The man you heard playing the organ in Leipzig?'

'Yes.' Granddad put the pin back into the palm of her hand, and gently folded her fingers over it. It felt warm, then hot, and then she couldn't feel it any more.

When she opened her fingers, it had gone.

Granddad winked. 'It's yours now.'

Now

Hannah's mom and dad did not get back together, I'm afraid. This is a story, but that doesn't mean it can't stay true – and some things can't be reversed. Two months later they sold the house, and Hannah and her father went to live in a smaller one on the East Side. It was a wooden cottage close to Twin Lakes Beach, with a guest room for when Granddad came to visit. He dropped by on the first weekend and gave Hannah a new sculpture for her room. It looked rather like the insides of an owl but she put it in a prominent position nonetheless.

Granddad was coming to town regularly at the time to covertly assist in the repair of the Giant Dipper, which people in Santa Cruz believed had fallen victim to vandals in the pay of rival seaside destinations. He waited until the crews went home every night and slipped in through the service door, achieving more in eight hours than teams of workmen could in a week. As part of this he disabled the hidden dial which allowed the machinery's speed to be increased. No one will get into the Behind from the Dipper's carriages again, though if you know where to look, there is now a way to charge your iPhone.

Hannah's mom returned to London to tell her bosses she

didn't want to work there any more, said goodbye to the man she had known, and finally answered her cousin's email. She stopped hiding. She still had to travel for work sometimes but she came back to live in Santa Cruz, renting a house on the West Side where Hannah stays every weekend, and some evenings too.

In time she started cautiously seeing a man from Los Gatos, a development of which her daughter took a dim view because she knew Dad still thought about her mom a lot. Kristen explained that occasionally girls had to be the bad guys, because bad guys are often just normal guys doing things that happen to hurt someone else's feelings; that life is short, and all you can do is take it page by page or even line by line; and that, as Steve had put it to Kristen recently, in their least shouty lunch so far, you are only bound in the same book as those you love, not always and forever on the same page.

Her dad didn't start seeing anybody else for a while. He seemed OK with this, though, especially after – to everybody's bafflement – someone at the network decided it might be fun to remake that funky cult classic, *Undertoe*. Thus it came to pass that Hannah's dad and Frankie the actor were reunited, and 'Fiasco!' became once more something of a catchphrase. The show was cancelled again after a (second) second season, when everyone realized it was still basically a crappy idea, but Hannah's dad earned enough for them to get by for another year – which, when you make things up for a living, is about as much as you can hope for.

Frank caught some lucky breaks and went on to enjoy a wildly successful career as an A-list action movie hero, finally scoring the Malibu beach house he'd always dreamed off.

On the deck of which he now sits, on some perfect moonlit evenings, vaguely wishing he was a cook.

*　　*　　*

Hannah went up to the city to visit Aunt Zo. They spent most of their time out doing stuff, as Aunt Zo's apartment was so tiny it reminded Hannah uncomfortably of what had happened to her old bedroom when it slipped into the Behind.

It was Aunt Zo who – over sushi in a restaurant where the food was delivered on little boats, which Hannah felt was absolutely the most sophisticated thing in the universe – managed to steer Hannah towards a place where she didn't glare suspiciously at her mother's boyfriend every time they met, and almost completely stopped muttering things at him that were supposed to sound like spells. It helped that by then Hannah's father had begun to be visited quite often by a lady he was working with down in Los Angeles. For a wolverine she had a very nice laugh, and was remarkably adept at juggling fruit.

Having discovered – through facing down a Fallen Angel, even if it turned into a squirrel – a depth of courage she didn't realize she possessed, Zoë is going from strength to strength. She is currently starring in a piece of performance art at a very small basement venue, during which she shouts at light bulbs. It's being received surprisingly well.

Vaneclaw the imp decided that, exciting though all the excitement had been, it was high time for him to return to what he was best at. He lurked around downtown for a few days, limbering up by causing a few minor traffic accidents, the permanent malfunction of two public toilets and the accidental dropping of a number of recently purchased coffees, before spotting a total and *utter* bastard who he believed would make an excellent target for a long run of disappointing luck, and launching himself at him.

He missed, and ended up splatted on to the roof of a passing car. He managed to cling on all the way up to the city, where he was drawn to revisit Madame Chang's grocery store. There in the stinking basement he encountered once more the angel that takes the form of a feisty squirrel with black fur and tufty ears, now released from servitude by his infernal master in recognition of recent services in the Behind.

A dark and intriguing deal was struck, the union of two entities weird and strange, both possessed of the power to affect destinies and shape lives.

Unfortunately Vaneclaw lost the notes from the meeting and so no one's sure what the deal was. He thinks it's either something to do with opening a pizzeria, or fighting crime.

But before any of that happened, three days after the adventure ended and when Hannah's mom had flown back to London and Aunt Zo had driven back to the city, on Saturday morning Hannah walked downtown with her dad.

When they approached Starbucks to buy his walking-around coffee, they saw an old man in a crumpled black suit sitting at a table in the courtyard.

'He's back,' Hannah's father said.

'I don't think he can ever really go away.'

A woman was in the chair opposite the Devil. She had long grey hair and a kind, lined face and was wearing jeans and a sweatshirt and looked familiar, though to be honest Santa Cruz is home to quite a lot of women who present that way.

'This is . . . a friend,' the Devil muttered. He looked as though he would have preferred not to have said anything.

'Hello, Hannah,' the old lady said. Her voice had the rich, friendly rasp of a woman who has been no stranger to good times.

Hannah glanced up at her dad. 'I'll get in line,' he said, and she realized her dad had the same gift as *his* father, and could hear things that hadn't been said.

'What happens about the machine?' she asked when he'd gone inside.

'Nothing, for now,' the Devil said. 'The Engineer says he is too old to build a replacement, though I'm confident I shall change his mind. For the time being, the bad that is done on Earth will simply have to remain here. It's been that way for some years now, and you've all survived so far.'

'But what can we do to stop the world getting worse?'

'Good,' the old lady said. 'You do *good*. The machine should never have been built. It is humankind's responsibility to make up for what they do – day by day and deed by deed – not give the power of restitution and redemption away to the gods.'

'I don't understand.'

'That's OK,' the old lady said. 'It's usually better that way. Comprehension so often confuses the issue.'

There was a quiet thud on the pavement behind Hannah, but she ignored it, having realized where she'd seen the woman before. 'You were in the airport when I went to Granddad,' she said. 'And in the restaurant, in the Behind.'

She was also, though Hannah didn't know about the event, the woman who'd spoken to her mother in a hotel bar in London.

'One does like to keep an eye on what's going on.'

'Interfere, you mean,' said the Devil.

'Why me, though?' Hannah asked. 'And why now?'

'Is any time, or any person, more important?'

'I guess not. Not to me, anyway.'

'But also – what makes you think this has been your story, and not your mother, or father's, or grandfather's, or that aunt of yours with the extraordinary hair?'

'I rather like her hair,' the old woman said.

'How do you guys even know each other?' Hannah asked. 'You don't seem like people who would hang out. At all.'

The old woman raised an eyebrow at the Devil, as if relishing his embarrassment. 'Would you care to explain, dear?'

'We were . . . together,' the Devil admitted.

The old lady laughed. 'For a *very* long time.'

'It didn't work out.'

'Irreconcilable differences.'

'And an infernal amount of bickering.'

'I kept the nice house. I made it, after all.'

'And I got this instead.' The Devil gestured balefully at the street, the people, the buildings, the world. 'Bad-tempered chaos, increasingly dire music, and a brood of turbulent angels that won't do a damned thing they're told.'

'They'll find their feet. Children always do.'

'What,' Hannah asked, 'are you two *talking* about?'

The old lady laughed raucously, and stood up. 'You know what the words "Santa Cruz" mean, don't you?'

'It's my home.'

'True. But it's also the Spanish for "Holy Cross".' She held her hands up in an X-shape. 'A cross is two things in perfect opposition, which yet form a whole.'

'I'm not sure they ever really understood that,' the Devil muttered. 'As I predicted at the time.'

'No, dear,' the old woman sighed, 'you were right. A circle might have been a better logo. Ah well. We stumble on. The truth is neither of us are real, Hannah. Not in the way that trees are real. We're what happens between you and other people, the ups and downs on the swing, the sunny days and dark nights. He's the blank page, I'm the words – or perhaps it's the other way around. I'll forgive your trespasses, but he *understands* them. I'm yes, he's no – but the wheel of yin and yang spins so fast that cold black and white blur into a living grey. There is never only this, or that. There are all the things in between. Humans will always charge where angels fear to tread. And life goes on.'

She walked away down the street, stepping around a dead bird lying on the sidewalk.

The line in Starbucks was even more epic than usual and so Hannah and the Devil talked a while longer, though nothing even started to make any more sense. Hannah decided it didn't matter. Somewhere between all the stories that have been told lies the truth – or 'a' truth, at least, as there are always several in play at any given moment. All we have in the meantime are hints and hopes, secrets and reveals, maybe-this and maybe-that. Best, then, to concentrate on keeping track of your own tales, and weave them as cheerfully as you are able.

As the conversation continued there were further quiet thuds, and by the end eleven dead birds were lying on the ground around the courtyard. Nobody but Hannah seemed to have noticed. The other coffee drinkers sat chatting about start-ups or consulting their smartphones, oblivious.

Hannah looked crossly at the Devil. 'Why do you *do* that? All the bad things? It's mean.'

'There is an echo after every footstep. When you take a cookie from the jar, a space is left behind. There must always be at least two paths – or there would be no what-ifs, no choices. No life. My job is very like your father's. The only difference is that in my tales, people really die.'

'So why did you help me?'

'I wasn't helping.'

'You were. You were inside the chef. And I think you were that wolf. And you kept looking at me when the machine was being opened . . . you were helping me remember what I could do.'

'I was a circumstance, Hannah, that's all. Good or bad – and I assure you that I remain extremely and appallingly bad – there are many angels because there were once many gods, pushing, pulling, hiding, guiding. Once we get through the fog and find a place that feels comfortable we look back and call their influence fate, and the destination our destiny. That's all.'

'Nuts. Admit it. You were helping.'

The Devil looked away, so she couldn't see him smile.

'Well. It's all been *extremely* interesting,' Hannah declared, standing to leave. 'But if I'm honest, I'd prefer my life to be a lot more mundane from now on.'

The Devil looked up at her. 'Are you sure?'

'I'm sure.'

'Then I'll see what I can do.'

All around them the fallen birds slowly stirred, and righted themselves, and flexed their unbroken wings, and flew away, soaring up into the clear blue sky.

Hannah Green has become involved in many other stories since then, and also now has a kitten, *finally*. She's currently busy with being very nearly twelve, and so it falls to me to round things off on her behalf.

Nobody talks any more about the events that happened in those strange days, and after a while Hannah came to understand that her parents and Aunt Zo didn't really even remember them. The tendency of memories to fade is both terribly sad and one of life's great blessings. There's always plenty of other things to worry about, after all, and to enjoy, so you put the things you want to keep safe in a box somewhere deep inside, and sit back and let the world show you what else it's got.

So there were gaps and edges in Hannah's life. Glimpses of the Behind. That's OK. She could fill them. If Dad was quiet sometimes she could cheer him up, as he did with her. He'd been happy before. He would be again, and some days already was. Hannah realized that, weird though life had become, it was a good weird sometimes. That the days on which you despair are as much a part of life as the ones on which you laugh or get ice cream – and often more valuable in the long run.

No, you don't get to rub anything out. But you can always turn the page and write something new.

So far, though he has still not left Santa Cruz, the Devil has kept his word, keeping Hannah's life wonderfully mundane. She has glimpsed him from time to time: as an old man disappearing round a corner; a black dog alone in twilight on the beach; and, once, as a passing chicken. The Devil is adapting fast, and considering some more modern form of loyalty programme. Maybe even an app. He's caused the untimely deaths of a few people who didn't deserve it, and is also toying with the idea of giving the San Andreas Fault a nudge sometime soon, which is not very nice of him, but I suppose it's what he does.

A couple of times Hannah has thought she's seen Vaneclaw, too, though it's possible it was just some other unfeasibly large mushroom. Wearing a cape.

Life goes on. Always. We make it, together. Hannah does, through learning to be herself. Her father – my son – does it telling stories that are untrue, the better to help people understand what *is* true. For myself, I build things.

I am the Engineer.

You might ask if, were I to have my time again, I'd choose to work for my master, knowing about him what I do now – and understanding that he would forever have a hand in our lives. I hope you won't be disappointed to hear that my answer would be in the affirmative. We all serve the fates.

Life will happen to us come what may. Not everyone gets to be a grandparent, but we're all someone's grandchild. We have no choice therefore but to carry someone else's weight, enacting their long-ago choices and duties of care. There's no point blaming others for what happens next, however: responsibility for shaping and unearthing our stories, following the bouncing squirrel of our destinies, lies with us alone. Our victories and losses, our gains and lacks, the challenges we decline and those we accept – all resonate through the generations that follow.

Nothing ever ends, and no one truly dies.

I'm unusual merely in that the deal I struck means that I have a body to keep living in, creaky though it may be on winter mornings. On the other hand I still get to eat peppermints. There are always upsides. And there is life.

But that's enough about us, for now.

How have *you* been?